# XD05

# XDO5

## WRITTEN BY
## DAVID W. SHERWOOD

All my work is Vampire/Zombie/Werewolf free.

The author requests that you, dear reader, review his work on Amazon.
1-5 stars; he just asks that you be honest. You may find him on Facebook
if you search for 'David Boo Sherwood'; it should take you to him. Thank
you so much for purchasing his work. Other stories he has written
include:

The First Book of Kalendeck–Young Adult Fantasy
The Second Book of Kalendeck–Young Adult Fantasy
The Red Queen's Gamble–Sci-Fi Fantasy / Virtual Gaming
Hopscotch–Serial killer / Thriller / Female Detective / Sick / Twisted
Darken French Road–Paranormal Romance
The Short Stories of David W. Sherwood–Contemporary Fiction
XD05–Sci-Fi / Space / Strong Female Lead / Coming of Age
Beyond the Vale–Urban Fantasy / Teen / Mid-grade / Strong Female Lead
/ Coming of Age
The Second Death / The Souls of December–Scifi / Strong Female Lead /
Revenge
Deuce–Rural / Strong Female Lead / Revenge
The Hells of Heaven–Novella set in an alternate universe. Based on a true
story.

My current stories on audible:
That D.Ar.N. T.O.D. (Days Are Numbered/Time of Death)
Deuce
A Life of Their Own
The Gift
Obendell's Tale
Butch

# ACKNOWLEDGEMENT

I have to give a huge shout out to Chris Phleks, A.K.A. Journeyman. Throughout the pages, there are many references to your work. Most of it is fictional or yet to be created. If you get the chance, check him out online. He's a fantastic performer with a lot of creative energy.

Thank you.

XD05, Day 1 - "Can you bind the chains of the Pleiades, or loose the cords of Orion?" Job 38:31

The black webbing held me to the red cargo seat. My legs were still too short to touch the floor, and when I felt myself pulling away, I was prone to clenching my legs. My Miss Piggy backpack stowed in a cubby by my feet bounced to the bottom of the seat from time to time, and I was happy. Even though they had cushions in the helmet, I could hear my breathing. It sounded loud. The rubber soles of my boots squeaked. The fabric of the new suit sounded like corduroy. Any little movement caused me to make a noise.

In the confines of the shuttle, I kept as still as possible, listening to the silence of space.

Priscilla hung in the air without a spacesuit. Being only tethered with a pink shoestring, my wrist to her left foot, she enjoyed her freedom. Her soft yellow-yarn hair was contrasting with the blue polka-dot dress she always wore. They assured me, several times, that being what she was, Priscilla would make the trip just fine. I knew to begin with. In the vacuum of space or air of the shuttle, she always had the silliest of smiles on her face.

The pink string would keep her safe, and with my care, no harm would come to her. I knew this, of course, but my imagination would run wild over some adventures I would have if I let her free. I watched her as she did a slow dance in the Zero-G, and it made me smile.

I tugged my free arm, and she tumbled back toward me.

With my other hand, I held on to Aunt Wendy's hand as best I could.

To make our trip from Homeport to XD05 more interesting, the pilots opened the channel feed to us in the passenger compartment. Most of it was jibber-jabber, but the pilots knew what they were saying. When they spoke, I could feel Aunt Wendy's hand tighten momentarily on mine. A simple reflex. Through the heavy gloves, it was hardly noticeable.

"X-ray Delta Oh Five, this is shuttle tree-niner-tree rounding your Twilight-side. We'll be at the portal in five. We have two pax with one return."

"Copy shuttle tree-niner-tree."

Aunt Wendy shifted in her seat, and I moved my head without turning my helmet. I looked up at her, and we smiled at each other. Aunt Wendy leaned towards me, and we touched helmets.

"You'll be okay?" she asked in a whisper. There was air in the passenger bay of the shuttle, and we did not need to touch our helmets to communicate. It was a comforting gesture for both of us.

I nodded and smiled once again. The concern in Aunt Wendy's voice was genuine.

"You'll see Mum soon," she offered.

"And Daddy too. I have some really cool space rocks for him."

She squeezed my hand once more and sat back up. The motion made us both bobble around.

As we neared the large ship, communication became a constant buzz. I felt some metallic clicks and then a sudden bump that really made me rise in my seat. The straps held me back. I squealed; although this did not frighten me, I was giddy with excitement. I have been on elevators that bumped more.

Miss Priscilla tugged at the string and spun downwards. Aunt Wendy smiled at me again.

It was not long before the door opened. A man came in, pulling himself in the weightlessness, and stopped himself with a tether just shy of our seats. He wore no boots, just black socks. The patch on his jumpsuit had the letters XD05 and two bolts of lightning. His hair was short.

"Whoa, you must be Miss Sally Weiss." He held out his hand, palm upwards, and I slapped it, and this caused him to drift back a little. "All right, thank you all for coming with us."

I gave him a thumb's up and mirrored his wink.

"Helmets can come off. We were just being safe in the shuttle with the suits. Protocol." I needed help with mine, but it came off quickly enough. The fresh air in the shuttle felt good.

"Mrs. Montgomery, will you return to Homeport?"

"Yes, I have work to get back to. I'd like to see the ship if I could?"

"Absolutely," he said with a broad smile. "Sally, you can slip this big ol' lumpy cocoon off, so you're more comfortable." He grabbed me playfully by the shoulder of my suit and shook me a little. My head bobbed. I stuck out my tongue and made silly noises. I knew what Miss Priscilla felt like when I tussled with her. "Mrs. Montgomery, gloves can come off, but we ask that you keep the suit on. It'll help the turnaround time."

He helped us with our harnesses and pulled himself back out the door.

* * *

Zero-G was something I was used to. I had used the tethers on the outer walls of the giant ring of Homeport many times as I explored. We had classes in weightless rooms as big as stadiums. We had to save Nelson twice because he drifted too far. Workers brought rocks the size of houses close to Homeport, and students could see what kind of work their families did. Aunt Wendy studied minerals, and Uncle Bob worked on robots. When class was over, we returned home to the spinning hub of Homeport. The spin brought us back to One-G.

Here at the Hub of the ship XD05, there was no gravity and no tethers nearby to hold me back. There was a term my mom used more than once: the kids were bouncing off the walls. With my spacesuit stowed in some compartment somewhere, I felt free.

It was a new ship. The bulk of the crew waited for our arrival back near Earth. There were few people around, and the sizable space of the Hub was all but empty. I could push off from one wall, float towards the other, spin, tuck my knees up close, and land on the bay window. I crouched and then pushed off again with the simple effort of stretching my toes.

Miss Priscilla, with her wild hair, rode with me in tandem.

Aunt Wendy and the soldier man were busy looking out the enormous bay window at the surrounding ship.

"Sally, come look!"

"It's a tube, Aunt Wendy. We learned all about it in school. It gets boring." Spinning just before turning, I grabbed Miss Priscilla out of the air.

"Tsk-tsk, Sally, two hundred kilometers to the far end, eighteen kilometers down to the surface in every direction. It makes this the largest man-made tube you've ever seen."

"She'll get used to it, I'm sure," said the soldier man as he used the tips of his fingers to keep him in place near the glass. Tethers hung randomly from the bulkhead. This enclosed area of the ship had no gravity, and it never would.

I paused long enough to point out the white band along the near side of the surface.

"If you picture XD05 just as a tube, this band runs all along the circumference, inside near the Twilight-end. We call it this because this is where our sun sets. From the edge of the wall to a kilometer inward, we made buildings that they will use for shops, homes, sports, and other businesses." This was the white band. The buildings were too far away to see individually. Beyond this, the whole rest of the tube was a grid work of white lines with the entire surface a blackish-brown color.

"I helped with creating the carbon on the surface." Aunt Wendy said with satisfaction. "Smashed enough rocks to coat it to ten meters thick."

I had stopped moving and let my hands gently brush against the window until I was all but still and listened as they spoke.

He whistled. "I thought it was just the standard meter."

"They plan to grow trees in this one. Fruit trees, pine, and deciduous.

Not just the run-of-the-mill gardens for food. Enormous trees, the ancient giants from Earth. They are already growing in a kim-two, um, one square kilometer, down on the far side. We needed the carbon-silica that was deep for the roots."

"That's why all the rocks."

"Yip," Aunt Wendy smiled. "Took a little longer, but it's worth it. This system is full of rocks, and they harvested as much as they could." I could hear the self-pride in my aunt's voice.

I heard a small beep, and the soldier looked at his wrist.

"I'm afraid it's time."

I looked between the two. A sudden sadness filled me. It would be a year before I could make it back to Homeport. Pulling on a tether, I drifted gently towards my aunt. My fingertips searched until they caught on the fabric of her orange suit, and we pulled each other close. Her hair smelled of bana-berries. The embrace was genuine. I would miss her as she would miss me.

Aunt Wendy kissed me on the forehead, and I kissed her on the cheek. After another quick embrace, we pushed from each other.

"Message," Aunt Wendy said.

"I will. I will. I'll let you know I made it, okay?"

I pushed off, grabbed a tether, and followed the soldier. The transport vessel was just big enough for one adult person. That meant that it was a little too big for me. Sitting in, I could stretch out a bit. When they strapped me into the green, single-person egg, I gave the soldier a thumb's up. I turned in my seat, looking over my shoulder, but Aunt Wendy had left already.

In anticipation, I grabbed the handles by the armrests.

The canopy closed and sealed above me, and the soldier tapped the glass, giving me another thumbs-up. The egg glided ahead into the chamber and stopped. My science teacher, Mr. Cromlich, said this part coming up was the coolest. The air cycled once again, and when the door in front of me opened, the vehicle was in a vacuum. There were clouds below. With the green light and a small chirp, I was suddenly rushing down the Twilight Wall, taking the eighteen-kilometer journey towards the surface on a magnetic indigo-colored ribbon.

Before I reached the atmosphere, I felt the tug of gravity pulling me forward. Were it not for the harness, I'd be up against the front window. The clouds looked solid, and I quickly passed through them.

Here the ship looked like a cut-down tree lying on its side. To the left and right lay rows of houses forming giant bands, not unlike the rings on the inside of a tree or a vertical city. All I could see of these were glass windows and balconies. Instead of having a rooftop, these homes had other homes above them.

The indigo ribbon I traveled on curved before I got to the bottom. It arced with the sides and surface of the ship. As the egg traveled down the ribbon, I could feel the gravity shift suddenly. It was no longer pulling me forward; it was pulling me downward. My stomach felt funny as I settled back in the seat.

When I reached the bottom, I was back with the familiar 1-G. Everything felt suddenly heavy again. Buildings zipped by. It would be just a moment until the egg stopped at Hotel Lima.

I tapped a button inside, and the canopy of the egg slid open. The rush of wind took my breath away. This air was no longer the stale air of the ships. This air made my head spin. Fresh and clean, it hinted of flowers and freshly turned soil. My hair whipped around my head in the sudden breeze. I laughed. It was an awakening like I had never known before. This is a wide-open space. So different from what I had previously known. I had been at the cramped Homeport for six months, and it felt good to be heading home.

I had the impulse to lift Miss Priscilla up so she could see. Not trusting my grip in the wind, I did not want to lose her.

I could tell the small egg had stopped. Its movement was quiet, smooth, and steady. The only way I could tell it stopped was the rush of wind was no longer there.

A female soldier waited for me on the platform to help me out. Other travelers stood around the front of the hotel. I wanted to say 'Again, again,' but I was too old for that kind of joy ride.

"Peep, peep." This response, I realized after I said it, was not grown up either.

"A sense of humor. I like that. Are you a little chick?" she asked me, and I giggled.

"I'm hatching," I said as I handed her Miss Priscilla.

"Well, well, well." I heard a lightness in her tone as she looked nonchalantly at my doll. "If it isn't the one and only Miss Sally Weiss. I'm Corporal Daniels," she extended her hand, and I shook it. She had to help me with the buckle. "Fantastic to meet you. Bring your things. We have a berth all set up for you. It's where you'll be staying during the transition."

"I didn't bring much," I said, climbing out, brushing back my wild hair. Daniels hefted my backpack with a minor effort. She handed me back my doll.

I looked at the sky. So much like Earth's, it was amazing. A bird, an actual bird, perched on a tree branch for just a moment before flying off. I watched it go and couldn't help giggling. The birds here carry the plant seeds faster than any person or machine could. They ate the seeds and then pooped them back out. Things we learn in science class. Humans controlled all things living here; birds, insects, and plants.

To my left and right, the white ring that was the working part of the ship with its houses and shops curved along the arc and disappeared into a haze above me. I could barely see the shaft that the sun traveled through in the artificial sunlight. I could only see the sky further down the tube as everything disappeared in the blue openness. The buildings hid the brown of raw soil. If I went to a rooftop, I could see it as it curved away and upward.

My eyes followed the ribbon of the track I traveled on. I could see its curve as it hugged the wall and went upward. The Hub was a little dimple way up there above the blue sky and clouds. If I squinted my eyes, I could barely make it out.

"Been on a ship like this before?" Asked Cpl. Daniels, waiting for me to adjust. The patch sewn on her shoulder matched the one worn by the other soldiers.

I shook my head and looked up at her. "Earth mostly." I tried to sound well-traveled. Although with me being just ten years old, I'm sure she has seen more places than I have. "I've been with my aunt and uncle at Homeport for six months. I've seen the ships being built but have never been on one. Looks like Earth, but turned outside in."

The corporal laughed and placed her hand on my back to guide me along. The sliding glass doors of the hotel opened. There were many people in the main foyer, and they all seemed taller. All of them were adults.

"Are there other kids along?" I asked hopefully while searching the people.

"Negative. Not a one. Most everyone has at least ten years on you."

"Oh." It came as a disappointment, and I could not help frowning. There are so many children at the school at Homeport, and now it was just me. I was hoping to have one or two to play with.

"Hey, you'll be ok," the soldier playfully punched my arm. "Three days' travel time, and we'll see you off to your family."

It was then I heard this loud screeching noise. We both turned. The sound echoed off the walls of the hotel foyer. I thought at first that there was an accident.

"What was that?"

"Someone brought a bird." She frowned, showing her distaste for the bird.

"Another living bird?"

"Yes, very expensive. He brought it to Homeport for a while. He's a bigwig who had to have his bird as he traveled. He…" The bird squawked again, interrupting her. Although the sound appeared to be close-by, I could not see the bird.

We walked away from the foyer, and I was thankful I did not hear the squawking again.

"Hey, you do this a lot?" I asked, looking up at her.

"Third transition. Fifth TDA, temporary duty assignment. It's a piece of cake with not much to do. We're just hyped up stewards, herding people to where they must go. We have a berth all set up for you. It's especially done so you may enjoy it."

We walked down a hallway and climbed two sets of stairs.

Daniels stopped in front of a door.

"Room three-two-one. Can you remember that?"

"Oh yeah, like a countdown."

"It's keyed to your thumb-print and no one else."

I placed my thumb on the pad, and the door clicked open. She nudged it further with my backpack. They had painted the room a soft pink. It held a bunk bed, dresser and mirror, desk, and closet. I had my own bathroom through a door to the side.

"Wow!"

"Big, huh?" Daniels giggled a little.

"My room with my aunt and uncle was half this size. And I had to share the bathroom." I stuck out my tongue.

"Oh my, aren't you the lucky one? It's yours. If I was ten, I would enjoy this room immensely. Enjoy it while you have it. They'll redo the colors after you leave."

She turned to go.

"Can I stay here for a bit?" I asked, checking out the bounce-isity of the bed.

"You sure?"

"Yeah. I'd like to stay, you know, stretch out."

"Okay, if you're sure. I'll be back later tonight. There is a big party scheduled." Daniels' eyes lit up at this.

"I'll stay here and watch vid," I said.

"I'm sure you can come along to the party if you wish. For us, it's a time for us grown-ups to unwind and get crazy before we get serious again."

"We'll see. Maybe later."

I was still bouncing.

"Be careful with doing that," she said in a stern voice, her smile suddenly fading. I stop jumping on the bed. She came close and looked me directly in the eyes. "Lights out at 2100 hours, wake up at 0500, barracks inspection is at 0600. Formation in the mess hall 0700."

My jaw dropped. "Seriously?" I asked.

"Ha! Gotcha!" she nudged my shoulder.

I laughed and bounced again.

"If I bounced on my bunk, Captain would have me doing push-ups." With that, she left.

I was alone at last. I tossed Miss Priscilla in the air and spun on my toes several times. Had the door stayed open, Daniels would have heard the giggles.

"Stand back… I'm about to do science!"

The Samuel Drives (SD) gave humanity what it so long desired; freedom. We could explore the galaxy with restrictions, but the doors it opened were ever so inviting.

**SIZE**: The size of the SD depended on the size of the ship. In simple vehicles used to shuttle people from place to place, the SD would be the size of a footlocker. They designated the smallest ships with the class of 0.001. The largest, to date, was class 2.008. These were the giants that reflected mankind's achievements. The Samuel Drives for the larger ships were as large as houses.

**SHAPE**: From a layman's view, the giant ships would resemble two tin cans, stacked end to end, rotating different directions in the vacuum of space. They needed the rotation to create an artificial gravity for those inside. This pressed people on the surface downward as someone might be as they rode on a carnival ride. It created an artificial gravity well. For them, the surface stretched away in either direction and joined at the top. It was a closed ship, accessed only through ports and airlocks at either end, where there was no gravity.

The two halves rotated in opposite directions to maintain the conservation of angular momentum. Once aligned, one end was always facing towards the sun, and the other facing away; they stayed this way with little correction needed to maintain stability.

**ENERGY USE:** Everything inside the ship depended on the never-ending energy from the Sun. Water boiled and evaporated at the Morning End, piped to the Twilight End to condense for reuse. This process guaranteed an almost limitless supply of fresh water. They emptied fountains, pools, and spas daily and refilled rather than using harsh chemicals to clean them.

The heat on the Sun side and the chill on the dark side caused convection to occur in the atmosphere inside the ship. Being able to control the temperature, the days could be a constant, comfortable 23°C (75°F) with the nights dipping down to 18°C (65°F). Rainfall and aridness are something they control. Lifestyles of the known ships differed from desert life, woodland, tundra, to equatorial rainforest.

In transition, they used a Burner—a nuclear device that acts like the Sun.

**SHIELDS/PROTECTION:** The normal shields used the basic principles to protect all ships from micrometeorites and space debris. One side of a normal drive shield generator pulled hydrogen molecules towards the drive. The other side would repel the same particles. Caught in an eternal struggle, the hydrogen would form a barrier several hands thick at about twelve kilometers from the ship. This barrier protected the ship from harm.

**NAVIGATION:** The Samuel Drive broke the molecules in the shield down further. So much so that the physical universe would lose its grip on the ship. The ship would wink out of existence, the galaxy would rotate over it, and the ship would reappear elsewhere in the galaxy. Held in the Milky Way by the gravitational pull of the supermassive black hole in its center, there was a corridor of space less than one Astronomical Unit (AU) wide, which became the limits mankind could travel. This was a spiral stairway, or beltway, that circumvented the galaxy—the beltway in the Milky Way.

Going "downstream" was the easy part. Ships would let loose their hold on the universe and slip to a secondary location. Coming back "upstream" was a little harder. They had to go against the current of the Galactic rotation. They needed just the right nudge to return the ship back to its "true position." The timing was so delicate that humans could not make the necessary calculations.

Circumvention of the Galaxy is not exactly the proper term. If they circumvent something, the individual will return to the starting point at some later time. This was not the case. Mathematically speaking, for every twenty-five seconds, the ship is outside the universe, approximately one Light Year, Calendar Year, (LyCy, which is coined Lucy) is traveled. One light-year traveled equals one calendar year back (Downstream) or forward (Upstream) in time.

They can only send messages over space at the speed of light. If you traveled four hundred LyCy and sent a message to those at your origin that you have arrived safely, it would arrive within seconds after your departure. You would be four hundred light-years away. It would take four hundred calendar years to reach them, which is about the same distance from the Sun to Pleiades.

When a ship travels the circumference of the Galaxy and returns to where they started, they will have traveled roughly two-hundred and fifty thousand years. Let us assume for a moment they started in a NEO (Near Earth Orbit) and traveled downstream. When they pop back into the Galaxy, they are, relatively speaking, at the same place they stated. However, the Sun, with our Solar System tagging along, receded a hundred and eighty light-years down the Orion Arm. Such a distance is unreachable.

As a side note, many weddings and funerals are at this location, in a suit, and tethered to a ship. The bride and groom usually toss a wreath of roses toward the approximate direction of the Sun. Likewise, many people have stated in their wills that they want someone to launch them toward the Sun upon their death. Statistically, there is almost no chance that the wreath of roses, or body, would make it to the Solar System or Earth. If it did, it would be a falling star in the night sky that burned before it ever touched the ground. The calculations needed to get the right trajectory over two-hundred and fifty thousand years are all but impossible. These relics will float in space for a very long time.

It was a common thought since the beltway intersected the seven arms of the Milky Way. There should be hundreds, even thousands of suns with worlds for humans to populate. Viewed from afar, stars crowd these arms. Once there, we found the truth, something we knew all along; space is a vast emptiness. Sol's nearest neighbor is Proxima Centauri. At just over four light-years away, it is still too far to reach by conventional means. A round trip to Saturn still takes several decades.

Three rotations around the Galaxy will take a ship seven hundred and fifty thousand years back in time. This is also, roughly, the location of the nearest G class star that travels close to the same ellipse the Sun will travel.

Scattered along this beltway like tourist attractions are many wonders we have only dreamed about.

**MAPPING:** They have sent probes both Upstream and Downstream. Winking in existence for a day, recording everything they can before making a one hundred second jump, and then easing back into the Galaxy. It was their task to gather data and samples before returning to NEO. They had sent one hundred out in both directions over a one-hundred-day interval—each leapfrogging over the last. Programmed to return when their data banks were full, they brought with them a treasure trove of information.

Mankind had placed a toe into the Galactic waters and found them warm and inviting. Alone, we began this great surge into an abyss we had only seen through telescopes and through the eyes of our imagination.

With little hesitation, the nature of curiosity took over, and we wade deeper.

Homeport, Day 0

Richard Porter, no relation to Elysian, was the senior director at Homeport. It was his job, through different department heads, to coordinate almost every task needed in the building of a vessel that would house and feed millions. From the pulverizing of city-sized rocks to gather the essential minerals and gases trapped inside to the manufacturing of the super dense metal that would make up the outer hull. Every person, office, or committee would eventually report to him.

For the past seven years, there had always been some activity on LyCy step negative 140357 'Homeport.' Upon this barren place, left to its own accord, a star will form in a few hundred thousand years from the swirling, condensing disk of the rock, gas, and dust. Planets are yet to take shape. In a few billion years, life may arise.

Like an army of termites on a fallen tree, mankind ravished the dwarf system with no mercy. Dubbed XD by those that be, mankind discovered it on its third and last sweep of the galaxy. They broke down and purified heavier rocks and elements from the inner system. Man slowly worked their way outward. They picked over and discarded much of the rocks by the first team. In a year, a second, and then the third wave of collection machinery came along. Even though this was a dwarf system, containing only a third of the mass of the Solar System, there was much to mine. Seven years of mining only scratched the surface of the wealth that this system could provide.

The disk of gas and rock still spun its dark, slow dance. Macabre and silent.

Nearly the whole time, from its discovery to the present day, ships were being built as a shelter for humanity's constant need to grow and expand. Most ships, once complete, would sit in space between Earth and Mars, mostly empty, to become vast gardens and farms. When the older ships become overpopulated, they cracked seals. After much fanfare and ceremony, families would be allowed to populate the newer ones. There were whole nations who gave up their rights of ancestral heritage on Earth and now lived solely on their ships. They called them ring clusters.

The building of a ship was not an easy task by any means. They did much between initial preparation for the inception of water and atmosphere. They designed and put into place pools, fountains, and artificial lakes, still void of water. A team of bots created homes, shops, warehouses, and business plazas in Zero-G and no atmosphere. The Shaft, with its coatings to keep out harmful solar rays, was up and working long before they installed the nuclear burner that would give the ship life and light. When the Samuel Drive kicked it out of this part of the galaxy and took it back to the Solar System, they removed and returned the nuclear burner. Natural sunlight would stream in.

Life.

For Director Richard Porter and the ten-thousand that worked beneath him at Homeport, no detail was too trivial. Like an assembly line cranking out motor vehicles from history past, a ship the size of XD05 seemed an easy matter.

This was their fifth. Four earlier ones now sat in NEO and housed millions. Five others sat with it in the dwarf system and were in various stages of completion. XD06 would receive the nuclear burner in a months' time. The light and heat would melt the ice on the inside, and it would create a basic breathable atmosphere.

XD09 was still open and raw in places. It sat motionlessly. In four months' time, strong electromagnets on both ends would start the tug and release, beginning its lifelong rotation.

With XD05 completed, there was a moment to pause and breathe a sigh of relief. Once again, they had done it.

The ship, navigated strictly by a computer and only staffed with a skeleton crew of trained military staff, had taken on a handful of passengers that would return to Earth. Director Porter's son, Brandon, was among those in transition. In his quarters, alone before the large screen that fed several live videos of the ship, Richard raised a glass of wine. After so much sweat and effort, he gave his people a silent salute. Another job well done.

In one corner of the video, a timer counted to zero. The Samuel Drives began to kick in. From a view from several kilometers out, a delicate shimmering egg formed around the two-hundred-kilometer long cylinder that was the ship. Starting at both ends, the shields trapped and released the subatomic particles. Slowly at first and then with ever-increasing speed, the silver-white form spread.

There was no sunlight in this system. The closest star was many light-years away and afforded no usable light. They had erected great beacons around the craft. Spotlights shone from each, casting the cylinder, now egg, in an eerie glow.

In twenty seconds, they could not see it; the shields were so thick. The communications back and forth between those in the system and those on the ship soon became erratic as goodbyes mixed in with the ever-increasing static.

With the egg now completely solid, the space grew silent.

Suddenly, as it was, the ship encased in the egg ceased to be.

Richard filled his glass once again and emptied it.

Homeport, Day 2


The buzzer was insistent. Richard opened one weary eye and raised his head until the pain in his forehead forced him to seek refuge in his pillow. There was always a farewell party given once a ship winked back. They had grown in popularity and creativity. The wine had poured freely, and even though he had tried to remain the social drinker, he had almost needed assistance to make it back to his quarters. Thankfully, he didn't vomit on the way. That came later in the privacy of his room.

The buzzer sounded anew.

Mable's voice was heard as the ConfVid brightened the room.

*"Richard?"* She tried, and when he didn't respond, she became more formal. *"Director Porter? We have a situation."*

"Is it urgent?" He mumbled, running his fingers through his hair. How could great tasting wine leave such a foul aftertaste the next morning?

*"They always are, Sir. This one is more so."* Her voice was calm. As his personal secretary, she was second in command at the station in everything but name.

He swung his feet over the edge of the bed and sat up, elbows on his knees. Sometime during the brief hours of sleep, the comforter had been kicked to the floor.

*"Sir, X-ray Delta Oh five has returned. Jumped out into normal space about an hour ago."*

Looking at her with one weary eye, he gave the ConfVid the command to dim to fifty percent. He rubbed his eyes again. If she had smiled, if this was some kind of joke, he would have killed the connection and went back to sleep. Instead, he brought up a second vid and keyed the main channel. XD05 sat in space. Respectively, it appeared much smaller, and there was a bit of graininess to the image.

"How far from us?"

*"From the central station, it's just under two mil. We thrust a few bots out on hard burn, and it has been confirmed. No holes, no wreckage. The unit is complete. Returned to us just as it had left us."*

"Light?" he asked.

*"The burner is still fired up. They'd still have ambient heat for a few days, regardless if it had fizzled out or not. They did have battery-powered, hand-held lights throughout the ship."*

"Have you called them?"

*"Lights on, but no one's home. Communication is out, oddly."* She looked off screen for a moment. *"We are continuing to ping them. We have*

*a team assembled. If granted, we'll send them out."*

"Granted," he confirmed the order. "Send out shuttles right afterward. We'll need to get those people back. My son's there."

He heard the tap of a few keystrokes. After a few seconds, the communication net began to buzz with commands. He heard it on his end and the echo from hers. The delay was notable.

"Where are you?" He asked.

*"A world away and then some. I was deep in-system when the call came up from below."* His head began to clear, and he noticed the timed delay he originally missed. As for 'coming from below,' when you are second in the chain of command, everything comes up from below.

*"Would you like to be there, Sir?"*

He looked at his watch and shook his head. "I'm not fit to make the shuttles. I want them there as soon as it's cracked open. No hysteria, no panic. If everyone is okay, send some techs out, fix the thing, and we'll retry sending the ship back to Earth. If it's a long delay, we can bring them back here to wait it out. I'll shower and be presentable when they dock."

*"Should word be sent?"*

At this, he gave pause. There were six such locations creating ships and returning them to the Solar System, or two other favorable stars. The launching of XD05 was widely publicized. The launching of interstellar ships was becoming as commonplace as the launching of oceanic vessels of history past, and so only a few thousand were watching the skies for XD05. With the launching of XD01, the known universe held its collective breath. Although it would be years until it sustained the millions it was created for. Now only a few farmers, scientists, and family members of those that hitched a ride back to the Solar System were waiting for the arrival of XD05.

"Do not send word yet," he said, keeping the caution in his voice. "There will be no heat, but if there is any backlash, it's on me. We don't wish to appear weak. When we figure out what happened, we'll send a detailed message back. The problem will be fixed, and they'll be on their way."

*"Very well. I'll keep the bots back when the ship is opened, and the human team will be first to enter."*

"Live feed?" He asked.

*"Always."*

"I'll call you after my shower."

She cut the feed on her end. Her corner of the screen suddenly turned black.

\* \* \*

All cameras were focused on the returned XD05. The CommNet was silent for a time when suddenly, a new voice was heard.

"Tommy Tom Tom, this is Big Dawg." The word 'Dawg' was drawn out with an impromptu deep southern drawl. "One hour 'til the big touchdown. How do you read me?" There was the annoying sound of someone snapping gum.

"*Lima Charley, Sargent Layne.*"

"Dang Tom, you almost sound like Major Ronca. Is it a late night for you or early morning? I have some Ole Tennessee in my locker you can gargle with."

"*Oddly enough, Sargent Layne, this is Major Ronca. Captain Tomas Klasnick is beside me. He says hello.*"

"Sir, m-my apologies. I didn't know…" incredibly, he managed another quick snap of the gum.

"*You didn't realize the whole Homeport, from the top down, would be listening to your conversation as your team inspected the unexpected return of XD05?*"

"Um, copy that, Sir. I thought it would be a visual feed only. I…"

"*Stand corrected, Sargent. Lose the gum.*"

"It helps keep my ears from popping during atmospheric imbalances, Sir."

The whole of Homeport heard an audible groan coming from Captain Klasnick.

"*You will survive.*"

* * *

Sargent Layne felt a tap on his right shoulder. He heard the hiss and a slight vibration at his feet. On point, as the shuttle docked at the center of XD05, he waited for the lights of the airlock to cycle through.

It had been a while since he had worn the suit. Normally, coolant pumped through tiny microtubules kept the body at a comfortable temperature. He had been sweating since his conversation with the Major. Like an itch he couldn't scratch, he badly wanted to reach down and adjust the temp controls a bit cooler.

Optics in the helmet projected a HUD that seemed to float in the air before him. In the bottom corner of his display, he saw a timer click off percentages. Two minutes after being attached to the great ship, internal monitors would adjust air levels, green light the airlock, and open it up.

"You are so busted," said Schmidt on Team Channel. For the last hour, his team was relentless in their jibes. He could hear everything they said, and it went no further than his suit. No one else could hear them.

Being team leader, his communications, everything he said and did, was broadcasted back to Homeport. Being Command's visual, as well as audio, he couldn't even make crude hand gestures. They didn't design suits to allow people to flip off others behind their backs. The suit was flexible, but it had limitations.

"Rotation of the craft is stable," he said. "A fall from the Hub to the surface would be... unpleasantly painful, and the person falling would have a long time to contemplate their end."

*"What was that, Sargent Layne?"* Came the Major's voice over the link.

"Sir, just making an observation to my teammates. Precautionary measures."

*"Copy, stay focused."*

"Sir."

* * *

*"We have people!"* His camera bobbed as the airlock opened. The blue suits of fifteen to twenty people could be plainly seen. They were motionless.

*"People,"* Sgt. Layne said to them after touching his external speaker, *"we don't have much room in the shuttle, but we can take most of you."*

They did not respond.

He reached out and grabbed the first one. They spun, and the helmet turned to him.

*"They're dead!"* He whispered, looking into the hollowed eyes. The person was old. Gray hair was pulled back under the cap; the skin wrinkled around the eyes was deeper than crow's feet. Mouth agape, they had several teeth missing. With a simple tug, he pulled this one over his head back to his team.

*"Central Hub, you're not going to believe this."* His arm came within camera range as he did a quick headcount. *"I have twenty to thirty people here; they all appear to be elderly, so far, none are breathing. The suits are dark."*

"Clarify," said Major Ronca.

*"Sir, if the suits were operational, and we were in this close proximity, I would be able to get a ping from each one. We would be able to know that there was a gathering of people in the airlock well before we got there. The batteries of the suits burned out some time ago. They're dark."*

"I have never seen that happen before," Mable said. "The suits we use are not your off-the-shelf, run-of-the-mill suits. We're deep in space.

Someone gets lost out here, then the suit better carry them through till they are found. Two-day air tanks, auto-magnetic soles and gloves, spider lines, and a four-day battery backup are second to none. Each one has a micro-beacon that would stay active for years."

"Do any of them have name tags? Are we able to identify anybody?" Director Porter asked.

"Sgt. Layne, are you able to identify any of the individuals by name tags?" the Colonel relayed.

*"Sir, they're all blue maintenance suits. There are no names. Seven of these are male, three are definitely female, and the rest I cannot tell from simple observation."*

"Copy that."

"Director Porter," Mable tapped him on the shoulder, "I dispatched three medical teams," she whispered.

"My son's there." He sat forward in his chair. "We've got to find him."

"We will." Mable touched him on the arm. "It's only been a day and a half to two days."

"We have no one that old on that ship or at the station," said Capt. Klasnick. "Director Porter, everyone over fifty, is usually cycled out. Am I correct?"

"We have kept older people from time to time who are more experienced and have unique positions. It's retirement age. These people," he nodded to the live vid, "were much older than our oldest when they died."

"Do we have any type of facial recognition software?"

"No, we have no need for it here. There are no vagabonds or derelicts here at the Central Hub. If you are here, you are accounted for. The screening of individuals takes place back on Earth."

"Sgt. Layne, look at each one so that we can get a clear view of them on the camera."

It took a second or so, but there was a sudden jerk to his helmet, almost as if he was being pushed playfully by one of his comrades.

*"Yes, sir. Remove the helmets, Sir?"*

"No," he snapped quickly. "They must remain suited up. They and you are under quarantine at this time. If it is some type of contamination, we must have it contained."

*"Dobbins, let's start with the first one and then work our way back."*

*"There, something right there. Um, Miller, shake him just a little bit. Yep, right there. Major Ronca, there seems to be some foreign object that this gentleman put in his helmet before he put it on his head. What the hell! Oh, it's a video recorder. We will mark this one, Sir. Looks like he had a*

*message to get out."*

"LOOK!" Mabel was on her feet. "Look at this one! Sgt. Layne," she keyed the mic. "The one you just spun, turn him back around."

Sgt. Layne did so.

"Do you guys see this? I couldn't quite place it before, but it's right there. None of these people have tanks. There's no way they could have made it from the location of the Mag-El to here holding their breath. Someone brought them here. They probably took their tanks back down to the surface after they stripped them off."

\* \* \*

One by one, they look over each body as directed. No external wounds could be seen with the suits on. Dobbins lashed each one in the shuttle after the preliminary examination. Besides one having the recorder, there was another one with a paper notebook in his helmet.

As he secured the last one, Sgt. Layne turned and looked toward the airlock door once again.

From his wrist, he keyed the shuttle to return to those who waited. In physical contact with the wall, he felt the vibration of the ship releasing. Another one was activated at Homeport. It would latch onto the same door within the hour.

*"Sir, do we have the authorization to proceed?"*

Major Ronca looked to Director Porter.

"If something went wrong, if there was some kind of outbreak of some sort within a few hours of them leaving, then we have to know. The worst-case scenario is that there are no survivors, and we vent the gases and have the ship sitting vacuum for a year before we begin to rehabilitate it."

"That would mean starting whole ecosystems from scratch, from the bare-bones," said Mable.

"That is quite understandable," Major Ronca said. "We cannot have any of what's in there getting to here before we know what is going on. I don't want to be dead like these people in a few days," he said offhandedly.

Director Porter nodded. "They, and anyone else we send, will remain quarantined until we find out what is going on. Again I say, my son is in there. They may move ahead."

Maj. Ronca keyed his mic. "Sgt. Layne, you have a green light to proceed."

*"Copy, Sir.*

\* \* \*

The airlock cycled through the lights, and the door opened. The tethers around the lock hung motionless. External sensors in the suits took readings. The lower right corner of his HUD lit up. Going through a quick rainbow of colors before it settled back down. Stats on common gasses were nil.

"Sir, my suit was screened and cleared out before I left, and everything is working properly. These readings are not due to a faulty suit. Everything is down all across the board. Readings are all low. There is no atmospheric pressurization in the Hub. Eighteen kilometers to the surface. There should be normal levels as the air here is controlled." Sgt. Layne looked at the floor to take in all that was conveyed by the HUD. This gave them a dark background to view his HUD. Had he looked in the glare of a window, some visual info may have been lost to those watching. After a moment, he reached up and grabbed a tether to pull himself through the lock.

"Lights are out. Harris, get to Hub Central and try to bring them up. With the burner online, it should be brighter here. Channel some light if you have to. Schmidt, find the internal comm. We'll find out where they are."

Harris pulled himself along toward his right, Schmidt over his head.

*"Sargent Layne, move closer to the bay window. I'd like to see what we can see from here."*

"Copy, Sir."

* * *

Sitting beside his assistant Mable, Richard watched the CommVids.

Major Ronca and Captain Klasnick were in their usual combat fatigues. Their dress uniforms were used mostly for ceremonial occasions. Richard had only seen them worn three or four times. When XD became operational, they were sent to Homeport as a police detachment. Although there was the occasional fight to settle, they, and those in their command, had it somewhat easy. They had taken over the duties of escorts with enthusiasm. It broke the boredom.

Mable gave Richard a tentative smile. She was the one that was the most nervous in the room. She fidgeted and tapped her fingers on the table. On her third cup of coffee, it would have been pointless to ask her to settle. Captain Klasnick gave her a look from time to time.

"Major," she said, leaning forward, tapping the CommVid inlaid in the table before her. The image froze in place. "There are no IPV's in the Hub. The system is in place that allows at least one shuttle to be in the Hub at all times. It's a fail-safe."

"How many IPV's on XD05?" asked the Captain.

"Four hundred fifty," Richard said. "Ten were being used by the people on board when they… well, two days ago. The rest were moth-balled on the far end, the Morning Wall, awaiting the ship's arrival to Sol. There were a few Pea Pods in use as well."

"Sir," Mable stopped fidgeting long enough to speak. "Send a second someone to Hub Central. One to work the Hub lighting, the second to contact the IPV's. If they cannot get any shuttles back, they'll have to descend to the surface manually."

Sgt Layne was contacted, and he dispatched a third person.

*"Sir,"* his voice wavered slightly. *"I'm looking out of the large bay window. There is one large crack running from bottom to center and has like a… like a film on it. Going in closer so you may pick this up on CommVid."* He wiped the window with his gloved hand and removed some of the debris. His camera panned around for just a moment as he looked outside the Hub.

*"Director Porter."* A woman's voice came over the open channel. It was not difficult to imagine that despite the workload, every able-bodied person at Homeport was watching the feed from Sgt. Layne's camera. The woman spoke before Richard could acknowledge her. *"From what I can see, it looks like the whole surface is brown. It's a lighter brown than the soil that we used. When the ship was sent off, we had a variety of plants there, but they only took up the first quad in the cylinder. The brown that is there is something completely different. Something took over what we once had."*

"What would you think it is?" Col. Ronca asked.

*"I cannot positively say without going down to the surface and looking. Might be some kind of plant system or a series of surface roots. I cannot tell."*

"How did these roots get here, Miss?" asked Colonel Ronca. "They could not have grown so quickly."

*"I am not sure why it is so over-grown. We have been working with fast-growing vines, but nothing this fast. They are aggressive if not controlled. They are meant to be pruned, tended to, and destroyed if need be; otherwise, they will grow rampant. They are a very invasive species. In a matter of a day, it would not have grown this much. We are talking years though. At least five to twenty years of growth."*

"I see. And who are you?"

*"Deborah McClanahan, Chief Botanist, Sir."*

"Deborah, where are you?" asked Director Porter.

*"I have set up a post on XD06. We have been pretty busy here."*

Captain Klasnick cleared his throat. "You are sure this is what they are?"

Silence answered him. He was about to ask again when Sgt. Layne's voice came over the VidComm.

*"Sir's, we sent a ping out to the IPV's. They are all non-operational. Schmidt, check the door."* Through Sgt. Layne's feed the soldier shoved off and floated to the nearest door.

"Sgt. Layne, what was that to your right?"

The camera turned back. *"The bottom part of a maintenance suit, Sir. There was a glove over there, and Dobbins found a sleeve. Someone undressed up here when the place still had atmospheric pressure."*

*"The power is still out,"* Schmidt replied. *"No way to open the door with it dead."*

"The Hub is a big facility," said Director Porter. "To get out into space, there are a handful of maintenance airlock doors that are magnetically locked, and they will have to cut through. The shuttle tubes lead directly out. There are four; one in each direction. Five to ten meters in length tops. Could you check on these, please?"

Sgt. Layne whistled, *"Schmidt, this one. Harris, there. Dobbins, there. I'll take this one."* Sgt Layne's hand reached out and pulled him towards a shuttle tube. In the darkness, his lamp came on automatically. Over the comm channel, he growled.

"A problem, Sargent?"

*"Foot caught, sir. Good thing too. Wall sides are smooth. I did not have much momentum, and it would be awhile until I reached the plug at the end."*

The camera rocked back and forth a bit, showing the darkness of the tube, and with a shove and slight grunt, Sgt. Layne pushed off. At first, the camera looked back the way he started. The dim light of the Hub grew ever more distant. He turned his head in the direction of travel.

He was able to rotate and land feet first.

He paused and looked back into the darkness. *"Sir, Dobbins and Schmidt did not have the forward momentum needed. They are, at the moment, traveling very slow and have made little progress."* There was a hint of laughter in his voice.

Mable spoke up. "Sgt Layne, use caution. Find a place to tether yourself to."

*"Copy."* His hand reached behind his back, and he tugged the spider line. With a metallic click, he was secured to the side of the shuttle tube wall.

*"Lamp off,"* Suddenly, it was dark. The glass at the end of the tube had a much heavier film over it was also in shadow. *"Lamp on."*

After a few moments, he radioed back.

*"Sir, the glass of the airlock has been shattered."*

"Something really, really bad must've happened. The damage to the window may have caused the depressurization of the Hub."

Sgt. Layne finished clearing out bits of glass, careful not to rupture his suit. He pushed each one of these outward, and they drifted away.

*"Oh yeah, that's a long way down."* The camera changed views, and they were looking eighteen kilometers down at a brown tangled mass that covered the inside of the ship. There were no clouds. Toward the far end, the Morning end, the sky turned a pale blue.

"Would you be able to make it to the wall? If you cannot go down with an IPV, do you think you can go down manually? There are magnetic elevators, but with the power being out, they will not work."

*"Um, sir, we are really close to the ship bulkhead. If we use the spider cables, I do not see that it would be much of a problem. Time-consuming mostly. We have to repel down the surface at two-hundred meters at a time once we hit the atmosphere. Even with gravity kicking in, we should be fine."*

"We have to see if the others are alive. Sgt. Layne, give us a nice slow shot of everything around you. Start off to the left and work your way to the right. Deborah McClanahan, if you see anything of importance, please let us know."

*"Yes, sir."*

"I see nothing green here. Everything looks dead; old, and dead." In a few moments, he was done. "I will head back to the Hub, gather my people, and will get to the ship's surface straight away." Sgt. Layne brought his head back into the tube, turned on an axis, planted his feet beneath him, and pushed off.

* * *

They kicked off from the Hub as a unit. Freefall very close to the wall was the best way to travel this long distance with no elevator. "Stay ready people," Sgt. Layne said. "We are dropping, and although it may look slow, things have a way of sneaking up on you." He kept rotating around, giving everybody a clear view from his camera of what was going on. People rambled over the intercom.

*"That's all brown. There should be some green throughout the vehicle."*

*"You think something poisoned the atmosphere?"*

*"If it did, there would be notable trace gas or gases. Nothing we have, nothing we know of can do that much damage in so little time and then*

*leave unexpectedly. We would have remnants of it throughout."*

"Sir, when they passed into the sunlight, we were able to get a better readout from the burner. The sunshine is down by five percent."

*"These things are built to last."*

*"This is true. There is no way that there can be a 5% reduction in sunlight within two days."*

"Sir, Sgt. Layne here again. We are starting to accelerate. The pull of G is catching up with us. Nothing bad right now. We will be hitting the atmosphere very soon."

"Hey Sarge," Dobbins came over the team channel. "At the hub, we were not spinning that fast. What if the ground is spinning faster than we are?"

"The ground is spinning faster than we are. If there were no atmosphere, we'd be a tomato hitting a fan."

"Hey! That's not even funny."

They were well beyond any help from tossing out spider lines.

"Don't sweat it, Dobs. When we hit the atmosphere, the arrow pushed against us. By the time we get to the surface, we will be up to speed."

"I hope," the desperation was out of his voice, "I wore my good suit."

* * *

The parachutes automatically deployed at one thousand five hundred meters.

"We had the wind almost a half kilometer early. Atmospheric pressure is quite oppressive. The suits make it bearable. It is super heavy here, but the suits are still within operating parameters." Layne said. His camera recorded and broadcasted the whole descent.

*"Where are you at?"*

"Sir, I believe this is near magnetic elevator number four, Twilight Wall."

*"We are prepping two other teams to send over. In addition, three medical units and also a third team to work on the magnetic elevators."*

"Copy, Sir," Lane said, looking at his feet dangling beneath him.

* * *

Richard sat back. "Send over some tankers. We have to get those guys to siphon off some atmosphere. Those gases are way too heavy to work with."

"Director," it was Debra's voice from X-ray Delta 06. "The oxygen content is too high. I believe that somehow if the plants grew at an accelerated pace, they used so much $CO_2$ that they eventually used it all up. In effect, they were suffocated. They suffocated themselves. The same would happen if they were thousands of people in a small, contained area. $CO_2$ levels would rise just enough to become toxic."

"Something like this just doesn't happen overnight."

"I do understand that. This type of growth, even if it were accelerated, with the amount of water on board and 20.5 sunlight, would take years to produce the results that we see here."

"Is there any chance that the vessel could rupture being as bloated as it is?"

"Sir, Jacob Michelson, here on '06 as well. The structural integrity of '05 is solid. It would take a lot more than that to hurt her. You take away the shielding, and that thing is meant to withstand quite a bit. Bleeding the access of atmo off will be a good thing, but it's not crucial."

Mabel leaned close and whispered. "He's a design engineer. One of our top people."

"How much time will take to bleed it off then?"

"That's a lot of volume to remove, Sir. If we added to what we have here, it will accelerate everything on '06 by several months. I think we are almost ready to bring down the containment and have a full atmosphere down the shaft. It takes a lot of time to build that up. If we combine the two and balance it out, we can get up to, oh, 32 percent. Give or take. As to your query, transferring it from there to here with tankers running continuously off the top of my head, I'd say about a month at the earliest."

Ronca tapped the glass tabletop with his finger. "If there is something harmful in the air, I do not want it transferred to another ship." Jacob cleared his throat.

"Will have a series of bio-filters in place and take only what is needed. We can have it filtered down to the molecule. Everything else will be filtered out and held for analysis."

"Well, we could wait a few months and get the atmosphere that we need, or we can pack it all up and send it to earth and let them divvy it out."

Even though she mentioned it, Mabel was not too happy about the prospect. Richard opened the channels so everyone on the site could hear him. "People, this is Director Porter. We're still working out the details of what is happening. At this time, I am uncertain of the fate of the people who were traveling on XD05 and heading back to Sol. I will set up a statement, and we will send word." His voice wavered slightly. "My son Brandon was among those on this trip, and it makes it very personal. We will do our best to continue our mission and also find out what is happening. I know everybody has questions, and we are all looking for answers. The channels will be open. If you have any suggestions, please go to your department head. I need help from everybody."

* * *

When Layne hit the surface, clouds of dust rose up around his feet as he struck what looked to be a dense tangle of vines. He sunk in almost to his knees, and the dust settled quickly.

"Whoa! I thought these things were solid. They turn to dust as soon as you touch them."

*"Can you pick one up?"*

The voice of the chief botanist what's-her-name came over from Homeport.

"Ma'am, as soon as I attempt to, they turned to dust."

*"The weather system is down,"* someone said.

With the channel open, it was difficult to know who was speaking.

*"If there was wind or rain, the water would break down like the soldiers are doing. For some reason, they don't have the weather."*

"Sir, Dir. Porter, we will have to send over as many people as we can get this vehicle up and running."

Harris was moving in circles, reaching out and touching everything that he could, but it all turned to dust at his touch.

"Sir, Sgt. Layne here. If this place is covered with deadlines, should we continue our recon?

*"If the weather is down, then these people may still be alive, surviving on rations. We have to find the survivors. Continue on the ground to Hotel Libra, and we will let you know from there."*

"Copy that, Sir,"

Parachutes were disengaged, harnesses slipped off, and left where they lay.

XD05, Day 2 - "I'm wasted, and I can't find my way home," *Blind Faith*

There was a party that night for everyone on board. It was their going away and coming home party wrapped up into one. All the grown-ups had changed from their working clothes into clothing that was much nicer. One man wore a fancy, well-tailored suit, and another wore a shirt that was very colorful with large flowers. The women dressed up nicely.

Unlike the others, I had no fancy clothes with me. Everything was as plain as it comes. I wore a red shirt with red sequins sewn on the sleeves. The pants I had were plain, simple, blue denim. They were a gift from my aunt because I had grown since arriving, and they were more comfortable than any of the thin jumpsuits I had worn during my six-month-long stay. It was a wonderful feeling.

Daniels had looked through her luggage and picked out something for me to wear. It was a large scarf that I wrapped around my middle, chest, and tied behind my neck. It felt different, but she said it looked great—a nice accent.

The military commander gave everyone the evening off from duties. Daniels had changed from her uniform into a pretty red dress. We both wore red, and we matched each other.

Everyone was happy.

It would take the massive ship three days to get back and once there, another three until the smaller tug-ships found it. The smaller but more powerful tug-ships would bring the '05 to its place in the solar system as other ships shuttled people on and off. My family would come, and I would be home once again. Daniels said the three days getting back to Sol would be time enough to recuperate from the party.

"Stay close," Daniels knelt and whispered so no one else in the crowd would hear. "And if you need to go pee or anything, you let me know, K?"

"K," I replied in a whisper as I held her hand. Being in a grand hall in the hotel, I could go back to my room. That's what everyone else was counting on. They were fortunate that they did not have to go far and could drink as much as they wanted to. Many, by the looks of it, had already started.

"If things happen tonight and we get separated, you know the way back to your room?"

"Yep," I have no real plans of leaving the hotel. If I went away from the hotel, I could not go far. My science teacher, Mr. Crumlich, told us that each block of the city was a one square kilometer section. There was no way to go beyond without walking through a gate under the ribbon of the track. They locked the gates. The makers did not want the guests and staff roaming around and making a mess of the ship before the port of call. There was little chance I would get lost.

"Go," I motioned with my hand. I had to smile at her. They told this soldier to watch over me, I guess, and she was doing her job to the letter. I could tell she was getting antsy and wanted to chat with her friends. "I'll be fine," I added.

The music was loud. Some people were dancing on the tiled floor. Many just mingled for now. A mechanical server at the bar gave me a fizz with ice, which I took to the side. I explored, found the steps to the balcony, and sat so I could watch over everyone.

For a hall this big, there were not that many people. I tried to do a count, but the people were always moving around from group to group. There were ten with gray in their hair. The rest were notably younger. Those who were soldiers stood out from the others. I could tell them apart easily.

A man entered with a large white bird on his forearm. He wore a red shirt, much like the one I wore. It sparkled like mine, as if there were sequins sewn on it. He wore bright green pants and blue shoes. He also had a scarf around his neck, and I thought at first he wore a hat, then I realized his hair was jet black and just slicked back with some oil or cream.

The bird was bigger than those they used on the ship. When it opened its wings, he had to hold it away, or the bird would have slapped his face. It bobbed its head a few times, and the feathers on top rose to make it even taller.

He held it up for everyone to see and made sure they looked at him, too. After a short time, I noticed that people seem to move away from him. Either they did not like him, or the bird, or both. I feel just a little sorry for him. His laughter was loud and quick. It carried over everybody, and I could hear him distinctly even from where I watched. He cleared his throat often. Moving from group to group, he made a flashy show before going to another. The bird shrieked a few times. When it did so, the conversation in the dance hall would suddenly stop.

The bird pooped once.

"Lawrence!" He scolded. Taking napkins, he covered the spot on the floor. "You're a very bad bird." He exclaimed, shaking his finger at its beak. He excused himself, and after waving to a few people, he entered the doorway beneath me. About ten minutes later, he returned without the bird and in a different shirt.

A man entered. Not tall, but young, well-groomed, and well-tailored. He smiled and waved at people. He shook hands, chatted, but always moved on. He never stopped smiling.

I drank my fizz and soon grew bored.

"People," the well-groomed man stood near the bar spoke. "Please. People, can I have your attention, please?" Everyone grew quiet, and they stopped the music. "I am Porter, Brandon Porter. I am not trying to fill my father's shoes, but I do want to pass on his warm regards. Thank you all for your help. X-ray Delta oh five is a crowning achievement to humanity. Soon the ship you see will be the home of over a hundred thousand people. Farmers, businesses, and families. From many nations and many walks of life. Food grown here will help feed millions more. Again, we are making history. Like the ocean-going ships created centuries ago, or the first airplanes built by our forefathers, what we do today will impact humanity for many lifetimes. I know I possibly sound like my father, but what we do and who we are, here and now, is monumental. Thank you all for being a part of this."

"We have currently dropped out of space. The galaxy is spinning around us, and we are traveling forward through time. In the morning, when we all sober up or not, the computers will turn off the engines, and we'll be back in normal space no worse for wear. I do not wish to sound nostalgic, but I hope this feeling, that we have almost conquered the universe, never goes away."

"A toast," someone said. Everyone echoed it. They quickly gave those without drinks whatever was available.

"A toast to…"

"Mankind."

"XD05."

"Home."

"Earth."

We all drank.

I sipped my fizz. The straw made a slurping noise, and, embarrassed, I quickly ducked back. I heard people laughing and felt my cheeks grow flush. It was dark here, and I was sure no one had seen me.

"Enjoy everyone," his voice echoed in the silence. "Music." He motioned with his hand, and someone started the music. They soon filled the hall with noise.

* * *

After my third fizz and some snacks at the bar, I soon got really bored. I did not return to the balcony, but instead took the elevator all the way up. Through a door, I found steps and walked out into the open air. On the rooftop, I watched the sunset. To my delight, several small birds fluttered around. It was good to hear them and watch them play.

* * *

The soft chime of the clock woke me in the morning. In my room, amongst some toys in a toy box, I found a soccer ball. Adults brought it, knowing it would help occupy a kid's time. Like a prized egg, or a treasured orb, I held the blue and red ball in my hands for several moments, marveling at its stitching and the contours of the hexagons.

I wanted to walk. Just walk. Not move back and forth through narrow hallways, not shove off from one wall to another. I wanted to walk in wide-open spaces where I could not touch the walls. To be in a place where there was nothing over my head but sky and clouds.

There were very few people awake that morning when the elevator doors opened. I tapped the ball with my foot out through the main lobby to the sidewalk and walking path.

They divided the city that ringed the whole of this huge ship up into a grid-work of walls. This gave me the space of a square kilometer (kilometer square, km2, or kim-two) to play in.

There were no vehicles down on the surface, just the shuttles on their elevated tracks above to carry people about. Once you arrived close to your destination, you had to take an elevator down from the platform and walk the rest of the way. Theoretically, you had to walk no less than a half kilometer from where the shuttle dropped you off at. The kim-two where the Hotel Lima sat had many broad walking paths and a stream that meandered through.

With it still early and the people recovering from the party of the night before, I could kick and chase after the soccer ball without them getting upset.

As I was doing this, I kept my head down to not miss a kick. Once, when my thoughts took me elsewhere, I happened to look up. Before me was the most beautiful thing ever. My breath caught in my throat. It was the simple things I found pure joy in.

I stopped suddenly where the gray cobblestone ended. My own momentum threatening to spill me over. Slightly off-balance, I raised my hands rapidly lest I fall forward. The ball carried momentum and rolled on a short distance in front of me.

Regaining my balance, I went to my knees and then lay down on the edge of the cobblestone path. My arms crossed beneath me, I brought my head down as far as I dared. There, just a few centimeters from my nose, was grass. A tender green blade starting from the dirt below me curled up as it reached to gather strength from the sunlight. There were more. Thousands more did the same. Young, vulnerable lives with roots intertwined were striving for the same purpose. This close, I could smell the good earth and the actual aroma of the grass itself.

I had been at Homeport with its recycled air for so long I had forgotten what this was like. In class, they had talked about it. The teacher had mentioned that mankind had a connection with nature, and it was part of his innermost being to find peace here once again. All I know is that I remembered I really enjoyed feeling its touch as it tickled my feet.

I giggled as I took my shoes and socks off. One quick look around, and I ran and spun. The soccer ball, now all but forgotten, I grew dizzy with laughter, and when my feet could no longer carry me, I lay in the grass laughing at the sun.

Arms at my side, I closed my fingers, and with a gentle tug, several blades came free. I held them up, and they fell from my grasp to land on my face.

I sighed. A few more days here, then a shuttle back to Earth, and I could do this to my heart's content when I returned to my family on earth.

I raised up on my elbows and found the soccer ball just out of my reach. My shoes and socks were still on the cobblestone, I laid back down and felt the slender blades tickle the back of my neck.

This was wonderful.

\* \* \*

I heard voices later. The adults were now waking up. I crab-walked over to the soccer ball and kicked it hard, so it rolled off the grass. I quickly followed it. With my shoes and socks back on, I kicked the soccer ball while watching it.

When I came to a building with its back to the wall, I stopped. The ball bounced on the brick surface and then rolled back past me. I giggled and went back the way I had come.

When I returned to the hotel, I was nearly breathless. Seeing others nearby, I picked up the ball. They would frown upon it if I kicked it inside the hotel or struck someone.

The people were quiet. They were talking in quick, hushed tones.

"Sally," Daniels called as she came over. She was back in uniform, and her eyes looked tired. She probably enjoyed the night and didn't get much sleep. "Hey, um, you doing okay?"

"Yip, just kicking the ball around." I wiped my forehead and lowered my voice to a whisper. I could trust Daniels with the secret. "There's grass, real green growing grass, right down that way."

"Are you serious?" Daniels replied with her eyes wide in awe.

"Shh, yes," I whispered with a finger to my lips. "Yes, I am. Only you and I know about this, ok?"

"I won't tell anyone," she smiled, but I knew she would keep my secret. I liked her most out of the whole bunch. She had freckles.

Daniels squatted down, so she was eye level with me.

"There may have been problems, you know, small things. A bunch of tech guys headed over to the Morning Hub to find out what the heck is going on," she said in a whisper, as if telling me one of her own secrets.

"Is the ship broke?" I whispered back.

"Eh, not a thing to worry about. They'll get us through. Heard we came through it all and popped back into space just fine. They couldn't reach the tuggers to pull us in. Hey," her voice went back to normal. She tapped the soccer ball I had tucked in the crook of my arm. "You've been kicking that ball?"

"Oh yeah, lots of fun. I love to run."

"Huh, me too. You must do a lap with me tonight."

I smiled back.

"Grab a shower and come back down, kiddo. They may have lunch ready soon. Everyone overslept, so we get what we get."

I nodded and, forgetting myself, bounced the ball twice in the lobby before I got to the elevator.

* * *

There was a meeting that night. Everyone seemed on edge. At first, they would not let me sit in, but Daniels brought up the point that it involved me as well. I promised to be still, not fidget, and to listen.

People had brought in folding chairs to the large room they had the party last night. They arranged these in a large circle. Many had drinks from the bar, but the mood was not happy. They gave me a fizz, but like the others, placed it beside me.

The man who had the bird last night was here, but thankfully he did not bring the bird. Like a circus clown, his clothing was as bright as ever. He took a seat and kept coughing short quick coughs as if he were hiding some noise.

"What do we have?" Someone asked.

"Um," began Brandon, the important man from the night before, who stood in the center. "To stop any rumors, I'll tell everyone what has happened first and then try to convey what we need to do. First off is that they scheduled us to jump back into space as normal. Something went wrong; we are back in space, but not where we should be. It seems the ship only traveled about halfway there before it slid back in."

"Was there a malfunction with the computer?"

"We've checked several times. Tom has been down at the command center most of the day. He believes that an influence on the outside caused us to jump back in. Our systems are all up and operational. Everything is nominal."

"What could influence the ship from the outside? Technically, they say we are not even in the universe until we reach home," someone said.

"A cargo ship left Homeport a month ago. When it reached Sol, the pilot stated that he must have been off in the calculations. He took an extra day of space travel to get to this port." Brandon spoke up and then stepped back. "I'll let Tom tell us all about his findings. Tom."

With that, a man stood. His shirt was a festive one. Bright and colorful with many flowers and leaves. He wore tan shorts and sandals.

"Something seems to have knocked us off course. As he said, the only thing I can figure is that a bump in the road caused the ship's computer to hiccup and drop us out on time, but not where we intended to be. If this happened, then there is something huge and slow-moving in our path. It may be awhile before we can go on."

"How big?"

"Massive. It would have to be. Bigger than a planet, a couple of suns in mass. It could be the remnants of a burnt-out star—a dwarf. A drifter just passing by. But it is an elephant that we cannot get around. We'll just have to wait it out."

"Is there no way around it?"

"We cannot return to Homeport. If we returned, we could have someone plot a different course and go from there. If this thing catches us in its gravitational pull," he spun on his heel a little, and his sandals squeaked. "Then we are traveling away from where we need to be. We are already here, and frankly, no one here knows about the part of the computer involved. The navigation part. They encrypt all of that and lock us out. They did not wish to have someone bumbling around and sending the ship to where it's not supposed to go. Security protocols."

"Is this thing going to hit us?" A woman asked.

"Um." There was a worried look on his face, and he paused. This is something that he may not have thought of before. "More than likely, XD05 would rotate around the thing, like in orbit, for a time until it lets us go or we break free from it. It will fling us elsewhere when that time comes."

A man stood so they could see him above the others. His business suit was clean and pressed. "How long will that be?" he asked crisply.

"It would all depend on the orbit. We could skip across its gravity field like a rock across the water or just settle in and stay awhile. I doubt we would get sucked in and destroyed."

"How likely would that be?" the man asked again. He remained standing.

"X-ray Delta 05 would have to be traveling fast, relative to this mass. We would have to hit it at the right angle and at the right speed to suck us in or to skip across it. So, it is more likely that it has grabbed us and is spinning us around."

"Again, you're not answering my question," the man said as he chuckled a little. "Based on your theories, how long do you believe we will be here?"

"Not very long. The ship, relative to the surrounding space, is not moving or is on a slow coast. When we were to pop back into the solar system, they didn't want this huge thing flying so fast they could not catch it. I'm quite sure everybody remembers Rada II."

The man in the suit remained standing. "How is it, then, that you know of this presence that pulled us out of space?"

Tom gave him a curt look that lasted just a second before he regained his composure.

"We have instruments on board inside the ship that enable us to look outside. They wouldn't leave us entirely blind."

"If I didn't know any better," said the man still standing, "I would say this thing, this massive sun, or black-hole, is just a ruse, and you really don't know what happened to the computers of the ship. You do not understand why they happened to drop us out where we are. It is something you made up to calm our fears."

"I'm sorry," Brandon said, taking the floor once more. "What is your name?"

"My name is not important, Brandon. What is important is that I have someplace I have to be and would like to be there as soon as possible. I cannot be here. It doesn't matter if there is something sitting in our path, or a computer malfunction, or a glitch somewhere else. What matters is that I need to get there at your earliest convenience. I did not board this ship to become stranded out here."

"We understand, sir. None of us wants to be here. We all want to be back home, and we're trying the best we can to see that this happens in a timely manner."

"Well then," the man paused dramatically. "I would think this is our top priority. We need to fix this thing and get home."

"We are working on just that."

"Let us hope it is enough. Point of fact, I cannot stay here." The man picked up a small case at his feet and left. He did not make eye contact with anyone. He muttered to himself until he was away from the room.

There was a murmur as everyone whispered. I did not fidget and sat quietly, listening.

"What it all comes down to is that we are here, and we should make the best of it." Tom clapped his hands once and sat in his chair.

Brandon stood. "Not that I like being here, but we should get in the mindset that we may be here for a while."

"What do you mean, a while?"

"It may take time for us to get things in order and back on our way." The noise level in the hall grew. Brandon was getting frustrated.

"People, this ship is a self-guiding ship. The computer must do the mathematics involved, and there is no way that human hands can do it. I don't have access to the computer systems involved. They locked us out. Once we get into them, then we can figure out how to start the engines and how to get home."

"Until then?"

"Until then, there isn't much else we can do. As they were building this ship, food was put on-board, ready for when the ship arrived in Sol. People could move right in. Homeport had planted a few hectares of crops months before we left."

"We have over twenty different vegetables alone," someone stated. I could hear a sense of pride in their voice. "They started growing trees well over four years ago. Some are bearing fruit."

"They planted about a third of the east end with fruit trees." said another. "It helps with the atmosphere. Why create it when you can grow plants to do the job for you?"

"People, we won't be here that long." A woman stood up and held her hands out as if pleading. "I am sure Brandon is talking just a few days or a month at the most. We can't be 'stuck' here. I don't think he means that long."

The hall grew quiet. Again, everyone looked at Brandon and Tom.

Tom took a deep breath. "We have what we have. We don't have rockets; we have computer-guided Samuel Drives. We will try to get in and work with them. We are stranded somewhere between one port and another. We should think about settling in for the long haul. If they found our signal, it would take time to get ships to us to get us home."

The woman sat down slowly. She cried a little. I looked at Daniels, and she had an odd look on her face. She gave me a quick smile and then looked back.

"So, this takes care of our food," a soldier said in the silence. "What about the sunlight thing? Will that last?"

Tom cleared his throat. "It's nuclear and will see us through for many years."

"Water?"

"We have enough water for everyone supposed to board within a few days. There should be enough here for hundreds of thousands of people. XD05 is one of the wettest ships we have to date."

Someone in the crowd answered for him. "Yeah, the farmers need a lot in reserve for their crops. We have enough water."

Brandon was looking a little harried. Tom looked back at Brandon, who only nodded and said nothing.

"Can we space-walk?" This question was asked by another man who was still wearing festive clothing. Like Tom, his shirt was red with white flowers.

"What? Um, they might have service suits, but that would be ill-advised. Because of the design of the ship, we could not physically look outside. We have no portal from which we can look out. Again, with safety protocols, I doubt that anyone should go down to the actual Morning or Twilight Hub."

Brandon nodded his head. They talked for a while longer, but most of the information was already given out.

"In a nutshell," Daniels leaned over and whispered. "They know something happened, but they don't know what."

"Will everything be okay?" I asked.

"It will," she smiled, looked down at me, and patted my knee. "It may be a little while before you see your family again. Are you going to be okay with that?"

I looked away and watched all the people for a moment. I felt her hand on my chin, and she turned my head so I could look into her eyes.

"I will be fine," I said.

"You will?" She did not let go of my chin.

"I will. They love me, but they send me off to visit relatives in exciting places when they can. So, I'm a little used to being away from them. It will be okay. And you?"

She gave me a puzzled look.

"Are you going to be okay? You are away from your family too."

"I am a soldier. My family are those who serve with me."

"You don't have a mommy and dad?"

"I do," she said, squeezing my hand. "And two sisters and one brother. They are all older than I am. One sister and I had a heated argument when I left. It's best if we let things cool down a little. When I get back to them, they will be happy to see me."

"That's good," I whispered. "I have no brothers or sisters yet. If mommy has more babies, I will be the oldest."

Daniels looked at me and smiled.

XD05, Week 1 - "Take a walk on the wild side." *Lou Reed*

"Air is on. They pressurized the suit," Cameron said.

*"Good."* Several people were checking out the suit, looking him over for anything out of place. They nodded from time to time and whispered amongst themselves. Everything seemed to be green. *"Freedom of movement? Wiggle your fingers, bend your elbows. Good."* A man to the side checked off several things on his clipboard.

"Communication check; can you hear me?" He said into the microphone in the helmet.

*"We can hear you, Lima Charlie."* Came the reply from a guy by one terminal.

"Huh?"

*"Loud and clear. Military, you know 'Lima Charlie'?"*

"I never served," he said forthrightly.

*"Oh, okay."* They looked over the suit one last time. *"Okay, now reach behind you to your left. No, with your left hand. Yes, that's correct. There is an oversized D-ring, feel it? Right beneath the air tank is 200 meters of spider cable. When you get into the airlock, as it is cycling through, you need to secure this on one tether. If you don't, and you drift away, heaven forbid, it will take a few minutes to get somebody suited up to come to get you. If it were to happen and you drift away over 200 meters, you are officially humped."*

Someone else slapped him on the shoulder. *"I saw no mobility packs here that will allow us to maneuver around in outer space. No one thought about doing any outside maintenance in transit. So, they didn't pack that suit."*

"So, you couldn't come get me?"

*"We could, but if you drift away over 200 meters, then as Ron said, you're officially humped,"* said the man with the clipboard.

"Gee, thanks."

*"Just hook the D-ring onto something as a precautionary measure, please."*

"Copy."

*"How is your field of view?"*

He craned his neck. "Yeah, I can see pretty good actually," he looked at them in the eyes. He moved around a little bit. "You know, for the size of these things, they feel light."

*"True, they design them so that the person could last for several days if need be. You can recharge tanks on the go,"* said the man with the clipboard. *"Okay, you're good to go. Are you nervous?"*

Cameron held up his hand, thumb, and forefinger close together. "Just a wee bit," he said.

*"You should be; I'd be shaking if I were in your shoes."*

"Glad I went to pee first," he said, and they laughed. It broke the tension.

He tugged on one tether and pulled himself toward the airlock. Drifting in, he grabbed another and stopped his forward momentum. He found the clip and secured it to the wall. Pushing back, there was a slight vibration at his lower back as the spider cable gave him room.

"It's like a dog leash," his voice shook a little as it came over the intercom.

*"It will maintain the slightest amount of tension. There are controls on the wrist pad if you need more or less. When there is less tension, it will retract back into the housing. There will be an audible beep when you get close to the end."*

The door closed with a click and then several more as the locks hit home. There was a change in the way the suit felt around him as it sucked the air out of the room. The surrounding noise of the ship itself became less and less until the only thing he heard were the sounds coming over the comm system.

A light behind him turned green.

He took a deep breath and pulled a tether with his hand. He slipped silently from the airlock. Vibration worked its way in through the spider cable at the small of his back.

So far, he could see only the darkness out there. "Can you kill the lights in the airlock? Light them up when I come back, but for now, they're blinding me a bit."

It felt dark when they killed the lights. He could see stars.

At Homeport, in the housing, and on the great ships, it was mostly rock and dust on the verge of condensing into planets. Ranging in size from grains of sand to rocks and ice the size of hillsides, it was an ideal way to work with them. There was no gravity well that they had to climb out of with payloads of raw material. Visibility beyond was very limited with the water so muddy, sort of speaking. It was hard to see through the cloud to the universe beyond.

"Well, we have definitely jumped back into the Galaxy. Wow, this thing is huge. I see a lot of stars here. Going to take a while to take it all in."

*"Ha ha, you're a funny guy. Get those hatches open. We gotta get those sensors started, so they know what they're dealing with."*

He floated still and silent for three whole minutes.

*"Cameron, are you still there?"*

"Yeah, yeah. She was right; there are no words to describe this," he whispered. Pictures, videos, 3-D; none of it can ever compare.

*"Come on, Cam, we're waiting."*

He turned, and hanging onto the hull of the ship, worked hand-over-hand down the outside. A beep came over the intercom.

"What was that?" He asked nervously.

*"50 meters."*

"I thought I had 300."

*"You have 200; it's the standard amount. The sound was just your cable counter telling you how far you've gone. You have 150 to go, but the access panels are not that far ahead."*

He made it to the place. A quick depression of the button and the panel opened. The cables were still there, just disconnected from the device. It was just a matter of reconnecting them with the wiring harnesses.

"Why would they not keep these connected?" he asked as he matched them up.

*"We do not know. Something about if they are active during transit, it will screw up the system. Like a magnet affecting the compass."*

"Do you think this is what happened to us? Made us go off course?"

*"No, no. It is a standalone system."* It was the voice of the man with the clipboard. *"It's not part of the navigational system at all. When the shell formed around Ex-Dee-oh-five and we spiraled back to Earth, they didn't want the system reaching out and gathering information. There is no need for it. If they know the position of the ship in the universe, then there is no need for this tracking."*

"But what I am reconnecting is a galactic positioning system, a GPS," Cameron said. "I find it hard to believe they would not use this to get us where we're going. If not the primary system, they would use it for a backup or something to check and make sure."

*"I did not design the thing, Cameron. I believe they felt so confident in their navigational computer they felt they didn't need a backup. The computer controls the duration of the time we are in the shell. We pop out of the galaxy, the galaxy spins over top of us, and then we pop back in. If these devices were working while we were in the shell, they would have false readings. They are looking for specific quasars, and if they cannot find them, the whole thing goes haywire."*

"Um, yeah, I kind of understood that. I think you gave me a lesson in Greek. I'm just an electrician; I'm not a scientist. Okay, it looks like that's it." Before he closed the lid, two small lights in the circuitry began the blinking green.

"I can only see part of the galaxy from the side of the ship. I hope it's enough."

*"The ship is spinning, so it should take an hour. It will have a whole field of view of what is around us. Also, there are other arrays scattered around. You connected the body to the brain. The whole ship is an antenna now. Coming back?"*

"Yeah, I'll be there."

He waited several more moments in silence before returning.

\* \* \*

The next day, they conducted another town meeting in the evening. With everyone there, they filled most of the seats in the main hall. Wide monitors dominated the wall and the back of the stage. They may show videos. This gave everyone a chance to see what happened.

"Okay, we have been able to reconnect the star system. It tells us exactly where we are in relation to the galaxy. I must remind everybody that when we travel through space, it's referred to as Lucy. LyCy, every light-year we travel away, we also travel one calendar year. Either forward or backward in time. We cannot beat this. We cannot jump ahead. Every light-minute jump ahead, we travel one light-minute in space. Every year we travel ahead in time, we travel the distance of one light-year. It gives us a spiral stairway in the galaxy we can journey up and down without meeting ourselves again. If we go forward 103,000 Lucy, we are the same location that we started from; however, the earth has moved on and is well beyond our range of communications. It's the same if we go backward. So, this gives us a nice, tidy, spiral staircase in which to work.

"A pulsar is a galactic signpost. We know all of them by their unique signatures. We can tell one from the other by the rate it is spinning. We also know which direction each one is traveling in the galaxy. Lining this up gives us a pinpoint of where we are on the Lucy staircase. Until now, that should have been more than enough information. We got some other sensors up and running and have found some very… disheartening news.

"There is no other way to put it but to tell everyone bluntly that we are no longer on the Lucy staircase."

There was an uproar that lasted several moments. Everybody had questions. The man in the suit from the night before sat quietly and watched. His fingers were steepled before him.

Brandon waited until it was quiet once more before he spoke.

"I do not know how it happened. No one here can rework the computer to send us back home. Those calculations are so far above anyone's head that if we tried to redo them, it would be folly. I think it is best for us to wait here for them to come to find us than for us to return home."

"How far away is the Lucy staircase?" Asked someone.

"Yes, if we were just one or two astronomical units away, they could find us and send shuttles out to get us."

Brandon waited until everybody was quiet. "I want to sugarcoat it; that's my first impulse. I want to stand here and say everything will work out and that we will be home with our families soon. But I cannot. Between us and the staircase, there is about half a light-year of space. If they send a probe to every step on the stairway, it will be half a year before they locate us, and that is only if they can detect us. We are not sure if the signal from the beacon can reach that far. It might be so weak by the time it gets there that the signal will get lost in the background noise of the galaxy."

"So, you're saying that we're basically screwed?"

"No, we're not screwed. We still have each other. Now calm down, please, people." After several moments, he went on. "We have a ship that they built to support almost a million people, and we are just over three hundred. They have designed the burner reactor in the tube above us, providing us with light and warmth designed to last thousands of years. We have food. Working with the plants we have available and the hard rations brought on earlier, we will have more than enough to survive. I can say it will not be easy in the time ahead, it will not be a party, and there is work for us to do. We can do this, people. Mankind has survived worse situations. We must work together. We must pool our resources and do this. We realize that we are on our own. If help comes, it will take time."

"HEY! PEOPLE!" The uproar died away as he shouted. "It is what it is. I wish I could change it. I wish this did not happen. Like the man in the suit from yesterday, I had things I had to go to as well. This disrupts my whole life as it does everybody else's. I will miss loved ones, I will miss holidays, but I'm not about to let this kick my ass. We will pick up what we have, and we will survive. It is what we do. I will form committees. We will do this to ensure things run as smoothly as possible. I will need a complete list of people on-board and your specific skillsets. Let us work with each other. Can we at least agree on that?" There was a long pause, and everybody was quiet.

"All the information they give me, I will give you. You can view all the data we have collected. It will be in the mainframe under a folder titled "Week One." Each week I will post updates as to our situation."

\* \* \*

I sat on my bed in my room. I looked over a collection of toys from the toy box, and nothing there interested me. I pushed them quietly around, trying to see if any looked like fun, but they were mostly toys for boys.

A knock came, and it shocked me to see Mr. Brandon standing there when I opened the door.

"Hello Sally," he came in and sat down in a chair. "Are you busy?"

"Hi, just looking over toys. It's all trucks and cars and stuff. Not what I'm into." I sat back to where I was on the bed and pulled Miss Priscilla into my lap.

"I came to talk to you today because I feel very sad about our dilemma. I noticed you in the lecture hall. Of all the people here, I want you to know what happened. Do you understand the big mess we are in?"

"Um, kinda, a little." He seemed unsure of how to talk to me—probably used to talking with adults. They talk like I don't understand. "We will not go home soon, will we?"

"It may be a very long time. I can only give you the information I get from other people, but they all say that we are stuck here for a while." He gave me a sad face.

"Can we return to Homeport, and can I go back to Aunt Wendy and Uncle Bob?" Why is it the child always comes up with the right answer?

He leaned forward, elbows on his knees, hands clasped together. "I wish it were that simple. I wish we could just hit the return switch and go back to where we came from. We have many people here from different walks of life. People who work on all parts of the ship. We don't have someone to work on the computers."

"Well, if they don't find us soon, we'll still be okay. This is an enormous ship. Plenty of space. Bigger than Homeport."

"That it is, and we will be okay."

He looked up at me then, and I smiled at him.

He cleared his throat before he spoke. "I want you to know, and this is very important. I want you to know I, and others, will always look after you. We cannot replace your mother and father, or your aunt and uncle. We will be here to protect you and guide you every day you are with us. I hope you can understand."

I nodded my head.

Homeport, Day 2 - "The Life of the Dead is placed in the Memory of the Living." *Marcus Tullius Cicero.*


Dr. Guspoderek shook his head. "We cannot do autopsies here. They did not design our facilities for that. We can't even do births here. No woman in the system can be fertile, you know. They must have the pill to stop ovulating before they get here. I mend cuts. I reset bones; I deal with abrasions and fractures and the occasional nosebleeds. But I cannot bring someone dead here, cut them open, and find out how they died. When someone passes on, we send them back upstream, and they take care of it on Earth."

Director Porter sat back in his chair and rubbed his hands through his hair. He absently looked over the screens in his office. One showed the ship, and two others showed cameras from three individuals searching the ship and their relative position. "If we cannot cut them open to find out what killed them, can we at least try to identify them?"

There was a pause as the doctor thought about this. "If it is the same people who left on '05 days ago, I should be able to identify them through DNA and dental. When the big guns get here, they can search the ship for trace DNA. I have heard the people you want me to identify are old. There may be substantial tooth loss or decay. I believe we have rudimentary fingerprint records on everybody. If we absolutely have to, we can go that route. Also, the x-ray here in the lab is big enough to take full-body images. We can identify if there are any broken bones or if any broken bones have healed."

"Thank you," said Director Porter, looking up at the video. "We are all in this together. I would just like to see if you could let us know what we're up against. I have all the departments working on this, and I need you there."

"As I said, I can look at them, but as far as pinpointing the exact cause of death, that is beyond my current capability. I will gather all the information I can. We can tag them and get them ready to send back to Earth," he stammered a bit. "Well, when we, um, are ready to send people back."

"The shuttle is coming back now manually, easy burn. Would you rather do them here or there?"

"I am on '07. Until we know what we're dealing with, I would like to have as much containment as possible. I can have one of the older NRST's brought up online and can do the work from there. If you believe there will be more people found, I can have the NRST directed out to '05 on a piggyback, and I will stay out there in the interim."

"Very good, that'll work. There will be nothing political to gain from this. This is not a 'you scratch my back, and I'll scratch yours' deal. In this, we must pull together and do our jobs. We knew these people, and we worked with them every day. They were part of our lives. It could be one of us out there. Help us learn what has happened and let us know how to fix it if we can."

"Your son?"

"My son ... yes, my son is with them, and I have come to terms with the fact that I may not see him again. I'll be happy if we find him alive. If they find his body, I expect no preferential treatment between him and the others. It is our belief that in death, we return to what made us."

The doctor looked at him for a moment, nodded his head, and shut the connection.

* * *

Bob was fixing a circuit board, and when his vid rang, he did not even have to look to see who was. He recognized the chime.

"Hey, Wen."

"Hey, you've heard the news?"

"Yeah, it's all everybody's talking about. I heard they are sending shuttles out to get the people. We'll get Sally back as soon as we can and send her on the next ride back to earth."

"If she's there," Sally's aunt said solemnly.

He froze in what he was doing and looked up at her for the first time. "What do you mean, if she's there?"

"There has been a rumor here that something terrible happened on the ship." Her voice faltered. "They say, um, they say there are no survivors."

"What?" He set the optic circuit board down. "What do you mean, no survivors? The ship is still intact; it's only been two days." He tapped the terminal and commuted the news feed. "There is nothing about that, nothing at all."

"I heard the rumor they found bodies, Bob."

"I've heard rumors too. We all thought they were people from Earth. The ship jumped there, came out on time, and jumped back to us. We're all under the belief that those people were from the tug operators."

"No, no. I've heard those bodies are some of our own."

Arms folded across his chest, he looked intently at the vid. She gave no hint of a smile. "Listen, Wen, I know it may be difficult, but I'm sure Sally is fine. There are several soldiers who were heading back on this leg. They would protect her at all costs. I mean, come on, she's so young, and they wouldn't let anything happen to her."

"I know, I know. I'm just so scared right now. I'm out here with McClanahan and looking at the still vid shots they sent back. Something is just not right."

"Look, they will call it an early day. Nobody can focus on what's going on anyway, and there are no major jobs to complete. Only three damaged bots are in on rotation, and it's macht nichts. Are you still out on '07?"

"'06, actually."

"Would you want me to come out there tonight?"

"You can. Would be comforting," she sighed, and he knew he should not have even asked.

"I'll be there then. I'll call you when I get there, and we'll hook up."

"That will be good. I'm just worried about how scared she is. I know she's fine. I worry that's all. I got my suit prepped and handy. They replaced the one oxygen valve. If they let me go because I'm family, I'll be able to hitch a ride out to greet her when they bring everybody back."

"True. Something is wrong. They will want to do a thorough work over. She'll be scared."

"Look, I gotta go. I'll see you soon, hon."

The vid went dark, and he stared at it for a moment before standing at his work desk.

\* \* \*

As the news changed, so did their plans. Considering the circumstances, travel away from Homeport was forbidden. They brought in all nonessential personnel from the outer ships.

Large enough to accommodate everybody nicely, the gymnasium became a giant community room. Bleachers were pulled out, and rows of cots were set up for those who needed it.

Wendy found Bob there, and they sat in the bleachers to watch events unfold on the large screens. Director Porter patched through the live feed. They had a living space at Homeport, just a twenty-minute walk from the gym, which they could have gone to, but they wished to sit here with others instead. It gave them a sense of belonging.

Exchanging news with friends, some accounts differed. Craig from Term Ops thought there was a mutiny. Although, that seems very unlikely as the journey was normally to last three days. There was no one on board who would be so unbalanced as to do such. Yumi stated that she had heard a breakdown in the water system had a domino effect that put all the water into the atmosphere. This hydrated the breathable oxygen to over 50% saturation. The ones who could not get to suits in time drowned slowly.

XD05, Day 3 - "Till death do us part."


The first three mornings, a man sat in the lobby. A thin man dressed in a simple business suit and I remembered him from the other day as the man who argued at the meeting. He sat holding his briefcase on his lap. He nodded to me as I skipped by with my soccer ball under my arm.

On the fourth morning, I stopped.

"Are you waiting for someone?" I was curious as to why he sat there.

"I'm waiting to return home," he said simply. His voice was sharp and crisp. His words, when spoken, were enunciated perfectly. "The same as you, young girl."

"But you should be out there," I said. "You are a grown-up, and there are other things for you to do."

"My dear child," he touched my arm. "I did not come here to do all that. I am here so I may go home. My sole purpose in getting on this ship was to leave Homeport and return to Earth. I cannot be here."

I looked at him for a moment and brushed my unruly hair away from my eyes.

"Well, if you need a glass of water or something while you wait, I can get that for you. My name is Sally."

"Thank you very much, Sally. If I have any such need, I will ask you for it. My name is Demetrius Stubbs." He paused for a moment and looked at me in the most peculiar way. "You realize that with you being the youngest here, you will see a lot of incredible things in your lifetime?"

"Like what?" I tilted my head to the side.

"Like things we can only imagine." His eyes grew wide. "I'm glad I am as old as I am and will not have to live through it as you do. It is a nice ship, but the people could be a better lot."

"Do you think they'll be bad things or good things that happen?"

"Sometimes, child, the good things are bad things, and the bad things are good things. It's all about what you take from the situation."

"Oh," I stood there for a moment. I really didn't like it when adults talked in riddles. "Well, nice to meet you, Mr. Stubbs."

He waved at me as I skipped to the elevator.

* * *

I woke early the next day and wanted to surprise Mr. Stubbs when he came down. I sat down in a chair close to his favorite. When he noticed me there, it would shock him, and I would laugh. This morning I beat him to his place.

The first person to use the elevator was a woman with dark hair, wearing a long blue dress. It wasn't a fancy dress, just something to wear every day.

"Why, hello there, little girl," she said pleasantly before she left the building. She looked around, and seeing no one else there, she sat down beside me.

"Your eyes are red," I said, looking at her.

"I'm sure they are," she said, touching them lightly with her fingertips. "I have been crying quite a bit."

"Oh, you're sad?"

She smiled weakly but nodded her head.

"I miss someone. We weren't supposed to be apart."

"Do they miss you, too?"

"He was supposed to be my husband, and we would travel back to Earth. Things became hectic at the last minute, and he had to stay."

"If they send another ship after us, if they send one on the same path, then he'll be here soon."

She cried again. Not sobbing, but a tear formed in the corner of her eye and rolled down her cheek. "You are so naïve," she said, touching my chin. "Were I so, then I could be happy no matter what. Don't you miss your family?" She sniffled.

"I do," I tried to sound strong. "They will see me soon enough, I'm sure. I have faith in the others."

"Again, that is you being naïve."

"Is that bad?" I asked. I knew kind of what the word meant, but I was not completely sure.

"Sometimes it is good, and sometimes it is bad at the same time." Again, more riddles from adults. I wondered if she had spoken with Mr. Stubbs. She sniffed back her tears and looked around the large foyer. Taking my head in her hands, she pulled me closer. I thought at first she would give me a hug, but I felt her lips on my forehead, and she kissed me.

"Stay that way. For as long as you can, stay that way. Do not let them take it from you."

I nodded my head.

"Are you waiting for someone?" She asked, suddenly curious as to why I sat there.

"Mr. Stubbs has been here for the last few days, and I thought I would beat him down this morning."

"I don't know him."

"He's the one who always dresses in a suit. He's kind of angry that we are going nowhere. He's also someone who has things to do."

"Ah, the fussy guy."

I looked around to see if anyone else had heard. "Yes, he is that one."

We sat a while longer. It was awkward for me because I didn't want to say anything to make her cry, and it seemed like everything I said made her cry. She was the adult, and so I waited for her to do something.

"Well, little girl, I must go." She cried again. Bringing her hand up, she touched her nose and sniffled. "If anyone asks you, I was not here. Okay?"

I realized it odd that she felt that she was not supposed to be in the hotel's foyer. I went along with her plan, though.

"I won't tell anyone," I said with a wink. "No one needs to know you were here."

"You are so special." Again, she kissed me on the forehead. "I wish I had a daughter like you," she whispered.

She stood, and her touch lingered for just a moment on my shoulder. She turned and quickly left. The soles of her shoes made not a sound on the marble floor.

I sat back in the chair and waited for almost an hour. Mr. Stubbs was late. In time, the foyer got busy with people coming and going about their morning chores, and still, he did not arrive.

XD05, Day 6 - "It is very queer that the unhappiness of the world is so often brought on by small men." *Erich Maria Remarque, All Quiet on the Western Front*

"Can I get a headcount, please? Eighteen, nineteen, twenty; okay, good, got everybody." Captain Everett paused for a moment as he thought about what to say. He looked at the troops and cleared his throat.

"There are things I need to go over this morning. I know you have questions, and I may not have all the answers, but I shall try my best.

"We were all in a period of transition. Some of us were on leave, some of us heading off to new duty assignments. I was heading to the Azores on Earth to join a transportation battalion there. It comes as no surprise that by a simple human error, we are not where we should be. All our plans, no matter what they may be, are all set back. It sounds definitely like a military operation." There were chuckles.

"Hurry up and wait," Cpl. Addison grumbled.

"Exactly. We find ourselves a group of twenty amongst almost three hundred civilians, laborers, and scientists. Like at Homeport, there isn't much for us to do. There at Homeport, we could look for trouble spots and keep the peace. Here, they will need us doing more than sitting around waiting for a bar fight. We will need to work in the fields, searching for supplies, using our strength where it matters the most. With no enemy to fight, we cannot sit down idly.

"At this time, I'm going to ask you all to drop military courtesy. We will be, in effect, disbanded, although it will be our nature to assist each other and to care for each other as brothers and sisters."

They raised hands amongst the din.

"Sir, what about our pay?"

"Brandon says it will be a long time before they rescue us. At such time, be it one year or two, you will receive pay for service for the duration of the time that we are gone. I am sure they can pay it to you in one lump sum. There is nothing to pay you with here. Except through sweat and toil, they will see to all your basic needs. Also, your rank will reflect your time served."

Instead of raising her hand, Cpl. Addison stood. "Disbanded, sir? The military is all I have."

"Well, if you don't wish to call it disbanded, then just say for the duration of your time here you can wear civilian clothing, you don't have to call me sir, and we must report to Brandon for your work assignments each morning instead of me. We can call it 'extended shore leave.' People, the only resource that is extremely limited here, is manpower. I have been in the service for ten years. My father and grandfather served, and both retired active Army. I wish things were different, but here we find ourselves. They need the extra hands."

They were mostly silent. There were a few whispers, but no other questions.

"I don't have to shave again?" Evan asked, rubbing his chin.

Capt. Everett paused, raised a finger, and then spoke. "You, Evan, have been a very difficult one with shaving. Your 5 o'clock shadow rivals on twilight. No, you do not have to shave. You can grow your hair, mind the hygiene, and keep fit. When we spot a rescue ship, I will bring us back under all the military rules and regulations.

"We have gone through training to get where we are." He reached up to his collar and unhooked the dam-it's from the back of his rank. "We have the discipline needed. We would not be here if we did not wish to help others." First one side and then the other. "We will augment what is already here." He pulled his rank off his collar and placed it on the table in front of him. "They do not need the military here. Strong hands, strong wills, these people have always been governed before. For the first time, we will give them free rein to do what they want. Brandon Porter has clarified that he is in charge. It may be hard to believe, but the military is also in place to stop conflict rather than fight wars. Brandon knows who I am; he knows who you are. I will stand beside him as a civilian to help lead. I will not use my military rank to hold power over other people. I expect you to do the same.

He scooped the rank off the table. "Now, if there are no further questions, I will change clothing, pack my uniform way, and grab a cold drink. Dismissed."

XD05, Week 1 - "For the sun that rises in the sky, for the rhythm of the falling rain, for all life, great or small, for all that's true, for all you do, Kumbaya."

A few minutes' walk from Hotel Lima sat a stone amphitheater. Bringing other bricks from a project that was still not completed, some adults made a circle about knee-high. After a few armloads of scrap lumber from the same project, they started the fire. There were many complaints at first, but Brandon could not see the harm in doing it for one night. After the sun touched the Twilight Wall and changed to the moon, almost everyone sat around.

The conversation went from one subject to the next, and it was a good time. I didn't have much to say. I just sat there on the grass and listened. I was trying to understand how they felt about everything.

I heard Lawrence, the bird that Uncle Butch had, squawk somewhere in the darkness. He had that bird with him wherever he went. Thankfully, he stayed away and did not come to the fire. Uncle Butch was different, and having the bird here, making noise, would have upset many people when all they wanted to do was relax quietly.

"A nice glass of chilled wine would be nice."

"It may take a few months to a year, but I think we could do it," a man named Jaughn said. "We have apples, some grapes. We could add some other fruits, plums, oranges, and things, and in time, we could have a nice sangria."

"Not only do we have original grapes and apples, but we have an abundance of grapples. More juice, less pulp, and less work." A woman said.

"I think there are pineapples down by the Morning Wall. Warmer down there. It would add a little tartness to it and enhance the flavor."

"Yum."

"How can it be warmer down there? The land is the same, no matter what."

"They have some greenhouses that they pressurized much closer to the sun. I'm talking within the ten-kilometer range where we are sitting at eighteen right now."

"If we had some hops, it would be nice to make a beer. Don't know about you guys, but I could really go for a cold beer right about now. May have to find a way to ferment something, anything, to get a good buzz on."

"Not just a buzz, but it would be good to have some just to relax."

"We could ferment a lot of things we need for good yeast. Shall have to look in the kitchens for that. They are bound to have some. We could do corn alcohol. Love me some corn squeezing."

A woman spoke up. "I worked with the planning of the farms. We have beehives set up. Lots of honey." She nodded to Jaughn.

"How much is a lot?" He asked.

"Your heart's content. We figured in a year or two that the honey bees would populate the place. They are the original pollinators, so we need them to help with the growing of the plants and harvesting of the fruits and vegetables. If there are only three hundred people, then much of the honey will go to waste. Even if you use it for honey mead, there will still be so much more than we will ever use."

"Could find some pails of industrial glue," a skinny guy with long hair said. Almost everybody paused for just a second, wondering what the industrial glue had to do with the honeybees. "Just stick your head in and whiff away," he explained.

There was some laughter.

"Pat Pat, we gotta keep you away from that stuff."

The skinny man, Pat Pat, smiled a big toothy grin.

"I had heard a rumor," said someone nonchalantly, "that there was beer stockpiled in a warehouse somewhere around the rim. They had sent it here so that when we arrived back at Sol, they could have a big party, get drunk, and slap themselves on the shoulders for all their accomplishments. I would not touch the stuff myself. I am more of a tea drinker."

"Are you English?" Again, some laughter.

"No, just my personal taste."

"Now see," Jaughn began. He was a taller, bald man with glasses and sat deeply back in the lawn chair. "I like that. Have not had a good drunk in a long time. Been working on the tubes every day, and have no time to get a proper drunk on, you know what I mean?"

"Jaughn, there's not been a day I've known you that you have not had a drink."

"Ah now," Jaughn looked at the man over the rim of his glasses. "I never said I haven't drunk. I'm no longer working on the tube, so I think here I can get me a good drunk on. Was hoping to get it when I get back home. I'm thinking we're going to be here a while, you know?"

"There might be some Albert tubes here somewhere. Might use those to make a beer."

"They may be too big," Jaughn said. "Not that I wouldn't mind having an entire Albert tube full of beer. It's just the logistics."

"I'm not sure what you're talking about," someone said. "What's an Albert tube?"

"Those things that supplies came in. The 'All Purpose Tube.' They call them Albert tubes. Easier to ship liquid things here in bulk. You've seen them. Hell, I used to work in one shop where they made it a dumping ground. These big containers are made out of plasti-lite. Strong and durable, they hold four thousand liters of liquid easy enough."

"What would we use them for now?"

"Whatever we want to use them for. With the lid sealed, they are airtight. Takes a lot to shatter one; I've never seen one break before. May have to go see if they have any still here."

"Maybe we should go around the entire rim and take stock of what we have," someone suggested. "We are here at the hotel and have enough food and stuff for a while, at least until we can harvest the plants. We've been here for a week now, and still, we don't know the full scope of what we are up against."

"Geez, guy, how long do you plan on staying? They'll be here to get us soon enough."

"Well, as you said, we've got enough food in the hotel to last us a few weeks. Not sure how long the plants have been growing, but it should last us until we harvest the vegetables. We have plenty of fruits."

"Yes, but if we find a couple of pallets of canned beef or a good stew? I'm sure they have stuff stockpiled here somewhere that they used when they were in Zero-G working on the ship. We can use these to supplement our diet. Won't have to work on the harvesting as much."

"Is Brandon here?" They looked around until he raised his hand. "Yeah, hey yo, Brandon, do we have to coordinate with you to do this?"

"I think surveying the place would be the correct thing to do," he said, rubbing his chin. He stood as he spoke, making sure they heard him above others. "If everybody's up for it, we can start off in the morning."

"Would you want to do it systematically? Take everybody, form a line, and go all the way around?"

"No," he shook his head. "We can get maps to know where things should be. We'll just have to go search for them. There is no need to take all the manpower and search places we know will house nothing. Anybody wanting to volunteer, meet in the hotel foyer in the morning."

"Shit, we're not doing anything, anyway."

"They don't 'technically' have maps," someone spoke up. "They have a pamphlet that has a simple directory of where things are. There were houses that contained personal items. Also, there are other hotels and homes on terraces up along the Twilight Wall."

"There are some at the Morning Wall. That's where the heavy industry is."

"Right," said another. "I'm not trying to snoop, but if we will be here a while, we really need to know everything we have. I have seen times where survival comes down to the smallest of things, and if we overlook houses or some businesses, we may overlook what we need to survive."

"I do not want to encourage looting," Brandon said solemnly. He shook his head and sat back down.

"It will not be looting if we only take what we need, and we do not hoard what is there. What should be clear to everybody is that when we leave here, when the rescue ship shows up, and we can go back home, we can only take with us what is rightfully ours. Everything else will stay here on the ship."

Several people agreed with this and clapped their hands.

More wood was thrown onto the fire, and sparks drifted through the night.

A woman with red hair raised her hand and stood. This simple gesture reminded me a lot of when I was in class. Although her voice shook a little, she spoke loud enough so everyone could hear. "I have a question I need to ask. I have enjoyed my stay at Hotel Lima. It has more than enough rooms to accommodate everybody; however, with everybody in one central location, it seems a little cramped. Is there a chance we can find another place to live? And when I say 'we,' I mean if I find a house, I don't want it overrun with many people. I grew up on a farm in Kaiserslautern, and I would enjoy solitude. You people are the best," she said, turning around in a circle. "But I enjoy my peace and quiet. With all the space used at the hotel, it's feeling a little crowded."

"She says it is true, man," said Pat Pat. "I mean, we're all bunched up here on top of each other."

Brandon stood once more and dusted his pants off. "The way they designed the system, we cannot just go to a place and claim it as our own. They assign them much like the barracks or the living quarters at Homeport. Everything."

Jaughn turned his head and looked at him. "Are you going to keep us at the hotel the whole time?"

Brandon paused for a moment. He folded his arms across his chest. "Well, if we were still on our way to Sol, then you would be strictly forbidden from scouting around. However, considering current events, I think it would be rather harsh of me to ask you to live only in the hotel. I must ask that if you want to live in a different place, seek it out, and let me know."

"Why do we have to go through you first?"

"Yeah, if I see an empty place, I should be able to move right in."

"People, everything is in lock-down. It's a safety measure they went through when they sent us on our way. They have not used most of these places in the time since they constructed them. They don't want people wandering around where they should not be.

"If you leave the hotel, I will grant you permission to live elsewhere. The basic duties still need done. If you wish to eat at the hotel, then I ask that you put forth an effort and help us as much as you can."

"You won't be leaving?"

"As of right now, no. It's a commonplace, and everyone will find me there. As Captain Everett will agree, there is still a lot to coordinate. Just let me know where you want to live."

There was a lot of excited talk then. People stood and left. If they would stake their claim, they wanted to get a good place, even though it was late in the evening.

I turned to Corporal Daniels to see if she was eager to leave, and she smiled at me.

"I will never let you go, Wee One," she whispered quietly.

"You sure?"

"Yeah, positive." She placed her arm around my shoulder and gave me a squeeze. "You are my one and only kid sister, and I must watch over you. We are in this together."

"Should I keep calling you Daniels? Sounds like a boys' name."

"You may call me 'Lena.'"

"Ah, thank you. And you may call me Sally."

She looked at me oddly. "That's your name, right?"

"Yip. Just didn't want you to call me Sergeant Weiss or something."

She laughed and hugged me again.

I had never had a sister before. Being mom and dad's only child, I was not used to having someone looking out for me the way Lena did. There were the kids at school who I chatted with, but it differed from having a sister. And everyone here was so much older. I felt a sudden deep connection to Lena that night. As I returned her embrace, I could smell a faint, lingering presence of her bana-berry shampoo. It made me feel safe with all these strangers.

"Thank you," I whispered, and I felt her nod her head.

\* \* \*

The gathering fell quiet after a while.

"This reminds me a lot of home," someone said. His voice was deep and carried well. Others stopped in their conversations to listen. "We used to do this when I was a boy. My parents would take me to the camp they had up in New York State, and we would spend the evenings sitting around the fire. Things were a lot different back then, and I don't mean in a good way. I'm not reminiscing as some folk might, just saying how I feel. I've been at Homeport for almost seven years now. I thought I would take a break and use some of my vacations, and so I wound up here. Lucky, I took an X-ray Delta back and not a shuttle."

"Enjoy your vacation now, MC," said someone who knew him.

"Yooooooo…" someone said, and he echoed it.

"Ah, so it is your fault we're in this mess." A woman said, and others laughed.

"Yeah, I might've jinxed y'all pretty good," he laughed. "Naw, I mean, shit, I'm sitting here the whole time thinking I'm burning up vacation when really I'm not sure this is my new home or not? I helped install the ribbon for the shuttles. With them here and working, I ain't got shit to do. I fix one if it breaks pretty good if I have the parts, but other than that, I'm all but useless. Too old to be retrained to do something else. Any y'all play spades? I welcome a good game."

"Do you play well?"

"Oh, I'm pretty good. People say I'm pretty good."

Brandon had gone to talk to people and returned to his seat. When he spoke, his voice carried over all who gathered. "Again, I say that we will need everybody's help, and I mean everybody, in the days ahead. You say that survival may depend on one item; a case of yams, or a warm blanket, or a bottle of water. But again, I cannot stress this enough. We will need the help of every person here to chip in to make this thing work if we are all to survive. If one person fails, then we all fail. I, for one, would like to see this through to the end."

Again, several people clapped.

\* \* \*

In a galactic time frame, we took a blink to explore our galaxy. In human terms, it took just five years to record the bulk of the data and another decade to sift through it all.

One set of recording probes equipped with Samuel Drives jumped one light-year/one calendar year (LyCy) backward in time and another set forwards in time. They would sit for twenty hours, one full standard day, and collect a multitude of information. A complete 360-degree panoramic holograph of their current point of view in gamma-ray, x-ray, ultraviolet, normal light, and infrared. Another sensor would listen for microwave and radio.

After twenty hours, the probe took the next step up the Lucy staircase, where it would stop and listen again. On average, the probes only did five such jumps before their data banks were full. Returning home, replaced with new storage, and inspected, we sent them away where they blinked to another time and space.

Combined, the five-hundred probes returned with almost a million-year history of our galaxy.

Within two years, the number of probes quadrupled.

And our insight expanded with it. We scrutinized every waypoint of each spiral arm as we traversed the void. Space is a paradox, it seems. Brimming full of stars and solar systems, they are tantalizing close but agonizingly very far away as we reach for them. One of the closest that we came to was a binary system in the Sagittarius arm. Slow-moving and in sync with our Sun on its arduous journey around the Galaxy. Had River 3 any planets, it would be a prime candidate for colonization.

After the first, second, and third sweeps, the probes let us know the truth.

We are alone.

Perhaps on a planet distant from our staircase lies a civilization in its infancy that searches the night sky as we once did. Either we have not heard them, or they are yet to make a noise we can hear. Sensors listen all along the staircase for something out of the ordinary and have found the Milky Way a quiet place.

The number of exoplanets, planets beyond our solar system, we have found the number in the tens of millions. If they have life, it is pre-industrial. So far, we are the only ones here. A fact both comforting and unsettling at the same time.

And still, we continue to search.

It would be a complete and utter folly to stop where we are. It is in human nature to look down the empty road and ask ourselves what is around the bend. With each new understanding comes an even greater sense of awe. Wars and differences aside, we are now a civilization of wanderers.

Homeport, Day 3 - "So take me down a lonesome road, point me east and let me go." *Joe Cocker*

It took time for maintenance to open the outer airlock door at the Morning Hub. The power cells there had degraded so much that there was no hope of getting them to work again. The soldiers, when entering the Twilight Hub, had much better luck.

Shining her light through the glass, Becca did a count of the bodies as maintenance worked. When they manually pushed the door open, she counted once again to confirm.

"Homeport, this is Becca on team two. Be advised the door is open here. We have twenty-four bodies. It's like they've all come here to die."

"*Or were brought for preservation. Do any have tanks on them?*"

"At first glance, no."

"*Give us a visual, if you can, of their faces.*"

"Gary, let's move them out. Maintenance, start on the next door. Homeport, we are moving them to the shuttle." She tried to keep her movements slow and steady, not knowing how many people were watching. She did not want to give them motion sickness. She recognized no one.

It was tedious work, but they got them into the cargo hold.

There was no air pressure on the inside of the Hub. The seals no longer worked or, at some point in time, had given out. This made it easier as the bodies did not tumble out into space as the airlock decompressed from the inside out. She shuffled bodies over while Gary waited on Maintenance to open the door. For her, it felt weird, placing them so tightly together.

Like the first door, Maintenance had to manually pry the next one open. Gary entered, and a moment later, his voice came over her comm.

"Becca, would it be possible for you to stop for a moment and come look at this?"

"I've only just started here. Did you find more?"

"Something different. There's something here that shouldn't be."

She went through the doors and floated there for a moment as she took it all in.

"Homeport," her voice was a little stressed. "We found a chamber of sorts, a burial chamber. Somebody died, and they had a real elaborate setup."

"*It's hard to see. There's a glare off the Albert Tube.*"

"There is a woman inside, white dress, flowers, and it looks like bedding beneath her. She's pretty. She doesn't look old. A lot of people in suits look much older than her. The body looks well preserved. There was a lot of love that went into this."

"*Can you identify her?*"

"At the moment, no. There are artifacts here in a tote. Hold for a few moments." The lid to the tote slid off with little effort, and she rifled through the contents slowly. Becca brought each piece to view, scrutinized it for a moment, then let it hang in the air.

"Central. If these are her possessions, I think we found her."

* * *

They could not bring the Albert tube out to the airlock. Sizing up the route they had to take, Becca realized that it was too big to navigate around the turns. They never designed the tube to leave the ship. It had been brought on board when the ship was still under construction, and then by magnetic elevator. It was never meant to leave. Messages bounced back and forth for almost an hour before they removed the woman from the tube and brought her home with the others.

The hardest part was taking the end off the tube. After several attempts, Becca hooked her feet into the bulkhead and inserted a pry bar into spaces on the lid. Gray had to work on the other side. Working in unison, they twisted the lid off.

They could then remove the body from its captivity.

"*Hold, Becca. Capture just the face. And... good. We shall see if we can find out who this is.*"

The two gingerly, and with as much dignity as they could, placed her in the holds of the shuttle.

"Hold tight," Gary whispered to the corpses. "Just a little longer, and we will get you home."

She had to wait a few minutes before the radio was silent. So many people were talking. "Homeport, this is Becca and Gary. Just be advised that we will search the Hub a little further before we send the shuttle back. How do you copy?"

There is a pause of a few seconds before Homeport replied.

"*We hear you loud and clear, Becca and Gary. If you could find all the personal objects and return them to the shuttle, we would appreciate that. It may help us identify who this is, who they are.*"

"Roger." She tapped Gary on the shoulder and motioned back to the Hub.

They collected all they could. There were no more surprises for them. Three hours later, after their second sweep, they had found nothing new.

There was no atmosphere on this part of the ship. When it was new and operational, they maintained air pressure at the Morning Hub. Now there was no need. With the power down, the airlock doors remained open to outer space.

With a few metallic clicks, the shuttle disengaged.

XD05, Week 2

I took Lena's hand and smiled. Lena had not dressed in her combat fatigues. This day she wore a loose shirt and shorts. They were very comfortable-looking clothing.

"Strong shoes?" Lena asked, and I lifted my pant legs so she could see. "Outstanding. Sturdy clothing. You have a backpack?"

I pointed to the side.

"Water? A snack?" as Lena said this, I rolled my eyes.

"Yes, I have them all."

"Your doll?"

"Miss Priscilla is staying in my room. She will be safe there."

"Good. Fantastic."

"Besides," I cupped my hand and whispered. "I'm getting a little too old for a doll," she was a soldier. I had to make myself look strong in front of her, and I know Miss Priscilla would forgive me for denouncing her. "I had her with me when I came to see my aunt and uncle. I was just taking her back, was all."

"Well, okay, if you say so. Do you understand what we're doing today? We must go all the way around this big ship to see what they have provided for us. Going to be a lot of walking. I hope you're up for that."

I gave her a salute. Instantly, her smile faded.

"You… you don't have to do that," Lena frowned and looked away. "We're, um, we are not soldiers anymore."

"Oh, well, I will always think of you as my soldier."

Lena held her hand up, and I gave her a high five.

"You see, the whole ship is one big circle. If we walk this way, West, we will go all the way around until we eventually wind up back where we started from. They lay everything out in perfect squares—Kim-two's. When the ship arrived at Earth, there would be a big celebration. Families and farmers would move in and work the land right away."

"But we are off course," I said, putting my hands in my pockets and looking downward. "Completely."

"Yes. So, we need to find out what is here. There will be plenty of vegetables to eat, but if there is more stuff that we can use to help us, then we need to know about it." Lena playfully tweaked my ear. "We have a bunch of people we must feed for a very long time. You don't want to eat salads every day, do you?"

I made a face and stuck out my tongue.

"Stay close, and we will solve this mystery of what we have here."

"May I bring my ball?"

"That you may," Lena smiled. "It will be quite something if you can kick your ball all the way around the ship."

There was a whistle. Others who milled around looked up.

Brandon stood on a shipping crate. Arms up, he motioned everyone to gather. "People, we will have seven groups of five. Each of these five will have somebody taking notes. As you walk, call out what building you come to. Be it a hotel, residence, school, business, or warehouse. Although most residential units are up along the wall, there still may be some here. You get the idea. I have heard around the upper side; there are places that are lavish. If, by chance, we get to these, they are gated and locked. We are still just passengers. We should avoid entering these places if possible. The other places we can have access to are supply warehouses and food warehouses. I can justify using these to the authorities when our rescue comes. It's a matter of survival. I cannot justify breaking into and defiling the homes of the rich.

"We will note when we find the locations of warehouses, and we will return later to get supplies. I would like to do this in an orderly manner. We do it willy-nilly, and we're bound to miss something."

"We will be camping out there tonight?"

"If we find a place big enough for everybody, we can stay there. I have a light lunch meal being prepared by those in the kitchen, and they will bring supper this evening."

"Why would they stock warehouses when this thing is not even back to Earth yet? Wouldn't they wait until we were back home to put food in this place?"

"As you all know, X-ray Delta 05 has been operational for the last three years. X-ray Delta 06 is still four years from completion, two years until it gets its own atmosphere, but there are things stockpiled there. It makes it easier to bring stuff in when they don't have to worry about threading it through airlocks."

"Can you give us a heads up on any alcohol?"

"Ah, is that all you guys think about? Is Jaughn here?"

"No, I believe he is cooking."

Several people laughed.

"There is a good chance that we will find alcohol. To make Jaughn happy will have to bring him a bottle. We are not here to get silly, stupid drunk for weeks on end. Same with the food. If we find any, we must use it in moderation because it is all that we have. We will have to conserve. We will have to ration. Please remember that all our supplies are finite. Our saving grace will be the crops we grow."

"Pssst, hey," Lena nudged my shoulder and whispered. "Which spot do you think we should take?"

"We get to choose?" I asked, looking up at her.

"We might."

"Oh, I thought they would tell us where they wanted us. This is great!"

* * *

They stood on the roof of a one-story office building that connected to a large warehouse. It was flat here, and they had ample room to walk around. I stood by Lena, and of the five people in our group, two of them were busy working on a window. They had a piece of a metal bar and were trying to pry the window open.

"Stop, stop." The two men sat back from their exertions. "If we put too much pressure on it, the glass will not bend as the window frame does, and it will shatter."

"The latch is just too damn hard."

One of them stood, cupped his hands over his eyes, and looked in the window again.

"They locked the window here. You see the mechanism? That's what's holding it. If we get the bar in and apply the pressure gently and evenly, it will strip the gears, and the window will open."

"No jerking movement. We'll just give it slow, steady tugs."

They tried it again. In light shirts and pants, the two sweated under the midday sun. When they had it back far enough, they inserted another bar in and applied more pressure.

I sensed that they were applying too much pressure. When the glass shattered, I squealed and turned away.

"Well, they'll just have to take that out of my pay," the one guy laughed.

"If it's broken, we may as well just take it out. We will deal with those consequences later."

They pulled pieces out gingerly and placed them on the roof, with a few falling to the warehouse below. They got the rubber gasket and pulled out even more, so the window frame had nothing they could get cut on.

"The thing is still too small."

"None of us can climb in."

"I can." They all turned to look at me.

"Sally, it could be dangerous. You may fall."

"The ledge is big enough for me. I can grip on that bar all the way around. The steps are just over there."

Lena looked between them all, weighing the situation, before nodding.

"I didn't bring you up here to do this," she said, kneeling. I could see the sincerity and sense of worry in her eyes.

"I know. It's okay."

"Bernard, you watch her."

"Okay, what I want you to do is to enter it sideways. Crouch down and stick your head in, arm in first, leg in second. You will turn your head to the side and then slip your way in."

I smiled at Lena.

I followed his guidance, and he led me through step-by-step. "Now, reach up. The bar is up just a little higher, just a little… Okay, there you go. Turn your head to the side. Look at me. Now, with your arm, pull yourself in."

"Does it feel too tight?"

"No, no. It feels… exciting."

Everyone laughed. When I stood, the bar came to about my hip level. I had to lean inward, over the expanse a bit, but that was fine. I took a few sidesteps and heard Bernard's voice close by. He was lying on the rooftop with just his head in the hole.

"Oh my, quite the drop from here, huh?"

"It's a little scary," I whispered. I didn't want others to know I was afraid.

Every time I slid my hands down the bar, a thin sheen of dust fell. When I got to the corner, there was nowhere else to go but down.

Still hanging onto the bar, I spun, so my body was inward. Down on one knee, I found a place where I could put my foot beneath me. Hard and sure, I could let go with my hands and ease my way down. A small jump and fall and I landed on a stack of pallets. I waved up at Bernard with dirty hands.

"Hey, the girl has some skill," he told the others over his shoulder. "Sally, if they set this place up like other places, they will not have locked the door from the inside to go out. Just the outside to go in. Do you understand?"

"Uh-huh."

"Probably beneath us is a way out. If you open those doors, it will let us in."

"Not the bigger doors?"

"No, we'll get those later."

It was quiet in the building. All those above were listening. I climbed down from the pallets and looked about. There was a lot here. Shelves towering above me held pallets of boxes wrapped with plastic. They told me it was a distribution center and there should be food here. I walked down one aisle, looking at all above me. Doing so, I almost missed the door. I undid the latch and pushed it open. The wind stirred the dust a little.

Lena met me there and tousled my hair.

I slapped her on the arm, leaving a dark stain of dust.

"Hey, you," Lena gave me a quick hug. The others came down, and they all smiled at me.

"Well, we got this turtle cracked open."

"Should be enough freeze-dried stuff here to last us a while."

"If there's any beef, I got dibs."

"If there's any beef, we all must share. Rules are rules."

They wedged the door open with a chair from one office. I used the bathroom to wash my hands, and by the time I went back out, somebody was already on a lift truck. It hummed in the most peculiar way when they raised the forks. A cheer went up.

It was a good day.

* * *

I was happy with the fact that although they let me and Lena investigate the buildings for a time, they also let me walk with the man who wrote the notes down. His name was Tang. He was not a soldier, but someone who worked on the frame of the ship. His penmanship was great because he drew on big papers. He needed his words to be readable. As the day ended, he allowed me to write about what the buildings were in the squares on the paper.

I took the job seriously. On the morning of the second day, they gave the chore to me as Tang scouted ahead.

By the time we walked the complete circuit and reached Hotel Lima, we found four other warehouses. Three of them had stockpiles of food and in the fourth were parts for machinery and work clothing of various sizes.

It startled us to find a small corral with several pigs. They had an automated feeding system, and they had a few week's supplies of food. Had we not gone out and did the search, the pigs would have eventually died of starvation.

Those who designed the ship had used birds to help spread seeds around. We thought the birds were the only other creatures on the ship. Now we had to deal with pigs. Tang said he had never heard of pigs in space before. Several people laughed, but no one would tell me what the joke was. They could leave the pigs on their own until the survey was complete, then we would decide how to deal with them.

There were two places we did not have access to. These were large homes of people who had a lot of money. The landscaping was beautifully done with decorative trees and fountains.

Tang lifted me up so I could look over the fence.

Besides those houses, we found many other places. There was a stadium, an arena, an open-air theater, several pools, and elevated walk paths. The place was ready for people to move in.

Other than the shuttle's used for transportation, there were bicycles found in stalls in the business area. I had never ridden a bicycle before. Several people pulled them from their racks and rode around. They were laughing and weaving back and forth. It looked fun and an easy thing to do. The bicycles in this area were all for adults. There were none for children. They reassured me several times that there had to be some bicycles set aside for little ones like me. They would teach me how to ride a bike when they found one.

One guy who was tall with big muscles was especially ecstatic when we found a gymnasium. He was happy. The windows were big so people could see out as they exercised, and they also reflected the man as he posed on the street in front. He made a show for everybody of going through this whole routine where he showed off his big arms and chest, the whole-time grunting. I half expected him to rip his shirt to shreds. I think the only thing that stopped him was because he had a limited supply of shirts.

It was a good trip. We took six days, as they wanted to be very thorough. It was just after noon when we got back to the hotel. I sat down on the steps, let my soccer ball roll wherever, and gave my weary legs a rest. I sighed and lay back with my arms out from my sides; I wanted to soak up the sun. Looking straight up, I could see where we had traveled, although it was too far away to see any detail. We were there. Just three days ago, we were walking right up there. Somewhere on the land, thirty-six kilometers above my head, were streets and avenues I had walked. Right in between here and there was the tube that carried the sun. I squinted my eyes and tried to find it; however, it was too small for me to see.

Tang came by and tapped me on the knee. "Hey, Wee One, you tuckering out?"

"Naw, just resting."

"Shall we do it again?"

I looked up at him as he stood there with his big, toothy smile.

"You did good," he said, still smiling. "We're all very proud of you. Come on; we'll get you a fizz."

I smiled and took his outstretched hand.

Homeport, Day 3 - "Can you hear me running, can you hear me calling you?" *Mike + The Mechanics*

The shuttle that had deployed soldiers out returned with the corpses of those who were in the airlock. Guided electronically, it locked onto Homeport. Several people waited in white medical spacesuits. The locks cycled through, and as the door opened, no one moved.

Dr. Guspoderek was the first to break the moment. He reached out and tugged on one of the blue utility suits. The corpse floated closer. He looked at the bleak, old, and dried skin behind the face shield. He could not identify who it was. Not that he was overly familiar to everybody on the ship.

There was one with a ribbon tied on its shoulder. He lifted this one and pushed it back over the others who, for the moment, had precedence. When there was only one remaining in the shuttle hold, he looked at it again. In this one, the video recorder lay. Had the suit batteries still held the charge, he could tap to buttons near the back of the jaw, and the faceplate would retract back into the helmet. Now he had to take the helmet off manually.

Two assistants came and, although it was rather difficult in Zero-G, the clasps eventually loosened. A quarter twist, two snaps, and the helmet released from the rest of the suit. There was no normal hiss of air.

Long hair, brittle with being frozen for so long, broke off in tiny strands. He deftly reached in and grabbed the recorder. Wordlessly, he handed it to the assistant with a nod. She turned, grabbed a tether, and quickly left.

Taking the magnetic-elevator down to the communication room, she passed it to a waiting tech. He checked it several times, looking for any damage. Seeing none, he handed it to his supervisor, who inserted it into the reader.

Without hesitation, he gave the command, and the computer played the reader from the beginning.

After a moment, he stopped it.

"Director Porter?"

"*Yes,*" the voice on the other end of the comm was worn and tired.

"We have the recorder, and it is intact. The video plays just fine."

"*How much have you watched?*"

"I have played it for only two minutes. It seems to be people sending letters home. We did this when we were in the military."

"*Is it one message?*" He could hear the desperation in the director's voice.

"From what I see, there are over two hundred hours of playback. One moment," he said. Advancing the playback in one-hour increments, he saw what he was looking for. "There are at least twelve different people sitting in front of the camera at different times, speaking, Sir. It seems as though the whole thing is letters home."

*"Outstanding. There may be news on there that we can get."*

"Should I channel it through to you, sir?"

*"No."*

"Sir?"

*"I want you to channel through to the whole station. I want everybody to see it all at once for the first time. When the two hundred hours are over, I want you to loop again. Give me a minute to prep everybody and then begin."*

The technician gave the command to the computer. "I will start in five minutes, Sir."

* * *

"Hello everyone," the screen displayed their director. "This is Director Porter. Yesterday, as you all know, X-ray Delta 05 returned with no clear damage. However, there seems to be some other malfunction. I will not sugarcoat it. I will tell you how it is, so there is no misconception. I have nothing to hide.

"It appears as though somehow or another that there is a big difference between ship time and our time. For us, only three days have passed since it left. For them, it was much, much longer. We were lucky enough that in the first group, someone had the forethought to place a recorder. They have retrieved the recorder and will play momentarily. Undoubtedly, you will recognize the people there as family, friends, and coworkers. This is the first time we have played this recording. You are seeing it as I am."

* * *

"Hello, hello, is the tape moving?" Asked the man sitting in the chair.

"What do you mean, tape?" A different man off-camera says this.

"Old joke," and the man in the chair chuckled. "A few centuries ago, they used magnetic tape to record sound and video."

"Ah, gotcha. Um, the system we're using is micro-diamond-etching. Once it records the video, nothing can damage it. In a few billion years, they will still be able to count the hairs on your eyebrows."

"Seriously?"

"Oh, yeah. MDE is the way to go."

"No, I mean seriously, I'm about to leave an archival message for when they find this ship again, and the only thing you can come up with is comments about my eyebrows? Just let me know when you start taping."

"I'm not taping anything. We have been recording you for about two minutes now."

"Idiot." The man sitting in the chair scowled at the person behind the camera. He shook his head and looked back at the camera. "Hello, again, I am Jacob Coleman. We drew lots, and I was the lucky one to get number one. With just over two hundred and fifty individuals left, this will be a long recording when it is done. Dan says with just over ten minutes each, we will still record for the rest of the week. People gotta get their speeches ready and figure out what they wish to leave behind in the message to others."

"I was, well, I had worked, on the big ships, '03, '04, and '05, laying down micro-fiber optics. I had started on '06, and my team would start on '07 in a month, but the end of my rotation was due. There were some new techniques involved, and I needed to go through some classes before they would allow me. I was heading back to earth to complete the tasks and then planned to head back."

The man behind the camera shifted a little. "You could have stayed back on earth and worked on the micro-fiber optics there."

"Naw, man, once you get to space, once you get out there and see the galaxy for what it is, what it truly is, you can't go back to living on the planet. There is so much out here. So much beauty, it never gets old."

"Five minutes left, already? You're shitting me. All right then. We three hundred have been out here for ten years now. I know that by now, my mother has probably passed. She was up there in years, and her health was failing. I was coming back to see her. Probably just a little too late for that. Ah, to my brother Ken, I hope everything is going well and that you are still married to Mary. I think I would've been a good uncle to your children. Sorry that I didn't get back and have any of my own. Whatever possessions mom has, I guess it's all yours now, and although there were a few things I wanted, I doubt I'll ever get the chance to see them again. There was a cookbook she had, and I know that it sounds corny, but I would've liked to have had that. Also, on the eastern side of the property, I would build a house. I guess that won't be happening. I have found a little kim-two here on '05 that I have called my own. It's bigger, and I've grown kind of partial to the sunrise from there. Can't beat the rent," he beamed. "It's free. To all the guys who have finished up '06 and '07, doing the math, you guys are probably on '12 by now; I could not work with a better bunch of people. Some of my supervisors were a pain from time to time, but I forgive all. I'm still impressed at the way the fiber optics here have held up—some fantastic workmanship, guys. I hope everybody is fine, and it would be great to hear your voices once again. Love you, Mom, and Ken. I miss you every day." Jacob nodded to the camera, and four seconds later, it went dark.

* * *

The screen darkened. Everyone in the gymnasium sat in silence.

Wendy squeezed Bob's hand. People whispered in the darkness.

"Miss you, Jacob," said someone off on the other side. His voice was loud and carried.

"Going to have a beer for you tonight, my buddy," said someone else in a different part of the gymnasium.

The big screen lit up again. There was somebody else sitting in the chair. It was an elderly gentleman.

"Hello everyone," his voice wavered a bit. "I'm Carl Sykes here on '05. I was a general laborer with building construction and plumbing. I'd like to say hello to my daughters Sarah, Jessica, and my son Albert. You were full grown when I left and probably have my grandchildren by now. I hoped that I would get to see them, but fate played a cruel twist. I miss you…"

* * *

Dr. Guspoderek looked over at the frozen corpse. Even though they had gravity where they were, he suited up to keep him safe from the effects of the cold. It was easier to keep them at this absolute temperature.

"She is lovely," said his assistant. Her voice came to him in his helmet on the closed channel.

"Yes, she was." Normally, in the few autopsies he had done in the past, he kept himself distant, impartial to those that he worked on. At her death, her caretakers took the time to make her right. Makeup applied lightly; the hair pulled back into a loose braid. This woman was lovely. "She has held her age for someone as old as she is. Scalpel."

With that, he began the examination and to remove the clothing the woman had worn for a very long time. He selectively cut the gown off her. It may come in handy later as part of the identification process. The seams sliced at the shoulders, and they could slowly and methodically slip the dress off.

"Much, much easier than the spacesuits," his assistant said.

"Indeed," he replied.

Because of the age and degradation, the spacesuits were no longer usable for any practical purposes. When he cut them off a body, they searched the fabric thoroughly and then placed it to the side to be discarded later. There was one suit that may have stayed warm for a while after the death of the individual. The individual had bloated inside the suit, and it was not pleasant.

"No tattoos or other marks. A small scar here on the shoulder, another one on her forearm. A thin slice that healed many years ago. I wish they were all this easy. We will send her through the AMRI and see if we can find anything internally."

His assistant looked at him, gave him a nod, and took her away. Only a few moments passed before a second assistant brought in another fully suited corpse on a gurney.

XD05, Week 2

They said they found a bunch of food rations in one of the bigger warehouses. Enough that would last us for a few months if we didn't gobble them all down at once. There were still many places yet unexplored up on the Twilight Wall. From where we walked, these places all looked like homes or office buildings. Lena said many of the magnetic elevators, or mag-ele's, were not built to take tons of food or equipment upward. So, there was little use in looking up there for stuff. Maybe another day, they would gather everybody again, and we would map that out, too. She even said they were many places over on the Morning Wall. That would be an exciting journey.

Brandon put a lock and chain on the warehouse with food. People were mad. He gave a big speech afterward stating that we needed to ration the food; otherwise, in years to come, we would run out. He said we could eat the food grown. We had many big squares of farm stuff ready to harvest. It was all grown in anticipation of farmers arriving and harvesting what we had. They normally did it this way.

Although he did not want to do it, we had to collect this harvest lest it go to rot. They assigned everyone tasks, and we gathered as much as we could. I was helpful. It gave me a chance to meet the others and to get to know people. They were very thankful to have me.

After four days, we rested. There was still so much to do.

* * *

We were in the dining hall one evening, and everything seemed normal. Almost everybody settled down with their meals. They had made flavorful soup with a lot of vegetables and, to the side, some dehydrated fruits.

Brandon, Mr. Everett, and the big guy with the muscles were sitting at a table when three men entered. They grabbed a bowl and went over to the kettle that had the soup.

The first one had filled his bowl and was getting ready to leave when Brandon stood up.

"What are you doing?" he asked loudly. Everyone in the hall grew quiet.

"We're getting soup. Dang, everyone else has some."

"Were you in the fields today?" was his second question.

"No, we ah, had a party last night and overslept this morning." The other two laughed.

"Don't let it happen again," he said in his adult voice.

"It upsets you that we take some of your soup?"

"It's not my soup," Brandon stated. He turned and pointed to tables at random. "This is their soup, and their soup, and their soup. By the effort of everybody here, the soup was made. They all took part in the gathering of the vegetables, or the cleaning, or the cooking. Tomorrow, if you do not make it to the fields, then you do not get to eat under this roof."

"Look, man, it's just a bowl of soup."

"Yes, to you, it may seem like a bowl of soup. To this man, and this man and that woman there, that bowl of soup represents a days' worth of work. A days' worth of work they did, and you did not. As I said, you may have the soup today. If you're not in the fields tomorrow, then don't expect to eat here tomorrow night."

"There's plenty of food out there," said the man, his arms wide open. "Enough for everyone."

"Then you find it, and you cook it elsewhere."

Brandon took his seat. Mr. Everett stood and clapped his hands to show his support. Others joined in, and soon everybody in the hall, except for the three men, stood and were clapping.

\* \* \*

I paused in the hotel's foyer.

The chair I remember Mr. Stubbs sitting in had been vacant for some time. It was sitting in a ray of sunlight, and when I went up to touch its arm, dust rose from it and drifted in the light. He had not been here for a while. I did the math in my head and realized that it had been over two weeks since I have seen him sitting there. I had been so busy doing other things; I forgot to look for him. I did not see him here or on the ship at all. He had just disappeared.

The same with the woman with the dark hair in the blue dress. The morning we spoke was the first and the last time I had ever seen her.

XD05, Week 2


"Brandon, you wanted to see me?" For this occasion, Lena thought it best that she wore her military uniform out of courtesy. It let Brandon know she knew where her place was.

He wore his hair cropped short, button shirt loose at the neck with the sleeves rolled up. It could've been a casual day at the office.

"Lena, come and sit down." He looked her up and down and smiled. Mentally, she noted he did not call her Cpl. Daniels.

"How are things with you?" he asked, leaning forward.

"Things are well, as expected. Being stranded here put a damper on my life. I was heading back home to visit with family and friends who surely miss me by now. But," she shrugged her shoulders, "what can you do? I have to wait this layover out like everybody else."

"We are all in the same boat. I heard of a television show that played almost two centuries ago where a group of travelers became stuck on an island, and although they would meet new people every week, they never made it home." She had never heard of anything like this before. Television shows, even from 100 years ago, were sometimes hard to stomach. An unlikely bunch of heroes rose from that era.

"That's odd."

"Yes, very much so."

"Unlikely as it was, people seemed to enjoy the premise of the show. I'm not sure if we have it on file. May have to look it up just to see."

"Um, Sir, did you call me here to talk over television shows?"

"No, I did not. There has been trouble lately. I did not call you in as part of the military to help solve it. I think we can find an answer without force. To the point, I must say you have become close to Sally. She is young to be alone here with no one to guide her, to watch over her. I need you to become almost like a surrogate mother. It would be truly a shame if something were to happen to her."

"I have been watching her, Sir. She likes the kickball and enjoys helping in the field. I have noticed no one else has taken an overt fondness to her."

"There are several men here that I would deem questionable."

"Really?" she thought but couldn't come up with any.

"Yes, some. There are a few that just seem creepy. I've kept her away from those. This is exactly what I want you to do. There is a lot at stake. So much so it would surprise you. As simple as some decisions are, they have huge ramifications. Some people are so steadfast and adamant about what they want that the consequences of their actions overshadow the dilemma we are in."

"I don't understand, Sir."

"I can't give you the full details now. It's commonplace for the government to be an elusive beast. But as far as this subject goes, at this point in time, I cannot get into any great detail. It will take time, but believe me, in time, you will understand. I must have somebody watch over her. I cannot let anything happen to her that is 'bad'."

"No, of course not," Lena agreed.

"May I trust you?"

"Well, of course, you may. It would pain me to see anything wrongful happen to her, or anybody, on the ship. I mean, putting the uniform aside, it is not my purpose to see other people harmed in any capacity."

"Good, great. I know that you two have spent a lot of time together. From here on, can you make it more so if such a thing is possible? Word has come that there may be people here who would like to hurt her, and I cannot have that."

"Hurt her? In what way?"

"Someone on board has a history of sexual abuse. I will not say what they have done. I cannot even say who it is. They did their time for their deeds, and in the face of our court system, they laid the matter to rest. However, out here, I hope they do not think they can take up old habits. We have no written law. The only law is of common knowledge. I do not believe people will overstep this boundary, but I cannot take any chances."

She sat back slightly in the chair.

"I will protect her in the time ahead by any means necessary."

"Good," with the tension eased away, he sat back in his chair as well. "Think of her as a mascot, in a sense. You've seen what lengths some teams will go to degrade or humiliate the other team's mascot?"

"Well, yes," she smiled at a memory. "Back at the Academy, we had our class mascot, an albino dog, covered with pink and red lipstick. It took a while to clean her up."

He folded his hands before him, elbows resting on the chair arms. "I know 'mankind.' I studied psychology for many years, and I know that even though we are only three hundred, inevitably, we will divide. Some people will align with other people and be against us completely. It is human nature. They will see Sally as young and innocent, an embodiment of all that has passed, and whoever has her on their side will seem strong. We must keep her from this turmoil as much as possible."

"Relatively speaking, it's a small place, Brandon. I won't be able to hide her completely from everybody or to keep her away without suspicion. Not just other people's suspicion, hers."

"I'm not saying we should do this right away," he said. "I'm not asking you to run off with her to one of the desolate kim-two's. I say that it will take time for divisions to form and for people to show their true nature. We need to be ready when the time comes."

"I will be with her always, then. Rest assured, I will protect her above all others."

"Thank you, Lena. I know she will be in good hands."

XD05, Week 3 - Lawrence, the naughty bird, escaped.


I was sitting by myself in the main dining hall of the hotel. I had found pencils and was drawing different things I noted around the space where we lived. I had the hotel with the correct number of stories, me kicking my soccer ball and the grass down the lane. It wasn't bad artwork. I didn't know where to put it when I finished them.

I heard something loud, and the commotion was such that it caught everybody's attention. I heard yelling and screaming and ran to see what was going on.

On the steps to the hotel, there were many people. Uncle Butch was in the middle. Dressed as usual in dazzling colored clothing, his hair was a mess for the first time. He was waving his arms in the air, crying to the sky.

"He's gone! He's gone!" I had never heard of an adult so upset. "Lawrence got away." He was doing circles and looking at people but seeing no one. "I… I was just trying to feed him, and I thought everything would be okay, you see. Can't you see? I thought he would be fine in my apartment, away from his cage. I turned my back for a moment and," sobs wracked his body. "He flew. They clipped his wings. I never knew him to fly before, but he did. Lawrence! Lawrence! I have his food. I have… everything he needs. Why would he go elsewhere?"

Uncle Butch went to one knee, and two people had to help him up.

He covered his face and sobbed uncontrollably.

MC, a taller man with no hair, rubbed Uncle Butch's back.

"We'll go find him. Yoooooo… everyone, let's all go see if we can catch him. I think with everybody here, we can do pretty good."

"No, no. You can't chase a bird like that. He'll just fly off. We need to trap him somehow. Find netting and capture him. He'll come back when he's hungry. I had a little bell he loved to play with."

"Maybe if we jingle it, he will come back."

Several people just shook their heads and turned.

MC glanced around, giving people a look of hopelessness. Somebody motioned him to move away, and he shrugged his shoulders.

"Look, look, young man," MC patted his shoulders. "We'll keep an eye out for him. If we see him, we will let you know."

Uncle Butch sat down on the steps and wept. Elbows on his knees, hands covering his face, he stayed there as everyone moved away. I turned as well, and head down, I walked into the hotel. It was so unusual to see an adult act like this. I wasn't sure what to make of it.

Behind a window and a tall fern, I watched him for a bit. He stood, and in a dash of color, ran haphazardly down the walkway. Of all the people I had seen on the ship so far, he was one of the stranger ones.

* * *

I grew bored quickly. Being the youngest person on the ship, there was almost no one else I could relate to. Everyone else had their things to do, and if I had food and checked in from time to time with everybody, they seemed content to let me be on my own. I explored and would often wander around the square, looking at the buildings and kicking my soccer ball.

I was going from one corner of our kim-two to the next, tapping it gently.

Sitting quietly on the bench was Uncle Butch. I did not notice him watching me until I looked up.

"Well, good afternoon Sally Weiss. How are you this day?"

"I am doing well. How are you?"

"I am still very sad that Lawrence has gotten away from me," he said coolly. "Would you believe me if I told you that he was in a place and has stayed there for several days?"

"Can't you go get him?" Not that I was overly fond of the bird, but I was eager to get him back to his owner.

"I could go get him if I could make it through the fence. Do you remember those properties that had the high fences?"

"Oh yeah, they were there to keep us out." I raised my hand and pointed my finger at him.

"Well, I must tell you that these same walls are keeping my Lawrence in. I know, I know that Brandon said we were not supposed to go there. If I were to get in, I could rescue Lawrence, and he would be with me once more."

I thought about this, and it didn't seem right to have him here and his bird elsewhere on the ship flying loose. They should be together.

He leaned forward a little. "I have his food here. I'm sure he's eating other stuff in there, something he shouldn't be. And what if we find a way back home? The rich people will come to the ship and their homes and see that Lawrence pooped all over the place. I can't allow that. Very disgraceful."

"Can we shoo him away?" I asked.

"We can, but I believe he'll just go right back. I must get him and bring him home." He pointed to a different building, and I wondered if he did not live at Hotel Lima.

"The fence is very tall," I said, remembering the places he was talking about from our walk around. "Do you need a ladder of some type to get in?"

"No, I think the people who built the place would expect somebody to come with the ladder to break in, and so they put in safeguards against that."

"Oh?"

"There is a way we can get in, but I am too big to climb under the fence. I will look and see if there's anybody smaller who could do this."

"I can probably do it." If it meant getting Lawrence back, I was all for it.

"Oh no, I need somebody brave and somebody willing to take chances. You are the youngest one here. I don't think you've taken any chances before, have you?"

"Um, yeah, I did. There was the one warehouse they couldn't get into. The windows were too small. We opened them up, and I climbed in all by myself. Hanging onto the pipe, I dropped to the floor and opened the door."

"You weren't scared?"

"Just a little," I had to admit to him. "But I knew it would be better for everybody."

His face got a little pouty, and he coughed in his fist just once. "Would you mind? Lawrence would be with me tonight, and we make the happiest team."

"It's a long way to walk," I said, remembering how far away the buildings were.

"Well, then, we won't. We'll take a shuttle."

He stood up and held out his hand. I looked at it for a second, looked at him with a smile, and then looked back at his hand. I did not take it. I knew I was now committed to helping him, but it would feel odd touching him that way. I turned and picked up my soccer ball. I would toss it from hand-to-hand as we walked.

He coughed in his fist again two times. It was almost as if he were hiding words he was forced to speak, but didn't want to.

\* \* \*

When we were in the shuttle, I did not sit next to him. He sat in a row of seats in the back, and I had to catch my soccer ball once as it rolled away. Except for the wind, it was quiet. I sat sideways in a seat three away from him. They were big seats for me. I sat with my back against the outside and my legs straight over three seats. I could only look over the back at him. He had his elbow on the window's edge, and with two of his fingers, he was playing with his bottom lip.

"Is everything okay?" I asked. He seemed a little nervous.

"It is. I am just weighing options on things I must do."

"Oh, okay. Do you think he'll still be there when we get there?"

"Who?" he looked really confused.

"Mr. Lawrence, your bird." I smiled, trying to lighten the mood. I almost added the words 'silly head,' but I do not think he would appreciate that. Uncle Butch looked nothing like a silly head.

"We will find him. He will be there."

He was quiet for a time. I rolled the ball in my hands and watched out the far windows as the world slipped by.

"Do you know, little one," he said, looking out from the window, "that with the ship lost as this one is, many people will enjoy this."

"They will?" I knew nobody who would enjoy us being lost. I only knew we would be out here for a long time before they rescued us.

"There are games that adults play with their possessions," he almost chuckled. "Much like you would with the soccer ball or your doll Mrs. Priscilla if there were other children around. Like, say, those trucks in the trunk in your room." I stopped fidgeting with the soccer ball at the mention of my doll. I wondered how he knew about the other toys? "If they cannot find a ship this size as it suddenly disappears off the map, then there are winners and losers." He coughed into his fist again. "Same way if there were a bunch of children and suddenly the soccer ball became hidden by a few. Those who once had the soccer ball would be at a loss; those with it would be at a gain."

I could understand that and nodded.

"You see, for some people who work constantly going nowhere, the only way they can gain something is by doing what they do best, wrong. It's these wrong twists and turns that eventually help them go forward. Sometimes, oh, dear sweet child, the best way to get forward is to go back."

"Is that a riddle or something?"

"I wish it were," he said, raising his eyebrows.

"What did you do?"

"Pardon me?" He asked.

"Everyone here had a job doing something before we got on the ship. What did you do at Homeport?"

He looked at me coldly, and for the first time, I was not sure if I should be here with him alone.

Closing his eyes, he shook his head. When he spoke again, there was no more laughter or happiness in his voice. "That is something I cannot tell you."

"Really? Was it a secret or something?"

"No, I cannot tell you because you would not sleep at night." Saying nothing more, he turned his head and looked out the window. I never dared ask him again.

* * *

There was a quiet chime just before the shuttle settled down on the ribbon. We got off, and I kept the soccer ball with him and me in the crook of my arm. I listened for any irregularities in his footsteps. Things about him put me at unease. I do not know if it was his flashy clothing, but for some reason, I had this bad feeling about clowns. He, of all people on the ship, reminded me of a clown.

The place he wanted to get into took up almost one whole kim-two. It was big. When we walked through a week ago, I was on a different street and had not seen this place. They had taken great care with the design of the space. All the pine trees remained neatly trimmed, and the grounds were just a bit messy since no one has been here to cut them.

He stopped suddenly, looking at the high fence.

"I like what they did with the stonework. You see, this is an actual stone, not milled prefab garbage. For the last billion years, these rocks were floating in space. Probably from some star or some planet that something had destroyed. Beautiful to look at. You do not own rocks like this; you merely hold them for a time. They will eventually belong to somebody else, and then somebody else, and then as the eons pass either, they will erode or become somebody else's." He ran his fingers over the hard surface.

"Do we go through the gate?"

"Since no one is watching, I could easily get a ladder and climb over the top. However, that would set off alarms, and not only would it notify anybody nearby that someone was here, it would also lock down security systems. If this is how I got in, I could not use any of the computers inside."

"I thought we were getting Mr. Lawrence." I bounced the ball once and caught it.

"Well, yes, he has been in one of the bigger trees. His white plumage stands out notably, and from his perch, he taunts me."

"That's good."

"Indeed. Beneath this one place right here, there are no sensors." He pointed to a place where the fence and the ground met. "The place is tiny, and it would take a wee person to climb underneath. They were not expecting this place to be open without security bots, cameras, or guards.

They expected a short transition and then people to populate the ship. In doing so, anybody would notice people being suspicious."

"You couldn't stand out here in your colorful clothing without being noticed," I said, understanding what he was getting at.

"Yes, quite true. Once you go through, if you would come down through to the gate, there is a gatehouse there. Unlocked, you can go in, and in the main terminal, you can request the gate to open. Can you do that for me? There is no one else on the ship small enough to do this."

He was right. Like helping them by squeezing in the window, I knew I could get into tight places.

"I sure can." I held out my soccer ball for him to hold, which he did for a moment with just his fingertips of both hands before setting it down. "What do I have to do?"

"You must lie down on the ground and put your one arm over your head. It will be too narrow for you to wiggle your shoulders in."

I did as he instructed. The chopped-up mulch was rough on my back. I'm sure some were getting in my hair as well. I looked at him once, and his broad smile and large eyes were a little unnerving. On my back, with my hand over my head, I kicked with my feet.

I found that I was only pushing mulch away with my legs. I could find no solid surface to push against. Suddenly I did. Craning my neck, I could see that Uncle Butch was standing there, and my boot soles were on the tips of his blue shoes. He was using himself as an anchor.

I had to turn my head to the side, or my nose would bump the metal.

"Your shoulders are almost too broad, child." He said coolly. I grunted, redoubling my efforts. Not sure if I was trying to get inside the fence or if I was trying to get away from him.

He was right, though; I could not get my shoulders in square on. I had to turn a little with my arm still outstretched and then moved to the side, and the other shoulder slipped through.

"That's it. Now all you have to do is get the rest of you there."

I brought my one hand up and pushed on the fence. In a moment, I could sit up with my hands beneath me, my legs before me.

He still had not stopped smiling. "You did it. You are inside."

I nodded and brushed myself off. I was thankful that there was a barrier between us he could not cross.

"Brush it off more; you still have some on your pants. Listen up. In the guardhouse, it will ask for your identification. Place your hand on the blue plate, and it will record your palm print. After it records your palm print, it will ask you your name. It will ask you for your identification. When it does that, let me know, and I will tell you. It is too long for you to memorize now, and we do not have time. You must get back to the hotel."

That brought me back. Suddenly, I remembered that they may look for me.

"To your left, sweetie," he said, and I turned. "No, your other left. This way," he pointed.

After I was out of the hedgerow, I came to a walking path, and I could see the gatehouse down the way. I did as he asked.

After I touched the blue glass and gave it my name, it asked me for my identification number. I stuck my head out the door and nodded to him. He was loud when he said it.

"2... 0... 8... 5... 8... 4... 9."

When I typed the last number, it cycled through to green.

I'm not sure what I had done, but I guess it was okay.

I gave him a thumbs-up, and he motioned me to come to him.

"There will be a terminal, and in the upper left-hand corner will be an icon for the gate. I need you to tap the icon, and I'll be in."

"Just like that?" I snapped my fingers.

"Yes," he tried snapping his fingers, also with little success. "Just like that."

I was hesitant. In no time during my short stay there, did I see the white bird in a tall tree. I took several steps before I turned around and then skipped. The icon was easy to see, and I tapped it. The gate opened silently. I went back towards it.

"Did you want me to help search for him?"

"Hmmm, oh, no. I'll look from here on out. Why don't you go get your ball and head home?"

Again, I did not hesitate. As I got back to the cobblestone, I felt a vibration. The gate was closing. I felt relief. I was forever thankful and happy that he was no longer near. The soccer ball was where he left it. Not wishing to draw attention to myself, I carried it until I was back at the shuttle platform. Even then, I looked over my shoulder.

The trip home was uneventful. Back at the hotel, my stomach grumbled at the smell of garlic and greens. Everyone was busy. They paid me little attention as I grabbed a tray, a bowl of soup, and an ear of corn.

XD05

I was sitting with Lena and Addy in the dining hall one day. They were talking about life before and how they had hoped their military careers would have worked out.

I wanted to hear what they had to say. When we get rescued, I will put some serious thought about becoming a soldier myself. The things they have done and the places they have seen all seem very exciting.

Addy was in the middle of a story when we heard the loud voice of Uncle Butch.

"Everything he does is so over-the-top," said Addy, shaking her head. Her story unfinished and forgotten, she watched him.

"Loud-clothing, loud-mouth. His hair is always slicked back. I mean, who does that anymore?" Lena was just as disgusted as Addy was. I had helped him a few weeks prior and got an odd feeling from him. As he walked up to get his tray of food, I wrinkled my nose at him.

"Watch his eyes if you get the chance," Addy said in a whisper. "He's always looking. I know that's what we all do with our eyes, yet it appears he is constantly taking things in. When he is talking with somebody, it's almost as though he is gauging strengths and weaknesses. He acts like a fop, to be sure, however…"

"He's just odd." Lena finished for her.

Thankfully, he took a seat elsewhere.

"I think we intimidate him," Lena cupped her hand and whispered. She gave me a knowing wink, and I winked back.

We ate quickly and hurried to get out to the fields. As we walked by the table where he sat, I happened to glance at him. As Addy had said, he was watching us intently. Eyes wide with a big smile, he did not nod in greeting, just stared as we walked by. I could feel his eyes upon me as we left.

\* \* \*

It was days later, when I was out with my soccer ball, I noticed Uncle Butch with a bucket and a square on the ground. He was mixing up something thick and pouring it into the square. He wore no shoes this day, and he had rolled his pant legs up to his knees. My curiosity got the best of me, and even though I had misgivings about him, I was very interested in what he was doing.

As I came closer, I noticed that several squares lay on the ground, not just one.

"What are you doing?" I asked, holding the soccer ball in the crook of my arm.

"Ah, good to see you. Uncle Butchie is making plaster impressions of things. If I put an object in this material, I will push aside the material and leave an imprint. The material will harden, and the impressions will stay forever."

I watched him as he smoothed out the material. He took an overturned bucket and sat down. He looked at me as he put his feet in the mixture.

"Ooooohhh, that feels good. Little cool feet on a hot day; that's what I'm talking about. That's the best. Did you want to try it?"

I wasn't sure if I wanted to or not.

"Slip off your shoes, and I will smooth this out. We'll get an impression of your feet. Come on. It's okay."

He grinned as I put the soccer ball down and reluctantly slid my shoes and socks off. I found it awkward sitting on the bucket, trying to put my feet in.

"No, no, no. You are doing it all wrong. It's all messed up. Gotta be perfect the first time."

Again, I tried, and again he was not happy. He smoothed it out once more.

"Here, I'll show you."

Without realizing what he was doing, I was looking at the mold and not him, but he went behind me. I almost cried out when he grabbed me around the waist. Too stricken to do anything else, I did not fight or push him away. To do so may have made him angry. One hand around my waist, the other hand around my bum. He picked me up and gently made an indentation in the plaster.

"See. Nice and easy." It was cold on my feet and did not feel as good as he led me to believe. I shivered a little. When he put me down, I twisted and backed away.

"See there, not so bad at all." Fists on his hips, he looked down at the plaster. "Perfect imprint of your feet. I think I'll keep these."

I walked backward, never taking my eyes off him. That he touched me, that he got so close to my circle, I felt that had somehow tainted me. I would not let this happen again. As I stepped away, I rubbed my feet on the grass, hopefully rubbing off as much of the plaster as I could. Still, I did not look away from him. I found my soccer ball and my shoes and socks by touch. Picking them up, I quickly ran from there.

XD05

It has only been a few weeks since we had been there. The stored food for the pigs was running low, and we were feeding them the scraps we didn't eat. It was barely adequate. Also, no one knew how to properly care for them. We gave them water and food, but the pen really smelled bad. To help them with their diet, they brought armfuls of vine from one of the far kim-two's. This, in turn, led people to believe maybe the vine would infect the city.

Then the idea came to them that instead of bringing all the vine to the pigs, why don't they take the pigs out to the vine and let them be?

It caused a loud ruckus.

There was a mother pig, a father pig, and several little runts. They had tried several times to capture the animals but could not do it. They tried roping them and walking them like pets. The little ones really squealed. The mother and father were not happy as they thought their young were being hurt. Renn almost got bitten by the father pig, the boar. He managed to rip his pants from his bum all the way down to his ankle. Only after we realized he was safe did we have a good laugh.

Wrapping them up in a tarp did no good, and even herding them did not work out. They found some shipping crates, and it took tact and good luck, but they could get the grown-up pigs in separate containers. It scared the little ones, but this made it easier for us to catch them. With the crates secured, we could lift them onto a wagon. Two people pulled, and three pushed from behind. It took all day, but we got the pigs to their new home. The parents were not happy until we brought the little piglets in and released them. Even then, they seemed a little agitated.

Someone mentioned that sheep were a lot easier to herd than a family of pigs. All things considered, they would rather have sheep than swine.

Someone else mentioned that if they wanted sheep so badly, they should eat a wool shirt and shit one out—their words, not mine. Many people laughed at this.

Given a constant supply of water, they had all the vines they wanted.

They gave the skinny guy, Pat Pat, the job of watching over the pigs. It was the only job he had to do, and he took it seriously. Not a day went by that he was not taking the scraps from the dining hall.

In two months, the mother pig had more babies. By that time, the younger ones were much larger. They moved them to a neighboring kim-two. There they ate the ever-present vine. By the end of the first year, we had over seventeen pigs. Pat Pat said one of the father pigs would make a great meal for the one-year anniversary.

There was a great debate on how to kill the pig and prepare it for food. I would sit and listen intently while they talked.

I only ate a little of the meat. There were so many people and so little to go around. They wasted nothing. It had a lot of flavor. We have been eating fruits and vegetables for so long that this was welcome. I ate each piece of my small portion slowly and was not ashamed at the end when I licked the plate. I was sad to see that this moment was over. Everyone assured me that this would not be the last. With the litter continuing to grow, in a few years, we could have a pig a week, and the group would not suffer. Tang called it sustainable farming.

Some wanted his skull to be on display at Hotel Lima. And just as many didn't want it displayed there at all. In the end, it was placed over the top of a door of a building in a different kim-two.

Birds picked at it, and there was a rumor that they even saw the white bird Lawrence cleaning meat from the skull. Uncle Butch waited there for many days for his return, but after a time gave up.

* * *

I grew. After the first six months, my shoes would not fit. My clothing became too small for me, and we had to search the ship. Jaughn, busy with finding stuff for his alcohol, heard of our search and could tell us exactly where to find clothing my size. Not really meant for someone like me, it was work clothes meant for a smaller adult. I could not find any shoes my size, but there were several pairs of clothing that almost fit me. I had to roll up the pant legs or the shirt sleeves, and I was fine. I wore a big old sloppy hat a few times, and they said I looked like a kid from the Great Impression. I did not understand what the Great Impression was about, and they never explained why kids dressed this way during that time.

* * *

Sam shuffled to the stage. There were so few people now. He once thought, and he was right, that his presentation on what was going on outside the ship was the event of Sunday night. He remembered a time when almost everyone showed up. Now the crowd was down to under twenty—a few diehards who were once spacers.

"Well, we are fast approaching our one-year anniversary. In the year we have been here, I have learned a lot. From all the signposts I studied, we are exactly 'where' we need to be. It's the 'when' that is a huge problem. Let me explain. We have the Lucy Staircase. If you remember, we pop out of the universe, and everything rotates over us, either upstream or down, clockwise or counterclockwise. When we pop back into the universe, space and time have taken us elsewhere. It is a nice, tight place where we have been free to roam. We have traveled light-years in mere seconds. Most of space is empty except for when we cross the galactic arms.

"Are there questions?" he asked.

Everyone looked at him oddly. To date, it was one of the shortest meetings he has had.

Jay spoke up. "What exactly are you saying?"

He breathed a heavy sigh. It's almost as if they were not listening. "With all the studying that I have done, I have sort of stumbled across this one conclusion. The computers brought us home, but rather than doing it as a stairway, they did it more like a fireman's pole. We did not circle around the galaxy to the Solar system. We took a shortcut and came straight across. We are where, exactly where we need to be. It's the 'when' that someone screwed up on."

"Shouldn't Brandon, Everett, or someone know about this?"

"If they wanted to know, they'd be here." With that, he walked off the stage.

\* \* \*

The news was all the rage the next day. Brandon sought him out and asked him to give a much larger demonstration. Everyone wanted to hear the news firsthand, and so they packed the place.

He brought up a still frame of the video on the large monitor. "The Samuel Drives we created to give us a way out of the Solar System. Not with unstable rockets, not with ion drives, or solar sails. We have this vast area obtainable to us. As the galaxy spins, those in the bubble of the SD's are stationary." He found it hard to believe he was explaining these rudimentary principles to them all over again. This is common knowledge they presented to school kids in classes.

"We should have been out at a different location. Three days and three spins later, our destination was the Solar System. We did the three days; we did not do the three spins. We took a shortcut. From one side of the galaxy to the other, we got the 'x' axis; we just didn't get the 'y' axis."

The auditorium was quiet.

"How do we get back?" someone in the crowd asked.

"We tried working with the ship's engines, and the computer system is so complex, it's beyond everyone's understanding. If we were stationary and not moving, it would only be a matter of time before the Solar System came back around, and we would be home. However, like a leaf in the water, we are traveling with the current once again."

"How far away is the solar system from us right now?"

"Yeah, can we see it?"

"As near as I can figure, it's on the opposite side. A hundred thousand light-years away. Also, we are caught between the staircase above and the one below. If our signal was strong enough, it would take thousands of years to get to the staircase, either one. We do not have the capability to transmit anything so strong. In analogy, it would be like looking for an ant on earth from a location on the moon, and those on the moon do not understand they should be looking.

"So, to wrap it up," he clapped his hands and took several steps closer to the edge of the stage. "We are here for the long haul. Rescue, if it comes, would be centuries past our lifetimes."

Brandon stood and cleared his throat. "I would like to ask if you could continue to look."

"I can do that. The equipment is exciting to work with. We are in a quiet part of the galaxy, which is good because there is nothing flying around. Does everybody remember Rada II? I doubt seriously that we will get anything like that here."

He grabbed his papers and again shuffled off the stage.

Homeport, Day 3

The buildings remained preserved relatively well. They carried a few broken windows here and there. Some surfaces crumbled, but Layne saw minimal damage.

"There can't be anybody alive in this," whispered Schmidt. His deep voice adding to the eeriness of what lie around them. "There is air to breathe, but food will not last like this."

"Dry out soon enough." Harris stopped and touched a form that had once been a bush. Parts of it fell away in a cloud of dust. Growling, he swatted and kicked at all the branches. It took just a second, and when he stopped, his suit was almost uniform brown.

Layne watched him with a smile.

"Feel better now?" Layne said, brushing what he could from Harris's intakes. "The food would need some serious preservation. With transport readily available to the higher atmosphere, it could be freeze-dried."

"Yeah, however, nothing can grow. The atmosphere would suck out the water of anything living and not sheltered."

There is a ping on his NavSat inside his helmet.

He held up a hand for silence.

"Maj. Ronca, we are on the last leg 'till Hotel Lima. So far, there is nothing. As stated before, everything is dry and crumbles as we touch it. No signs of life. No signs anything has lived here since it dried out."

*"Copy that, Sgt. Layne. Be advised a second and third team have arrived. Everyone else is on the Morning Wall. They found more people there. We will keep in contact and let you know if there are any changes."*

"They will come down to the surface?"

*"Negative. Civilians recovering bodies and Burner teams. However, more are in route to assist with the search for bodies. Medical and a second reconnaissance are inbound. ETA about an hour."*

"Copy, sir." He clicked his mic off and walked onward.

"Sgt. Layne," Dobbins called him. "You've been here for some time. Did you know any of them? I mean, I remember Burroughs. He was the one that would laugh all the time."

"He had that scar on his ear?" Layne asked, touching the side of his helmet.

"No, that was Mohammado. Burroughs had this laugh that was high-pitched, and I believe he laughed all the time because he was short on time and getting ready to cycle out."

"Other than the shift rotations, I really didn't talk to them much. That crew was on the way back. Kind of unspoken that you keep to yourself."

His foot caught something, and he almost went down. He stumbled a little and brought up a cloud of dust. The vine had, at one time, covered almost everything, and it was difficult to see what lay beneath. Finding a piece of rebar leaning against a column, he swung it back and forth before him as he walked. This enabled him to avoid other unseen dangers.

"I will resort to my tanks," he told his team. "Gotta close it off. You should too. If the suit is constantly pulling oxygen in it, dust will settle on the intakes. If we use them more, it will get pulled further in, as the suit has trouble filtering out the air. The engineers did not design them for this much fine dust. We'll have a couple of hours of reserve. We can refill them when we get above the vegetation."

"Yeah," Dobbins said, smacking his lips. "I am picking up this faint taste. Mine are already getting overloaded, and it's cycling the dust through."

"Stop breathing then," Harris chided.

"Oh, that was a good one," Dobbins shook his head.

They came to the first platform that led to the ribbon track. Station-N. It was the first station at the bottom of the curve. Taking the steps up, they cleared the tangled mess that was once plants. Here, few had reached, and they made less of a commotion as they walked.

Layne blew a burst of air out of his intakes to clear them. After a few breaths, he keyed the pumps, and his tanks filled again.

"Never seen a place with humidity this low."

"They have recorded zero percent on Earth."

"Yeah, we did a desert module in training. Did you guys ever get that?"

"We all did." Layne tapped the ribbon of the track. Even though it was paper thin, it still had its strength. Free of the vine, they could make good time without the risk of getting injured by unseen obstacles. He turned on his heel and surveyed what he stood on. It did not surprise him to see that a huge strip had fallen away up near the Hub.

"The power is out. That much is clear."

"Shuttles are down. Nothing will be coming or going. If you think we must spend as little time as possible here, we could run the distance."

"No need." He turned. Using the piece of rebar as a walking stick, he began the walk.

\* \* \*

Everything was intact. Something cracked one window in the upper left-hand corner, but at first glance, that was all. Hotel Lima stood a quiet tomb. Before they tried to enter, Layne and Dobbins went around to the left. Schmidt and Harris to the right. As with many other buildings, it held true.

At the front again, Layne paused.

"Maj. Ronca, this is Sgt. Layne. Sir, Hotel Lima is secure. No sign of anybody."

"*We can see the vine has been undisturbed.*" They had been watching from Homeport the whole time.

"That is correct. All the surrounding ways, we're the first ones to be here in a long time.

"*Hold tight, please.*" There was a long pause as they waited.

"*Sgt. Layne, attempt the doors. It is highly unlikely that they are operational. If you cannot open them, then there is a service entrance to the back. Use what means you can to gain access. We understand that the place is in ruin. We will search the place for some answers; however, we want as little damage to the structure as possible.*"

Harris and Schmidt were already walking toward the entrance.

"Understood, Sir."

\* \* \*

A room by room search yielded what they already expected. There was no one alive. Dust settled ages ago with no disruption since. The hotel gave no signs of anyone being here for a long time.

They had to be thorough in their efforts.

The first floor, the entrance foyer, the kitchens, the dining room, and the other staterooms were all empty. There were tables set up in the conference room; it looked like they had played cards. Discarded bottles littered the floor, and there was a tall stack of crushed cups in the corner.

Schmidt picked up a small notepad from the table. He dusted it off with his gloves and gently flipped back through the pages. "Once they reach 500 points or over, they start a new game. What game do they play where the winning score is always over 500?"

"Spades, man."

"It's a good game. If you play enough, you can get really competitive."

"This says here that MC cheats." Schmidt looked up and chuckled.

"Does it give a name?"

"No, they used only the player's initials." He laid the tablet gently back down on the tabletop.

\* \* \*

On the third floor, they found the first body. Laying in the room's center was a corpse. They covered it with a sheet up to its waist and a shirt up to its neck. Layne knelt and looked closer. The shirt just lay on top of the body rather than having been worn. Body fluids discolored the cloth of both. Around it were flowers of some type that had turned to dust.

"Should we try to move it?"

Layne held up his finger.

"Maj. Ronca, we found a body. As of right now, I cannot tell the sex of the individual, and by a preliminary look around the room, I cannot identify any names or possession. Do we have permission to move the body?"

*"Negative Sgt. Layne. Leave it as is, and I will send a secondary team."*

"Copy, Sir. Room number 341, one individual."

* * *

When the hotel was operational, all the doors were closed with magnetic locks. With the power gone, the mechanisms deteriorated until all the doors were open.

Layne was the one to find Sally's room. The walls remained a very light pink. Things laid around that could only be hers—an old soccer ball which had deflated. A rag doll laying on the bed was only identifiable by shape. The thread that made up it and its clothing had rotted beyond any form. On a small child's desk sat an empty bottle, which may have at one time held wine. It, like the world, was bone dry.

*"Sgt. Layne, there is writing on the wall. Look at it, stop, and hold."*

He did so as they took a snapshot of what he saw.

*"Good, got it. I see names and dates?"*

"That is affirmative. It appears to be all the dates in the future. I see where it says 'Xjan, 05 February 12, heart failure. This must be a list of those who have died," he whispered.

*"There was a man by the name of Xjan on the itinerary."*

There was a pause of almost two minutes as he looked over the names.

"Here it says they lost seven in one day. Magel accident."

*"Who is Magel? I'm not sure if there was anybody on board named Miguel."*

"I have no idea."

*"That is almost everybody's name there. Director Porter's son is there."*

"Ah, yes, found it. 04 March 20."

*"It does not start off chronologically."*

"No, the dates are jumbled at first. I guess they were not expecting to make a complete list."

*"The very last name has a date."*

"Um, yes, that is correct, 'Sally Weiss,' 12 December 2217."

*"Her date is the last one. She outlived them all."*

"If that was the last date, I wonder who wrote it?"

There was silence for a time. *"Keep searching."*

"Copy."

\* \* \*

Layne looked through drawers. One held sheets of paper, which he gingerly pulled out. It was a child's drawing of the hotel; they had gotten the number of stories correct, and a little girl was playing with a soccer ball on some tall grass. The artwork was not that bad. Whoever did this had some real talent. He placed the papers back into the drawer so as not to disturb them further.

\* \* \*

Richard Porter sank back in his chair.

His son had passed. Somewhere on that ship lay the bones of his son. Although it had not happened yet, although the date was twenty-three years from now, his son's name was there on the ledger on the wall in Sally's room. Somehow, in the single day, the ship had been gone. His son had lived to an age older than Richard was now.

Even though he and his ex had divorced fifteen years ago, he still had to get word back that her child had passed on.

Emotionally, it was stunning. He and his son were close. It was good to see that his son was following in his footsteps and had this desire and knack to lead men.

There had to be more; there just had to. How can you take one person's life and sum it up in a few brief notes? The days he missed, the years that went slowly by. He could not grieve for the death of his son. According to the records, he lived a very long life, and hopefully, it was fulfilling. To Richard, his son passed away yesterday at the age of forty-five, but according to the ledger on the wall, his son lived to be almost seventy.

\* \* \*

Sitting before her conference vid somewhere on '06, Deborah McClanahan looked frayed, and Richard wondered briefly how he, in turn, looked to her. It had been a long day, and things would not get better.

"Director Porter," she said. "I don't mind that you destroy the vine. It will be a nuisance, and it will hamper any form of rescue or understanding of what happened. What I'm concerned about is that perhaps the vine may have mutated just a little in the years it was left there. I'm asking for just a few hours for my team to settle down to the surface to find out what exactly happened. If this catastrophe was plant induced, then we owe it to ourselves to gather as much information as possible."

He shook his head. "We cannot find anybody, or anything, with this heavy layer of the vine. It crumbles to dust when we touch it. We need to get rid of it. We have vacuum units coming from in-system. They will collect all of it."

"It is several million tons of biomass that clutter the surface."

"I understand that."

"Do we have time then to investigate from our end?"

"They will bring them here, and we'll have them operational within a few hours. We will start in the city, on the Twilight Wall."

"Are they slow-moving?"

"I would say they are. Others have told me they are incredibly thorough and will not move on until it completely clears a space."

"Well, that will give us enough time, I guess. It covers the whole ground. I can take my team to an isolated kim-two, Morning Wall, and we'll search there. Up and running, we can collect our samples and be out well before they arrive. Do we have permission?"

Mabel nodded to Porter. "We need to find out all the answers. If this was the act of nature, then we need to know."

"You have my permission to proceed," he nodded. "Stay well ahead of the vacuums when they arrive."

"Thank you, sir."

\* \* \*

It was like a huge octopus struggling on dry land. Each vacuum had about ten flexible tubes extending out robotic feeders that would suck up debris and send it back to a holding chamber. Chiefly designed for space, it was easily adaptable to the gravity of XD05. When they deployed them in space, gathering dust from asteroids, the chamber would fill up about every two days. On the surface of the ship, it was under three hours.

Programmed to fly less than one meter from the surface, drones kicked up vast clouds of dust. The vacuum traveled right behind. Tubes, two meters tall and reaching back to the vacuum collection vehicle (VCV), made it look like one giant arachnid. It sucked all the matter that was picked up in the air. In the collection area, specially designed hydraulics compressed material that was brought in. They pressed out much of the air and what remained was a brick. One-meter square, it weighed several tons. Like a giant slow spider, the VCV moved on.

At the end of the second day, it operated. Someone noted that even though this was the only way they could clean the surface of the ship, it would take a very long time.

XD05, Year 1 - "Three potato, four."


Sebastian liked his new apartment. He wanted a home close to Hotel Lima, where it seemed like it would be the major hub of everything. He would've taken a place upon the Twilight Wall, except that he had a fear of heights, and the way they built homes there gave him a bad sense of vertigo every time he looked at it. He found a building on the surface that suited him nicely. It had large windows looking in the opposite direction of the wall, the big open floor space. He could put the gym equipment in one corner and be able to look out on both sides at the rest of the ship while he was doing his daily workout.

He got clearance from Porter, and if he harmed nothing, it would be fine. Mirrors, large plasti-lite mirrors, hung on the walls of several of the other apartments. With his strength, they came off those walls and installed on his easily enough. He could now check out his physique from every angle with all the privacy he needed.

The ship had four gyms. Yes! He confiscated a different set of weights from each one. Nobody here looked like they lifted, and they wouldn't miss them. Hell! The things would rust before anybody here would use them.

Once he completed his day of work in the fields, he had nothing to do all day but lift.

He needed protein. A diet of just fruits and vegetables just wouldn't cut it. He needed something more. If he didn't get the protein, he would lose his bulk. That was bullshit. He needed to keep his weight. The scales showed that he was already down almost three kilograms. Because he had so much muscle, his body was tearing itself down to survive. If he continued this course in no time at all, he would lose all that he had gained. That was not acceptable.

Tonya, his girl back at Homeport, would not approve.

At night when everybody was sleeping, he would dress in black and go on a raiding party. Even though the other gyms were almost twenty kim-two's away, he did not use the shuttles. They had interior lights and running lights that were bound to draw someone's attention. No, if he would take something from somewhere else, he had to rely on his own strength.

The first night he went east. The computer granted him entry to the gym easily enough, and he looked over the weights he would take. They went into a backpack, and he slipped it on. Readjusting because one hit him in the spine. He shook his shoulders vigorously until they settled down.

And he walked right out the front door. No questions asked, no one chasing him down. This journey was half over. By the time he made it back, he was exhausted and sweaty, and it was an awesome workout for his thighs and calves.

He spent that evening working on his arms and letting his legs rest. It would not do to have two leg workouts right in a row. Non-conducive to the perfect body.

The next night, he did the same. Same gym, same location, and he walked out with the same number of weights as he did before.

Some people in town were bellyaching about the length of the trip or the long layover they would have to endure. He had no issues with this. Little runts anyway. He would ask Brandon if he can get a position in security. Because of his size, people automatically respected him. He knew he wasn't a brainiac like some of these guys; however, he was intimidating, to say the least. If they had a problem to solve, he would be the one they asked to solve it.

As he flexed in front of the mirror, he would whisper silently. "Yeah, I will own you guys. Come get it, bitches. You know you want it. Yeah, yeah."

He got bolder as time went on. If he ate early enough, he could travel when it was still daylight. The gym to the West was so far away it was easier to take a shuttle. He broke down and did this several times rather than walk it. Nobody questioned his actions. Normally, if he had been in the city with millions of people, he would have to share the ride with others. Now, it was just him. It didn't take him long to raid the gym. Sometimes they would not call the shuttle, and it still sat waiting for him. Going back to his flat, he saw no one else. And this was a superb thing, as it made everything so much easier.

He decided to travel to the one that was almost directly overhead. The ride in the shuttle lasted about an hour. He had his headphones on, and the music was intense. The ride was so smooth and effortless that he reached up to the bars that the passengers would hold and did some awesome pull-ups. His head almost touched the roof.

This gym was a little bigger than the others. The first floor had mats laying out for cardio. Probably a dance studio because there was the horizontal pole in front of the long mirror so the ladies could watch themselves spin and pirouette or hop around.

There was no elevator, oddly enough. Taking the staircase, he found the second floor held an appropriate gym with free weights, machines, and ellipticals. Yeah, this will be great.

He looked things over and was about to pack when he remembered that the stairway did not end here. There were at least three more stories above. If they created this place for people to come to exercise, then what did the upper floors hold?

His curiosity piqued, Sebastian went back out to the landing.

* * *

The third floor was literally a carbon copy of the second. In answer to this, he gave an enthusiastic thumbs-up. There would be more weights and several racks for him to put them on.

The fourth floor was storage. Plastic boxes were all stacked nice and neat. They mostly held stuff for the first floor. There were giant rubber bands and a bunch of those ballerina shoes. Some talc powder he put by the door to take home with him. Tucked away, almost as an insult, he found gloves for the weights and belts. This now, he was psycho about.

There was a cabinet he saved for last. At first glance, he thought they locked it. The latch on the front looked serious enough, and he was sure he would have to use a pry bar to get it open. He had every right to do this. The other losers would not even use the gym. They would bring their sorry selves in here and look at the mirrors, all the while laughing and giggling.

This was his gym. He claimed it.

He looked at the handle of the cabinet, expecting it to remain stationary. It lifted easily. The doors swung open. There, sitting all this time alone and unbothered, was at least, *at least*, twenty jugs of protein powder. High-efficiency, maximum output, vanilla-flavored protein powder.

"You have got to be shitting me," he whispered. He brought one out and twisted off the lid.

There it was. He opened the safety seal and brought it up to his nose. A deep breath was all he needed to verify that this was the real McCoy. His hands shook as he put the lid back on. More precious than gold, more beautiful than anything he'd ever known. These twenty would see him through for some time.

He put the container back on the shelf and closed the door.

"Yes, yes," he screamed. He took one of the plastic boxes of ballerina shoes and tossed them the length of the room. "Ha, bitches. Whoo!! Dammit, WHOO!!" He mimicked how he had seen a ballerina dance once. Hand on top of his head, he spun on his tiptoes as best he could. Coming down on a knee, he grabbed the ballerina shoes and tossed them in the air once more.

Forget the weights today; forget everything else. He had to get this back to his place before anyone else found it. They would scarf it up for sure. This had to be his secret stash and no one else's.

He wrapped his arms around the cabinet. Squeezing and lifting, he found that he could carry it with no effort. It pumped him up beyond comparison. He walked forward, and as he did so, it was difficult to see beyond the cabinet. He first looked around it to the left and then looked around and to the right.

"Hey," he said to himself. "This is almost like prom night."

Sebastian made it to the landing before he placed it down.

An elevator would've really helped.

"Bah, imbeciles," he muttered. Leave it to somebody in the lab coat to design a gymnasium.

At the edge, he wrapped his arms around the cabinet one more time. He hefted it a little higher and had to adjust the center of balance, but this allowed him to walk down the steps without having to duck walk.

He stopped at the landing on the third floor. Finding a fountain, he drank deeply. He poured water in his hair and shook his head vigorously.

He growled deep. "You can do this, Sebastian; ain't no pussy here." He thumped himself on the chest with his right fist and then his left.

A second growl escaped his throat as he picked up the cabinet again.

It seemed a little heavier than he expected, and he had to carry it a little lower. He knew if the building was fifteen stories tall, and he had found this cabinet on the top floor, he would still carry it down. By the bottom, he would be dragging it, but he would never give up, he would never quit, he would persevere.

By the time he made it down to the landing of the second floor, he was sweating profusely. He set it down heavily and smiled.

"I got this, man," he said. "I got this."

One more set of stairs and he would be at the bottom and home free.

To make it easier, he thought of doing it a different way this time. Instead of having the bulk of the weight in front of him and having to lean back to bring it back to center balance, he thought it would be so much easier if he kept the weight uphill. This way, his body, legs, and buttocks would support everything rather than having his arms and back do all the work.

He would not have to duck walk.

Heaving up the cabinet, he turned, and like a diver on the edge of a diving board, he put his toes on the edge of the top step.

Without warning, the cabinet shifted.

"Shit!" He exclaimed as he lost his balance. Even as his feet faltered, he would not let go of the cabinet. It was far too valuable, and he would not lose it. His right foot came down on nothing, and he fell backward.

He reached backward. Quickly trying to grab the railing. His muscles clenched, bracing himself for the inevitable impact. Muscles would take most of the blow, and hopefully, no bones would break.

His left leg overshot the step, skinning the shin on the edge.

There was no saving himself now.

He fell backward. Trying to hold the weight of the cabinet, he lost.

He twisted his ankle on the landing, and his momentum carried him backward. He fell then with the cabinet right on top of him. Two of the small metallic legs were beneath a step, and two were above.

His head against the wall, the cabinet caught his mid rib cage just beneath his pecks.

Under different circumstances, he could have pushed the cabinet aside. However, now he was trying to regain his breath. Taking small breaths, he could have lasted for some time. His body was screaming for oxygen that his lungs could not provide. He tried to breathe deep. The cabinet offered no resistance. With his massive hands, he tried to push it up, not to the left or right, and it was no use.

"Well, this sucks," he grunted between breaths.

It was a battle he was losing almost before it began. With pain screaming in his chest, he felt the world suddenly darken.

* * *

When we got back from working the fields, someone said they found Sebastian. I didn't know who they were referring to until they aped the way he walked. Arms stiffly out to the side, shoulders hunched up to hide the neck. It was the guy who I watched when we had our very first bonfire.

Although many people went to go see the body, Lena said it would be best if I did not. I guess wherever he died, he had been there a while.

On earth, where nature would take its course, insects would've found him and, within a few days, ravished his body. Here we had no such insects or carrion birds. His body stayed where he was and bloated in the heat.

Two brave souls donned spacesuits, and with their air systems sealed, they could wrap him up in a sheet of plastic. It was very gruesome.

They dug a grave for him in a kim-two near the Morning Wall. They sealed the kim-two from the ground, and the only way to it was by track. He was our first accidental death.

After they laid him in the ground, we were all asked to come out for a service to honor him.

* * *

Once again, Brandon, Mr. Everett at his side, stood before us.

"This is overly shocking to all of us. Sebastian stood out from everybody. He was the embodiment of mankind. He was strong in both mind and physique. We will miss him. To put it bluntly, he is the first of us to pass away accidentally. We can only assume that he died because he wanted the cabinet of protein food. He could've taken them out one by one and made the load much lighter. If you wish to have something that is here, please don't hoard it, I beg of you. He could have saved his life, but for this simple basic impulse. And I cannot sugarcoat this. I cannot tell you that there will be a happier tomorrow. Let us live our lives and do the best we can to make it through. All we have is this ship and each other."

He motioned to the men with the shovels, and they filled his grave.

Homeport, Day 4

"Hello everyone. My name is Brandon Porter. My father is Director Richard Porter, no relation to Elysian, who oversees Homeport. I miss you, dad. Thank you for your guidance through the years. It has helped me when things were not going so well. I would like to think you would do a much better job than I, but that would mean that we would have to change places. I do not wish this castaway on anyone.

"By the time this reaches someone who has a suitable reader, it would not be hard to assume that many years have passed. We have tried to find out where in the galaxy we are, and our best estimates tell us we are so far off the staircase as to be unreachable by another ship in a single lifetime. We all know we are stuck, and this will be where we die, eventually. We have tried to make the most of our situation. The resources we have been given are more than adequate for the handful of people we have. We still have a bounty of food. The vine they planted years ago has become a nuisance. We combat that every day. If the ship had gone back to the solar system, they would have destroyed the vine after setting down a deep, rich layer of biomass. Now, we must keep it at bay. The pigs are fond of it, and they have helped us out.

"I try to keep things quiet. After the initial shock of us being here and not being able to get home, there was some chaos. Our lives have settled down to farmers rather than those who build great ships. I would like to keep things peaceful here. However, our lives have not gone without the turmoil created by ourselves.

"I cannot point fingers at anyone. It would be wrong of me to do so. It would taint the memory of these people to the ones they love, and I believe everybody deserves a fair chance. I must tell you, we have lost about five people a year since we have jumped back into the universe. I have the list here, which I will read. Some have been so distraught about being away from their families and loved ones that they committed suicide. We have been lucky and have only had three accidents that resulted in a loss of life. The rest are death by natural causes.

"There is a cemetery in kim-two 2626. We have blocked it off so that the pigs will not get in there and disturb the bodies. To date, the remains of everybody who has passed are there. I will try to see that we bury everyone there. There will be a ledger in my room and Hotel Lima with a map of our plots.

"The first one we lost to an accident was Sebastian, Randy Sebastian. He lost his footing on the stairs and a locker he carried pinned him with its weight on his chest and neck. It was a while before anybody found him.

He died of asphyxiation and blood loss." Brandon paused for a moment as if he were gathering his thoughts. "He was a good man."

He unfolded a sheet of paper.

"I will read the rest of the names. Ruth Sheehan, suicide. She and her fiancé were traveling back to Sol to get married. He had to stay back at Homeport and would catch up with her in a few days. She died the first week we were here. Timothy Carlson, suicide..."

\* \* \*

*"Sgt. Layne?"*

"Sgt. Layne here, go ahead."

*"How far are you from kim-two 2626?"*

"We are still looking for survivors here at Hotel Lima. Should we go?"

*"One second... Negative, that kim-two is almost opposite your position. Search and standby."*

"Copy that. Someone found what?"

*"A cemetery. Brandon Porter kept a room there at Hotel Lima. They say that there is a book there. We need to find that and send back information on the pages."*

"Sir."

\* \* \*

It did not take long. The green ledger had seen many years. Settled in Brandon's room, it lay untouched for an untold time. The fastened door kept out the dust and other foreign particles, mostly. Although sealed in an air-tight crypt, it could not stop the passage of time and its effects.

Layne opened it and began to slowly go through the pages. Though frail and brittle, they held up.

On the first page was a series of small squares within a larger square. Most of the smaller squares had numbers next to them.

*"Pause, okay turn, pause, okay turn."*

"It looks as though he wrote a few notes, just a little, about each person."

*"Sgt. Layne? We received word from Director Porter that he does not wish us to release information in this ledger to the public."*

He paused, fingers ready to gently turn the page over. "Should I stop looking through?"

*"No, you may continue. I have paused your video. He feels that, as a leader of the people, his son may have written information in the ledger*

*that is not for the eyes of others. The messages home are one thing. This may hold thoughts that are only privy to those higher up. He will review these pages and release them afterward. Proceed when you're ready."*

And he did so. The whole book took him over a half hour. He could not fully take in everything they had written.

When he finished, when he got the okay from admin, he gingerly placed the book back down exactly where he found it.

XD05, Year 1 - "Take one down, pass it around…"

While he was not working in the fields, Jaughn would wander. The others could have the Twilight Wall. He liked the solitude of the lake and the Morning Wall 120 km away. Even though 300 people lived in this place meant to hold many thousands, the place seemed crowded sometimes. Not that he was a loner or an isolationist, but he needed his space.

Besides the lake, the Morning Wall had a thin band of buildings around its space and up the side. These are the ones that Jaughn was interested in. He peered into one massive building that held shuttles. He looked around briefly but saw nothing that would help him as almost everything here was shuttle fleet maintenance. Back in the day, he worked on the water flow systems, not the shuttles.

He would take one day a week and search a kim-two completely. Not alone in his efforts, others would come out and look around on their own. They would talk for a while, compare findings, but just mostly let him be.

He stumbled upon about fifteen to twenty Albert Tubes in a warehouse. Taller than he, they had girth, so much so he could not put his arms all the way around them. Light enough, he could pick one up easily by himself if he desperately wanted to. The caps at both ends were removable. Once sealed, they became watertight and airtight. If taken to a Hub, sealed in a vacuum, and brought back down, the weight of the atmosphere would still not crush them. They engineered plasti-lite to be thick and durable, and Albert Tubes became a multipurpose container. It was just too bulky for what he needed right now.

He was looking through a shed that someone had rummaged through before. The gardening supplies were a little disheveled along the wall. Probably a maintenance shed for when they built the '05. Under a shelf, he found several boxes that remained sealed. He pulled these out, and lifting the lid off, he smiled.

He had found it.

Therein were six three-liter glass bottles with lids. Five boxes all the same.

He looked upward and gave a silent prayer.

"Thank you, Lord, thank you, Lord Jesus," he whispered. He could carry one box at a time and set them outside the mag-ele entrance. When he finished, he took off his red ball cap and wiped his brow with his forearm.

"I can make this work," he muttered to himself. Copper tubing would be a treasure beyond comparison.

Once they were all there, he carried the bottles inside the mag-ele and selected a destination for the residential areas up on the wall.

The elevator took him to a place that was much cooler because of the elevation. This would be perfect for his wines. They fermented slowly over time. In the short version, if you wanted to make hard cider, you must grind your own grapples, seal it in a jug, and place it in the basement out of the light for about a year. Occasionally, you get one bad jug that didn't take properly, and that one gets tossed. The rest, though, are excellent. Here he had more than grapples. His experiments ranged over many fruits. Grapples with a hint of oranges, or some carrots, or bana-berries. Figuava juice had something to it that soured the mixture pleasantly.

As he carried the jugs to a vacant home, his mind came up with all different possibilities. He made a mental note of the house number and location. Stowing away a small bushel of fruits every so often, no one would notice.

Two of the jugs became a constant home for yeast. Grown and cultured from ground sorghum seeds, he slowly amassed all he needed. As long as he grew the yeast, he was in business.

* * *

By the end of the week, he had everything he needed. He spent his two days off creating mixtures that would eventually become wine.

With everything locked up, he would come back and check his stash every other week. They were all sealed properly for now, and he was happy.

After some further exploration, he found a whole pallet of glass jugs down in a storage warehouse well past the lake. He brought these back on a shuttle five at a time. Unlike musclebound Sebastian, he knew his limitations and made several trips to lighten the load. By the time he finished, he had almost one thousand liters of different ciders and sangria's going.

This made him happy.

XD05, Year 2


One kilometer in from the Twilight Wall, they built a second wall. Here '05 became strictly farmland with deep, rich soil. To make all things equal, and so that there was no squabbling, they divided the surface area up into lots one square kilometer in size. Fences on the bottom sat in the shadows of the mag-ele supports. The carbon-nano ribbon stretched taut between supports gave travelers a smooth ride wherever they went. Stashed in the corners of these kim-two were small homes and utility sheds for the farmers who would work the land. Designed, so the farmers had eight neighbors with which they could trade produce if they desired.

Every three kim-two away from the homes of the farmers, the engineers created a series of beehives. Ideally, a queen bee would find the empty hive desirable, and a new colony would arise. Now, the second year since the Event, most of them remained empty as there were not a lot of plants covering the inner kilometer kim-two. We spotted plants growing about twenty kim-two in. Time, things always took time.

Jxan would suit up every morning and make his rounds, which was ironic as his rounds were the circumference of the ship. Originally, two others had shown interest, but they have since opted to work elsewhere and left the collection of honey solely up to him.

There were over sixty-two stops per kilometer of circumference, which kept him busy. Some hives were more productive than others. The ship never had a shortage of honey. Used as a sweetener by itself or to enhance the flavor of other foods, it was a natural food they loved. Jaughn confiscated liters of it and took the containers to his place weekly with which he had made honey mead. The mead itself took time to ferment. Jaughn, through trial and error, had just started the process of fermentation.

The designers of the system introduced ants and worms into the soil. The birds kept everything under control. Were it not for them, the insect population would grow considerably, eventually tipping the balance and causing a catastrophic failure to the whole ecosystem. Checks and balances were needed to keep the system stable, and these other forms of life were needed to break down the matter and help enrich the soil further.

So, here he was, day after day, bringing back the golden nectar. As the mag-ele came to a stop, Jxan placed the helmet on his head, sighed, and grabbed an empty container. It beat working the fields any day.

Homeport, Day 3

Helmet lamps on, they searched each room, yet it was all the same. Bodies made twelve rooms crypts. Someone had lain most of them out with articles of clothing, flowers, and other offerings. With some, the bodies lay in different positions as if no one bothered to disturb them after death.

It took over two hours, and when Layne and Dobbins finished, they went back down to the foyer.

"Sir," Layne keyed his mic.

*"Go ahead."*

"There is no one down here at the hotel alive. All rooms checked, twelve deceased, no signs of struggle or foul play."

*"At the present time, we have no further locations for you to investigate. Not going to have you go clear to kim-two 2626. We are sending several other teams over. Our priority now is to get at least one of the mag-ele's on both ends working. Be advised we have sent the vacuums in. It will get real dusty quickly. Retrace your steps away from the hotel and if the elevators are working, bring one back up. Return to the Twilight Wall."*

"Dobbins," he tapped him on the shoulder. "Find Schmidt and Harris. We gotta get back out. Sir, rounding up my team; will be there as soon as possible."

* * *

Schmidt brushed off a control panel. Back in, under the wall, the elevator stayed sheltered from the outside world by several doors, and yet dust still had found its way in.

"It's dead. There's been no juice in here for some time."

"Maj. Ronca, this is Sgt. Layne. We are at the bottom of the gravity well. All systems here are nonfunctional. Suits are checking in at 85%. What do you advise?"

There was a delay of several moments. *"Sgt. Layne, I have taken you off live cam. With the VCV's removing the dust. We have nothing else for you until they are cleared. There is a team up at the Hub working on getting you up. It may be a whole day before we can get you out. Would there be a problem with you staying at your location?"*

Layne looked over the confines of the elevator booth. "Sir, we have rations enough to stay here." Harris rolled his eyes and shook his head. "The atmosphere is dry but breathable. We will need to remove the suits to use the head. We will recon our current location and report back if we find anything significant."

*"Copy, Sgt. Layne."*

\* \* \*

They shrugged the suits off, letting them hit the floor in a heap. Doing so, they powered down automatically. Layne unclipped the communicator and stowed it away in his pocket. It would not be wise to be away from communication with Maj. Ronca or Capt. Klasnick, although they were probably very busy now. They would not have any need of him for a while.

"Okay, listen up. They have told us to stay here. By that, I am under the understanding we should not venture out into the main space of the ship. The cleanup crew is coming through. You can roam here, no roughhousing or damaging anything. Believe me when I say we are just an exploratory team. They will come down shortly with a fine-tooth comb and look over everything here. Stray, but do not stray far."

"Why are you looking at me?" Dobbins was rubbing his hair. Being in the suit for so long, it had become flat, and his scalp itched.

"Dobbins, come on, we all remember," Layne looked at Dobbins and raised his eyebrows. That's all he needed.

"Hey, they told me to wait for the last vehicle. I didn't know the last vehicle to leave was the last vehicle. They never told them to stop and pick me up. You think walking twenty clicks back into base was exciting?"

Layne shrugged his shoulders, and Harris hit him on the bicep.

"Two groups of two. Just remember that we are still soldiers. Recon, if you wish. If you find anything, report back; do not get into any trouble."

\* \* \*

They terraced the buildings here, one above the other. There was evidence of extensive water damage at one location. The erosion was catastrophic. At one time, a massive amount of water had once flowed freely through the hallways. It eventually found weak spots, wore out holes in the floor cascading, over time, from one floor to the next. It took its toll and destroyed many buildings.

Layne retraced the damage and came across a burst pipe more than a kilometer above the surface.

The structures he went through showed no signs of occupancy. In one building, there was significant evidence that birds had nested there. Mummified remains, feathers, nesting material, and even eggshells littered the place. A broken window, common now, may have been how they got in. As he was about to leave, his foot kicked an irregularity in the floor. It slid from its resting place. Picking it up, he found that it was part of something else. After he took several photos, the classification came back. It was part of a shuttle. Namely, a piece of the harness that kept it on the ribbon.

Testing the floor, he shuffled carefully to the empty window. This building sat almost in the shadow of the indigo road the shuttle's traveled on. There must've been some catastrophic accident that caused it to throw pieces of the vehicle here.

"What the hell were these people doing?" he whispered, and not for the first time.

Homeport, Day 4

Space rippled.

From literally out of nowhere, a ship appeared. Small, compact, they used it for the transport of soldiers and their supplies.

"*Homeport, this is TTS Marsic. How do you copy?*"

"Communication Center here at Homeport, TTS Marsic, we read you loud and clear."

"*Could you notify Director Porter and Major Ronca that Gen. Bidwell and Director Reed are en route?*"

"Shall do. Is there any other information I can pass on?"

"*At this time, no.*"

* * *

Director Porter, Mabel, Maj. Ronca, Capt. Klasnick and several others waited just inside the airlock. Mabel fidgeted a little.

When the doors opened, no one moved.

Director Reed was the first one to speak. "Richard, why am I here?"

"We have had trouble, Sir, to say the least. '05 has returned unexpectedly. They have lost all hands. There were no survivors."

"Wait," General Bidwell held up a finger. "Are you saying they have lost all?"

"Yes, sir."

"We have families on the other side who are waiting. My God, three hundred people, just like that?" He snapped his fingers. "What happened? Was it catastrophic failure? We saw the ship as we came in. It looked fine."

"Should we review in the airlock, or do you want to go to the conference room? Sorry again for my bluntness," he nodded to both. "It's been a very hectic three days."

"Give me what you have along the way." Director Reed grabbed a tether and pulled himself forward. Richard and the others followed.

"XD05 departed three days ago with three hundred pax, ten hours later it returned in system. We sent soldiers out to shuttle the passengers back here while we found out what went wrong with navigation. Upon opening the airlock, they found bodies."

"Were the people trying to leave?"

"No. From what we can gather now, that someone placed them in the airlock after death. The bodies were of elderly people. Upon further research, an undetermined amount of time had passed on board the ship. We are getting into the workings of it now, still not sure how it happened.

The best guess, at present, is from the Burner of all things. Based upon the half-life of the materials used, we have determined that anywhere from a thousand to five thousand years have passed."

Director Reed looked at him.

"How could this have happened? A ship just does not leave for ten hours our time and come back five thousand hours ship time."

"I do not understand the data, sir." Richard grabbed another tether and pulled himself. "I can only interpret what they give me."

"Is it just the Burner in question?" asked Gen. Bidwell.

"There are many other signs. Something has consumed the water on the ship. Atmo is down to 0% humidity. The rivers, the lakes, there is absolutely no water left. There is a significant biomass that has covered every square centimeter of surface area. Some type of vine had grown rampant and died out when it devoured all the water. We have mapped the surface with drones and are now proceeding to vacuum the biomass from the surface."

"You can just suck up all that biomass?"

"With the atmosphere down to 0% humidity, everything has dried out like old parchment. The plants, although dead, still hold their original form. There is no wind movement. It is all dust. Rigid and holding its shape, it's still just dust. Bringing up this biomass, we can see what lies beneath."

It was quiet for a while.

"We've made startling discoveries. The three hundred pax lived for some time after the departure. Most lived until their elder years. The ship did what we designed it to do. Although not at the right location."

They were leaving the Hub of Homeport. Arrows along the wall showed them which way was down. The tethers gave way to rungs, and eventually stairs. Within a few moments, they were all walking downward to the outer shell.

"I must ask Director Reed, Gen. Bidwell, and pardon me for my frankness. Again, I have had little sleep in these last few days. Are you here to assume duties of Homeport?"

"No, we are here to assess what is wrong and report back. If what you say is true, I see there is no wrongdoing on your part. I'd like to see the raw data, though."

"I lost my son. He was a passenger returning to Sol."

"I'm sorry for your loss. Were you close?"

"We were. He was going back to attend the University and to take classes. I had hoped that he would have made his own way in the universe. I did not want my influence on others to help him. I was very proud of him."

* * *

"What is everybody thinking on the other side?" Richard asked, taking a seat.

"We did not understand what happened," General Bidwell said. "We know it's been three days since we received a communication from here. The ship did not arrive, and with everything dark, we came to imagine the worst."

Elbows on his knees, Richard rubbed his temples slowly.

"Mabel?" He said a little too loudly. "Mabel, alert communication. We must send back a message globe. That another ship has come through unscathed is good news. We will send back the probe. We must see if it makes it through or not."

She nodded. "I will have them prepare a message. Not to undermine you, gentlemen, it will let everyone else know exactly what happened."

"Is that wise?" asked the general.

"It will let everyone else know something went wrong. It will let family members know they can stop waiting and that people need to be cautious about traveling. I do not know, nor can I tell you right now, that the computer may have caused this, or it may be something external. If it is just something wrong with the computer, then hopefully, it's isolated to just '05. If it is something that is external, then perhaps the whole staircase may be in jeopardy."

"It is doubtful that the staircase is in jeopardy. We have been using this system for many years."

"I understand this. A week ago, I thought our system was infallible, and yet here we are. They have sent a team over to see if the computer system still works. All other non-essential personnel are being sent over to look for clues. For the first time, they have vacated the other ships. We need to find out what has happened."

"Who is this on your video?" Director Reed nodded toward the video playing on the screen.

Richard looked up. "In one of the suits, we found a diamond etched recording of letters home. The people found the recorder and sat down to send messages back. They did not know we would find it. All they were doing was saying goodbye."

There was a woman there. Mabel turned up the volume.

"… sick and tired of vegetables. An apple a day keeps the doctor away. I've had so freaking many that he'll never come to visit. There are only so many ways you can prepare one thing before you become redundant. I think Doc has almost given up on fixing everybody's food.

"Anyway, I'm Joan Abigail. I miss you, Tom and Amanda. Be good in school; try to have a good life. You are all adults now, and I hope you find your own paths. Stay out of trouble. I pray for you every day. Love you," she blew a kiss to the camera.

Richard nodded to Mabel, and she muted it again.

"I have been letting it run nonstop since we found it. Most everyone there had a family or a significant other here. Mabel, we should copy this and send this with a message globe."

She nodded. "General, Director, is there anything you wish to add to the formal statement?"

"Let's send one back to notify everyone what happened before we send the letters home."

"True, we must make sure that the probe returns and that everything is safe."

\* \* \*

They sent the globe. On a hard burn away from Homeport, it engaged the Samuel Drives as soon as it left. Sixty kilometers was the average distance before it winked out. Just a computer guidance system with broadcasting equipment strapped on a Samuel Drive. They programmed it to quickly climb the stairway, and when it arrived in Sol, it would transmit its data to the appropriate channels.

They talked for about an hour before someone in the communication room contacted them.

*"Director Porter, sorry to bother you. We have another ship just arriving in the system."*

"Well, at least we know that everything in-coming is getting through properly."

"Is it a supply ship?"

*"Sir, no, sir. Ada Iadanza is requesting a meeting. She says she has come here looking for her nephew."*

"Who is this?" Richard asked. He appeared genuinely confused.

"She is prominent in the Iadanza family," Mabel said, shaking her head. "On the ship '05, they had a significant presence. Although '05 was a farming community, they held a good bit of real estate on-board. There was a rumor that this is where they would move the family business."

"So much for a quiet neighborhood," he whispered quietly. "Gentlemen, do you wish to sit in?"

"Ada knows me from a long way back," said Director Reed with a grin on his face. "I do not wish to see her again. My advice is to not sugarcoat it and let her know everything you know about '05. If she's here ten minutes, it's ten minutes too long."

"We will not keep you," General Bidwell stood. "If this globe returns successfully, then we will leave. We will send over men and supplies as needed."

"Thank you, gentlemen. I have no secrets, nothing to hide. I wish to see this through to the end."

They shook hands and left.

* * *

At a young age, Ada learned that feelings often left you hurt. She suppressed hers as far down as she could. The middle-aged woman who walked into Director Porter's office had an air about her that seemed very cold and uncaring.

"The Iadanza family has considerable assets on '05." She said without preamble. "Not only the real estate involved. We had placed a lot of what we own there, thinking it to be a haven. A sure bet. And now we hear from your communication center that something may have gone wrong on the ship."

"Something went wrong, and we are working on cleaning it up."

"I'd like to send one of my boys down and see. You know, make sure everything is where it should be."

"I am sorry. That will not be possible." By the look on her face, she had a difficult time when someone told her 'no.'

"Director Porter, you don't seem to grasp the severity of the situation. I can make it very profitable or very difficult for you." She leaned toward his desk, her voice above a whisper. She nodded to Mabel as well, including her into the deal. "Not just now, but over the long haul. You can leave this backwater area and live the high life once."

"Point of fact," Richard was undaunted. "I know how severe this is. There has been a loss of life, and I cannot and will not let anybody on board that ship who is not furthering the investigation. There is nothing here that you can do now. You can go back to your ship and wait there, or you can go back to Sol. Either way, you, or your people, will not have access to that ship until I deem it appropriate."

"Loss of life?" she leaned back and folded her arms across her chest. A hint of a smile came across her lips.

"Yes. Sadly, we have found that there have been no survivors. Friends, family, co-workers who we knew just a week ago have all perished. If you would please respect us now and give us our solitude and the chance to figure this out."

"Everyone... died?" The smile she gave was as cold as the vacuum outside.

"Yes," he said again. "I have not hidden the fact that we lost everybody."

Her strong façade broke then. The tough girl attitude slipped away, and her smile deepened.

"Well," her mood lightened. "Looks like there is a silver lining to every cloud. Director Porter, I will trouble you no more."

With no further words spoken, she left the room like a whirlwind.

Mabel sat back in her chair, attempting to suppress a chuckle. "That is an odd group of people."

"They definitely run in different circles than the rest of us. Who on board would she know? I mean, personally?"

"There are a few names that come to mind."

XD05, Year 2, Day 210

The grapples ripened nicely and lay heavy on the trees with such an abundance this year. They asked for my help in the harvesting. I found two wagons and rotated them one at a time, laden with grapples, to the shuttle. The grapples would tumble into another basket, and I returned with an empty wagon. Often, I waited a few moments for the other one to fill. The process started all over again.

Working the body worked the soul, as Tang often said. It was good work. I was hot and sweaty, but it felt good working the muscles. By noon, when the sun globe was directly overhead, we broke for lunch.

I continued after they ate and did not spend much longer in the orchards, as the harvest was nearly done.

It tired my hands and legs. I knew after a nice meal and a hot shower, I would sleep well tonight.

With my legs curled beneath me on the seat, I leaned out an open window daydreaming, as the shuttle pulled along quietly on the indigo magnetic tracks. The other adults sat back and chatted amongst themselves. I was so glad to help them. It helped with the day-to-day boredom. They never gave me too much work to do. They were proud people.

The shuttle settled down in front of Hotel Lima. I waved to Jeff and Renn, who were sitting on the benches near the back entrance. And, once again, I helped bring the grapples into the kitchens. I only made one trip, as there were many there to help.

I washed my hands with the others and giggled as everyone tried to grab the slippery bar soap at the same time. Instead of drying my hands on the towel, I flicked my wet fingers at Joan, and Joan flicked hers back. Everyone had joined in, and it was a happy time.

* * *

It was quiet in the hall that night. The others did not share my light mood. Everyone seemed quiet and subdued as if something really terrible had happened.

A man, I did not know his name, approached the table where Everett and Brandon sat.

"Everyone is here. We can ask her now?"

"Troy, please. This is neither the time nor the place."

"Oh, I'm sorry. I believe this is the perfect time and place. I think we should ask her now instead of dragging it out further."

Tom spoke up. "Troy, we will handle it differently. We will approach her, just not today. I know it upsets you, but it's how it is."

"Another day goes by? We are getting older, Brandon. We must settle this once and for all. Wouldn't you agree, everyone?" his voice carried over the dining hall. There were a few people muttering words of encouragement, but no one stood with him.

To my surprise, he motioned in my general direction, and I could have sworn that he looked right at me.

"People, we need to stop avoiding this issue," his voice was louder and unwavering. Arms up, palms outward, he spun in a slow circle, making sure everyone heard him. "I say now, right now, tonight, is the right time to speak up. If another day goes by, then that is a day we are all closer to dying."

"You are out of line." Everett stood, and he and Troy were just a hand's breadth apart. I thought they were gonna fight. "We will talk to her. We know the time is near, and we should do it, but this is not the way."

Lena wiped her hands on her napkin and stood. She came to my seat and knelt.

"Sally, we should go," she whispered in my ear.

"I'm, I'm not done yet." I looked over my plate of food, at Lena, and then back to Troy and Everett.

"Why are we waiting?" Troy asked loudly.

Lena grabbed me by the shoulder and turned me. "Sally," her voice is very forceful. "This is something I do not want you to hear right now. These people here will have no qualms if I pick you up and carry over my shoulder to get you out here. We can do that, or you can walk."

I had never heard Lena so intense. I hesitated just a heartbeat longer and felt Lena's hands on my shoulders. She wasn't picking me up; she was just turning me around. I tossed my fork on my tray and stood. The two of us walked out together.

"Oh great, wonderful," Troy's voice trailed out loudly after us. "Another fine missed opportunity. People, we must seriously decide this amongst ourselves then. With her gone, I demand an open forum on this. We must ask…"

And the doors to the dining hall closed. I could no longer hear his rant.

We passed the grassy octagon and crossed beneath the first tram-way and continued. Time passed, and we still did not stop or slow down. At first, I thought Lena was taking me somewhere when I realized that she was just walking to get away from the hotel. I looked over at my friend several times, and her face was stoic.

"They have no right," Lena whispered, finally breaking the silence.

"It's me they're talking about?"

Lena nodded. Looking at me, she did not stop walking.

"What do they want to ask me?"

"It is a simple question, but it has huge ramifications. Well, beyond a simple yes or no."

In the silence that followed, my mind reeled. Searching for everything I knew, I could not fathom a question so important that the whole town would want to ask me. By the look on Lena's face, I knew Lena would not give up information.

Lena stopped abruptly and turned to me. "I will not ask you the question. I cannot even hint at what the question pertains to. It is not my place, nor is it my right. They will ask you in due time, and all I have to say is that you must be true to yourself and no other. Okay? Can you promise me that?"

"I…"

There was a tear in the corner of Lena's eye. "Listen, Sally. This isn't like Earth, all right?" her voice was loud and echoed back to us from the buildings' walls. And she cried. When she spoke again, her voice was much quieter. "We don't have people we can go to for help. We are all we have. They will ask you a question, and either way, it will change the life here on the ship." She sniffed a little and wiped away a tear. "Someone has put an idea in their head, and there are some that believe quite strongly on both sides. They may harass you, but you do not let them. You remain true to yourself. Promise me that."

"I do. I will remain true to myself, but what does it have to do with? What could be so important…"

Lena shook her head and walked again. I was quick to follow.

\* \* \*

That night, we stayed away. It was my first time sleeping away from Hotel Lima.

Lena took me to a house that clung to the side of the Twilight Wall. We had taken the mag-ele so far up that there was a chill in the air. We walked two blocks behind a decorative fence they meshed into the stonework. Accent lighting lit our way as we walked.

She stopped in front of a house, and when she placed her hand on the lock pad, it scanned her fingerprints. "Lena Daniels," she said, and the door locks cycled through.

"Sally, place your palm on the screen."

I did so, and it scanned my hand.

"Authorize Sally Weiss," Lena said.

"Hello Sally, please state your name for voiceprint identification."

"I, um, I am Sally Weiss."

"Very nice to meet you, Sally. Will Sally always be welcome here?"

"Yes, she will."

I smiled at Lena. Here, she found a house where we could sleep. The house had several rooms that were empty. Only the master bedroom had a bed and other furnishings.

The view was incredible. I'm not sure how far we traveled, but I could not see Hotel Lima. I thought it would distinctively stand out. Standing at the window, I searched for some time. With my finger on the window, I traced the track for the shuttles. But I still could not find the hotel. The streetlights below were coming on like clockwork as the sun traveled down the tube. The house was so close to the wall we were now in shadow. The sun would go through its own transition, and the moon, the sun at one-quarter brightness, would start its journey back to Morning Wall.

"You stayed here before?" I asked, noting that the house had a 'used' look to it.

"I have," she said from the bathroom. "Sometimes it gets too loud at Hotel Lima. Some guys get obnoxious, even my old comrades, and there is plenty enough room to go around on the ship. I've picked this place as my own. Many people have done it. It gives them a sense of being settled in. The hotel is a place of transition. A home is a place of your own."

"Oh, I see," I said, looking around at some stuff she had collected. "Have you ever brought any guys here?" I could not contain the smile on my face. I was trying to lighten the mood from earlier.

She peeked around a corner. "No, silly Sally, you are the first person I have ever brought here. It is a place that only you and I know of." Even though I was much taller than when we had first met, she tussled my hair like she had years before.

"I will change into something more comfortable. We can talk," she said, going into the laundry room. "Nothing too serious, and we must not, under any circumstances, talk about the question Troy was talking about." It was a warning to me.

"Gotcha." I meandered into the kitchen and found some fruit and nuts in a bowl.

They had cut my supper short, so I grabbed some grapples and an orange. I left the only chair in the living room to her and sat on the windowsill, and ate.

\* \* \*

When we returned to Hotel Lima four days later, something had changed. I could not quite place it until the evening meal. Looking around, I noted that there were a lot fewer people present.

"Where is everybody?" I asked in general.

Tang was sitting near, and he looked at Lena before he spoke. "Some people have decided that it is better if they don't stay here at the hotel with us anymore. They have their own group and live North of us." When he said 'North,' I knew they live directly above us on the ship. If I had a telescope, I could look upward across the kilometers and see them living their life upside down from us.

"Why did they go?"

"There has been a disagreement of sorts. These people feel strongly about something, and if they were here, it would be very uncomfortable for both sides, so they choose not to be here."

"Does it involve me?" I ask, still curious what the argument was about.

"It involves everybody, Wee One," said Lena, leaning in.

Tang licked his fingers free of bana-cado. "We are all family here."

XD05, Year 4

I was about to get on the shuttle with others and head to the fields when Lena came up.

"We have something different in mind for you today."

I motioned toward the shuttle and the other people waiting. "We are going to go to the orchards. Doc says we need more grapples, and a few bushels of plums would be nice."

"Not today. Sorry people," she waved to everybody already seated in the vehicle. "We have other plans for your little Sherpa."

"I'm not little. I'm 14," I said under my breath. I felt Lena squeeze my shoulder.

With only a little sadness, I watched the shuttle head down the ribbon.

Lena did not move, and within a few moments, a second shuttle arrived.

"Should I buckle in?" I asked, taking a seat.

"No, we're not going up the wall. We will meet someone today. She worked with plants back at Homeport, and you would do well to listen. It is my job to watch over you. It is your job to shadow Stacy for a few days. She will teach you."

"Like school?" I could not hide the disappointment.

"That's exactly what it is. Do not be sour or upset; I'll make you do push-ups. Your elders have a lot of wisdom you need to learn."

It was a short five-minute ride that took us out to a kim-two just beyond the city line.

* * *

I do not remember Stacy at all. The whole time I had been here, she must've kept to herself. She met us on the platform as we got off the shuttle. Seeing her, I know that I would never forget her. Tall with straight, graying hair pulled back in a very loose knot, she had a very soft smile. Her whole demeanor was calm.

Listening to Lena and I talk, she guided us to one building in her kim-two. She had a large room with a variety of plants and seeds laying out on tables. She handed me a notebook and a pencil. With no further instruction, she spoke. She went on about how to extract and germinate the different varieties of seeds. Grapples being the most abundant, then common apples, oranges, pears, and plums.

Back in civilization, the fruits we bought at the store were all sterile. You could still grow trees from them; however, they would never produce fruit. All the plants here on the ship were viable. The plants and trees grown from them would produce a crop naturally.

She had been talking for almost an hour as we wandered around her place. I still carried a pen and tablet in my hand at my side. She stopped for a moment and asked me if I had questions.

"Why do I have to learn this?" I asked.

"Because," she said simply.

This answer did not satisfy me, and I pressed her further.

"Because, why?"

She stepped forward and placed both hands on my shoulders before she spoke. "Because, child, in time, this world will be silent except for one soul. You will be the unfortunate one to bury us all," she said this so calmly, so matter-of-factly, that it took a few moments for the extent of what she was saying to sink in.

"Now, avocados," she went on as if the weight of the world was no longer on my shoulders. "There are several ways to plant this tree. I will show you my favorite. They bear fruit at about 3 to 4 years, so you'll want to keep an eye on that."

* * *

I found it hard to believe she had so much common knowledge about every type of food we had on the ship. The first day was just an overview. When Lena and I arrived the second day, she replaced the fruits from the day before with vegetables.

I brought a high stool over in front of the first table. Climbing up, I laid the notebook on my lap open to the first page. I sat ready with my pencil.

"You don't want to zip through this like we did yesterday?" Her eyebrows raised, she looked genuinely concerned.

"As you have said, I need this and," glancing at Lena, "my survival will depend on what you teach me."

She looked at Lena, and with a slight smile, nodded.

"Not just your survival. We help others with what we do. When they planted food here, while we were back at Homeport, they did not concern themselves with diversity. They wanted large plots of crops that would soon ripen for harvest. I wish they would've thought of more variety. To sustain us, we have ample amounts; it's the different tastes on the palate that bring a richness to all that is bland.

"Let us start off with one that is a diverse staple. Cabbage"

Slowly and methodically, she went over every vegetable we had. By the time lunchtime came around, my hand had started to hurt from all the writing.

She made a meal of boiled pork knuckles and cabbage. We three sat outside under a shade tree and ate.

The rest of the day we spent outside, and I helped her plant onions and garlic. She had several rows of rhubarb and celery.

"You see, Sally, it's not all about the harvest. We must make sure we sow the seeds for next time. I take these potent vegetables into Doc every so often to help vary the meal. Each plant offers its own unique flavor. Some are compatible, and some combinations are to be avoided."

* * *

I was looking over my notes again later that evening when I noticed on the first page Lena had written a message to me. One phrase that simply said, "Always the student."

I smiled at this. It reminded me a lot of when I was in school, back when we were amongst civilization.

Sometimes I missed my family dearly. Mom and dad were forever in my thoughts. I wondered how they would see me if they could see me now. It has been over four years since we've come aboard the ship. I try not to be slack. Daily I worked in the fields and rested only when it was my time. I'm sure that my parents would look at me with a sense of pride. It is possible that Aunt Wendy and Uncle Robert felt they were to blame for me being on the '05 at that fateful time. I wish there was a way I could tell them I still love them, and I hold no remorse or no regrets for what has happened.

My hand ached from writing. Placing everything down, I held my hands before me and looked at them. So much would come from these fingertips. I flexed my fingers a few times and then made a fist.

I told myself from time to time, 'Oh, what I would give to see into the future.' To see what I would create. Would I be proud of myself if I could go to then and there and see what I did in the here and now?

* * *

I had never before been told about the wondrous plant called sorghum. When I harvested it in the fields, I did not understand what it was. It gave a pleasant odor, and for some reason, part of me at the time thought it was for making candles or something. Of all the plants she spoke about, she highly praised this one. They grow it in four neighboring kim-twos where she meticulously tended to it.

With the seeds from the plant, you could grind them up and make flour. It's what Doc uses to make our bread, muffins, and tortillas now, as there is no wheat on board the ship. If they press the seeds, they release oil that you could use in cooking, which is better for us than the pork fat that Doc has used. If you heat the seeds in the oil, they will pop like popcorn. I have had these frequently and did not know what they were. They were tasty.

Word in the rumor mill said this was Uncle Butch's secret to keeping his hair slick.

She mentioned that this is where Jaughn got all his yeast for fermenting his alcohol. Some of his brews were created from what yeast was on board the ship, but most of that was used by the time he had his equipment ready. He cultivated a bunch of it and has kept a continual supply on hand.

Corn has many uses as well. They modified the sorghum, and it grows quickly, in about half the time it takes corn to produce. The yield is much heavier and feeds more people.

Stacy says even with all the land we have, it takes a little finesse to feed the people that are here. Diets should not be bland. She has done a lot to spice things up just a little.

If the ship had gone back like it was supposed to, then this whole land would now be occupied by dedicated farmers. The land would be green with crops or blooming with bright flowers for the bees to germinate.

For us here on the ship, sorghum has been a lifesaver.

\* \* \*

By the time she finished teaching me, three weeks had passed. I had used two pencils and completely filled the notebook from cover to cover.

I asked her why I had to use a pencil and paper when there were other forms of storing information. She told me that what the hand creates; the mind learns. I found that very profound. Also, and this kind of burst my metaphorical bubble, she said everything we used relied on electricity. If, in years to come, things begin to fail, I would still have the notebook. Writing it out longhand would help me remember better.

Looking at her place, I realized that she was not big on using electricity. Wind chimes brought music. Mirrors, small and large, reflected sunlight. Her home was unique.

When I finished with the notebook, I tucked it away in my room at the hotel. Kept there safe. I would hold on to it until I needed it again.

\* \* \*

Stacy was not one of the people who were heading back to earth and going elsewhere. They had commissioned her specifically to stay on '05 for several years. When the new farmers arrived, she would instruct them on what to grow and where to grow it. Some fruits and vegetables complemented each other; some did not. The ship would have to be set up in a certain order and not just have crops grow 'willy-nilly' as she put it. In the time since we were first stranded, she worked in the fields religiously. Our meals in the evening were because of her.

\* \* \*

One day, Stacy motioned me to come with her on a walk around her kim-two. There were many diverse plants.

There was a row of red, heart-shaped berries amongst green leaves.

"What are these?" I asked.

"These are original strawberries."

"Straw-berries?"

"Yes, they are a distant cousin of bana-berries. Many years ago, to save the bananas from fungal infection, engineers came up with a way to incorporate the banana and the strawberry. They made a hybrid that was highly successful, and it is what we have today."

"They are so red." I peeked in through the leaves and did not touch them. Usually, in nature, red means bad, and I was hesitant to do anything else.

"They are. Lena, come, you may try one too."

Lena had a look of pure delight on her face. "I have not had one of these since I was a child. Sally, you're in for a real treat."

"Pick one, go ahead."

I reached in and tugged it gently with my fingertips. It fell from the stem easy enough. "These are... seeds?"

"Yes, the seeds are on the outside."

"Should we save them? Do we take them off?" I looked at all the seeds that covered the fruit.

"Just eat." She tapped my elbow with her hand.

I took a small nibble at first. The fruit was small enough I could've set the whole fruit in my mouth; however, I wanted to savor this as much as possible. It had a burst of flavor. It took me aback. Tart and sweet at the same moment, it was a wondrous thing. For me, it was so pure, so natural. I had bananas before, and I had eaten bana-berries since before I walked. This flavor I tasted was so much more than either.

"That, my dear, is a strawberry."

Three bites, each one larger than the last, and it was gone. I shook my head in wonderment. Lena was looking at me in the most peculiar way, with a smile on her face. She was still holding hers by the green stem. When she ate hers, she ate it too fast. I watched her eyes close, and she had the most wicked smile. When she finished, she looked at me and shivered.

"They are that good," she said, wiping her mouth with the back of her hand.

"These are special treats that are very rare here. Those that I have, I started from just a few, and it's taken a little finesse to get these."

"Why haven't you planted a plot out on the ship?" I said, motioning with my hand.

"They take a lot of work, and the bana-berries are easy to grow and harvest. The bana-berries grow in clusters like grapples, only smaller. If you want, I can give you one more, and we can pick a kim-two to plant these specifically."

"Really?"

"Yeah, with everything else I'm involved with, I have little time to do it. It would be something you would have to take care of all on your own if you are up to it."

Lena chimed in. "I'd help her too," her eyes were wide. "It's been a very long time since I've had a strawberry, and I think we can do it."

Stacy smiled as she rummaged through a cabinet for a container. Lena, with a broad smile, nudged me on the arm.

XD05, Year 4

What spoiled us was the sheer size of the land we had access to. We would have a whole kim-two of just one type of vegetable. Tomatoes were not only a staple for us, but for the pigs that we kept in captivity. With the corn, they ate the stalks and everything. In the early years, they erected trellises, and we could just walk between them or underneath them, collecting the tomatoes we needed. Same with peppers, cucumbers, squash, an amazing variety of berries. They had set the whole ship up as one huge farming community. With everything in place, up and running, we didn't have to dig for irrigation or run pipes. It was all there for us.

Sometimes we had a break between the cycle of crops and had no other chores. It was not all hunting and gathering. Lena would accompany me when I explored buildings more often than not.

Today she grabbed a few towels from the hotel laundry and threw them in a pack.

She slapped me on the shoulder.

"Come on, kid," was all she said as she tossed me my shoes.

She keyed for a shuttle before we left the hotel lobby.

"Where are we going today?" I was unable to read the look on her face.

"Learned of a very cool hot spot. You'll see."

"How far away?" Usually, we walked if we had places to go.

"Morning Wall."

There was a rush of air, and the shuttle settled before us.

\* \* \*

I looked at her over my shoulder as she lounged, stretched out, in her seat with a foot upon her knee. Her fingers tapped out a simple beat to a song that only she could hear. I enjoyed these rides and loved to cross my arms and lean out the window. The wind was so inviting. I closed my eyes and daydreamed a while. Transition eventually came, and in a moment, we were traveling on the Morning-side of the ship. The Twilight-side, the side we all lived on, was behind us. It was notably spinning counter-clockwise.

There were more and more green spots as plants reached out and took hold. Several of the orchards, raised in perfect symmetry, could be seen to the left as the land arced. I think Tang said they were orange trees. The grapple trees and the pear trees were two kim-two away. With all the pollinating to do, the bees were having a field day, as Jaughn would say.

The sequoias were taking their good old time getting tall. From the ones I had seen before in the history books, I kind of expected them to reach higher and higher in no time, yet, it seems like they have been growing forever, and they have not grown notably taller at all. In time, they said. In time, they will be the giant landmarks reaching to the skies.

It took almost an hour before the shuttle stopped.

I had dozed a little. With my arms folded and my head out the window, I had closed my eyes and daydreamed. There was no sudden change in movement as we stopped; it was the loss of the wind that made me notice.

We were near the lake. Sure, there were smaller ones here, rivers connecting them all, but this one was the biggest. Stretching to the left and to the right of us, I could see the ends as it curved up the wall. We were still a good two-and-a-half kilometers until the actual wall. It was a familiar sight seeing the ritzy homes, offices, and businesses on the wall like rings of a tree.

This stop was the last one before the ribbon of the track went in a slow arc upwards to those places.

"We've gotta walk two kim-two down. Thatta way. Is that okay?" Lena asked as she hefted her pack.

I nodded my head.

The shuttle would stay where it was until someone called it away.

"The wind is different here," she said, incorporating a small lesson about the ship. "When we are on the Twilight Wall, we're always getting the wind from the burner. Here, beneath the burner and near the water, there's a little bit different kind of convection going on."

"It's not a huge difference, though, is it?" I asked.

"No, not really. It would just be a little different from what we're used to."

"Oh, you come here often?"

"Some days. Swimming is fantastic for you. It helps tone your muscles." She flexed her arm with the backpack. "Mark comes out here every day and swims from pier to pier and back. There's one further down. It keeps him fit. Also, I must warn you that others will be here and, although they may be a little crass, pay them no mind."

"Crass?" I asked, unsure of the word.

"They may say things or make gestures to embarrass you."

We walked down some side streets and past buildings still sealed tight.

In no time at all, we were standing on the shores of this great lake. There was a pier extending out about twenty meters. Backpacks and piles of clothing dotted the wooden planks. As we walked down its length, I could see about fifteen people in the water.

I recognized Jxan, Connor, Helen, and Viyona. Even Avery, as old as he was, was enjoying the water. Helen was topless, and with this realization, I felt my cheeks flush.

"Warm?" Lena asked, shedding the backpack.

"Always!" rose a cheer from several people.

"Can I have everyone's attention, please?" It took just a moment for them to grow quiet. Connor was insistent on playfully splashing everybody. "We all know Sally." She turned to me and spread her arms wide as if I were some type of consolation prize. "I brought her here today to allow her to enjoy herself. Let it be known I am here protecting her, and if anything should happen to this young, fair lady, then you will have to deal with me."

A series of catcalls came and a whistle from Viyona.

"Are we to do push-ups?" someone asked.

Jxan lay backward and bringing his legs up. I could see that he was completely nude.

"Hey," Lena yelled at him. "Keep it beneath the water, buddy." Upon hearing this, he spun around and gave us a clear view of his backside.

"Sorry, sweetie," Lena whispered. "There are no bathing suits on the ship. They have been coming here for some time doing it this way, and I guess you could say it's tradition now."

"You don't have to come in," Helen said, swimming to the ladder.

I looked at Lena, smiled, and shook my head. "No, it'll be okay."

"We'll watch over you."

To my amazement, Lena undressed shamelessly.

"Guys, you make her feel self-conscious. Could you please turn away until she's in the water? Guys? Hello?"

There were groans, but they all turned around and faced away from the pier.

My hands shook as I worked the buckle of my belt. Lena was quick to give me help.

"Hurry, they won't stay turned around forever. Do it quickly and jump in the water. It's about ten meters deep here, so there's no chance you'll hit bottom."

"Anything in there that could hurt us?" I asked, looking over the edge and biting my lip.

"No, just bottom feeders living off the algae is all. Other fish to eat other fish, but nothing our size. A small, tight ecosystem."

I looked her in the eyes once more, and she smiled. In the water, everyone had their backs turned. Sighing, I undid the snap, and without a sound, my pants fell to the wooden planks.

"It would've been nice to know beforehand," I mumbled as I slipped my shirt off. For a second, I hesitated and was reluctant, feeling the wind on my skin as I had never done before. Lena slapped me on my bare backside, and taking a quick step, she dove in. I followed as quickly as I could. The sound of Lena's splash broke the silence, and I was sure they were going to turn around. Before she surfaced, I was in the water.

\* \* \*

"Did you ever swim to the wall?" I asked everyone out of curiosity as we bobbed there.

"They strictly forbid swimming to the wall," said Jxan in all seriousness. "It's about a kilometer away. Unless you're very fit and experienced, it would be a bad idea. Also, right in the center of where the water touches the wall, there is a drain." Even though he and I were not even close, he held his thumb out of the water and squinted with one eye. "Right about there."

I looked a little frightened. "The pond has a drain? Yikes!"

"It's not a pond; it's a lake. It is huge. The water is gravity-fed through a series of screens to the drain. This keeps the fishies from swimming in and mucking it all up. After it passes the smallest one, there is a quiet pool that is about 20 meters across. At the bottom of this, now hear me out people, is hell on earth. There is something akin to the burner. Forever hot, this water pours down on this thing, it evaporates immediately and travels down these huge pipes clear," he turned in the water dramatically and pointed to the Twilight Wall, "down to the far end where the steam collects into liquid and nature starts the process all over again."

"This is where we get our drinking water?" I asked.

"It is," he nodded. His wet hair was now a wild mane. "It is also where we get the water to flush toilets, to bathe in, and for the fountains. In days past, they used chemicals to continually reuse the water and to keep the growing algae at bay. Now, we drain the pool or the fountain every night, and fresh-water comes in."

"Well, ain't you the bright one?" Helen, swimming behind him, splashed him. He twisted and grabbed her by the waist. She screamed playfully, pretending to try to get away.

\* \* \*

I saw white, pink, and blue lily flowers. Tethered to the soil beneath with long stems, I swam to them. A frog, sitting on a lily pad, jumped in before I got there. My presence startled him. Stopping before I got to them,

I tread water and slowly went amongst them. There were a few bees collecting nectar from the flowers' open faces.

I stayed for a bit, and soon, my curiosity quenched, I swam back to the others. As I did so, the stems touched my feet. This startled me. For just a second, I felt as though something was down there trying to pull me under the water. Bringing my knees up to my chest, I used my hands to stay buoyant. That's when one touched my arm. I did not want to scream, but it's what I felt like doing. I bit my lip. Thrashing and kicking, I got away from them, but not before I felt them touch my legs again.

When I got back to the group, Viyona must have noticed the look in my eyes.

"You made it out alive, girl," she said with a knowing smile.

\* \* \*

We swam for some time, and then one by one, people got out to dry off. Lena and I were the last. Even though they had seen me in all my glory, I was still self-conscious. I was beneath her as she exited the water up the ladder.

Climbing up after her, I peeked over the edge to make sure that everyone had left. We toweled off and dressed.

"Anything else you want to do today?" She asked.

"Er, no, not really."

"Thought we'd grab lunch before we head back to the Twilight Wall. There's a lot over here."

I finished putting my shoes on before she did. Jumped up and motioned to her.

"Lead the way."

Homeport, Day 4

"Diana?"

It took a moment for his supervisor to reply to the voice over the radio.

"Yeah, go ahead."

"Flynn here, um, we were checking out the air intakes on the Morning Wall. Going over it with a blue light, checking it for anomalies, and something fluoresced. A closer look reveals somebody has written graffiti up here at the edge of the PNR."

"PNR?" she asked.

"Point-of-no-return. Another meter or two, and the wind would be so great the person would get sucked into the air intake. Whoever had done this was either extremely brave or idiotic."

"What does it say?"

"They originally wrote it in red marker. Friction from the wind removed the writing itself. The only way we can see this is because the oils in the ink permeated the paint. It reads, 'Sally Weiss was here,' and then several dates beneath it; '14 January 2166, 12 May 2171, and 15 December 2189. Doing the math, for some reason, she kept coming back for many years."

XD05, Year 6–"This little piggy went to market,"

We had pigs like never before. There was the first generation that we had found on our tour of the ship: the boar, the sow, and seven little runts. With a lot of help and some ingenuity, we could get them from the pen they were in and into a kim-two that had a lot of the vine. Before they cleared that kim-two of vine, she had more babies. Then, a short time later, when we expanded their domain to an adjacent kim-two, a baby from the first generation had babies of her own. Within six years, their number had grown tremendously.

It's hard to believe pigs are smart. They would watch Pat Pat as he came to feed them scraps. They loved the vine, but when he brought buckets of grapples, they were ecstatic. You could see it in the way they moved. The bigger ones would contend for the position at the trough, making the little one's work for it.

They watched him come and go. They knew somewhere beyond that door were more grapples, a lot more grapples.

Pat Pat was cautious. Diligent in his efforts, and as skinny as he was, he made sure they had food and water every day, shade from the sun, and shelter from the rain. They had no choice but to be content. So, when they got out, it was to everyone's surprise.

We really don't know how it happened. Joan came up with a theory that perhaps one of the bigger boars had dug a mudhole near the doorway. For some reason, they would gather at the door and wait, even though he would not arrive for hours. This may have formed a deep hole that allowed one of the smaller ones to get out. A sow, suddenly realizing that one of her piggies was on the other side of the wall and unobtainable, became frantic. She may have worked at it for an hour before the door finally gave way. This is all theory, as no one knew for sure.

All Pat Pat could do was shake his head at the aftermath. The designated kim-two was empty of pigs. And they now wandered the streets.

Our gardens were well beyond where they roamed. Half of XD05 spun clockwise, the other half spun counterclockwise, whatever that means. There is a place right in the center that they call the transition point. It is a ring that circumvents the ship. There is no way that the pigs could get past this. A good bit of our crops are on the Morning-side. The birds, gifted with the ability of flight, can fly over the ring. They have the freedom of the whole ship.

The pigs had somehow gotten into the city, and even though they ate a bunch of vines there, they also left messes. We never domesticated these animals, and they have always been feral. Brandon believed it was only a matter of time before a pig got upset with a human, and bad things were bound to happen.

We had trouble enough with the birds causing messes. We did not need any more.

* * *

I stood at the second-story window of an office building and watched. For the moment, I was a lookout. Just a little nervous, I tapped my wooden staff on the window. Then, realizing that the pigs might hear me, I stopped. The little buggers had exceptional hearing. Also, somebody may mistake it as a signal.

A boar and his pride roamed the walk paths of the business district below. He was an older one, might be one of the first litter. The sow traveling with him had grown hefty, and we could not underestimate her. We would let her live. We needed her to have more babies. When this day was done, we would cart off her and the litter of piglets to some other kim-two away from the city.

It was our chore today to kill him and pen her and the babies. Little did the big one know, he was living his last hour. I felt sorry for him in a way, but this needed to be done.

I raised my eyes up. The brown curve of the ship was turning green. Brandon theorized that if we let them all loose to eat the vine just on the Twilight-end, within five years, they would outnumber us. In twenty, there would be so many that we could have one a week, and it would not hurt the group at all.

This was only one kim-two of the three thousand. There were so many places that were showing signs of the vine. It was hard-pressed, keeping it away.

My thoughts came back around. Jonathan was across the way, crouched on a wall almost right above the pigs. He held a spear in his hand, but the wood was more for show rather than actual killing.

He had changed a lot since I first knew him. Hard to imagine that he wore those brightly colored shirts all the time. It was as if he was on a constant holiday. As time went on, that clothing became threadbare, and now he wore the traditional utility clothes with a tight weave. Comfortable and rugged, this clothing lasted a very long time. He would bring out the colorful ones only on special occasions.

He had thinned a bit since year one. They all did. I grew as well. Surviving from plants and vegetables, there was very little meat or car-boro-hydrants, or some fancy name, in our diets. Tonight, there would be a feast.

"*Filthy swine,*" I whispered, echoing Paul's words.

This was not the last batch, either. Franco and Jon had spotted at least three more families further down the curve. It would take a few days away from gardening, but we would get them. I would feel a lot safer knowing they were out of the city.

If they were more domesticated, not apt to get into the crops and leave their scat where they pleased, it would be good sense to leave them to roam where they willed and eat the grass that sprouted in the cracks and crevasses. All in all, they had their use in the scheme of things.

I pulled back from the window, letting the plastic shades fall into place, and left the room. Passing other empty offices, I took the stairs to the street level. I hefted my spear, testing the weight. Made from broken furniture, the tip, wooden, not metal, I sharpened recently.

I smiled.

"*Sally, you there?*" Jon's voice came through my earpiece.

"Here, Jonathan," I vocalized. "Mom, dad, and the little runts are right beneath you."

"*Copy. Seen them. How many runts? I didn't get a count.*"

"Um, eight at least." I would go out the back door but opted to go to a front window. Not that this was pertinent information now. Seeing the family on the street, I began the count. One, two…

"Nope, I'm wrong," I said. "A litter of six. Pint-sized."

"*Copy.*"

"Derwin, they are heading to the end. Make some noise and send them this way."

The pigs had been slowly walking into a trap. The avenues of escape that they could take were getting smaller and smaller. Also, we had placed crates that we could climb up on if the boar happened to charge. The sow might turn aggressive to protect her young. I had seen that happen before. The memory of Jay's death was still fresh.

The door to the back alley opened with a little effort. I paused, listening. They were not coming this way.

"*Sally, you safe?*"

"Always. Be with you in a minute, Derwin. Avery, I'm coming your way."

The door closed, latched, and I continued down the alleyway to where Avery waited.

"Hey," he said when I neared. He stood on the cage. We covered it with a tarp and other scraps to make it look like a den. It was something that would make the pigs feel secure. A trap they would unknowingly run to. He tightened his grip on the cord used to hold the hatch open and gave me a weak smile.

"Hey," I said. I took the position to the side. Back in the day, as they were fond of saying, the space was meant to be a meeting area between office buildings or a place to have lunch. Now, though, that had all changed. With three of the four exits barricaded off, the others would chase the pigs in, seal the exit, and it was just a matter of getting them in the cage.

Avery looked at me quickly.

"All set," I vocalized into the mic.

He gave me a quick thumbs-up.

*"Derwin, bring them back."*

There were shouts and a loud clattering of cookware. Squeals followed.

Avery rocked nervously on the cage. His hands anxiously worked the cord. It was mid-day and warm. Beads of sweat rolled down his forearms.

The sounds beyond the building were getting louder.

*"The boar is a bugger. Whoop..."* some screams and then laughter. *"Almost got me on that one. Next time we get stuck in outer-space, someone bring a gun. Cha! CHA!"*

*"He's moving again."*

*"Runts are coming at ya, Avery."*

*"Copy."* He crouched low behind some office paneling. Still able to see, he waited.

Three little piglets were the first to run down the alleyway.

As easy as can be, the mother sow and the rest of the piglets ran into the courtyard. She was grunting. I'm sure it was very traumatizing to her. Looking for another escape route, one of the three little ones ran for the cage. Two others followed, and in the darkness, they hid. The mother sow squealed. Being boxed in clearly agitated her. She wanted to leave, but the little ones would not come out from the cage that was their shelter. The rest of her litter came into the courtyard. Like the others, they ran to her and then found solitude in the darkness.

"Drop it?" I whispered to Avery.

He tested his grip and shook his head. "Mommy," he mouthed and held up four fingers, making circles. We needed all of them.

I placed my stick down and grabbed a length of rebar. Heavy in my hands, I tested my grip. I jumped down from the crate to a crouched position on the cobblestone. I held the bar level in front of me.

The sow watched me.

Avery hissed his disapproval.

I held up my hand, telling him to be quiet.

"Shhhh," my tone was low. I stood, making my form as big and as intimidating as possible. "Hey, we're just trying to get you and your babies somewhere else so they won't be in our crops and on our streets. Do you understand? We'll still feed you our scraps," I stood. "You have some little runts. Get you behind those walls, and you can have a whole section to yourself. Would you like that?"

The sow seemed indifferent.

"Do you know how far you are from home? You're not the first pigs in space, and I doubt you'll be the last, but you're here now, and we have to deal with this problem. You have the prettiest ears," I murmured.

The mother sow was squealing less. I was calming her down. The trouble was we had never domesticated these things before. Wild as the day they were born, they were feral.

The rest of the team was still talking in the headset.

"Your babies are waiting for you."

The sow grunted a few times and looked around.

"Go on in," I cooed. "We don't wish to harm you, just want to move you elsewhere," I tapped the rebar to the one side, and the sow turned away.

"Go to your babies," I said. There were tiny grunts from the cage.

When she was almost in, she stopped and would go no further. I ran forward and smacked her hard on the rump with the rebar. The sow squealed and turned. Avery let loose the rope. The door fell, and the sow's snout banged against the wire mesh.

I caught her, she knew I caught her, and this pissed her off.

I wiped the sweat from my brow with my forearm.

"Wasn't so bad." I smiled up at Avery.

"*Avery.*"

"Yeah."

"*Boar coming your way.*"

"Quick." He held his hand down and pulled me up. The cage rocked a little, but we managed not to fall.

\* \* \*

With a clamor behind him, the boar ran into the courtyard. It was bleeding from some cuts on its back. Avery and I stood motionless. If we spooked the boar, it may have turned and bolted the way it came in. The others would have a time of it herding it back in.

The team members rushed forward. Sweating and harried, they had crazed looks in their eyes. Two carried panels, which they dropped quickly and used to block the exit. The boar tried to escape once. Felix was there with pots and pans making a ruckus, and the boar turned away. It huffed, doing small tight circles, but could not find the way out.

He grunted and squealed, but clearly, the chase exhausted him.

Once we contained him, we used what we could to kill him.

He was soon too weak from blood loss to fight back. Derwin ran forward in a blur of movement and slit its throat. Like an ancient tribe on earth years ago, we howled and danced. Even I joined in.

\* \* \*

It took time. We could not find a pole long enough to carry the pig with. We could find a table, and after we broke the legs off, we worked this underneath the boar. We had to call in some other people. It took six men to lift it, three on either side, and they carried it back to the hotel. Had Sebastian still lived, this would have been the perfect opportunity for him to flex his muscles. I walked in front, still carrying the length of rebar. I could hear men call out occasionally as those carrying the boar were swapped out when they grew tired. Mostly, it went smoothly.

As we neared Hotel Lima, I ran ahead.

"We got a boar!" I exclaimed and pointed in the direction they were coming. They looked at me but did not share my enthusiasm. I tried again to arouse their interest, and they all seemed indifferent.

In the foyer, I turned to the stairs and sought Lena. I knew she had her place up on the wall, but there was a chance she may be here. The boar hunt brought many people.

When living in the hotel, residents left the doorways to their personal rooms open to keep the breeze flowing. Doors are usually closed only when they sleep or were otherwise engaged. Many left doors open to signify that they had abandoned the room, and it was available. I was pleasantly surprised to find Lena in her room on the third-floor writing in her paper journal. She enjoyed writing her thoughts down on paper. Her journaling calmed her.

I stood there for a moment, not wishing to disturb her, and looked at her. Five years had changed us all. Gone was a soldier's uniform that she had worn until it degraded so far that, out of respect for the uniform, she had to dispose of it. They all had four pairs of uniforms. Lena kept a brand-new pair stowed away under her bunk. She still wore her long hair back in a ponytail, black T-shirt, denim jeans, and sandals instead of combat boots. She looked good.

The memory of her nude at the swimming hole came back, and I blushed. We had gone several other times, and I had almost grown accustomed to seeing her naked.

My thoughts switched gears to the matters at hand.

"Did someone die?" I asked. Lena looked up from her notebook. "Everyone seems upset, very somber."

"The Others have sent one of their own as a messenger," she said, placing her pencil down. "They feel that it is time and want to come to talk."

"Do you think they'll join us again?"

"Sally, I can only speculate what they wish to ask."

I paused a moment. "Maybe they want some of our boar," I stated.

"That's the consensus. They exiled themselves to the other side, where they have only had fruits and vegetables. Now, they want to share in our spoils."

"It's only one boar," I said. "We could give them a whole group and let them have their own."

"It is just one boar, but it is a significant kill. It is something we should be proud of, not them. The fact of the matter is, they had no hand in this whatsoever. Brandon expects that they will get very pissy over this. They have been quiet up until now. They could make things terrible for us."

"How did they know we had the hunt on today? Do you think they had some watchers?"

"That," she tilted her head to the side, "or perhaps somebody is telling them what we're doing."

"A snitch?"

"A mole, somebody who has dug their way inside."

"Humans will always become divided," I whispered. One tip of my metal staff was on the floor; the other rested on my shoulder as I leaned in the doorway.

The din down below grew louder.

"They are here by now," I said excitedly. "I'm going down to watch them prepare the boar. You gonna be down?"

"We shall see."

* * *

More people gathered below. They brought the boar with the tabletop to the steps of the hotel as if they were paying homage. They placed it down and stepped back. They agreed that they would not gut and skin the animal in this kim-two but rather take it to the next. They did not want blood on the hotel steps.

I followed them, and many people asked me questions about the hunt. They treated those in the group almost as heroes. I heard Derwin's laughter often, and Avery's deep voice made people pause and listen.

They searched the archives, and there were only a few references on how to properly skin a pig. With a crane, they hoisted the boar up in the air over a vat by its hind legs. It took about an hour and was very messy. I had seen nothing so bloody.

* * *

They hung the body of the boar up in the air. Two hooks in the hind legs just before the hooves, a length of rebar between the hold these apart. Three men were working on the hide, meticulously stripping off the carcass with sharp knives. They made small lacerations in the space between the skin and the muscle, and the hide came off centimeter by centimeter. They caught blood, gore, and entrails in the vat.

I watched it in fascination. This is not the first time I had seen something butchered. We had killed pigs before. It was almost too difficult to look away.

I stayed to the side and watched it with many others. Lena came over and stood beside me. Her arms were folded across her chest, and she seemed very preoccupied.

"Kinda gross and fascinating at the same time, don't you think?" I asked. "I mean, that thing about took a bite out of me two hours ago." Although I stood next to Lena, my eyes never left the men skinning the boar.

"Sally, I need you to come with me."

"Seriously?"

"Yes, seriously," Lena turned with no further explanation. I thought she was in one of her moods again, and it was best to humor her.

After we had walked for a time, Lena's demeanor changed slightly. She seemed to soften.

"The kill fascinated you?" She asked offhandedly.

"It is really something to watch, you know? I understand pigs are smart and that they can sense things and feel pain; however, I wonder what they think when those last moments come."

Lena just shrugged her shoulders, not answering. I went on.

"It's the first death I've seen, well, since..."

"Yes, I know. To several people, the blood and such may bring back memories of the accident. I see the blood, and all I can think of is Jay. We weren't there when it happened. We were in the field, as usual, but I did help in the cleanup. I thought it was my duty as a soldier to step forward and help with the things that were harder to do. I still get dreams from time to time, you know? Seeing the blood today may make it come back."

"Would a drink help?" I offered to try to lighten the mood.

She shook her head.

"I don't think I'll watch another butchering," she said dryly. "Most people do not wish to see how you prepare meat. They would rather see it when it is fully cooked rather than during the process. I haven't become desensitized enough to it yet."

"I can understand that." Hands in my pockets, I specifically walked through the grass. "It will feel weird when I have a bite of him. It's been so long since I ate it, I can't remember what beacon tastes like. Funny that way."

"We tend to forget a lot of things." Again, she was not in a pleasant mood.

"So, why have you called me away?" I was curious as to what was so important as to pull me from the butchering. I knew it wasn't to talk about trivial things.

Lena looked at me but did not stop walking. She pursed her lips, looked forward, and then looked back at me.

"The Others have come today. They will ask you some questions, questions I believe I know the gist of, but I cannot tell you about them. I have sworn to them, and to Brandon for that matter, that I will keep this information secret."

"The Others wish to talk to me? What about?"

"Sally, I cannot say. Things are changing. How we handle things in the future will depend on these next few days," Lena stopped on the footpath and reached out. She took my hand. She looked at me in the eyes before she spoke again. "All I have to ask of you is that you please, primarily, please be true to yourself. You are you, and they can never take that from you. Follow what is in your heart." I broke eye contact and looked down. "Can you promise me that?" A hand under my chin and our eyes met again.

I cleared my throat. "I can." I kicked the dirt with the toe of my boot. "I am not really dressed to do this. I didn't bathe this morning, and I've been sweating all day."

"Like a pig?" Lena asked.

I smiled, and it broke the spell.

"Come on. It won't be so bad. We'll get this done and over with. Maybe we will have that drink and celebrate with a bottle of Jaughn's sangria tonight." We turned, and Lena put an arm on my shoulder as we walked along the footpath.

"The first generation of his wine is superb," she said, smacking her lips loudly.

\* \* \*

There were many people at the hotel. They talked in hushed tones, and when they noticed Lena and I walking up, they grew quiet. They cleared a path. I felt awkward, to say the least, being in the middle of so much attention.

"Go on in; they have a seat waiting for you. I'll wait out here." And then, in a whisper, she said, "Remember, be true to yourself."

She stopped and pushed me lightly. It seemed like everybody was here. I nodded to some, and there were some I had not seen in a while who had gone with the Others. I smiled. Ben and Evan, who once were soldiers, led me through the crowd of people to one of the large conference rooms.

They packed the place. I expected a few people, but not this many.

I looked around the room to see who I could identify, and Troy was sitting there. Seeing him gave me a start. Sitting calmly at the large table in the conference room, with crisp, clean clothes, his facial hair neatly trimmed, he watched me. His stare was, so that I had to turn my gaze.

Brandon cleared his throat as I took my seat. "We shall, ah, get it started. Now that Sally is here. Sally, do you know why we have gathered here?"

I felt very nervous with all eyes upon me. "Um, I kinda think I do," I said. "We have to work something out between us and the Others. I take it they want pigs to raise and eat. Um. Maybe we could trade them for fish, perhaps," my hands fidgeted on the table. I silently wished that they would have given me time to clean up. My fingernails were dirty, and I curled my hands into fists to hide them.

Elbows on the table, Troy leaned forward slightly. "Sally, that's not why we're here at all. We…" he began. Brandon interrupted.

"We agreed, Troy. She knows me, and I will speak to her. I will ask her the question." With a nod from Troy, he went on. "What Mr. Gavin is saying is that he believes there are other matters more pressing than these treaties for food. I must find a common ground to this one pressing issue, something we can all agree upon, after which the tension will ease.

"Do you remember Homeport, which we left when you were just a child?"

I nodded.

"You should, of course, you do. You lived at Homeport for several months with your aunt and uncle. They designed homeport to hold only so many people. Before we left, there was an influx of people to compensate for our departure. As usually happens, it packs the place for a while until the ship leaves, and things get back to normal. The services at Homeport are modest. I am not sure if you remember the delays at the end of quartermaster services; meals, laundry, and such.

"They limited the healthcare that they provided. If accidents happen, they could treat the injured people, but they did not have the services to treat people long term. Do you understand this?"

Again, I nodded.

"If there were long-term illnesses, if they diagnosed someone with cancer or a severe sickness, they sent them back to Earth where they have the facilities to treat them. Do you remember the guy who lost his hand?"

I did not respond, curious as to what he was leading to. "I, um, I really don't remember."

Brandon went on. "There was almost an equal number of adult men and women at Homeport. I think, and I'm quite possibly wrong because I do not have information readily available, but there were about four to five thousand people living there. With the number of young couples we had, it would not be far-fetched to say we could have a pregnancy every few months. Homeport could not cope with this—the prenatal care, the actual birth of a child, and the visits afterward. You only got to visit Homeport because of your age. A few years younger, and they would not have let you come at all."

Troy breathed heavily as if it bored him. "Can we please get to the crux of the problem?"

"I must give Sally the background, sir. I cannot thrust this upon her."

"But thrust upon her it has," Troy mumbled with a chuckle.

"Sally, everyone here, all the adults you have met on XD05, had a position at Homeport. You were the only child going back to Earth on this trip. Of the three hundred, you are unique.

"In human anatomy, a woman has ovaries that create eggs which, if fertilized, they would make babies," he was clearly uneasy about speaking of this. "They gave every woman here a pill to stop the eggs from forming. We do not have the other pill, the antidote, that would reverse this process. As a precautionary measure, they just never sent any to Homeport, and there would be no reason we would have some here. We were just on a mission to transport the ship back to earth. It was not meant for our permanent habitation."

Troy anxiously tapped the tabletop.

"What I am trying to say, Sally, is that of all the women here, you are the only one who can have children."

I sat back in the chair, too stunned to speak.

It took a moment for the scope of what they're saying to sink in. It was then I realized that he was correct. At no time since we have been here had any of the women become pregnant. Sex was commonplace in some respects. I had gotten so used to people being naked that now it was almost routine.

That they chose a forum so openly to discuss this filled me with so much emotion. I could feel the anger build inside me. I wanted to smash something, break a window, do anything, and leave.

"What he is trying to say," Troy injected. "Is that we need you to have children. *You* need to have *our* children."

Brandon cleared his throat. "We have the facilities here and plenty enough people to care for them. Your children would really liven up the place," he smiled weakly. As a salesman, he was doing a terrible job. "It would bring laughter back."

I breathed deeply and looked at my fists on the tabletop. "We have not lost the laughter," I whispered.

With a remote, Troy clicked on the screen behind him.

"In this first slide," Troy held up his hand needlessly, "we see a chart depicting the inhabitants of our home. We have lost nine people already in the short time we have spent here. There were suicides, and then the loss of Sebastian, Randy, and Jay. These are accidents that we have learned from. If our research is correct, then, based upon our numbers, and if everybody lives long healthy lives, we should see on average we will not lose people to age or illness for another twenty years. We must be careful, and there will be no more accidental deaths.

"If you have children now, then in those twenty years, they could have children of their own. There would be no struggle for them, to be sure. With ample fruit, vegetables, and meat, they will flourish. The colony can survive."

I looked at the chart, and of all the red lines present, there was one red line longer than all the rest. I believe it was my line. Troy clicked the remote again, and a second chart came up.

"This chart depicts the number of people we would have at the same time if you agreed. As you can see, over the course of the next seventy years, the red lines drop off significantly; however, the blue lines take off and continue to increase exponentially. If the conditions are right, then it is easy to assume that by the time of your passing, there will be twenty to thirty of your offspring alive. Children and grandchildren." he smiled at this, trying to win me over. "Within one hundred years, the colony will have grown to over two-hundred. This ship is meant to feed and house over a million people. It would reach that capacity in about a thousand years.

"Theoretically, you could give birth to a whole nation of people. To ensure diversity, there would be different fathers, of course."

I sat there in the room of people who were eerily quiet.

Everyone was staring at me, and I looked at my hands once more.

"You are expecting me to decide something of this magnitude today?"

"We would hope for a quick and easy outcome," said Brandon. "I would like Troy and his people to return to their side of the ship as soon as possible."

"Or if we resolved the matter in our favor, then we could stay and enjoy. We, the people of the ship, would be whole once again." Troy looked at Brandon but did not smile. "This is a very serious issue."

"It truly is," I nodded to both. "You are telling me I have to birth the children to whoever you please? That, without doing so, we will die. Isn't this the point of life to begin with? To grow old and die. It's inevitable. These children will not extend the life of you or me for one moment."

"But Sally," Troy spoke up. "We will need these children in years to come to tend to us as we grow older. Besides, it would truly be a shame to waste a ship of this size just on one person."

"Ha," I tried to laugh, but it came out more like a croak. "It would be a shame to waste a ship of this size on three hundred people, and yet here we are. I can head off and claim a whole kim-two as my own, or a whole square four-kilometers and no one would give two shits."

"Sally," Isaac, one of the Others Troy brought, cleared his throat and spoke. "I don't think that is the point they are trying to make."

"I'm sorry." I brushed a lock of hair from my eyes. "But is it so hard now? They schedule the rains. The fruits and vegetables grow year-round, and we can pick them as we need them. I'm sure the fish are of an abundance as we can harvest them by hand, and with no predatory animals, there is no need for weapons."

"There are the pigs, and that damn bird, Lawrence."

"Yes, in time, I suspect they will become difficult to kill. If we can herd them into several kim-twos, then they will be more manageable. We can, I don't know, make a set of pulleys to pluck one up every so often when we get hungry. But I do not think you want me to birth children so they can kill pigs."

"It's just a matter of procreation," Troy looked at me calmly. "Look at how quickly the pigs have flourished from just a simple few. One family, Sally, one family was all it took. As a species, it is something we need to do to survive. If we do not do this, then in fifty to sixty years, this could all be a barren wasteland. Plants would take over; this whole city would be in ruin."

"Isn't this place already going to ruin?" I could not hide my contempt for them. "We were tearing apart buildings for wood for the campfire. Name me one building we have not justified breaking into? We have no way to mend them. What happens if, in time, the burner goes out? The artificial sunlight fades, and X-ray Delta 05 goes dark? There could be a million souls trapped on board with nothing to do but to die. We don't even know how to fix the thing. We can't even fix it. We can't get back home.

"I am sorry," I went on, tapping the tabletop with my finger. "X-ray Delta 05 is a beautiful place, and if there were other children here, then I would not mind raising children of my own. We would really enjoy it. But I do not wish to become a mommy machine. Popping out babies for the whims of the state. My ovaries, my uterus, are mine and mine alone."

"Sally" as Troy spoke my name, I heard murmuring and looked up. I was so focused on Troy and Brandon that I had forgotten everyone else was listening. They were relaying my message to the people who could not hear.

I felt my anger rise. Here, I thought they would be discussing one thing, and they completely turned around, and it's on me. I felt this deep-seated emotion I had to get out.

"I feel highly insulted, Brandon, by you and others, that you would even entertain the idea that this is something I want."

Brandon held up his hands. "I am not in agreement with you having children or being forced to have children." His voice rose slightly, and his face turned red. "I have been adamant from the start that we drop the discussion. They persisted, and that is why they left. It was to keep the peace."

"Also," I turned to Troy. "If I had chosen the other option, would we get started right here? I mean, everyone would know when I was having sex with somebody because they would wait for the outcome." I slapped Troy on the arm. "What say we get the show on the road? Let me get naked, and we'll get started right here." I jabbed him in the arm a few times. "You going to be the first of this, or is there a line?"

There were chuckles from a few people. Brandon and Troy exchanged glances.

"Well," said Troy, obviously dumbfounded. "This is really not what I expected. You say you are turning down the opportunity to become the matriarch of something beautiful?"

"Yes, that is exactly what I'm saying. You have shown me the light, both of you." I looked between them. "I see now I need to be more conscious of what I do in my personal life. The implications are simply staggering."

"I must ask Sally." Brandon sat up and leaned forward. "Is there anyone on board who you have been promiscuous with?"

I looked at him and could not speak.

"Good heavens," exclaimed Troy with a bit of humor. "With no one to look after her morals, she could be with anybody."

I cleared my throat and looked around the room. "I must tell you,

Troy," I said, leaning forward, placing my hands on the tabletop. "That, yes, if my virtue is in question, then it's already ruined. My flower has indeed been plucked. By whom? I will never tell, but I must say that it is none of your business."

He held his hands up. "Whoa, whoa, whoa! That's not what we're saying. We're just…"

"No," I said sharply. My voice cut through the air. "It is exactly what you're saying. I can see it in your eyes. Some of you want me pregnant; some of you don't. I can tell you right now that it will not happen. I will be more cautious with whom I entertain my time. I'm not here on the ship to give birth to a multitude of children. I will live my life the way I see fit, and no one else can tell me what I can and cannot do."

"If you do not have children, then we are all doomed," Troy whispered.

"We are all doomed anyway, are we not? When was the last time we checked the radar to see if anybody was at least on their way? I remember before, Sam, the radar man, would come back daily and give us an update. Is he here? Sam? No, he's off doing something else. He has given up any hope of anyone finding us, and so he is no longer listening to space outside. If they make it to the right step in the Lucy stairway, they still have a long way to go to get to us. Ain't nobody going home. All this fuss over me. You all should be ashamed of yourselves honestly and truly. I will not birth your children."

"But Sally, the ship"

"No, the ship is our home. It is my home, and it will also be our grave."

Troy looked around and raised his hands. "Well, that didn't go over well," he said out loud.

Brandon looked at me and then turned to everybody in the room.

"I need everybody to leave. Troy, that means you too. I wish to have a word with Sally alone, and then I'll be out to make a formal announcement."

They were slow at first, but eventually, everybody filtered out.

"Troy, we were expecting this."

"I guess my problem was in my presentation, Brandon. Had I been a salesperson or a lawyer rather than involved in warehousing, I could have been more persuasive." he paused at the door as if he would say more, shook his head, and left.

When the room and the hall were empty, but for Brandon and I, he spoke. "Sally, I am sorry this had to happen." My hands, balled into fists, were shaking. He cupped my hands into his. "It is something that they have wanted to bring up since after the first year. It was only my influence that held it at bay. I would find it morally wrong to condone such behavior. We put up a good fight, and we won. There may still be some time in the future where he tries to influence you, but it will not work."

I nodded and bit my lip.

"With this now in the light, you understand that you are special above all others. I hate that this has to be. Believe me, life would be so much better if we didn't have to deal with this issue. Life will go on. We will live day by day as best we can and do everything we need to do to survive. Nothing has changed; nothing will change. No one will harm you or ridicule you in the days ahead. I need you to feel safe here.

"I will go talk to everybody. You stay here if you wish, as long as you wish, and come out only when you're ready."

I looked at him and nodded. Still too stunned to speak, I could only look into his eyes and search for understanding. My anger was not for him; above all others, he helped me.

"Go," I whispered. "I will be fine, honestly. Just a little shaken, but it will pass."

He squeezed my hands and stood.

I stood with him. Reaching out, I held him close for just a moment. He returned the embrace.

"We must look out for each other," I whispered. "There may be times coming where we need to let the anger and the hostility go. In the end, we are all we have."

I felt him nod. We parted.

As he turned, I followed.

"You don't want to stay here?" He asked. "Get yourself composed?"

"No, I want them to know I am strong. That if they want children to help them out in the time ahead, then I am the only child they have. I must be strong."

"You'd make a great politician."

\* \* \*

On the steps of the hotel, in the sunlight, everyone gathered. It had been a very long time since I had seen this many people in one place. MC stood a head above the others. Uncle Butch, still without Lawrence, stood to the back. His arms folded, he watched over everything.

"We all know what happened here today." Standing on the top step, Brandon's voice carried. "I have to say such divisions in society are not uncommon. Mostly, they are expected as people have different ideas on how things should go. Sally, the youngest of anyone here, has bravely given her choice and not buckled to pressure from either side. I ask that we respect these wishes and hereby state that the issue is resolved.

"For those who lived elsewhere because of this, I am extending the offer for your return. We do not 'need' you back to help with our labors. With the abundance of food they have given us, we are self-sufficient. We 'want' you back as friends and as part of a peaceful people.

"She is now an adult individual of our society, and we will not force our beliefs on her. I shall punish anyone caught doing so."

"The same goes for those coming back if they do so. There will be no anger or bitterness toward them. They felt that they were doing the right thing. We will not break down and become heathens. People, in the scheme of things, we are so few. Let us bury our differences. There is no need for them."

\* \* \*

People were slow to disperse. Late in the day, it was a day we lost from the fields. They brought the remains of the boar to the kitchens, and Doc and crew immediately cooked. The aromas were overpowering, and, although slow, the mood lifted.

I was never alone. Lena stayed close. Arms folded across her chest; she would constantly watch the crowd. I guess she was looking to see if anybody would start an argument. Others stood by, and even Addy, the strong female soldier, remained close. She was very intimidating in her own right.

People who I have not seen in a very long time meandered by. Corey had changed quite a bit. An older man to start with, he looked frailer than ever. Derek had let his beard grow, which was not altogether uncommon, but his had grown exceptionally long. Mostly gray and hunched over, it was fantastic to see him. I had forgotten how much they were once part of our lives.

Troy came over and sat. Lena and Addy tensed up.

"I am not trying to sway you either way. You have made your decision, and I will take a bow and back away. I thought maybe things would work out better, and, no, it would not be as crude as I led you to believe it would be."

I nodded my head.

"The issue is over." he looked at me and smiled. "I will never bring it back to light." At this, he nodded to Lena and Addy.

In a way, I was still leery of him.

I set my resolve and did not falter when I spoke to him. "Even though the matter was just given to me this morning, I gave my answer, and in my heart, I know I made the right decision. If ever it changes in the future, very, very doubtful, I will address Brandon."

He extended his hand, and I took it. "Truce," he said. "Truce," I echoed.

Homeport, Day 4

When the video starts, the chair is empty. Someone younger comes in. It's a girl in her late teens, which is so uncommon because everybody so far was so much older. She's wearing jeans and a light-yellow shirt with soil stains on the arms and shoulders. Wendy grabbed Bob's arm needlessly. She tugged his sleeve twice until he reached out to hold her hand.

The girl nodded at the camera before she spoke. "Hello, I have never seen this done before. Tang showed me what's going on. My name is Sally Weiss."

Wendy brought her hand up to her mouth and tried to stifle the cry.

"They say we have been here for almost six years now, and I like my home," Sally beamed. "I miss Earth, but this is okay. There are some people who get really annoying and pushy, but I don't let them bother me one bit." Sally fidgeted. With her hands on her lap, she constantly fussed at the seam of her jeans. She was nervous, to say the least. "I want to say hi to Uncle Bob and Aunt Wendy, and if this makes it home, I want my mom and dad to know I'm okay. I don't know if I have any more brothers or sisters now. So much time has passed, and so much could've happened. Mom and Dad, 'I love you.' I am being strong for you. I have never forgotten you. There are so many adults here that I feel they are my surrogate family. I wish I would've carried a photograph of you all with me so I could see what you look like and remember.

"Some people here wanted me to have children of my own," she stuck out her tongue and grimaced her face. "Can you imagine that? Me having children? They had a big 'to do' about it, and I had to go into hiding for a bit until things calmed down. Lena has been awesome, and I do not know what I would do without her. She is my rock." She clasped her hands together. "Anyway, they had split into two groups. We stayed on the Twilight Wall West side, while the other group stayed on the Twilight Wall Eastern side. We have given each other boundaries, and although they are not formal, we stick to them. I truly hate that there is so much infighting because of me. Thankfully, there have been no deaths, no killings because of it—just a lot of people who are stubborn and angry.

"I did not want to have children. Nope, not happening here. Maybe if I were back in the world, then things would be different. I didn't want my children growing up in this world where catastrophic failure could happen at any time and wipe them out. They asked me to take my time to answer, but I bluntly told them 'no.' Besides, I didn't want any creepy old guy getting his jollies on me." She smiled nervously. "Nuff that." She waved her hand.

Sally held up her hands so the camera could see.

"I work in the fields almost every day. We have a lot of reserves of food, and everybody has got down to the pattern of helping. We have enough pigs here that we can have one about once a week now. Not that there is a lot to go around, but it helps break up the diet. Maybe somebody has already said this, don't know. I like to say I'm very proud of what I do." she held up her arms and flexed her biceps. "Keeps me in shape."

"What? Two minutes? Oh, okay, um, in closing this letter, I want to say I love you all, and I will miss you all for as long as I live. We are doing our very best here, and I think everyone would be very proud of me knowing what I'm doing. I'm not slack. All these people rely on me for help, and that makes me happy. Until next time," she blew a kiss. "I love you, Mom and Dad; Aunt Wendy and Uncle Bob miss you dearly. Love you too. Buh-bye."

* * *

"She grew up," was all Bob could whisper. Wendy squeezed his hands tightly.

"I knew she would get older before our eyes and people say they blink, and suddenly their children are grown, yet I expected nothing like this." There was humor in Wendy's voice, and she gave a chuckle. "Sally is so strong," she whispered. Standing, she raised her voice to the screen, although it had grown dark. "We love you, Sally!"

XD05, Year 7 - "Here cometh April again, and as far as I can see, the world hath more fools in it than ever." *Charles Lamb.*


I was not there when it started. I rarely am somewhere when exciting things happen. My days and months had fallen into a routine. I would work in the fields for three days and then have two days off. It was the same with everybody. We were all on different rotations, so everybody did not have the same time off together. We found this way to be the most productive. If I work over three days in a row, I get wiped out and become grumpy.

The fields we travel to all cornered each other. The kim-two with the cornfield and tomatoes shared a corner with three others. Green beans and snap peas were in one. Onions, radishes, and cucumbers in another. Potatoes, yams, and brussel sprouts in the last. They enclosed them so the pigs could not get in.

They were not the extent of our food by any means. It's just that this is the one where I commonly worked. A few more minutes down the track were four more sets of fields, and then you had the orchards further on. Lena enjoyed picking grapples, oranges, and mangoes. Tang was one to gather nuts, and that suited him just fine.

I had kept myself distant from everybody. They gave me a chance to let my thoughts settle. They were older than I, and the concerns they had were not my concerns.

I was taking my basket of beans up to the shuttle platform when I heard someone singing. It was Jxan. He was sitting on several empty crates, drumming the bottom of a bucket, and although his voice was off-key, he sang to several others who were working.

I stopped and smiled.

When he finished the song, people clapped their hands, and that only encouraged him. Lost in thought for a moment, he sang again, and to my surprise, other people who knew the song sang with him. Sometimes they stumbled on words, but that was okay. As they sang the last words, everybody gave a cheer.

"You know we should do this more often," he said, turning the bucket upright.

Others agreed with him.

"We have not had a festival in a while."

"We should ask and see if we can have a music fest."

Viyona laughed and shook her head. "I don't think there's permission needed to have a music festival."

"You know any other songs, Jxan?"

"Oh, I know hundreds of songs. Come on! You're talking to the fantastic Jxan here. Who doesn't know music, huh? I used to go out into space and wrangle big rocks to bring in to Homeport. Nothing to do out there in the void but listen to music."

\* \* \*

A day or two later, everyone was talking about the upcoming festival, and looking at the calendar, they held off for a week while people gathered stuff for homemade instruments. It so happened that the date they had planned on was April first.

The term going around was April Fools' Day, although I did not understand what that meant. I asked, and no one else really seemed to know except for it was a day to get silly and have fun. It also just happened to fall upon one of the three days I was working in the fields, and I welcomed having the time off. To coin another phrase, I needed a vacation.

Lena sought me out the day prior as I was working in the kitchen.

"Wee One," as she said this, she must've seen the look in my eyes. It was a name she had given me years prior, and I have grown older since then and now almost stood eye to eye with her.

"Yes, Lena,"

"There is talk of some kind of music festival they are putting together. I should tell you, fair warning," she repeated herself when she saw me smile. "Fair warning that I have every inclination of getting more than a bit tipsy. Is there any misunderstanding about this?"

I laughed.

"Honestly," she held her finger up to me. "It is my understanding that they will tap more than one keg of beer. I'm were not talking Jaughn's flavored water. I'm talking honest-to-goodness beer that can be found in no other place on this side of the Milky Way. I have not had one in so long." She smacked her lips. "I find it hard to even remember what it tastes like."

I looked at her quizzically. "So, you want me to help you drink it?"

"No! Well, you may have a sip or two, but I need to tell you that if things go as planned, I will not be there to watch over you."

"You don't have to watch over me." I stood there with my hands on my hips. Not that she angered me or anything, it's just that I was getting old enough now I didn't need her to constantly babysit me. "I'm a big girl, and I can take care of myself."

"Yes, I've noticed how much you have grown. Gotta find a new nickname for you. I'll add it near the top of the 'to do' list. In the meantime, I want you to watch out for yourself and be mindful of others.

Do you remember before I told you that some people just give me bad vibes? They have gone nowhere. They are still here, and they still give off these bad vibes. I can't shake it. I know that you are old enough to take care of yourself; however, over time, I have gotten your back. Just saying that for tonight, and tonight only, I'll not be here to do that."

"I thought it's supposed to be a fun time?"

"Oh, it will be. I am just saying, be mindful of who you chat and are friendly with."

"All right, all right! I got it. I will only sit and eat and listen to music. You do what you're gonna do, and I'll do what I gotta do."

"Just making sure we have an understanding. Capiche?"

* * *

It was after the third hour of music. I must admit, I had two glasses of beer and found the taste and the texture of the drink interesting. It differed from anything I have had before.

Addy, for as strong and muscular as she was, could sing wonderfully. Growing up, she learned how to sing from her mom. The military taught her cadence and rhythm. She had always intimidated me from time to time. Now I looked at her in a different light.

Brandon, seeing such a demand for the beverage, allowed another one tapped. They took this with much enthusiasm. Everybody let out a cheer.

I caught sight of Lena every-so-often, and it was good to see her at a distance. I was happy. I knew after all this time; she missed her family and friends back home, but this was something she needed. I knew she said to watch out for people, which I did; however, there were so many here. Everybody was in a fantastic mood.

* * *

We were all scattered about, sitting on the field in front of the stadium. Jeff and Joan sang a woeful duet when there was a commotion at the center, and everyone turned to look. Connor stumbled towards the stage. Someone tore his shirt on the back and sleeves, and his left eye was also notably black. Blood dripped from his disheveled hair, and there was a second stain of blood on his stomach.

Someone screamed.

The music stopped playing.

"What happened? Connor, you're hurt!"

Some stood to aid him, yet he held his hand up, and they stopped.

Clutching his stomach, he almost doubled over. He groaned in agony and looked up at the sky.

"Please, please," his voice wavered. He held up his hand again and looked as if he would be sick. "Brandon! Brandon!" His voice trembled. Everyone who had gathered was now silent. He looked at Brandon, who was standing. "Could you please tell them to... to... have a happy April Fools!"

And he laughed.

"Gotcha," he jumped into the air and came down nimbly with a bow. "Boo, you're an ass."

Even though there was a lot of laughter, some people were booing him. Someone, although they have never found out who, tossed a tomato at him. It caught Connor in the shoulder and spun him a little. He looked into the audience but could not tell where it came from. There were vegetables and baskets all over to show the bounty of our harvest.

He ran to the nearest one, and all that was there were cucumbers. Grabbing one, he strutted with this thing pointing out from his waist. Everyone laughed. And, as expected, this drew a few more lobbed tomatoes. He found a basket with some and returned fire.

That's all it took.

With no other encouragement needed, there were suddenly tomatoes flying through the air. I got hit with several and grabbing mushed tomatoes from the ground; I threw them randomly.

No one was immune. They chased Jeff and Joan off the stage. After trying defiantly to remain clean, they were both soon covered in tomato. In a show of good sport, people picked them both up and paraded them around, kind of like a king and queen on parade. Even though they were easy targets when they were on the shoulders of the others, no one threw tomatoes at them.

There were screams of delight, laughter, and happiness. For the first time in a long time, I felt content being where I was.

Although it seemed like forever, I'm sure it was just over in a matter of minutes. The mood had lightened, and they filled their glasses once again.

Lena came skipping by, her arm hooked my waist, and we spun around, almost losing our balance.

"This is wonderful, Wee One," she said coyly. "Everyone is dancing."

She let me go and quickly moved away. I tried to follow her with my eyes. In a moment, I lost her in the sea of people and commotion.

Derwin lay on the ground, rolling in the mashed tomatoes, cucumbers, peppers, and chives. He covered himself from head to toe and laughed the whole time. Brehm had his shoes off and seemed to be fascinated by the feeling of tomatoes on his toes.

"Feels like Buddy bombs." He said to no one in particular. "I had a big dog named Buddy, who would shit the backyard."

Viyona had a cucumber in her shirt wedged between her cleavage. Anna had curled two small ones into the locks of her hair. Her shirt was close to bursting with the vegetables she tucked in.

They danced and chased each other.

Two more people took the stage, and after cleaning their hands, they picked up the instruments and played.

* * *

They pushed me then.

Someone, I don't know who, hit me in the back, and I went down on the ground hard. My arms pressed downward as I tried to keep from falling to my stomach. Someone stepped on my foot, and I pulled back on reflex. It didn't hurt much, but it brought me back to the here and now. Everyone else had drunk quite a bit. Of those gathered, I think I was the soberest one.

I limped to the side. I had to find a place to sit down for a few moments. I climbed to the second floor. I found an open window and sat on the windowsill. As I sat there overlooking them and nursing my wound, I could not help feeling depressed. It came over me like a wave, and I could not stop.

If they all lived their natural lives, if things kept on course the way they were going, I would outlive everyone here. The noise of the ruckus they made today would be gone someday, and all I would hear would be silence.

I tried to bring the laughter back, but it only made it worse. Evan, with his long hair and beard, put a cucumber between his teeth and shook it until it fell away. I looked at him and nearly cried.

Maybe it was because I was much younger than anyone here that these thoughts came to my mind. Had I a group of kids my age to spend time with, my thoughts would've taken a different route. But here I was the youngest; I was the last born. I was part of them only because I was here with them. We did not belong here; none of us did. I did not belong with them because of my age.

Perhaps I had not drunk enough beer. To me, it tasted a bit harsh. Maybe next year, when I was older, I would drink it, and the flavor would come back to me once more. I would remember the happy times, like this day.

I heard a couple come in, and by the sounds, they wanted their privacy. They chose a different room and were into shedding clothes as I tiptoed out to the stairs.

* * *

I was sitting in a corner on the edge of the stage listening to someone play songs I had never heard before. The fire had gone out from the group, and everybody was winding down. The music reflected this. Gone were the energetic songs from earlier. The songs the people sang now were much slower. Some were downright depressing. There were a few talented musicians in the group. The ones now who sang the songs sung without instruments and were mostly off-key. I would've loved to have heard the songs they sang, from the professionals, rather than from my friends.

Evan searched for me sometime later. I wasn't hard to find. He wanted my help with Lena, who was in no condition to do anything. Having more than her share of alcohol, she had all but passed out in the grass. The world did not follow our schedule, and it was going to rain in a few hours. Those that could, who were considerate enough, were rousing up the rest and making sure they had shelter.

He reached up and tapped my leg.

"She can barely walk," he said, offering me a hand down.

His hair was a mess, and so was mine, I'm sure. He had stuff in his beard. Everyone could use a good shower to rinse the sticky vegetable juices off us.

We walked through the mess side-by-side.

He put his arm around me briefly and gave me a hug.

"I hope you enjoyed this," he said.

"I don't remember April Fools' Day," I admitted. "I think I remember there being jokes and things and pranks, but nothing to this extent."

"Well, I'll be the first to admit that this was one of the best April Fools' Day's I've had. We've never had music or food from the field before. That part was wonderful. We must do it again next year."

"Yeah, I think next year there will be more vegetables."

He laughed.

"Connor had black eyes," I mentioned, and he laughed again.

Lena lay on the ground on her side, curled up a little, and still holding her glass. She was a mess.

Evan pulled her by the arm, and with a slight wince, lifted her. He placed her arm over his back and held her by her waist. She brought her head up. I got on the other side and carried as much weight as I could. I'm sure Evan hefted more than I.

"She doesn't stay in the hotel, does she?"

"No, she has a place up in the temperate forest."

"If we get into a shuttle, do you think you can get her to her place?"

"I'm strong, but I'm not that strong," I looked over at Lena. "I'd end up dragging her."

"Can't have that. I was a soldier with her. We stick together. Lena? Lena? I need you to walk with me for a bit, okay? We can do this. One block to go until the stairs. Gotta stick with me, dear."

We took a few steps, and she seemed to come around a little.

"Hey." she gave Evan a glassy look. "There you are. It got dark out kinda quick, you think?"

"Sure did. Walk with me, one foot in front of the other. One minute it was full sun, and I blinked, and suddenly we're at full moon," he laughed halfheartedly. She looked upward as if trying to find the moon. I felt her weight shift. Her head bubbled around, and I heard her groan.

"Yeah, best we not do that," Evan offered.

"Where's m' Sally?" She tried to turn in his grip. "Is she left out on the field?"

"I'm right here, Lena," I felt her arm tighten around me.

Evan cleared his throat. "Metzger, you member Sgt. Metzger?"

"Me, are you talking to me?" she asked sluggishly. "I remember him. Boot laces broke, and I had to run that damn track for a week. A freaking week. Not my fault, rat bastard."

"Well, we have lights out in half an hour. I got to ask you, Cpl. Daniels, got to ask you to pick it up. I can't do this on my own. We get you in the bunk before he gets there, and it's fine. We're golden. We miss lights out again, and we're humped."

"Ah shit, you serious?"

"Cpl. Daniels, we gotta move. Dig deep, focus, dig deep."

And she did.

By the time we got to the steps, she was on autopilot, and he was just guiding her.

On the steps upward, she almost stumbled, but he caught her.

"Ah, damn," she laughed.

Sensing we were on our way, a shuttle arrived as soon as we got there. He sat her down on a seat, and she slumped to the side.

"Open the windows. She'll need fresh air."

The shuttle lifted.

"It will take a day or two of recovery," he whispered. "Should be fine." And he gave me a thumb's up.

"Did you have a lot to drink?" I asked him.

"I had my share," he nodded with a half-smile. "I used to have a big tolerance for alcohol, and I'm sure it has somewhat changed over the years without it. I can still handle it."

We were about to start up the wall when Lena suddenly opened her eyes wide.

"Out the window," Evan yelled. "Out the window."

She sat up and turned. I thought she was looking outside for something when suddenly her whole body heaved.

She vomited.

"This is a good thing for her. The alcohol is a poison that affects the body, and this is the body's way of rejecting it."

"This is *good* for her?"

Lena heaved again. It sounded disgusting, and I did not hear it strike the belt. If it cleared there, then it would be like a ten-meter drop to the surface. Fortunately, the chances would be rare that somebody would get hit.

"The more that is out of her system, the faster she will recover."

She spat a few times to clear her mouth. I could hear her moaning softly.

"Oh God, oh God," she whispered. And then she got sick again.

I went to her, upwind, and held her arm while patting her back.

Tears ran down her face.

"Hey," I whispered. "Are you okay?"

"Yeah, oh yeah, I'm fine."

And with that, she hurled again. I felt her whole-body spasm.

I held her hair back, sticky with tomato, and did all I could for her. Evan sat to the side and was mildly amused.

When our destination came, we pulled her back from the window.

"It's colder up here."

"Yeah, it feels good sometimes after being down in the heat."

She was out of it, yet knew what was going on. We strong-armed her out of the shuttle, and I went ahead to her house. I palmed the entry pad and turned the lights on before he got there.

"Couch or bed?"

"Put her in bed. It will be fine."

He did so, and she unceremoniously fell into a heap. He grabbed her feet and straightened her out as best he could.

"Watch over her, make sure she sleeps on her side or stomach, not on her back. If she gets sick again, do not have her lying on her back. She'll choke, and it could kill her. I've seen it before. We lost Dunbar that way."

"You won't stay?"

"No, I need to get back and retrieve one or two more people. You seem a little down tonight? Is everything okay?"

I looked over at Lena once more and stepped out; I closed the door.

"Um, yeah. Just depressed. After the tomato fight, I got into a mood and couldn't shake it."

"Dollars,"

"What do you mean? What's a dollar?"

"A dollar is something they used to use for currency. If I work so many hours, I'd get so many dollars, and I could purchase things. The actual word dollar comes from an old term that meant hills and dales, highs and lows. You get to this high spot, and to come back down, you must go lower than you were before. We used to call it 'dollars.' It's natural. Back in the day, there used to be a cycle. People would try to compensate by having stronger and longer highs. It rarely works."

"What do you do?"

He shrugged his shoulders and turned to go. "The best thing to do is ride it out, come back to normal."

"I miss home, I guess."

He stopped at the door. "We all do," he paused again as if he would say something else and left. After the door closed, the panel lights cycled from green to red, and it locked.

* * *

The mushed vegetables on her had dried considerably. I thought maybe just removing her shoes would make her comfortable in bed, but as she lay there curled up, I knew I had more work cut out for me. I undressed her with no resistance from her. I tossed the clothing in a pile at the wall.

"Lena," I breathed.

She moaned a little.

"Can we get you to the shower?" I asked softly.

She opened one eye slowly, and she then looked at me. I could tell it was hard for her to focus. She shook her head.

"Sleep," she mumbled.

"Let me wash your hair, then. It's a mess."

I felt her nod slightly, and I quickly went to the kitchen, where I found a pot to fill. I brought it back in with soapy water. It took time, but I cleaned her hair. It was acceptable. When I finished, I took the towel from under her head and put that with the pile of clothes and into the laundry. I emptied the pot, refilled it, and washed her body. I know that doing so would disturb her, but in the end, she would sleep better. Starting on her shoulders, I cleaned her arms and her back. There was a scar of some type just above her hip, about the length of my little finger. It looked like it had been very painful.

When I finished, she curled her legs up a little and made small tight fists, which she held to her breasts. I covered her with a blanket. She moaned slightly, nestling in.

I scared myself when I looked in the mirror. I looked like a vagabond. I had matted hair, and something had left a stain on my forehead. I showered and changed into a pair of her comfy clothes.

She had not moved, nor had she vomited again.

It tired me. It was a long day, and much had happened.

I lay behind her, spooning with her. Draping my arm across her stomach, I snuggled close. She reached down and took my arm. Her grip was strong and sure. She wiggled her hips a little, working herself back against me. I found comfort in this. It was an intimacy that calmed me. Giving in, releasing the tension of the day, I slept.

* * *

When I opened my eyes, we were lying face-to-face.

"I was watching you sleep," she whispered, gently brushing a lock of hair from my eyes.

"You were?"

She smiled. Her arm under my neck tightened and pulled me closer. The first kiss was a surprise. Unsure of what she was doing, I was not ready for it. My kiss was an awkward return, and my eyes were open while hers were closed.

Something awakened in me.

I remember kissing my parents, and I gave uncle Bob a kiss on the cheek before I left; it was nothing like this.

Lena's kiss was stirring; it drew me in.

Feeling her lips on mine again, there was a heat in my chest, and I felt wetness. Shifting, her leg slid over mine.

"I'm not sure I'm ready for this," I said, whispering over her cheek.

"Neither am I." her breath was hot in my ear. "Let's sleep some more." Her arms tightened around me, drawing me closer, and we did just that.

Homeport, Day 5

"Richard, there are so many fail-safes that this ship should not have returned here."

"We need to get that department on the line, Mabel. They should have reported in."

"Not a word yet." Mabel brought up the diagram and trickled the request downward. It took almost a quarter of an hour before she got a response.

"The one we're trying to locate is 'Michael White.' He is at the top of the hierarchy with the guidance system."

"How big is his department?"

"Um, just him, actually. The whole thing comes with a diverse set of presets, and there are only a few things they let humans intervene with. Everything, almost everything, is pre-selected beforehand by people back home. I guess we would call him a liaison here. They integrated the software into the computer systems here, and then they went back home. No real reason to keep a huge department here except for one person who is the liaison of sorts. When he gets the order, he starts the countdown, and it does everything automatically."

"Was he ever on the ship?" Richard asked.

"Um," she looked at her screen. "He logged in at the Hub on '05 two months ago, stayed for two days, and then returned to Homeport by shuttle."

"And? What have his activities been since then?"

"We are checking; however, it does not seem that he has done anything of importance."

"What do you mean? He must have done something. It must be a real cushy job if all he does is program ships to go back home every couple of years. From what you said, he does not work in a big office, but he has to have a record of what he has done here."

"Still looking, Sir, but his name or employee number does not show up anywhere after he returned here."

"Nothing in the mess hall? Nothing at any of the recreational services?"

"Um, nothing. It's as if he disappeared on his way back from '05'"

"He could still be there," Director Porter whispered.

"If he stayed there, and it's very rare, he was a stowaway."

"Could he have been the cause for all of this?" Director Porter waved his hands at the screens showing the ship sitting in space.

"If he had access to the computers there, then he was up to no good and has done something rather bad. Understatement. Not pointing my fingers at anybody until we know for certain, but his name is at the top of a very short list."

"Well then, if he's here, then we must find him. If he is over there, then he is still there. Is there anyone else in-system who knows how to work with the computer guidance system?"

"No, and I really wouldn't say he knew how to work it. It's just that he knew which buttons to push to get the whole thing going. I doubt he would know the programming aspect of the computer system. You know, which buttons to push to make your coffee in the morning? You cannot reprogram the coffee machine to give you cocoa."

"Can we do a headcount of everybody in-station?" It was not the first time today he thought about doing so.

There was a notable pause.

"We could. It would take just a little to set up. I do believe we have a department set aside for census purposes. They could tell us exactly who is here and if we're missing anybody. With this," Mabel waved at the screens, "it will be some time before we send anybody back home."

"A lock-down."

"Well, yeah, I guess in layman's terms, we could call it a lock-down," she offered.

"I don't see our safeguards as being all that lax, Mabel. If he reported that he was on the shuttle to leave '05, then he should've left. How could they misplace human cargo?" He asked, rubbing his temples with his fingertips.

"It may be a simple mistake on their part. However, if he came back on a maintenance run and didn't make it, he could've always caught a second shuttle. His being there, if that is where he is, this action is something he purposely did. Our attention to detail and the need for security have not slacked off. We may need to come down on people a little harder and tighten things up."

"Let's get going on this, then. I want everyone accounted for. Send me whatever you need, and I will look at it and approve it as necessary."

XD05, Year 8

The building had caught my eye only because it was larger than the others. Not larger in the sense of height, as this was a business district, a city hub, designed for offices and for people to commute to for work. Most buildings here were twenty to thirty stories high, whereas this one was only two to three. With its colored glass façade, it would beckon to people on a busy day as they walked by. The openness of it caused people to want to look inside and investigate further. Possibly just a venue that served food and places to eat. Young trees planted here offered shade as they grew to maturity. MC had used the term 'oasis' once or twice, meaning a place to find life or a refuge from the outside. I could see why they built it at such a location.

I circled it slowly, testing each door, nudging each pane of glass, looking for a weakness I could exploit. At first, I walked with my right hand touching it all the way around until I was back where I started from. A loading dock in the back was locked up tight, as was the rest of the building. The design, like most everything, was secure and meant to keep people out.

I stepped back and walked to the other side of the street. Again, I circled the building, noting once again every door and window. The obvious choice to gain entry would be to simply smack a window with a hammer, breaking the glass and letting me go inside. There are several problems with this. First off, it would be frowned upon by the others. They wanted to preserve the place. If we were rescued, it would look terrible for us if the place was in complete shambles. We had a sense of pride that carried with us from the days before. So, breaking one of the big windows here at the bottom of the building would not sit well. Also, it was glass. It would leave shards and splinters all over the place. I didn't even want to think about what would happen if I slipped and fell onto a pile of broken glass.

The doors to the loading dock were heavy-duty roll-up doors with thick wooden panels. If I broke one of these open, then anybody could come and go as they pleased.

This was my building. I admit it; I was greedy. I tapped the pane of glass lightly with my knuckles; this was my walnut to crack.

At the corner, I stopped and looked up. The roof of my building was flat. There were plants growing up there, and it seemed unlikely that they would grow there already. It had only been seven years since we first started our journey. The plants up there grew well beyond that.

To break up the symmetry of being so square, the designers of the city used a series of catwalks above and pathways on the surface. The one building down to my right and one building down to my left had a catwalk going between them. This overlapped my building with about a twenty-foot drop. The corner of my building was a pillar for the catwalk, and although there were no steps or ladders leading downward, I could remedy that.

I smiled.

There were four such catwalks, each touching the corner of my building. Now, instead of having to try to make it into just one building, I had to figure out how to get into just one of eight.

\* \* \*

The door to the roof was unlocked.

Stepping back, I held the door open with my foot. A few steps down, and there was a landing. Beyond this, stairs went downward into the darkness. I could see the small blue panel of light that had been glowing all this time. Located at the bottom of the stairs was a light switch. I retreated just a bit and found a heavy planter with a dead tree in it. I put it in front of the door, so I would have sunlight. I wiggled past, and after my eyes adjusted, I could find the light panel again easily enough.

After two more rooms, I came to one with many cubbies. These were square storage shelves, each with two flat pieces of plastic with straps. I tried to fathom what their purpose was, but in the end, was just more confused. My investigation of this room stopped short as another place beyond the plexiglass caught my attention. A set of swinging doors opened to a very large room. The sound of my shoes on the wooden floor echoed back to me.

"Wow," I said. I whistled and paused as the sound filled the space. I thought at first it was so dark that the light did not touch the ceiling, but I was wrong. The ceiling was intentionally dark. From it, lights and some globes hung down. When it was working, it must be a wonder to look at.

This was a fantastic find. I was thrilled to explore all that it offered.

Seeing every part of the place took the rest of the day. There was a control booth of sorts with steps in the back and large windows that looked out over the great room. I turned on one switch that looked important. The air stirred in a sudden rush—something that tugged on me even through the sealed glass. A strong breeze was coming from beneath the door. I turned the switch off immediately. It was something too big. I had done something I shouldn't have. When the air settled once more, I breathed a sigh of relief.

I found I could bring up things, and through careful testing, I could bring up the lights, make a few of the colored one's spin so that the globes, which were thousands of tiny mirrors, would reflect a rainbow of light on the walls.

I left the lights on, and they played silently for a time. With a giggle, I raced out the door and down the steps. This is beautiful. Every color imaginable glued to my skin. I looked at my bare arms in my hands. It was magic; I was light; I was dancing in the beam of light. I spun on my toes, and my hair whirled. The individual strands caught the light.

I danced until I could not stand anymore. Spinning one time, I tumbled and lay on my back. One strand of hair fell on my face, and I blew it away. I lay there beneath one of the mirrored globes, watching the colors above.

With all this brightness and all this color, I could not help feel a sadness creep in. No one would get to see this. The thousands of people who were to travel through this building daily could never enjoy this.

Finding the master control switches, I shut everything down and was in the darkness once again. It was how it should be. My presence in this building interrupted the order there. Where once there was nice manageable darkness, I brought the chaos of light and color.

Before I left, there was a secondary room on the other side that I wanted to investigate. Also, with windows looking out over the great room, it had a specific function. I found the hallway that circumnavigated the great room behind the wall. Those below would never see a person leaving the control room. It led all the way around and to another unlocked door.

Here, there were several sets of very large headphones. I had seen these before. Not here, of course, but when I was younger, I remember the pilots and the navigators for the shuttles would wear these. They blocked out the noise of those around you and let you hear only what you wanted to hear.

I slipped a pair on my head, and although they were bulky, I snugged them up with a few clicks. I tapped them several times with my fingertips. The big room was quiet and still. The muffled noise of my fingers tapping was loud.

I tapped the screen on the terminal. A list of numbers came up, and it took a while, but I realized that it was a list of decades. Scrolling down, I could see it went from the year of the Event all the way down to 1950. Tapping on one, 1970, all the songs were of a light blue. I almost tapped one, just to see how it would sound, but I held back.

I scrolled back up through and went to the 2030s. Here the computer shaded song titles in different colors. Presumably, they were color-coded to different genres. I double-tapped one and waited. There was no sound. Nothing changed.

I tapped another one, and another one after that, when again, nothing happened.

Taking the headphones off, I looked at them. Perhaps they were broken. It was then I could hear, as if it were off in the distance, the lightness of noises. Setting these headphones down, I picked up another pair by the cup and listened. It took three tries, but I finally found the one that the music was coming from. Low, barely audible, an upbeat rhythm played by people who were recorded almost six decades earlier.

The rhythm of the song was quick, and when the artist sang, I could barely understand what he was saying. I listened intently, trying to catch the words. A few I could, but the rest were just spoken too quickly for me to form into sentences.

I picked another song; something shaded a different color and listened. Immediately, the tempo slowed way down. There were no words, just music. The simple beat of drums and reed instruments made me sway back and forth. It pulled to me from my very core. I found my head bobbing, my feet tapping, my hips swaying.

I close my eyes and let the music fill my mind. It could've been an hour. It could've been days, but realistically I'm sure it was just a few moments, and the song was over.

These people, when they recorded this song, were back home, back with civilization. On any given day, they could step out of their home and be in contact with hundreds, maybe even thousands, of people whom they have never met before and will never meet again. Mothers, daughters, wives, husbands, sons, fathers. I would never know this, this feeling they took for granted.

They denied me music, like so many other things. Jxan sang frequently in his native language, and I could not understand him. He explained to me what the words were at times, what the meanings were behind them, but I never heard the deep harmonious cycles, the way just a simple sound could enhance a section. MC would tap things with a stick, but the sound never compared to the beat of the drums, which now played in my ears.

I shut the lights off in the booth. I could see well enough with the glow of the terminal. Holding the volume control in the long cord of the headphones, I pushed the chair aside and lay down with my back on the floor. Closing my eyes, I immersed myself in a world I never knew existed.

* * *

Rather than walk back home, I summoned up a shuttle and rode back with the twilight wind in my hair. I needed the silence. I had heard so many new and uniquely different songs that, like a meal with many flavors, my brain needed time to digest a bit of what I've heard. I rested my chin on my hands and watched my world slip by.

Lena was worried as I had missed the evening meal. I waved off her concerns. With the sensory input, I was just numb.

She had saved me a plate, and she sat in the window as I ate at a table. Baker came in with some cold drinks he pulled from the refrigerator, and we all sat and talked for a while. She questioned me about my day; such was her nature. I told her I went exploring the city, and I let it be at that.

I patted her leg and gave her a quick hug to show her that everything was okay.

XD05, Year 8 - "A one, a two, a one, two, three, four..."

I found that it was very difficult to control myself. I wanted to listen to music as much as I could.

Back in the big building where I had originally found music, I explored. Behind the counter of the room with the little cubbies, there was a display rack that held smaller headphones in plastic cases. They meant these to be sold. I picked one and tore open the plastic. These things would fit snugly in my ear. There was a second part to these: the controller. It was a little display that was small enough to fit into my pocket. Figuring out how to work took almost a week. The instructions were pretty much gibberish and offered almost no help. It asked for things for which I had no reference.

Back at the hotel, as I ate supper or when I was working in the fields, I would bring up things in conversation with others.

"I'm just curious," I said to Stuart one day as we were digging potatoes. "There's been a name from the past that keeps coming up, and for the life of me, I don't remember where I heard it. Do you remember what an 'input jack' is?"

"Huh? Oh sure, a jack is a round circle with receptors on the inside. My grandfather, when he would reminisce, spoke about a 'telephone jack.' This was when they would connect telephones to walls. The cord would go from the telephone to a telephone jack in the wall."

"Why would they call it a jack?" I had pulled several potatoes up and was brushing off the dirt.

"You know, I do not understand. I know they call spacesuit 'spacesuits,' yet why do we call a suit? Yes, we dress in it, but we do not dress up in it. We don't look fashionable when we do. Imagine one with a tie and cufflinks.

"What's a cufflink?" I asked, looking at him oddly.

He shrugged his shoulders.

I steered him back around to the original question. "So, a jack is a hole, and you place the input jack in this?"

"Yes, if the device does not have wireless capability, then there will be a wire, and you connect to the input jack. You can then retrieve or send information back and forth."

"Hmmm," I said, trying to show I was very interested.

"Pavlina had a degree in historic communications. She may help you better."

"Oh no," I said nonchalantly. "The name, just something about the name, that's all."

We finished the potatoes. I had my basket full. I was very eager to finish so I could take a shuttle back to the big building.

* * *

The earphones were small, and I knew no one could see them unless they were close. I had to change my hairstyle. Instead of keeping it back away from the face with pins or a hat, I let it fall over the ears.

When working in the fields, I would often go off by myself or work well ahead of everybody. Turning around so my back was away from them, I could keep an eye on somebody coming close. If they got too near, I would stand quickly and go empty my basket.

I tried not to hum; it was so difficult. Not tapping a foot, or a finger, to the beats I constantly heard in my head took every bit of control I had.

It plagued meals with fits of anxiety. I would turn the volume down, but not completely off. I did not want to stop the flow of this new sensory input. I would get frustrated with people if they wanted to speak with me. The song was playing. How dare they interrupt the song?

Frank had come over one time as we were eating and spoke to me of the flowers blooming in the transitions' shadow. The engineers designed the buildings there, so that they angled their walls. When the light of the morning showed on the windows, it reflected down to the hidden places below. In all the years he has been here, he had never gone to the transition wall to see this.

When he spoke to me about this, everything fit perfectly with the song that was playing, and I looked at him for a second, holding my finger up for him to be quiet.

"*What are the worlds we live in and the sky above? Who will tend to the flowers if there is no love?*"

He smiled, but I was unsure if he knew the song, as it was well over fifty years old.

He said back to me, "*If it were not for the trees, we'd have no place to be, and our love would be so as dust, and wind, and snow.*"

It was my turn to smile and pause.

It was so unique speaking to him in the secret pose. Another human being had once delved into the world that I found so fascinating. Then again, like the day when the people came into the arena, suddenly someone else had trod upon the sanctity of something I held dear. I could not let him know these paths I traveled. I did not want to travel them with others; rather, I relished letting my bare feet find the earthen path and carry me on the journey alone.

He could see my smile fade.

I pulled my hair over my ear once more and went back to eating.

"I believe the name of the band is Phleks, Kris Phleks," he said, trying to pull me back into the conversation, but to no avail. I looked at him once and nodded. "He's the Journeyman," he concluded.

It was a name that would start to haunt me. One of the greats from recent history, he dominated the music industry for a very long reign. Like the group Top-Flight, or the instrumental melodies of Tamanoski, Phleks captivated my senses. There were songs of his I would listen to and some lyrics I really had to pay attention to in order to get the right words. I would sit in bed at night, and some lyrics I would play again and again.

As with the reference to the input jack, I had no reference to what he was saying. In his one song, 'Lavender Wall,' I had to listen to one stanza countless times before I realized he was singing 'In good company.' The way he said the word 'good' differed from what I was used to. Perhaps it was his native accent, or if he purposely put the inflection on the different syllable. When I understood, finally, what he was singing, I started playing the song from the beginning again. I confess I must've played that song at least twenty times a day.

To say that it hunted me was an understatement.

* * *

I was in my room getting ready to sleep when there was a soft knock on the door. Lena came in quickly before I could give a reply, and she noticed my hand moved to my pocket.

"Is everything okay with you?" She asked. "Turn it down; you'll hurt your eardrums. Is everything okay with you?"

"Yes, it is. I'm doing quite well." *Quite well, but sinking slowly like a feather that somehow fell.* Lyrics filled my mind like a second voice. *Once silent, it is now awakened.*

"Why the sudden change in behavior? You hardly talk to anyone anymore, you stay away in the fields, and we cannot even get you involved in any activities."

"I have been distracted lately. Been busy doing stuff here." I motioned to my room with a wave of my hand, but clearly, I had not cleaned the place for some time.

"Is someone bothering you?" She asked, raising her eyebrows suspiciously.

"No, that's not it." *Sit down on my windowsill, and I will tell you.*

"Honestly, you can be totally honest with me, and it will not upset me. If somebody is bothering you, I need to know. We must take care of it."

"Lena, no one is bothering me."

"What is it then? You have many people curious, and when these people get curious, they also get edgy."

I breathed deeply. This is something I did not want to share with anybody. I guess that I could not cover my actions much longer. *Oh, can you hide our love from the sun above?*

"I have gone to the stadium," I sighed. Looking into her eyes, I needed her to understand. "It was something, you know, like a prize, something. I had to see what was inside. It is so different from any other building in the area or on the ship, for that matter. I, um, found a way in through the roof. No, I didn't break in. The door on the roof was unlocked, and I could get in. I was not sure what the place did or what they meant it for. I managed to find a library there, of music." From my pocket, I pulled out the player. "I have this, and the earphones, and I'm able to listen to the music. How could you guys not have told me of this before? There is so much richness in our past culture and history. Some of these groups are just phenomenal."

"They played music during the festival."

"Yeah, homemade instruments, and we had to listen to Helen and Tang do duets. They were about as in sync as his left foot to her right. I mean, come on, the people on this player are professional. It's what they do. It's what their lives depend on. The people who sang at the festival had no motivation whatsoever. Everyone was drunk. This is music, actual music. It's so beautiful and mysterious and... empowering at the same time. Have you listened to the album by Phleks?"

"Yes, as a matter of fact, I have," she folded her arms across her chest. "Which song in particular?"

I held up my hand to stop her. "All of them, geez Lena, I know you've heard the songs, but did you ever actually listen to them? I mean, deep down, listen to a song stanza by stanza, note by note. You can see how they flow from one to another. There is a magic that these people have created, unlike anything I have ever heard before."

Clearly, I could see that I did not impress her.

"Have you heard 'Inter-twined' yet?" she asked, sitting on the edge of the bed.

"I'm not really familiar with this one. I've only been listening to the songs for a few weeks now."

"If you listen to his music, there will be a song of his that stands out above all others. You'll know it when you hear it."

"Do you want me to let you listen to what I have?" I reached up and was about to take my earphone out.

She held up her hand for me to stop.

"Sally, there was a brief time when I was in school that I worked in an air arena on earth. I did it to earn some money. Do you want me to show you what it's like?"

"What do you mean?"

"What do I mean? You actually asked me that? I cannot believe she actually asked me that. Grab your shoes. We'll go and light the place up."

* * *

She went through the list on the terminal of the shuttle. Selecting entertainment and the air arena from the list given; the shuttle lifted quietly.

I was giddy, and I could not contain my smile. I tapped my legs with my hands and bobbed my head back and forth.

"So, you've heard of Phleks?" I asked.

"Yeah, back in the day, his music was quite popular; it still echoes in today's culture."

I was curious. "In his one song when he sings, *'Down the road I will amble, thinking of the red queen's gamble. Walking the sidewalks of the streets at night, head held low from the terrible fight.'* What did he mean by this?"

"A deck of cards has how many suits?"

"Two," I said and then realized I spoke wrongly. "Four. A deck of cards has four suits." MC, just a few weeks ago, tried unsuccessfully to teach me how to play Spades. I got the basic concept, but I thought he might have cheated a little."

"Two black suits, two red suits. There are two red queens and two black queens. The two reds are diamonds and hearts. I have always come to believe the gamble he spoke of was between a woman he loved. Be it the queen of diamonds, someone with power over money, or the queen of hearts, someone with power over him. He lost the fight and is now walking the streets, thinking of his fate."

"He sings 'fight', not 'fate'."

"He lost the fight. The red queen lost her gamble. Now he has to accept his fate and deal with the consequences."

"Early in the song, he sang of *'Someday I'll bum a ride home again, I bring a smile and my bum geek again.'* What did he mean by that?"

Lena laughed. Don't get me wrong, it was awesome to hear her laugh, but it still confused me. I could not share her mirth and just sat there looking at her.

"I'm not laughing at you. I'm honestly not. When you hear the song, you must know what he is referring to, and then it makes sense. In this, you are naïve, and that's quite alright. Most songs want you to feel sympathy for who the song is about. This one is no different. In this song, the person is far away from home. For them to get home, they must have somebody else bring them. That is where the phrase 'bum a ride' comes from. A bum is destitute, with little or no possessions."

I nodded.

"The next part, you must listen to slowly. There is a type of wine called 'Plum Gekkeikan.' I have had it before, and it is very flavorful. It became popular after the song came out. Again, you don't have a reference to this, so you would have nothing to relate to in comparison. I can truly understand why you got the words 'bum geek again'."

"You mentioned one of his songs, 'Intertwined'?"

"Ah, the guy was a genius," she said, sitting back in the seats. "One year, ok, he came out with a song called 'Inter.' It was fantastic. Whoot! The lyrics said a bunch of things, yet, taken as they were, they didn't make much sense. It was music, and a lot of times in the lyrics, you do not have to make sense." She was getting quite excited. "Ok, now jump forward several months. He came out with a second song, 'Twined.' It had the same beat as the first song, and many people really connected with the feeling of the song. It didn't take long, maybe two months, before somebody realized the obvious. They realized something we had been missing all this time. If you start the first one and the second one simultaneously, not only are the beats the same, the whole song suddenly meshes. Song one links in with song two, and you come up with a third song."

* * *

There was a ping from the shuttle, and we had arrived at our destination. By the time we were on the street, it was dark. The sun had traveled the twelve hours down and was now taking twelve hours to go back, but at one quarter its brightness. Instead of yellow, it was more of a silver color.

Lena slipped her hand into mine, and it was good to feel her warmth and her strength. She made me feel very secure. We walked in step. I could guide her.

"We've walked past the arena," she noted.

"We did. I must go into this building up around to the catwalk and then down. They locked the ground doors."

"Ah, I see," she said as the darkness enveloped us. "You know your way around, I take it?"

"Yeah, I've been here a few times."

"Anything I need to look out for?"

We had slowed, and I could tell that she had her one hand out, being careful not to bump into anything.

"The halls are wide, the ceiling high, and we will be near the stairwell soon."

"Is that from a song?" She asked, and honestly, I cannot remember.

* * *

Instinctively, Lena touched the panel to bring the lights on.

I ducked down. It was something to turn them on during the day when the light would not travel. Here and now, people above the horizon would see them from any distance.

"Lena!" I hissed at her.

"Hey, it's all right. There is no rule that we're breaking on being here and turning a few lights on." She whistled, looking at the place. "This is a little bigger than what I was used to."

"Really?"

"Oh yeah! The one in Tallahassee was much smaller."

I went to the edge and peeked over into the darkness. She had just turned on the hallway lights, and their glow did not travel far over the railing. I heard a noise and turned to see her sprinting down the hallway.

"Lena!" I yelled after her. She giggled loudly and kept going. I chased after her. Deep in the pit of my stomach, I knew it was wrong to bring her at this time of night. We could have waited until morning. We could've waited until sometime tomorrow. I regretted that she brought me here now.

She was fast. There was no way I could catch her. I put forth my best effort and reached the door a few seconds after her.

"Ah, the maestro's booth. He controls the music. Kept in sync with," she pointed with both hands, "the other control booth. They try to put forth a good show. There are some better duos that really get the crowd going."

"Is it just music?"

"It's music that is alive."

She went into the booth, and after a few switches, music coursed through the air.

"You like Chris Phleks?" she winked. "I'll play you some Chris Phleks."

The volume started at number four. The rhythm filled me. I knew the booth had to have some order of soundproof. I could still hear it loudly. She took the volume from four all the way up to 6.57, and I could feel it reverberate through everything solid.

I tilted my head back and laughed. This was beyond comparison. Why was I the only one to find this place? Didn't these people care about music?

She tapped me on the shoulder and pulled me close. "We must go to the other booth." She whispered in my ear. "There are more controls there that work what is happening below."

I nodded.

Again, like misbehaving school children, we ran down the hallway.

At the next booth, she brought up the house lights, and we could see the arena below. The music here was just as loud.

It took just a moment to familiarize herself with what she was doing. She turned the bright lights out over the floor, brought the lights up inside the booth, and then brought up the colorful lights outside. It displayed every color of the rainbow. Reflecting off the mirrored globes above and sending them back on the walls in a dance of color and light.

When the music slowed, so did they. When there was an up-tempo, the lights reflected it. I was in awe. Like first hearing the music, this threatened to overwhelm the senses. When I had headphones on, the voice of Chris Phleks sounded as though it was in my brain. When it played now, with the light and the vibration of the beat through the floor and walls, it felt as if I was the music. As if it was flowing from me to an audience, I could not see.

"Ya like that?" she asked loudly.

I could not speak; I could only barely acknowledge that she had spoken. When I nodded, she smiled.

"That, sweetheart, is not all of it."

"There's more?"

Without hesitation, she hit the button, and I felt the tug of the wind.

"What did you just do?" I asked. This happened before, and at the time, I quickly shut it down.

"Everything's on automatic now. Follow me."

She led me outside to the stairway door. We took the steps quickly, and at the bottom, I wanted to go out onto the floor. She pulled me back. In the third room near the ground floor entrance, she pulled out large flat half disks out of cubbyholes.

"Strap these on." The pair she handed me was red. She grabbed a pair of her own, green and tan camouflage, and sat down on a round mushroom shaped seat with her back to me. She could not contain her excitement. The half disks were awkward to put on, but I did my best.

"There was a game played centuries ago called 'air hockey.' A little disk would float above a wooden surface as fans blew air through pinholes below. This is something like that. Although generations more advanced than anything they could have dreamt of then.

"It has been a while since I have aired," she said loudly over the music. Phleks still played. I think the song was, 'Full Moon Night Owl.' "Like riding a bicycle, though, everything comes back to you naturally. I remember when my mom and dad first brought me to one of these. I had no clue whatsoever, but it was exhilarating." Working the laces, Lena looked up and around. "A place like this would have hundreds of children running around, you know?"

"So, you did this a lot when you were younger?" I asked.

"Yippers. I think when I was 12 or 13, I spent every weekend in the air arena. Dad finally got me a season pass, and I used it as much as I could. You see once you start…" She had finished tying her half disks on her feet and turned to me. "Seriously? Sally, the curve part of the disc goes on the outside, not the inside. Are you trying to break an ankle? You have them on backward."

I undid the laces. She helped me as best she could. "This one goes here, that one goes there. Lace them up tight, and I'll go get the caps."

I thought when she walked away, she would do a duck walk, but the way she had them on her feet, she could walk naturally. A little cumbersome, but not bad at all.

She returned with two cloth caps in her hand. She handed me one, and the other she slipped over her head, hair escaping from the sides, and with a quick snap under her chin, she kept it in place.

"It will be windy?" I asked.

She just looked at me and smiled. She leaned in close and gave me a quick embrace and a kiss. Her voice came loud in my ear.

"You must remember, above all else, when you lock your knees and your feet are together, the disc is solid, and you will hover. Any inflection forward or back or to the left or right will cause the disc to move. It's all in the stomach muscles, the thighs, the knees, the ankles. Hold your arms out for balance if you need; however, you are being watched from above by the computer system. If you happen to fall, it will shut down the air in that area. When you regain your balance, it will come back on based on your skill level."

I said nothing, just nodded, knowing she could feel it. Her hair tickled my nose.

"Right, knees and ankles together, right."

When she stepped back, we gave each other thumb-ups.

As I walked to the floor's center, beneath the rainbow of swirling lights, and with the music surrounding me like the gusts of wind, it felt magical. I stood there and watched her.

Lena leaned forward slightly. I thought she would fall.

Hands down to the side, she traveled forward without falling, gaining speed. It seemed as if she would collide with the wall. As she neared, she leaned her body backward, brought her feet forward, and I swear the discs were centimeters from the brick. She traveled in an arc from the right side of the arena to the left. With the wall behind her, she pushed off smoothly.

She neared me and smiled.

Leaning in, feet back beneath her, she circled me effortlessly and as smooth as can be.

I reached out to touch her, but she held up a finger for me to wait. Traveling back to the center, she adjusted her feet. Spreading her legs, she broke the smooth plane of the disc. Left foot tilted forward, right foot tilted back, she began to spin. Bringing them back slowly at an angle, her arms once held up to her side now came together until her hands touched each other above her head. She spun there incredibly fast.

Five seconds, ten seconds, fifteen seconds. She adjusted once more and slowed. When she stopped, she was looking at me, arms bowed perfectly to her sides, and breathing hard.

The song had ended, and for a few seconds, there was silence.

"Now it's your turn," she reached out a hand to me.

'Falls the Lady' came on, and I thought how appropriate. *How can we dance if you won't let me run?*

I had been standing subconsciously, with my knees and feet apart. It was a comfortable stance as I watched her. When I brought them together, I could feel a puff of air beneath them, and I rose up. Hands clenched into fists to my side, and I squealed like a giddy schoolgirl.

"Lenaaaa…"

She came close but did not touch me. Adjusting her feet, she did slow circles again. I could feel the residual wind.

"Slow and steady, Wee One," she gave me a wink.

* * *

I found my air legs quickly. Leaning forward, knees bent, arms out, I could guide myself easily with just the slightest difference of pressure on the disc. Leaning to the right or left put me in a curve. At one point, I did a Nautilus. Starting off with a wide sweeping arc, I adjusted slightly and tightened it. Closer and closer, I spun around the central point until I was almost horizontal with the floor. It was now Lena who stood there spinning slowly with her arms out, and I was in a tight circle two meters wide.

She held her hand out, and I clasped it hard. The computer had the choice of slowing me down to her speed or to bringing her up to mine. It chose the latter. She leaned into it, and just once, her feet swung over her head. She told me later that they called it a 'slingshot.' If I would've let go, it would have lifted her in the air, and she would've flown for several meters. I held on, and we spun. Our hands, binding us together, were the central point where we pivoted. I felt her warmth and could see her happiness.

I'm not sure if I adjusted or if she adjusted to compensate, but I slowed. I could not stop looking into her eyes. With her cap and windswept hair blowing around her neck, she looked wild and yet so impossibly beautiful.

I tightened my biceps and pulled her closer. Mirroring what I did, we found ourselves face-to-face. I was unsure if the music played or if the wind had died. I could see the smile in her eyes and feel her breath on my cheek.

We kissed.

"Thank you, Sally. Thank you so much."

"For what?"

"For being who you are," she whispered in my ear. "For being who you are and being no one else." She hugged me fiercely. "God, I love this girl."

"I love you too."

And I did. I knew it deep inside and felt it as madly as she.

\* \* \*

"We must go home," she said sometime later when the music had turned low.

"Why?" I shifted my feet, and the wind responded.

"We've lost track of time. There are no windows here. It's dark intentionally. I believe, if my internal clock is correct, the sun is about to rise."

"No shit?"

She kissed me again. "Yeah, no shit."

\* \* \*

We quickly unstrapped and placed the discs back in the cubbies. I went to the music control booth, and she went to the other. The place was suddenly dark and silent. We met simultaneously at the front door after shutting everything down. Before we left, she keyed the access panel.

"You won't have to climb the catwalk to get in again. Your name is now on the register."

\* \* \*

We did not go back to the hotel. We took the shuttle back to her place up along the wall. We showered and had some food from what she had stored. My back, my legs were sore when we climbed into the bed.

\* \* \*

"There was talk years ago of making powerful hover disks," she whispered. I thought my mind would not let me sleep, being on sensory overload. I found, however, that I could not keep my eyes open. The night of skating on air had exhausted me. "You would drop them to your feet, jump on, and wherever you wanted to go, you pointed your feet in the opposite direction. Simple design. I believe they're still trying to work out the kinks. Pretty cool, huh?"

She lay on her back, and I snuggled close. My arm draped across her chest and shoulder; hers wrapped around my back.

I nodded, thinking mobile hover disks were an excellent idea. For some reason, my mind switched gears, and I thought the discs would be an excellent thing in the fields for harvesting.

"I wonder how much corn they could carry?"

Drifting off to sleep, I realized that the question made no sense whatsoever.

\* \* \*

Understandably, we missed breakfast at the hotel.

We woke mid-afternoon, and after putzing around for a bit, we got dressed to eat with the others. This change of pace made it seem like the weekend.

When we got there, almost everyone else was eating. Lena whistled to get Brandon's attention.

"I am sorry," she said loudly. The hall had quieted when everyone heard her whistle. Her voice carried over everybody. "Sally and I missed the field this morning. Something came up, and I have been instructing her. Put us down for Saturday. We have some catching up to do."

Brandon raised his glass in acknowledgment. I thought it was kind of out of place, but I assumed that Lena wanted everybody to know we weren't slacking.

\* \* \*

It was during the meal I heard the tingling of silverware on a glass. To my astonishment, I realized that it was Lena, once again, drawing attention to herself. Everyone became quiet, and even Doc in the serving line paused to listen.

"I have an announcement to make people," she stood so that everyone could see her better. She cleared her throat before she spoke again. "I do not know when it happened. I do not know the specific date of this momentous occasion. One of our own, Miss Sally Weiss, has discovered something that is very profound." I felt the blood drain from my face. I did not know what she was doing. I felt she was setting me up something embarrassing. I wanted to sink under the table.

"Many of you may have noticed, as have I, over the last two weeks or so, she has withdrawn from us and has enjoyed her solitude. Some of you may believe it is what a woman goes through during life's challenges, and I must say that it is very far from the truth. Sally has discovered 'music' of all things. We have denied her all this time, and suddenly, she cannot get enough. She craves it. She has almost blown out her eardrums on occasion. She has this insatiable appetite for the music of our people, of our past. Therein lie emotions and feelings she has never felt before.

"She has wept, she has laughed, her spirits have risen, the darkness has grabbed her heart. It makes the heart patter; it makes your head spin. It makes the body gyrate," which she, unfortunately, did just then.

"Lena!" I said, completely embarrassed. That she was doing it in front of everybody made it even more so mortifying. I hid my head behind my open napkin, and several people laughed.

"Yet," Lena looked at me and shook her head, "yet she cannot stop it. Once the door opens, it can never be closed." She tsked and shook her finger at me. "I'm letting everybody know, so they are forgiving and tolerant of her in the days to come."

Several people clapped. Lena bowed her head and raised her hand. As she sat, I hit her on the shoulder, and she laughed.

* * *

The next morning, as I got my meal, everyone was unusually quiet. No one made eye contact, and even Doc seemed a little grumpy as he served my food. When I asked for silverware, he pointed to the side and turned away. I asked about the orange juice, and he waved his hand.

I grabbed a fork and a spoon for my applesauce, honey for the muffins, and sat.

Hand on my forehead, elbow on the table, I fumed. If they didn't want to look at me, I didn't want to look at them. You know, I thought to myself as I forked a cherry tomato, why do people have to be so moody?

Then, I heard a beat. I didn't even know the dining hall had speakers, and yet there were sounds coming from the four corners. I looked up, but still, no one looked at me. The drum solo at first, and suddenly, a guitar jumped in and played an amazingly deep riff.

Evan, who still had not shaved since the day they disbanded the military, stepped forward with something that looked like a guitar. It was made of wood and steel bits. There was no way the thing could have made any kind of music. He twanged it in rhythm nonetheless. Wanda and Tony pulled Avery out on a cart. Around him were metal drums and glass jars of various sizes. When he hit them with sticks, he was so out of tune as to be comical.

Jxan came in from the entrance and sang as though he were serenading me.

"Baby," he lip-synched the song that was playing. "Where have you gone, leaving me all alone? You went away onna warm April day, and I've not seen you at home. Baby, don't do this, I beg you, sweet miss, your sister has come by, and I don't think I can resist."

I can say forthrightly that I had never heard this at all before. Others in the dining hall joined in. Renn rose from where he sat and played an air guitar of his own. Jeff and Joan sang loudly. I searched the room for Lena and found her in the back corner. Her arms were crossed over her chest, and she had the biggest smile on her face.

"Baby, I need you to need what I have…"

Whoever sang the actual song and played the actual music was so over-the-top. If I thought the song was bad before, it went downhill quickly. The tempo picked up; however, the guitar music stayed the same. The performer sang the word 'baby,' again and again, so much so I thought he would sneeze. When he finished, he sang the lyrics so fast. Jxan was half crouched over where he stood, rubbing his chest and doing tiny erratic steps with his feet. It became hilarious. Everyone else had picked up the rhythm perfectly and continued to clap. I looked at Lena in the corner, and she was clapping just as hard as anyone.

Suddenly, the music stopped. I thought the song was over, but the drum solo continued. Jxan stood there looking upward, eyes closed, head tilted back. He waited.

"Baby, you found me before; you can find me again. But what the other man do, I can do to."

Evan stepped forward and played the guitar as another riff came over the speakers.

"Your silence kills my heart to the bone-e-e-e-e." Jxan grabbed his chest and fell to his knees. The drum tempo picked up again before suddenly stopping. Avery, missing his cue, continued to tap the glass jars.

* * *

Everyone clapped. My meal was forgotten. I joined in, thanking them for the performance.

"Ladies and gentlemen, I am Jxan, and that was my rendition of 'Sleepless Nights' by On Targett, a one-hit-wonder from 2020. Sally, you're welcome."

I saluted him with my glass of orange juice.

He was about to sit down when he turned and spoke again. "You know, Sally, there is a tendency for everybody here to forget where we were when we were as old as you. We have been stranded out here in B.F.E. for over fourteen years now. I am 41 and must really stretch my mind and try to remember what life was like when I was your age. Myself, I was just getting ready to finish high school and head off to college. There was talk and rumors that they built these fantastical things called 'Samuel Drives' that were supposed to free us from planet Earth and take us to the stars above. I was just as excited as everybody else was . I wanted to explore.

"But back to my point, we need you here. We are sorry that when they rolled the dice, we were the ones who boarded the ship. I am sorry that you have gone through everything you have and that you did not get your chance to live a normal life of a preteen and a teenager with so many others like you. This part of your life is so important for development later on and has been denied. You got stuck here with us. Pretty sad once you think about it.

"You bring back what is missing in us. Yes, we had April Fools' Day and the shenanigans therein, but we don't have music in our lives. We don't have soccer balls or that doll you had with you when you first got here." He turned in a slow circle. "Everyone, let's tone things down a bit. This is our life now, and we're stuck here. Let's get the work done, but let's play as well. We need it. Sally needs it. And we need Sally. Let's all act like teenagers again." He paused and looked at me. With his hands over his heart, he spoke again. "We love you, Sally."

I was speechless.

The only thing I could think of was raising my glass of orange juice once again in salute, but even that paled in comparison to the love I felt for them.

I stood so my voice would carry. "I love you all too," filled with emotion, my voice cracked. I coughed in my fist and spoke again. "Quite honestly, not a day goes by that I don't wish I could go back home. If the star-ships were approaching, I would be right out there on the hull in my spacesuit waving them down. It is a dream I have, it is a dream we all have, but I do not think it will come." I looked at them each individually. "Even though there have been ups and downs, I am happy that I have you in my life. To be honest, I wouldn't have it any other way. You are my friends; you're my family."

As I took my seat, I could not be certain, but I think it was Lena who started clapping. Jxan came over and gave me a hug. He kissed me on the cheek.

"Never change," he whispered in my ear. "Never grow old."

XD05, Year 10 - "Mama always told me not to look into the eye's of the sun, but mama, that's where the fun is." *Bruce Springsteen.*

The carrots were huge. With the slow, gentle tug, I brought them from the ground. I stretched out my palm and laid them down. Measuring half the length of my forearm, I smiled. Our best harvest yet. The plants reacted nicely to the nutrients in the soil. If what Stacy was saying was true, this would continue as time went on. Once we reintroduced the excess waste from other plants into the soil, the native plants grew bigger.

I shook the dirt free and placed the bunch of carrots in the basket. A few more, and I would take it up to the cart. Ants scampered around the basket, and I shook it to knock them off. Little buggers. The basket was not their home; the earth was. I hate to take them with me, and I wondered, not for the first time, if their family and friends would miss them.

My efforts in digging the carrots caused a worm to come to the top. I held it for a moment, let it wiggle in my hand before putting it back into the hole I created. With a gentle pat of my hand, I buried it. It returned home once more.

The wind stirred.

Pulling through my hair, ruffling the fringes of my sun hat, it made me look up.

Addy came by with her own basket.

"Hey," she said in passing. Even after all this time, she remained solid. You could tell by the way she walked that she had time in the military.

"Hey," I answered.

"Looks like a storm's coming."

"Early today." I shielded my eyes from the sun and looked upward. Clouds were forming on the light side and were coming down.

"Yeah, seems like a strong one. Better hurry."

I looked at my row and realized that I was close to being finished.

When the rest were in my basket, I lifted it and went as quickly as I could to the shuttle.

"I don't like it," said Jxan.

"It's not natural," Avery huffed.

"Go help the rest out," said Derwin. "We need to get everything back soon, or we will get dumped on."

I looked to the sky once more and turned to go to help those who still worked in the field. Evan and Tony were the furthest away. I jumped the fence and landed squarely on the other side, avoiding the rows of potatoes.

They looked up at me with concern.

"Storm's coming," I explained. "Need to help you out. Derwin says it will be an early day."

"K," Tony gave me a mock salute.

\* \* \*

I was brushing the dirt from my hands as I rode back when the first raindrops came. It was an oddity to have it raining during the daytime, as before they always scheduled the rain to start after midnight to maximize the water intake of plants and flowers.

Evan let out a whoop. He held his head out the window and closed his eyes. The wind brushed his long hair back, and I could see water droplets on his face and in his thick beard.

Others joined in, and I laughed.

By the time we got back to the hotel, we were all drenched. Almost everyone bailed out, and I stayed and helped Cyn hand the baskets down to others. A basket of tomatoes tumbled. Brehm came out and quickly gathered them. With the transport empty, he offered me a hand down.

"Thanks, bud." I slapped him on the shoulder. He smacked my butt as I ran past.

\* \* \*

Besides the early rain, it was a day like any other. We brought in the veggies and cleaned them. Doc and Keys, knowing the food was on the way, began the prep work in the kitchen earlier. They boiled water and added salt. When the transport arrived, everything was waiting.

The baskets dripped water near the back entrance. Joan, Troy, and a few others on kitchen duty washed the dirt off. I heard Joan smacking the sink, and the only thing I could think of was an ant did not stay where they were supposed to. She killed it before it caused trouble.

I looked over the place quickly and realized that they did not need me. My chores were in the fields that day, not the kitchen. I slipped out the back, and rather than brave the rain and go home, I went to my old room.

I must say I had an odd feeling walking down the hallway again. It's been several months since I have moved out to live with Lena. Everything seemed smaller than I remembered. Things that were so familiar before became somehow new, as if I had forgotten them and was seeing them again for the first time.

The panel lit up at the touch of my fingers and chimed the old familiar chime.

Fortunately, I kept a pair of clothing here for just such an emergency. This particular set of clothing I laundered and folded about a year ago. I had to shake the dust off them first. I shed the wet clothes and slipped the other ones on. They were dry. It was a blessing.

The whole room was slowly becoming a shrine to the past. It's where I kept things that once meant a lot to people through the years. Captain Everett's rank sat on the table, a ring that Sebastian wore on his hand that fateful day when he danced with a locker on the stairs, the identification card that woman had who killed herself within weeks after the event, a feather from Lawrence even though the naughty bird was still alive, simple things like that.

I stored the soccer ball and Miss Priscilla in a bin under the bed.

\* \* \*

As we ate, Doc brought up the change in weather to Brandon.

"Odd to have rain in the daylight," he said. Directed as a general statement, he looked towards Brandon as he spoke.

"It is. I have talked with some people, and now we are not sure what is going on. They have informed me of several places on X-ray-Delta Oh Five where we have control stations. The light end, the dark end, and one or two others throughout. I would ask for volunteers to go look. Would you like to head the team?"

Doc stammered. "Me? Oh no, I gotta do my work in the kitchen, boss."

\* \* \*

After the meal, as I was helping with the cleanup when Brandon came and pulled me aside. I was holding a pot with unwanted mashed potatoes destined for the slop barrel.

"There are several workstations that deal with the inner workings of '05," he said, holding my elbow. "We have a guy named Dan who knows the computers and should be able to fix this. On board, we were lucky enough to have about four or five who can deal with this type of situation."

"Have they looked at the navigational computers?" I asked.

"It's a whole different format," he shook his head. Letting my elbow go, he rubbed his hair. "I've had them up at the Hub, and they looked things over. But tending to the inner workings of the ship is a lot different from being an astrophysicist and trying to find the right codes to get us back home."

I nodded and lowered my eyes.

"What we must do is concentrate on the here and now. We are getting together with about two or three people, just Dan and a few others, to go out and see what is going on. I would like you to go too. Dan will explain everything to you so that if the need arises in the future, then you will be able to do it without the help of others."

I knew what he was implying.

"What you're saying is that in years to come, I will control the weather and fix things."

Brandon just nodded and shrugged his shoulders.

"When do we leave?" I asked, shifting the weight of the pot.

"When would you be ready?" He asked.

"Give me an hour. I want to go home, grab a set of my field clothes, and a shower would be nice."

"I'll let them know then. Meet back here," he said as he took the pot from my hands. He stuck a finger in.

"Brandon!" I exclaimed.

"What? Get moving." He grabbed a handful of the mashed potatoes. Without meaning to, I squealed. "I gotta flick these at you to get you going?"

Hands up in my defense, I backed away with a smile on my face. "I'm going, sir." As I got to the door, I looked back. He was walking away, but turned back. Hand raised, a smile on his face, I did not know if he would follow through with the threat of flinging potatoes.

* * *

Brehm sat in one of the folding chairs, leg brought up, foot resting on his knee. He and another were listening to Brandon. I smiled. Brehm was pretty cool in his own way. Tall, misshapen teeth, and sleepy eyes. He was great to hang out with and was wicked at a game of darts.

I recognized the other man but could not recall his name.

The doors to the dining hall were slow to close, and when they did, everybody looked at me. I paused just a second, conscious of this, before walking to the table.

"Sally, this is Dan. Back in the day, he was big in the hierarchy of things. His expertise has been invaluable, and we're very fortunate to have him aboard when the Event happened."

Dan was younger than I expected. He had always helped in the fields, and I had no idea he had worked with the system computers. I never asked people about their previous lives and assumed he was just another traveler. Fitting in with the background of life and gardening so well, I never knew he was a computer person.

"Hi," I waved to him.

"Hi," he waved back.

Brandon spoke up, "We have everybody, then."

\* \* \*

The station we needed lay at the base of the Morning Wall. It was the closest that I had been. It was closer than the swimming hole. I sat in the shuttle's front, arms on the windowsill, with my chin resting on the back of my hand. The warm air rushed through, blowing my hair about. I closed my eyes for a time, and when I opened them again, the indigo road before me and the wall were all I could see. I looked upward, tilting my head back. I looked at terrace upon terrace. From what I could see on the lower levels, just the basic grass had taken root. To the left and to the right, there was a green ring about two hundred meters up. Beyond this, there was a definitive line where nothing had yet taken root. The soil was rich and had lain untouched for years. The wind was not powerful enough to lift the grass seeds to such heights. The birds were smaller birds and did not take seeds up there. With no natural predators, they stayed close to the surface.

I grabbed onto the window frame, stiffened my arms, and looked upwards. As high as I could see, the wall had no end. I could barely see the small silver thread of the tube that carried the ball of sunlight. In another hour, the ball would be at the Twilight Wall, directly above those still there. Once reached, it would begin its twelve-hour journey back to Sunrise with the aperture only open one quarter. It would be nighttime on the ship with a full moon above.

I turned. Brehm lay stretched out over three seats and presumably sleeping. Dan was looking through a black notebook.

"Should this be difficult?" I asked.

"No, not terribly so. Once I get into the computer, I can set up the passwords and create an abbreviated home screen with everything you need. The computers run everything here and rarely need human intervention to operate. Not needed and unwarranted. I believe the weather system needs just a little tweaking, and everything will work out right."

"Will computers last a long time?" I asked.

He paused before he answered. He looked at the interior of the shuttle, out the window, into the land beyond. "That's not the question I thought you would ask. I would like to say the computers will run indefinitely. Believe it or not, the computers do not control the whole weather system. They work to keep the ambient temperature steady, the wind, and the rain. But mostly, it's all a series of convection and wind currents. Once they have started it in motion, it takes a lot to stop it."

For as close as we were, we still had a short while to go before the wall—about ten minutes. I leaned back in the corner, letting my arms rest on both sills.

"They designed them to withstand anything but have never been put to the test of time. There's no way they could have tested for this scenario. These are the new holographic drives. They have made the system with two or three backups running simultaneously with the main system. I guess they feel that redundancy is the best thing. It was their belief that if one of these failed, there would be enough warning to install a new one. With us being out here, there is no way we could go somewhere and get new ones. We have all we have, as you've heard so many times before."

"So, if these computers don't work, we die?"

"No, years ago, we disengaged everything but the primary computer. We were holding them on standby, not running them, to save them for when needed."

"Is the primary failing now? Should we engage another?"

"Perhaps when we are all gone, and you have lived many years, you may engage the backup. The primary is still fine."

* * *

When the shuttle stopped at the station on the indigo road, I could see no further than the terraces and apartments right above us. We were so close to the wall that it was all that was there. Brehm stirred when he felt the shuttle settle. There were a few small clicks beneath our feet as it locked itself in place. Had this place been bustling with people, it would've left as soon as we stepped off. Now, it waited for our return.

Brehm took in the view for a moment on the platform. Dan went downstairs, and I followed. Brehm caught up, and we three walked side-by-side.

It was quiet here.

Before we got to the building, Brehm held his hand out cautiously. I looked at him and then back at the buildings before us.

"This isn't right," Dan whispered. "Even with a degradation of the buildings, there should be no way any part of this building would be open to the elements."

And then I noticed it. The door was slightly ajar.

"Of all the abandoned buildings here, someone chose this specific one to break into."

"Hardly random at all," said Brehm.

"True," said Dan, looking up and down the rows of buildings. "This is the only one that seems disturbed."

"Don't you think with something so important, they would secure it better?" I asked.

"They had done a lot of the things half-assed. They were probably waiting to get back to earth before they worked on major security. It is a big ship." He looked to the left and right. "There are literally millions of buildings in this city."

"This is true," Dan uttered. "Thirty-six kilometers straight up to the other side. Times that by pi, and we have a city one kilometer wide and almost one hundred and fourteen around."

Brehm went to the door and nudged it open with his foot. It was quiet.

"Are there other things housed in this building?" Brehm asked Dan.

"There are several systems housed here. Now, I can say the weather system is the most important. There are computers here that control the flow of water from the Twilight Wall to the Morning Wall. It vaporizes the water and sends it back to us in the form of clouds."

"Is that what is wrong with the weather?" I asked. "Something blocking the water from going back and forth?"

"I don't think so," said Dan. "It may be something simple, but I doubt it. As I said, they tried to make these things as easy as possible. The more working parts you have, the more chances of failure. If you have heat at one end of the tube, it creates convection, a stirring of the air currents, that brings the water in the form of clouds to the other end. At this end, it will condense back to a liquid, and we send it back down to the reactor. By recycling the water, they could have fountains that always have fresh water. The swimming pools don't need harsh chemicals and are drained and refilled every day."

Brehm cleared his throat. "I remember on Earth they tried to make man-made structures that could change the course of superstorms that met with disastrous results. They should just let nature do it on its own."

"They have done that here," Dan said, stopping him with an arm. "This is a controlled environment. If they want more wind or more rain, they fiddle with the controls and turn up the flow of water. If they want a drier climate, they turn it down. I heard a rumor that XD07 would be a desert. They were making an ark for desert wildlife."

Nothing looked out of place in the foyer. There were offices here behind glass doors. The names were long and scientific in nature. I tried to read them but gave up due to their complexity. With Dan leading the way, we went upstairs, checking for anything else amiss, and eventually made it to the fifth floor.

Walking down the hallway, we encountered broken glass on the floor.

"Well, this is not surprising." Dan shook his head.

"Damn, just shows you the lengths they will go to."

The shattered glass lay beneath our feet.

Brehm looked around the room and chuckled. "I expected everything to be in shambles. If they would take a blunt object to the door, why save the computers?"

"I am sure whoever did this realized that we would need the computers in the long run."

\* \* \*

Dan tapped the screen twice, and many icons came up. He selected one. After several charts and colored graphs appeared on the screen, he stood back. He turned to me and smiled.

"There is a lot going on here. The simple ebb and flow I was telling you about sometimes is not so simple. Sally, I thought this would be an easy learning exercise, but unfortunately, Anderson had other ideas."

"Anderson?" Brehm asked.

"He was in here last. There is a record of everybody who has ever used this terminal. Anderson was here multiple times." He brought up a directory and looked down the list. "Actually, in the last three years, he's been the only one here."

"There's no way there could be anybody else?"

"No, they could not bypass several layers of security that he had to go through. We have voice recognition, facial recognition, and finally, a password that only he would know. Why he would do this is something I do not understand."

"It cannot be that bad."

"It is. For some reason, he is trying to control the weather, um, to change it somehow. For what purpose? I do not understand."

Dan backed out and was on the main screen again. He tapped an icon.

"Sally, I will deputize you. Stand here and tap here. It will take a recording of your voice. All you must do is read what is on screen. We will leave, and you can choose your password." He stopped me as I was about to speak. "Your password is something unique to you and you alone. Make it something you will remember, and if you wish to change it later, you may. We will go back downstairs. When you're done, just yell down to us."

"Gotcha," I said. I looked at Brehm and smiled.

I heard their footfalls receding, glass crunching on their feet, and took a breath before tapping the command on the screen. I stated my name and read the statement about a quick brown fox jumping over a lazy dog. I stood still for a moment concentrating on the little red dot in the display's center. When it finished, the computer asked me for my password.

So much had happened in the few years I had been there. The names of several types of food came to mind: people I have known, places I have seen, none of these seemed fitting. Other words popped into my head: swine, boar, hunt, X-ray Delta 05. I struggled for a moment, trying to remember my aunt's name. Finally, I settled on a childhood friend—someone I had not seen in a while.

"Miss Priscilla," I said. I paused for a moment with my hand poised over the erase button. The little doll was a memory I had rarely revisited.

With a sigh, I pulled my hand back from the screen.

"Brehm, Dan," I yelled down the stairwell.

"Yo, yo, yo," said Brehm in his cheerful voice.

When they came back, I was leaning on the terminal. "Good to see that you're still logged in. I want to walk you through some procedures, nothing fancy, and we'll go from there. Please note that anything you do here will have world-altering consequences once you step outside the door."

Brehm punched me lightly on the shoulder. "Way to go, kiddo."

I smiled at him as Dan began his lesson.

\* \* \*

When we finished my lesson, Dan put a lock on the computer so no one else could use it from this location. The lesson lasted just over an hour, and when we exited the building, it was well past twilight into nightfall. The sun globe was now a light-blue orb 120 kilometers away at the Twilight-end.

\* \* \*

We walked quietly to the shuttle platform until Dan spoke up.

"When they designed this place, they did not design it, with one terminal being the one and only spot where they gave these commands. There are four known ones, and I know personally of a fifth one that is very hard to get to. If other ones are compromised as well, then I believe Anderson is trying to sabotage the ship."

"To what end?" Brehm asked.

"Well, I don't know." Dan stood there and shook his head. "If everything is running smoothly, why destroy the harmony? We may go for another twenty or thirty years with no disruption. They designed the system to literally never fail. Why, then, would somebody purposely do this? It would destroy our food supply and our warm habitat. I mean, let's face it, fifteen or twenty degrees in any direction, hotter or colder, would snuff us out quickly if we didn't prepare. If there is more and more rain, we would have a bad harvest and could ruin a whole year of crops."

"Anderson is trying to snuff us all out at once?" I asked.

"It would look that way. He may be tired of living and wants to take everyone down with him."

Brehm sighed and looked at us.

"Well, I guess we must find him before he can do anything else."

"Sally, it may be a few hours before we can check the other terminals. There are two on this end and two on the other end. It may be a little dangerous. I am not sure what lengths this person will go through. We can drop you off at the hotel on our way by. We've locked into the computer and finished your lesson."

"Well, I can go with you." The thought of being left out of something this important made me feel upset. I didn't want to wake up in the morning and go out into the fields only to find out what happened through rumor and speculation.

I pouted, and I think this persuaded them to let me go.

"Brehm, watch her. If anything happens, we must protect her at all costs."

* * *

At the second, third, and fourth terminals, it was all the same. They cleverly broke into the buildings and destroyed what he needed.

Brehm, on an impulse, brought up the surveillance archives. The cameras were motion censored, and so there were a few video clips. One of the first, dated three years ago, distinctively showed a white streak in the air. We had to watch it three or four times before Dan realized what it was.

"That was Lawrence," he said, pointing at the monitor. "You see, through here he tucked his wings in and right here, at the very end, he begins to unfurl them for a flap." We all smiled at each other.

"That damn bird will outlive us all," Dan chided, and we chuckled. "I'm not sure how old he was when Uncle Butch brought him on the ship, but that species lives long lifespans."

In a video capture recorded three months later, a man is walking down the street with his head down. With no other discernable features, it could've been anybody. He was not scoping out the buildings. Just somebody going from one destination to another.

The next one was the person breaking into the building in broad daylight. They were bold. Tool-bag by their side, they set it down and immediately began to pry the door open. It took time, but they did it.

Brehm sped up the video. Just over an hour's worth of work with the right tools.

Brown ball cap with a handkerchief tucked up underneath to protect their neck from the sun, overly large shirt, baggy pants, and work boots, which were common on the ship.

"There is nothing here that tells us who it is," said Brehm, peering close at the screen. "He works the whole time, never once looking for the camera or in any direction so we can get a profile. See here? As he's turning here, he lines up to give us the perfect shot of his face, yet his arm comes up and with it the fabric of his shirt. He stretched right at the proper time. This is very frustrating, to say the least."

"You think he knew?" Asked Dan.

"If he knows how to get into the building, he knows their surveillance on the outside and the inside. Here, though, his movements are so, I don't know." he stood back and rubbed his fingers through his hair. "It's like he choreographed it. In every single shot, his features remain hidden. The wind does not blow the handkerchief, so we can see the color of his hair. Even though there is nothing covering his face at any moment, we cannot see his features at all. It would be painstakingly slow, but if I had the outline of the nose, I could go through the archives of everybody we have onboard to check and see."

"And still we have nothing."

"Yep, not a damn thing."

"I may be able to get his height, but even then, if he has been so deceptive so far, then manipulating his height with the hat or boots would make it pointless."

I yawned. Not that the thrill of finding out the identity of this person was boring, but it was getting late. It shocked me to see that the clock read almost midnight.

"Send these to Brandon. We will look over them in the morning and see what we can do from there. Sally, I thank you."

I nodded.

"Please, I ask that you do not mention our findings to anyone. There are few who know what we're doing. We must find the guy. We must make sure he does not do this anymore."

Again, I nodded my understanding.

Lena was very excited when I got back home. I sat down with her after my shower, and we talked. She was a little upset. I had put myself in danger even though I had reassured her several times that the culprit was not there any longer.

We kissed and held each other, and although I wanted more, it had been a long day. I fell asleep holding her.

* * *

Dan pulled me aside the next afternoon.

"Sally, we could not discern who was in the videos. As much as I want to, I must say I still have no idea. Others are considering it. Everett, the military captain, has a background in intelligence. He has become incredibly useful in this; however, it is still the same.

"We have one terminal that Anderson may use. It's up to the Hub."

This really piqued my interest.

"You want me to go?" I asked.

"No, I would really like for you to stay here. However, there is a lot at stake, and if in time, if in years to come, the ones down here break down, then you will have to use the one up there."

I could barely hide the excitement in my eyes.

"Brehm is taller. He went to look for a suit his size, and we should be able to find a suit for you down at the Twilight Wall."

"I don't think I would fit the one I came here with."

"Yes, definitely." He looked me up and down. "You have grown."

"When do we leave?"

"We can leave now."

* * *

Brehm met us at the station at the Twilight Wall. In a side room were many suits still in their original packaging.

"Slip these on," he said, handing me a bundle. "Skullcap first and then work your way downward. They are straightforward and secure automatically. We'll get your tanks when you're done."

I found that the pieces were too bulky to slip over my work clothes.

"Oh yeah, you shouldn't do it that way," Brehm said as he noticed me struggling. "Things bind up for guys and make us walk funny. We get parts pinched. I'm sure it's kind of the same for women. There's a changing stall back that way."

It fit much better with the extra clothes off. The top went on first and bottom afterward. When the two ends touched, there was a little movement, and they sealed tightly on their own accord. Each boot did the same. I waited on the gloves for now.

There was a small screen nestled into the fabric on top of the wrist. When I tapped it with my fingertip, it came on. It pictured the suit, and there were blinking red outlines around the hands and the head. These would shut off when I put the helmet and gloves on.

When I walked out, it was good to see that they were both dressed. They both look quite dashing, wearing the black skullcap.

Brehm took a set of tanks down off the wall and motioned me to turn around. Worked into the upper body of the spacesuit was a harness. Strong magnets kept them in place. All he had to do was to hook it on my back and run the tube down to the side. It connected and sealed just above my hip. I thought they would be heavier than they were.

"Now, reach behind you," Brehm said, standing in front of me. "No, with your other hand. You feel that? That's a spider line. Each set of tanks come with them as a standard piece of equipment. Pull it out just a little." I did so easily. "If needed, just repeat the motion. At the end is a magnetic, nonconducting 'D'-clip. If you tumble, just toss it out, and chances are it'll grab on something to keep you secure. Once it's out, hit the tab on your sleeve terminal, and it will retract."

When I looked at the screen terminal, there was a counter which read 0.5 meters. I tapped that part of the screen, and the spider line zipped back into its harness. The surprised look on my face must have been comical. I felt like I had just been 'goosed.'

Brehm slapped me on the shoulder.

"Say, for instance, you are up out of the atmosphere. The suit will initiate airflow when you seal it completely tight. It will recognize that you need air, and it will come on automatically. When you have the suit on down here, and there is breathable oxygen around you, the tanks fill themselves. It takes about twenty minutes from start to finish."

Dan stepped forward. "This saves the workers a lot of time. They would come back down to the surface for their lunch breaks and then head back up with a full tank."

"What about going to the bathroom?" I asked.

They both stopped and looked at me.

"I… went already. I was just curious."

"Good," Brehm chuckled. "That's always best."

We could have taken the shuttle all the way up, but we opted to take the magnetic elevator. They told me before about buildings in our past that would have tons and tons of cables pulling the square elevator cars up and down. That would not work here. We had about eighteen kilometers to go up. A cable that length would be too heavy to lift itself and would undoubtedly snap. They based these elevators upon catch and release of magnetics. The magnets above would catch the car while the ones below released. Working in unison, it was smooth.

After we got in, we put our gloves and helmets on. The magnetic elevator had scanners and would let no one travel above a certain altitude without being sealed up—a safety precaution. The makers did not want you traveling up and imploding when you reached zero atmo.

After a certain point, Dan brought a finger up to his face-plate.

"We need to maintain radio silence. If we communicate and someone else is in range, then they will hear us."

"How far do these transmit?" Brehm whispered.

Dan held up two fingers, signifying two kilometers. We nodded.

* * *

The airlock was open. This far up, there was no need to have the room pressurized unless people constantly maintained it. Seeing the gaping hole in the Hub's smoothness was the first sign that someone was there.

A man hovered over a lit consul. His suit was a deep blue, that of an engineer. He was busy for a moment and must have seen us drift in. He turned his head and looked at us. Dan was the first to speak.

"Anderson, what the hell are you doing?"

"I… I was wondering if anybody would show up at all? How are you doing, Williams?" his voice came to my ears through my headset in the helmet.

"Why are you doing this? Anderson, they set this stuff so we cannot mess with it."

"I'm not the one who changed it." he looked back and forth between the three of us. He nodded to me before he turned his attention back to Dan. "Oh no, someone has been tampering with the terminals, and I am correcting everything. They erased the backups, all of them. You should see the drives that have nothing on them. When they did this, they went deep. I think I have it almost back to the way it was before." He corrected himself, "Then I will make an external backup and keep it secure down on the surface."

"Move away from the terminal, please." Dan did not raise his voice. He lifted a hand, palm outward, but made no other motion. "You're not tweaking it, Anderson; you're putting the whole thing out of whack. For all it's worth, just a simple nudge here and there, and you screw everything up."

"It's in the process of resetting itself, Dan." Anderson put a lot of emphasis on Dan's name. "It's going through the cycles, and in a short time, everything will be back to where it was." Anderson smiled. "I am not the one you are looking for." He reached out a few times as he was talking and touched the screen.

"Anderson, stop tapping the screen. Move away. Please."

Brehm grabbed a tether. He pulled himself a little closer and to the side.

"Dan, you just don't get it, do you? At the main terminals, the weather is not the only thing you can access. When I say you can access everything from these terminals, I literally mean everything we have. Working the right channels, a person can get to not only data on the Samuel Drives, but the information regarding where we are. The navigational program is at the very core of what is here. For someone to slip in, for some variables to be re-coded, which has been done recently, takes a lot of expertise." Still, he did not stop tapping the screen. "There is someone else sneaking around. Using the weather to get to another door. And it is not me," he paused, looked at us, and continued. "I'm on your side."

"You broke into places and tampered where you should not be."

"What? No, I only began my search a few weeks ago. Someone accessed and meddled with the data years ago. When I say years ago, I'm talking about right after we first got here, the big event, and that kinda leads us to several questions. Questions that nobody has asked yet. Why are we out here, and more importantly, how did we get here?"

Dan shrugged his shoulders. The motion was barely perceptible underneath the suit. "I really do not understand."

"Operator error, computer malfunction, or, I've come up with a new one; was it somebody's intent? I have come up with several possibilities of who on the ship would want to be a way out here and nowhere else."

"That's just ridiculous."

"Is it so far-fetched? You, of all people, should be rational enough. Just humor me for a moment. What if someone was trying to get away from something in their past? What if our being stranded here is because of one individual's intervention? Was someone working on the inside trying to stop our program from going home? Are, somehow, the rogue nations still upset from the events of the war. It's been over a very long time, but sometimes the slap in the face may still sting. What better way to get back at us than to destroy, or incapacitate, one of mankind's crowning achievements?"

Dan shook his head. "The programming required takes time. The boarding of passengers started just days before we left. No one can simply just get on-board, get access to the computers, reconfigure them, and act as if nothing happened."

"What if they never left? Stacy has always been on board." he then looked directly at me. "Not that she had anything to do with it. What if there was a stowaway from a while back? They could've worked on it for months, years, as they prepped '05. Perhaps not everybody left the ship when they were designated to."

I heard Dan scoff. "They accounted for everyone. We had to go through all the security to get here. They have records of who was here working, and those who left. If there were any discrepancies, they would've searched the ship."

Anderson seemed distracted for a moment as he tapped the screen.

"It's a big ship. If a group of five can stay hidden on Rada, or when Hudson laid low on Renée's ship, believe me, they can do it here. I mean, look at the size of this place. Lately, I've been watching everybody. When I say everybody, I mean *everybody* on board the ship. I am good with faces. I'll find the one."

Again, I saw Dan shrug his shoulders.

"Or perhaps a different angle to look at. Do I have to do the thinking for everyone? Someone found a new technology that can send the ship almost anywhere in the universe. They've expanded the spiral stairway, making the steps bigger. Perhaps they wanted a big show to impress everybody, and this may have been just a trial run. They will work it for the first time, possibly, on the ship as big as 05, to either get rid of somebody or to get a point across. Sometimes in mankind's past when they would sacrifice someone in a high office, Caesar comes to mind, to drive a message home to those who have survived."

Still, his hands continued to work the terminal.

"Anderson, you're stalling, wasting oxygen."

Brehm drifted a little closer.

"That still explains nothing," said Brehm. His voice, deeper than Dan's or Anderson's, was heavy.

"A back way to get in is through the weather system. Once I get the system to reboot, there will be time where I can go in and find out who has been here. This part of the program leaves the data dump of everything accessed. I compare this list to the list of people supposed to be in here, and I will find out who has tampered with the computer."

"Rebooting the whole system is just plain stupid, putting it bluntly."

"There is no harm in rebooting the system. Once I figured out this is what we were supposed to do, it's only taken me about three days. It will take about another three days for the sequence to run to its course, and everything will return to normal. The rain shower that afternoon was a little irresponsible of me."

The whole time, he continued to touch the display.

"Anderson, I must tell you that you need to stop."

"Williams," he chuckled dryly. "Back in the day, you may have had authority over me. Here, now, you have nothing. Go back to the surface. I'll be there when I'm done. I'll talk with Brandon. I'm not tampering with the system. I'm restoring it."

"I have asked you to stop."

"No, not going to."

"You have no idea what you're doing."

"Oh, but I do."

"Brehm?" Dan made a motion towards Anderson.

Brehm tugged hard on a tether. Bringing his knees up, he hit Anderson on the side.

"NO!" In a weightless dance, Anderson spun away from the terminal. "Just... just a few more. Dammit!" Brehm carried forward by momentum, brought his arms around to get a grip on Anderson's bulky suit.

Brehm had him, but the man was quick. With a push, he slipped downward. Brehm reached for him but only got the sides of his helmet. He could not hang on. He rotated a half circle and planted his feet on the door frame. Pushing hard, he caught up with Anderson and gave him another bear hug.

"Come on, guy," he grunted.

"No, you don't understand... these things have... to finish. Once set in motion, we must follow through. Dammit Dan, get... this guy off me and listen to reason."

He could not contain Anderson. They had drifted down to the bulkhead, and with his feet together beneath him, he sprang upward. I leaped, reaching for them, and grabbed Anderson's feet. My momentum gave them a slight spin, and we hit the bulkhead away from the door.

"Slippery little guy," Brehm whispered.

With a second shove, we spun away and hit the far bulkhead. Anderson was reaching out, trying to find anything he could hold on to. Tethers drifted near, but he could not grab them. Brehm tried to pin his arms down to his side. The suits were thin and versatile, designed for movement in working environments, here they hampered Brehm. He was tall with long arms, but Anderson moved around too much.

When we hit the far bulkhead again, Anderson squirmed and again tucked his feet beneath him. I drifted down. I could see the look of exertion on his face behind the glass. With all he had, Anderson kicked back. I grabbed his foot, and his momentum carried us all away from the wall. We went through the first door of the airlock. Anderson flung his arms and legs outward. Brehm was too busy to notice. We hit the last door of the airlock hard.

Anderson stopped.

I looked up. Brehm was drifting back. With nothing to hold on to, there was only the empty vacuum expanse of the ship. His arms flailing, his feet kicking. There is nothing he could do.

"Williams, Sally, I need some help," he said in desperation.

Dan shoved Anderson to the side. Reaching behind his back, he tugged at the D-ring to the spider lines. Securing it to a tether, he jumped after Brehm. It was a bad jump. He could not get the full force he needed.

I watched. Dan was just not fast enough. He would run out of cable. I looked around, and without hesitation, I hooked my D-ring on Dan's cable. I grabbed a metal frame of the outer airlock. I squatted, and with one massive thrust, went after them.

"Dan, I'm coming right behind you," I gave him forewarning. For a few seconds, he and I were side-by-side.

It was only when his line became taut that I felt the hum of my own line being drawn out. When I grabbed Brehm, we were helmet to helmet.

"Hey, you," he said, his arms keeping a tight hug around me.

A beep. We were at fifty meters already.

"Grab your line and give it to me. Hook it somewhere. On my line." His arm let me go as he reached behind himself.

"The other side! The other side! To your right!" This made me smile. I remembered the lesson he gave me just an hour ago on the surface.

He grabbed the line and pulled out a half meter.

"I can't reach yours," he said

"I will hold it." I looked at him then, his blue eyes and the scruffiness of his chin. He smiled a weak smile.

There was a second beep. We were at one hundred meters.

"Sally, you cannot hold me. I've got too much mass. Too much girth," he chuckled.

"Ah, you think your broad shoulders will get you in trouble again? I got this. I helped kill a boar. I have the strength."

"If you wrap it around your wrist, I'll likely rip your arm off."

"No, they designed the suits stronger than that."

"You breach up here. It'll be bad."

The third beep. We had only fifty meters to go before I ran out of spider line.

Snatching the cable from his hand, I wrapped it around my wrist three times and hooked the D-ring back to his cable.

"We got this," I said, looking into his eyes. "Today is not your day."

He nodded.

"It wasn't his fault," he said. "We had a tussle, and things happened."

"Ha, don't get all sappy on me," I quipped.

"Sally, I "

My cable ran out. Brehm's momentum ripped him from my grip. My arms and legs dangled in front of me.

"Reel it back in to slow yourself down." My fingers tested my grip on his cable. Holding it tightly, I reached back and held it to my chest.

I could work my own controls, to reel myself back in, but it would only hasten, not prevent him, from slowing down. He tapped the controls on his forearm.

"It's a small motor. It's not designed for this."

"Do it, Brehm."

"Sally." It was Dan speaking behind me. "If you wrap it too tightly, it will rip your arm off."

"The suit is strong; it will hold me."

"He has way too much mass for you to stop so quickly. Unwind it from your arm…"

"Sally," Brehm said over Dan. "Let it go. You can catch me on the other side."

"Brehm, you gotta trust me."

"It's not a matter of trust. How do you think I would feel if I didn't stop, but carried your stump with me? Sally unwind it. Twenty-five to go."

"I… I," I unwound it from my arm then.

"TIME!" he yelled.

When the D-ring pulled from my grasp, it went with such force that for a second, I thought it ripped my hand off inside the suit.

I brought my hand back, shook a few times, and tried to feel if anything was broken.

"Well, you straightened me out a little," there was a touch of humor in his voice. "I felt the tug. Are you okay?"

"Ow," I said somberly. "And that's putting it mildly." It hurt to move my shoulder, but I could bring my hand close to my chest, and I squeezed each finger. I could feel the pressure on each one. I made a fist and clenched it tight. Pain shot down my arm.

"The spider lines are too thin, little darling. They would have cut through your suit and your hand like a cheese cutter."

\* \* \*

He fell away. His trajectory took him with the tube that housed the sun.

"I'll make it to the far side," he said. "You slowed me down some, so when I get there, the landing will not be as rough. It may take me a day or so, but I'll meet you back at the hotel. We'll have a drink."

"Dammit, Brehm."

"We'll find him again, Sally," said Dan. I felt a tug and knew he was pulling his line back in.

Brehm was little more than a speck against XD05.

"The sun will beat me to the far wall. When I pass it, the globe will come back through and only at twenty-five percent strength. Nighttime. It won't be strong enough to fry me. I'll leave my cable out, and as I get close to the end, I'll try to lasso something. I gotta tell ya, though, this really sucks."

It was the last we heard from him that day.

* * *

The fight had left Anderson. When I got back to the airlock, he floated in space, and I could've sworn his suit was empty had it not been for subtle movements, a turning of the head, a shifting of the arm. He held himself steady between the two tethers.

"I will go now," he said, holding his hands up. "What's done is done. I think I got what I needed. Dan, I am not the culprit here. I was just looking for the back door they used to get into the navigation system. I did not wish"

I pushed off the far wall with all the strength I had. I hit him with such force that when he struck the panel, his eyes rolled to the back of his head. He spasmed a few times and then remained still.

Dan cursed at me, but did nothing to interfere.

He still breathed.

"Sally, you cannot do this. Help me get him to the lift. We must get him to the surface."

"He hurt Brehm."

"Brehm is still fine. We must get down to the surface and let them know what happened. With any luck, they can send out a group of people, and I'll be able to find them. He was right. With twilight just an hour away, he will glide by the moon, and we can pick him up. We fully charged the suits. He will have air for almost two days. When they get in close proximity, we will ping his suit and find its location. Sally, there is nothing more we can do here."

* * *

In the lift, Anderson and Dan faced the proper way. A sign with big letters and an arrow told us which way gravity would pull us as we descended. I hung in the air with my feet pointed toward the ceiling. I stared him down for several moments. He looked at me once or twice, trying to reciprocate, but then looked away. He could not match my gaze. I tapped his helmet with mine a few times. When I felt the inevitable pull, I twisted and settled with my feet first.

* * *

Still in his suit, helmet off, Dan keyed the button on the terminal of the shuttle.

"Is anyone listening?"

The white lights on the roof lit the interior of the shuttle. He checked the radio once or twice to make sure everything was operational. The signal would just not reach as far as we needed it. There was so much left of the ship unfinished. Communication was one they would finish back at Sol.

Powerful magnets carried the small ten-man shuttle down the ribbon at 100 kilometers per hour but would go no faster.

I sat across from Anderson, elbows on my knees. Helmet beside me with the gloves tucked inside, and I looked at the bruising on my hand. The first two fingers were still numb.

"Hello, is there anyone listening back at the hotel?"

"Brehm was a good friend, you know?" I whispered. Inside the suit, my foot would not be still, and shook with nervousness. "We did a lot together."

"What Dan said was true," he said, as if he were pleading a case. "I mean, Brehm will have nothing to do for a day or so, but we can still get to him. It's not all lost yet." His words were shallow and empty.

I squeezed my hand again until the knuckles turned white

"You had no right to do what you are doing. I'm sure there's a way to go through and find out who was on the damn computer without resetting the whole thing."

"There were other ways that are more time-consuming. But I could not find the information I needed. If you could only understand the layers of security they have in this thing, then you would understand."

"Is there a reason why we need to know this? We're here. We have been here. We will be here for a very long time. If you have this information, are you going to radio back to some part of the galaxy to see if we can hopefully find someone who is listening?"

"The person who did this to us is still here. It may be somebody we see every day. I do not know."

"But you said you had the information."

"I had part of the information. I was working on getting more when Brehm grabbed me. It still sits up there. Another ten minutes, I could have had it."

Dan was still trying to get someone on the radio. "We have a few more minutes till the transition point. Should be able to pick them up afterward."

"Are you going to run?" I asked.

"To where?" his laugh is dry, and he shrugged his shoulders. "I do not need to run." When he looked at me, his eyes seemed exhausted. "If the people I'm trying to find are still on board the ship, then they will not want me to speak because everybody will be angry at them."

I studied him for a moment and looked down at the floor.

The transition was coming up. Completely automated, it took just a moment for us to get to the Twilight-side.

* * *

"This is Dan Williams. Can anybody hear me?"

"*Hey, Dan. Yes, we can read you. What's up?*"

"I have a bit of a problem. We were at the Morning-side. We had to go to the Hub." he looked at Anderson. "While we were there, Brehm drifted off. When we tried to save him, it accelerated his speed slightly, and we could not retrieve him. At this moment, he is above us outside the tube."

"*You're shitting me?*"

"I wish I were. We must send people up to rescue him. He'll make it through the night, but we need to find him before sunset tomorrow."

"*Aw, geez, okay, copy that. I'll get the word out and will get people up there. Everything okay on your end?*"

"Yes, tell Brandon that I wish him to be at the platform when we get there. About forty-five minutes."

Anderson sat forward with his hands on his knees, and his head bowed.

"I do not think Brandon had anything to do with it. Director Porter and his family are too high on the pyramid. I believe this is somebody mid-level trying to make a name for themselves."

"You should be safe then." Dan ran his fingers through his hair. "I will tell Brandon and no one else."

"Thank you," Anderson said with all sincerity.

* * *

Anderson took the steps down to the platform, with Dan right behind him. They had taken just a few when the door closed again. I sat at the controls and strapped myself in. They had the most peculiar looks on their faces as the shuttle accelerated past.

* * *

I stopped at the 3009 terminal, the last station before the arc upward.

Looking up at the moon, I knew I had time. I took the suit off and used the bathroom. Methodically, I checked everything as I began to suit back up. Taking my old tanks off, I replaced them with new ones fully charged. I knew the Brehm said they would be full automatically, but I didn't trust them completely, so I grabbed a whole new suit. I drank just a bit of water before I put my helmet and gloves on. My stomach rumbled.

I stopped the shuttle one kilometer from the Hub. The door opened, and I floated out. I pressed the key on the outer hull to return the shuttle. I kicked back a little as the door closed. The rigging up the wall was such that I could go hand-in-hand away from the track.

"Brehm?" I ask tentatively. It would be nearly impossible to have Brehm's arc in a straight line from one end to the other.

There was no reply. He was not in range yet.

It was beautiful here. Quiet, serene, the curve below was less pronounced. I looked above me into the sides and could see the gentle blueness of the moonbeams. Following the running lights of the ribbon back to the surface, I could see the area of Hotel Libra. Beyond that, I could barely make out the lights of the transition point. Beyond that, there was darkness.

"Brehm? You there?"

Of course, he would not be here yet. Now, he probably had not even made the transition.

The suits needed some type of beacon or something. A small, flashing light that would help them find people adrift. I pulled on my spider line and flung the D-ring onto the metal. It clicked and held me tight. I did not wish to slowly drift down to the surface as I waited.

"I will wait here for you, Brehm."

Here, where no one could see me, or hear me, where I could not wipe my tears away, I cried.

* * *

The light woke me.

One hundred and twenty kilometers away, the ball of prisms and mirrors began its daily journey down the glass tube. In ten hours' time, the place where I hovered would be unbearable to a human being, suit, or no suit.

My right arm had drifted upward to a comfortable position as I slept. When I moved it, I screamed in pain. As if my shoulder had caught on fire. The feeling had come back to my hand. I wiggled and flexed my fingers, just to be sure.

I checked my gauge, and by the time I had hovered there waiting and watching, I had used just one-quarter of my oxygen. It was lower than I wanted, but not critical yet. I still had a few hours.

"Brehm? Brehm, can you hear me?"

I looked down at the tube, but there was no movement.

*"Who is this?"* came a feminine reply. It wasn't Brehm's voice, but somebody else's. *"Shhhh, quiet people, I have someone new."*

"This, um, this is Sally," I replied. I looked around but could see nobody. "Who is this?" I asked.

*"Everybody, Sally's up here with us,"* she said to others as they relayed the message. *"This is Jen. A bunch of us came out well before sunrise to get situated. Where are you at?"*

"I'm up here." I realized that against the immense backdrop of the Twilight Wall that I would be hard to see.

*"Can't see you. Can you wave or something?"*

I waved my good arm frantically. My short spider line grew taut and brought me back.

*"Nope, I still cannot see you. Is there anything near you? Are you near some kind of landmark or something? Hold on a second. People, I'm talking."*

"I am close to the indigo road. Route 1, I guess. It leads down to Hotel Lima." I still couldn't see anybody.

*"Whoa, how far are you from the Hub?"* Jen asked.

"I stopped the shuttle about a kilometer from the Hub and got out. I figure I could see him at that distance. He didn't have much of an arc when he drifted. It was on this side on the Morning Wall where he drifted off."

*"She says she's about a kilometer from the Hub. I don't think there is anybody with her. Sally, we have about twenty people scattered around. The suits have a one-kilometer distance for the radios. We have a pretty big net down here. Everyone's a little lower than you are. Is there anybody with you?"*

"No, I've been up here all night."

*"No, she says she's alone. How's your suit doing, sweetie?"*

"Um, oxygen is good. Seventy-four percent left. The battery hardly shows being used. Well above the green line."

*"Good, very good. We haven't heard a peep from him all night. He's probably conserving his battery pack until he gets closer. We thought about heading back down to the Morning Wall and pushing off even faster than he. This would give us a little faster advantage, and if the tube was much longer, even with this little advantage, we would be able to eventually overtake him, but we didn't think we had the time."*

"What are we going to do, then?"

*"We're going to spend the day and wait and pray. If I don't get him*

*on the radio, then we'll see if somebody else can. Every few moments, we will call out and listen. Jaughn said he found a device years ago when he was looking for bottles. There's some optical equipment he told them about located in the foxtrot kim-two. It's something the designers had used when they were building this thing that will detect anomalies. The computer can scan up from the Twilight Wall and let us know if there's anything out of place."*

"That's good." I breathed a sigh of relief. "Will it be in place soon?"

*"Well, they left town before we did, so we should be good."*

\* \* \*

We waited. I watched the clouds below, the shadows, and the sun as it took its journey.

Every fifteen minutes, I would call out to Brehm.

They passed word around that they had found the device and brought it in place. They were scanning the Twilight Wall. They had found everybody up here who watched, but still no sign of Brehm.

*"It's noon, people,"* Jen's voice came over the radio. *"It will soon be too risky to stay up here."*

"Jen, I gotta piss like nobody's business," I said. "I don't want to leave him. I don't want the only chance of him making it be taken away because I must watch out for sunlight."

*"Sally, they are set up to keep an eye out. The scanner can run for days, weeks if need be, but it's getting too risky for us to stay up here. We cannot stop the sunshine. It will get too dangerous here for us."*

I checked the gauges. Oxygen was half gone. I could jump to the Hub and do a quick switch and stay another night if needed. The problem was my power level. It was near the border of the yellow line. As the sun warmed up, the suit would spend more and more energy trying to keep me cool. I looked up at the tube a kilometer above me. When the sun got that close, I would be in trouble.

"BREHM! BREHM!"

My cry drowned out all others. I tried to keep the desperation from my voice and failed. "I didn't mean for you to die. Forgive me, Brehm. FORGIVE ME! Dammit. Come back to us!"

I did not go then. I stayed there for some time until the movement caught my eye. It was not Brehm drifting in from the tube; it was Jen, nearly weightless, coming up the wall hand over hand.

With her coming so close to me, it cut her connection with the others. I was no longer in range with everyone else.

*"Hey, girl,"*

"Hey," I reached out with my good hand and drew her in. In the backdrop of all the people here, I remembered only speaking with Jen once or twice. She grabbed my suit by the shoulders. Her momentum carried her feet above my head, but she held on.

*"None of us want to lose him. None of us wants to lose anyone. We are all going to ride this out to the end. You have done all that you could do. Do you understand that?"*

I nodded.

*"No, no, don't just simply say you understand. You must know that you put forth every effort possible to avoid this outcome. And you must know that we will not stop. Were things different, I would like to know you wouldn't stop looking for me. If I was floating between here and there, I would take comfort in knowing you have my back. That any moment you will be that hand that reaches out and pulls me to safety."*

I wept then, frustrated once more that I could not wipe my tears away. Jen had to watch me cry. We touched helmets for just a moment, and Jen clung in an awkward hug. When we drifted apart, Jen had tears of her own in her eyes.

*"I didn't know Brehm. I was not part of his circle, but if he was here, he was a good man. If he is who I think is, we played darts last week. You should feel lucky that you spent the time with him you did. Your life is that much richer."*

I nodded again.

Jen unhooked my spider line.

With a tight grip on my shoulder, she pushed off. In a matter of moments, we were outside an airlock at the Hub. In the command center, I requested a shuttle. We could sit in the vehicle, listen and call out to Brehm and still remain shielded from the sun.

"Five minutes till it gets here. You've been favoring that arm. Everything okay?"

"I'm fine," I said without turning.

Jen undid my helmet.

"No, no." I pleaded.

"It's okay. They pressurize the Hub, the other end not so much. Can't have this on if you gotta use the bathroom. Remove the suit. We'll get you a new one."

We had to take it slow. My arm throbbed. Thankfully, we could get the suit off in pieces. The gloves drifted away and were soon followed by the sleeves disconnected at the shoulders. With the front open, I pulled my good arm in like a turtle and gently eased the suit over my bad arm. Damn, it hurt. I wiggled out of the bottom part after I kicked off the wall.

* * *

Jen had a new suit waiting for me when I returned from the bathroom. In the short time, the small motor had pulled in enough breathable oxygen so that my tanks were completely full. I dressed quickly. The pain in my arm flared up, and I winced.

She had taken her helmet off, and her hair was a red mane circling her head.

"I need to go back out," I said, drifting up to her and grabbing my helmet from where I left it.

"You know Sally, we, I am not ready to give up on him. Brehm was a good person as well. I heard nothing bad about him."

"You'll join me then?" I said, working the clamps in place.

"But the place, the tube running from one wall to the other, is no place for someone without proper shielding."

I looked at her and just nodded. "Jen, if it were you or I, we would want the same. Life is a precious thing, even more so here when there are so few of us. We must do everything we can to save him."

She nodded, and I started to put my helmet on when she held up her hand for me to stop.

"I was one of those who wanted you to have children. I am at that age biologically where if I wanted to, I could, and I was heading back home hoping to settle down there and find a husband and have children. At times, some women feel this basic need to have children. It's a yearning, it's a deep desire, and it's a call that is very hard not to answer. I envy you for your decision. Looking at the small picture, I can see how easy it would be to give in to them. Believe me; if I could, we would have dozens of the little heathens running around now. But looking at the big picture, this is a huge machine we live in. It is man-made, and therefore prone to error. If you were to have children and in a hundred or so years, a metal spring snaps, and the whole thing starts a downward spiral, thousands of humans would perish without knowing the reason why."

I looked away. She put her hands on my face and looked into my eyes.

"It was a very brave and strong thing that you have done. It is equally brave you have not given in, and that you live your life, day-to-day, in and amongst the same people who would bend you against your will. A lot of us are behind you in this, and we give you kudos."

I nodded again and could only whisper a silent, "Thank you."

"Now, let's go find him. That bastard owes me a beer. We played darts last week, and he has reneged on his promise. Hard to believe someone like that's a sore loser, eh?"

"I will go," I keyed my mic. I did not wait for her and pulled on a tether. As I drifted, I checked my suit to make sure it was sealed. Satisfied, I turned and landed on the bulkhead feet first. Grabbing the handle to stop me, I keyed the door to the shuttle. I had to wait just a few seconds for her to arrive. Her helmet on, she was ready. I tapped her on the shoulder and smiled.

"Brehm? You there?" I said as soon as we were inside. I tried several more times before we stopped the vehicle on the indigo road, but all I heard was silence.

Homeport, Day 5 - C'mon, lucky number 7's. Baby needs a new pair of shoes.


"Mabel?"

"*Go ahead.*" you could hear the difference in her voice. The stress was taking its toll, and her nerves were on end. She had probably been up for a very long time coordinating everything.

"Team 7 reporting in. We are down to the surface, Twilight Wall, outside of the housing building. It appears to be undamaged. Still some dust, however, not enough to worry."

"*Power?*"

"Power is down ship-wide, except for the Burner. Using the manual keys in three... two... one." There were three of them, each using their own key. They turned perfectly in unison.

"I'll be damned," the expression slipped from his lips. "After all this time, with this corrosion and exposure to the elements, they worked. Reed, Amy, good job. Mabel, we are in. If we had this little trouble getting this far, I foresee no problems from here on in."

"*Do what you do and get that back here.*"

"Shall do. I will keep you posted if there are any changes."

The doors needed persuasion to open. A pry bar they brought with them did just that.

Reed looked at the door. "I was here four weeks ago. Came down the mag-ele, walked the same route I did, and walked right through these doors." He slapped the frame with his hand. "Now, we must resort to this."

Their destination was not far.

Three floors up, they came to the unit that housed the brain of the guidance system. Set on a pedestal, they looked at it beneath the plasti-lite. Reed removed the housing bolts.

"I remember the first ones. Housed in a liquid mix in a container about a half meter deep, they were thousands of thin wafers. The electricity coursed through the liquid, and at the time, they thought it was close to the human brain and its trillions of synapses. Over the years, they condensed them. Quadruple the size and a tenth of the space. Now, we have a shoebox."

Amy paused before she touched the surfaces.

"Should we worry about an electric shock?"

"The ship is dead. The only thing that works is the Burner. Power has been out of here for some time." Needless to say, he touched them with the back of his hand. If he had done it with the palm of his hand, the electric current could have closed his fingers and tightened his grip. He would die grasping the metal. He was cautious, not stupid.

He felt no current, not in the slightest.

Even contained under so much protection, the gel had the color and consistency of tar where once it was as clear and slippery as liquid soap. They reached in and slowly worked it to the top. Raising one corner to break the suction, they coached it free. It fit snugly in the tote they brought.

The gel did not cling to human skin, and he wiped it back into the housing.

They gave one more look around. The bare room held nothing else they needed.

"Kind of anti-climactic."

He shrugged his shoulders.

* * *

The robotic spider-mule waited for them. With no internal power, the mag-ele was down, as were all the shuttles. The team climbed into the tight space, and it carried them up the wall. The RSM was not fast, but it was safe. It kept four points of contact with the ship at all times. By the time they reached the Hub, another team had arrived and was working on returning power to the mag-ele's.

* * *

"First off, I must say I have never claimed to be an expert on shoeboxes," said the tech, looking over the shoebox. "I have used them, but never had to deal with their inner workings specifically. As you can see, there is almost no way I can open it up. Everything is solid-state. Hopefully, it shut down slowly, like a shriveling balloon and not like a bursting balloon. I've never seen ends like this so fragile."

"Will it work again?"

The tech shook his head. "They design these to last for a very long time. Although no one has ever specified how long 'a long time' is. If we can resuscitate these old bones, then it will set the precedence for the rest."

* * *

To say the shoebox 'perked up' was an understatement. They let it soak for two hours in the immersion liquid. From there, they started with the lowest possible electrical setting. The gel became energized. They were like Dr. Frankenstein trying to raise something from the dead. Rather than have one huge massive electrical shock, they did it slowly, coaxing the components that were so long asleep to wake back up.

* * *

In an adjoining room, several techs sat around and waited with extreme patience. Lights turned down, and chatter kept to a minimum; they watched the terminals in sublime anticipation. The hours passed, and still, they waited.

It was as they were getting ready to go to lunch when a terminal gave a slight chirp. Although barely audible, you could have sworn it echoed. They huddled around the screen at first. In an upper corner, the first letters appeared. 'XD05'.

The cheer that went up was deafening.

* * *

The unit was old, to say the least. On a second housing pedestal, they brought one that was identical. Empty of all information, they would back up the original and use the new one as a slave, keeping the master in isolation. Four months ago, the units sat side-by-side. Now a few thousand years separated them.

* * *

The lead tech once again sat before Richard and Mabel.

"What do you need to know?" He asked.

"Who accessed the system last?"

"Sally Weiss. There is nothing major. She logged on to the system and looked up some information on people, basically browsing photographs of individuals who were on the ship. Based on the date and time, she was in her mid-60s. The people she looked up were undoubtedly dead at the time.

"Anyway, after this, she checked out the weather. She increased the precipitation by point 02 percent, the water flow exiting the lake decreased slightly. In the overall grand scheme of things, this would do absolutely nothing. You never really see a difference in things unless you get up into the five percent change. Something as small as this is quite insignificant, a token gesture, pretty much." The technician sat back in his seat. "The evidence shows she suited up and did this several times. Over the course of a few years, she did it about twenty times."

"Why would she have to suit up?" Mabel gave him a quizzical look. "She went up to the Hub to do this?"

"They locked the other computers out. This one terminal located there was only one she had access to."

"What is the last known recorded time from the shoebox?" Richard asked.

"Ah, let me check." The tech looked at his screen. "That is the last time that Sally accessed computers. After that, almost thirty years later, there is a record of a pipe bursting. It may sound trite, but this is one of the main ones, Morning Wall, Western side. For over ten days, it gushed hundreds of liters per hour before the computers realized there was a problem and shut that pipe off. After that, we have spikes in certain gases. There were alarms going off about four-hundred years later because of the decline of water throughout the ship. Other than that, I see little else."

"Could the computers erase data over time?" Mabel asked.

"No, after Sally passed, there is no one else aboard the ship."

"I don't mean that if any human could have erased it. I mean that if it would have done it by itself."

"Ah, I see. No, these systems are newer, and there's no way that any of the data could corrupt itself. If a person goes in, they can manipulate and erase it. With no human intervention, the computers sat idle all those years and recorded only information given to them by their sensors. For some reason, about a hundred years after Sally was at the Twilight Hub, there was a slow build-up of pressure. Point 02 percent for over five years until the seals could no longer contain it. That's what broke the glass. That and the pipe bursting and the decline of water were major events. There are literally millions of bits of information that the computer recorded on a day-to-day basis. The information that we received is invaluable to what we do and how we will plan for ships in the future."

"You could copy over every bit of information, then?" Richard ran his hand through his hair.

"Yes, very little, if anything, was lost."

"We can reconstruct the time-frame of daily lives?"

"A lot of the people did not access the computers. Most were busy with their day-to-day lives and had no need. I do show that there are cases where people accessed buildings that formed a permanent record. There is a listing of who called up shuttles for transportation. Authorization of certain tools and machinery. It is all there, buried under tons of data."

"Thank you," Richard said. "We must look it over."

XD05, Year 10

They held Anderson's trial two days later.

He wanted everybody to hear what happened. He did not want one or two people to judge him; he wanted everybody on the ship to judge him.

The kitchen made a big meal and fed everybody at one time. It was quite something to have everybody together in one place. Usually, there was rotation in the fields or people out doing other things. It reminded me of the first days here or the inquisition that I went through.

From what I could gather from the rumors going around, they found a place to shuttle us to other than here, somewhere in the city. Thankfully, they found a theater in a different kim-two that could hold everybody. We could see him as he stood on stage, and he could present his case without being misunderstood.

It was the most shuttles I had seen being used at one time.

The commander of the troops, Captain Everett, had an actual print out with everybody's name on it. He stood at the door and checked off everybody's name as they came through. Lena, my constant companion, came with me. This always brought the attention of others. Out of pure chance, we sat down just a few seats from Troy. I smiled at him. Not being a smartass, just showing him that even though he had strong beliefs, I showed him no ill will. Then again, he probably took it as being a smartass. He waved back to me with a smile, nonetheless.

When Brandon took the stage, everyone grew quiet.

"As you well know, Anderson asked us to come here today to tell us his side of the story. Dan is here also to provide his insight. When he finished, he asked us all to vote on his being guilty or not guilty in the death of one of our own. Of Brehm, there is still no sign. If he were unconscious and breathing very shallow, the air in his tanks may have carried him through. However, with normal consumption, we do not believe he would have lasted over 20 hours. The suits we have are all maintenance suits, not deep space. The heat from the Burner, if he were close, would have proved fatal. They're not designed to withstand that kind of abuse. From what others have told me, the battery pack would have gone into overdrive trying to keep the suit cool. That alone would have caused it to use the battery up in just over an hour."

The hall was quiet. We all knew this, of course, but it was something else hearing and spoken out loud and affirmed by someone of authority.

In the darkness, I bowed my head. It was my tenth known death aboard the ship. The number just popped into my head, and I was ashamed of myself for keeping count.

"I have no other news," he said, clasping his hands in front of him. Looking to his left, he nodded, and Anderson and Dan came out from behind a curtain.

There were two chairs provided, and they both took seats. With microphones clipped to their clothing, when they spoke, their voices were much louder than Brandon's.

"My name is Anthony Anderson," his voice resonated in the large auditorium. He seemed strong and sure. "And I must tell you, every one of you that I am deeply sorry for what has happened. I did not know Brehm personally; however, I remember him from time to time when our paths crossed in the common areas of the hotel and the ship. I remember that he was always good at a joke or a laugh. We will miss his presence. As with those who went before him, this world will be a lesser place without them.

"I wish to first explain why I was up there at that time," hands folded before him. He had the air of confidence as he spoke. He wore a pressed shirt and ironed pants. A throwback to the clothing we had before the Event. I wondered if he pulled it from storage.

He cleared his throat once, gathering his thoughts before he spoke. "For me, it began with the anomaly with the weather. I have worked with these things before, and I would like to believe I am more in tune than most people with the workings of the ship. I noticed subtle differences in temperature and the wind currents a while ago. On a day I was not laboring in the fields, I chanced a journey to one terminal that is tied directly to the weather. Someone had broken the glass of the door. Understand, if you will, that this was no easy task. It was in a secure office building, and the glass was tempered so the weather could not damage it. If there was unrest, tossing a chair and or hitting it with a hammer would warrant the same result. It was a building to house the government, and they made it so that if a madman came in with a weapon, they would do as little damage as possible. Whoever did this knew what they were doing and knew exactly how to destroy such a glass window.

"They then had access to the computer system that controlled the heart of the ship. It was in their power to slow the burner process down. If they slowed the cycles down by a quarter, it would eventually drop the temperature of the ship. The climate would change, the waters would freeze over, and we would find life here very difficult. To keep warm, we would have to live in suits; however, we have only enough food on hand to last us a month. His tampering would wipe us out without question. Thankfully, he only used these functions to access other areas. A door opens to one room to go to another. This is a double-edged sword because it limited the places he could be and let me know the remaining places where he would be.

"I had to find him." Not reading from notes, he watched us as we watched him. "I searched the other places where he could have accessed the system. At the other terminals scattered throughout the ship, I found evidence he was there. The glass was not always broken, but there was damage.

"When I visited the last place on the surface, finding it the same, I knew he could only be in one place. The Hub, at the center of the ship on the Morning Wall, was his last stand. That is where Dan, Brehm, and Sally found me. I had been there for some time and was working on the code to lock him out. When I worked on the ships back in Homeport, I had access to the highest security clearance. Apparently, he did too, because he could slip in and out of the system with very little difficulty. He was destroying the systems that could grant me access. I had to lock him out of the program.

"This is what I was doing when the three came up to the Hub and found me. I was almost there. I was so close to the end that just a few more keystrokes would have clinched the deal. Dan became upset with me being at the keyboard and didn't understand who the culprit was at the time. Brehm and I got into a scuffle, and I must tell you, in Zero-G, that is no easy matter for anyone of any size. Brehm had considerably more solid mass than I, and he knew how to use it. He had his arms around me and he pinned me against the bulkhead. I pushed off as hard as I could, thinking he would strike the opposite bulkhead and release me. Instead, we hit the open door. I could grab onto something to stop myself; however, Brehm was not as fortunate. He went back through the door and drifted away. They made efforts to retrieve him, but to no avail.

"I did not, in any way, wish to harm him or to kill him. That was never my intent. I had to complete what I had started with the computer. With that done, it would have locked the other out, and he would never get back in. I was saving everyone here from being under the thumb of this madman." He was silent for a moment, and his head bowed.

"Who is this madman?" someone asked.

"Point him out," said another.

"His name is Michael White. I believe he has two identities. His real one and the one he created. He knew the inner workings of the ship. And not only that, but his job when he was back at Homeport was with the guidance system. He is the one who programmed the computer to send us on this journey. Without his actions before, we would not be where we are today."

"Bullshit!" someone challenged.

"No, I tell you the truth."

"Then where is he? He's not on the itinerary. He has to be in this room."

"His name would not show up. He is a stowaway or hidden under a second identity. I do not think he meant for the journey to be this long. I believe he wanted to bring us out here, away from the staircase, to prove a point and then send us back. For some reason, that didn't work, and he has been in hiding ever since."

"Somebody would've seen him by now."

"Of the people here, we see many every day, and we assume they belong here. We know them as soldiers heading back, or people retiring, or people who once worked on the ribbon keeping the shuttle's running."

"Yooooooo" MC's voice, so help me, came over the crowd, and there were a few chuckles despite the weight of the situation.

"People, I must tell you that what happened to Brehm was a pure accident. A few centimeters to the left or right either way, and he would still be here. There was a struggle in a place where we should have moved cautiously. They have signs up all over that area, saying that spider lines need to be in use always for our security. In that I was negligent, Brehm was negligent, and so were Dan and Sally."

Silence filled the hall.

"Are you saying that Sally is at fault?" Lena asked loudly.

"Well, yes. Brehm had drifted into space, and when she pushed off to grab him, she gave him her kinetic energy. Had she done it differently and not used so much force to get to him, she could have caught him and brought him back."

Everyone was quiet. I looked at him intently, not sure if what I heard was correct. I felt a movement at my side, and Lena stood. When she spoke, I could hear the anger in her voice.

"Anderson, you're telling me that Sally did this?" Annunciating her voice, she made every word clear.

"Well, I..."

"Are you telling me that Sally caused this?" she snapped at him.

"I am saying..."

"No," I tugged on Lena's arm with my good hand, but she would not be silent. "A simple question, yes or no."

"Well ... yes."

Others, myself included, had to hold her back. Seeing too many people down the row of seats, to the left and to the right, she started to climb over the seat in front of her. We held her.

"Sally is not what caused this." I knew it was on her breath to say more, and only her training in the military held her tongue back.

Anderson, defending himself, was yelling back, "All I am saying is that with proper training on rescue in zero gravity, she would not have done what she did. With no training, she overreacted, and his death was a result."

Lena struggled harder. I had to calm her down.

"Hey, hey, hey," I said to her. "Listen, Lena. It's okay. Let him believe what he wants to believe. Okay? Don't let him make you angry," she struggled more. "Well, angrier than you already are. It's words, Lena, just words."

I did not think she would calm down, but she eventually did.

She sat in her seat, crossed her arms, and just glared at Anderson. I am thankful she had no weapons.

* * *

Brandon took the stage once more when things calmed down. "Are you saying we should look for this person?"

"No, this person has hidden here for so long that finding him would be all but impossible. He has blended in so well. If they live amongst us, we would accept any story he told us. If they lived in the city, we would have to systematically check every city building, block by block, above the surface and below, and all the homes and businesses up the wall, at both ends. And if we didn't find him, there we would have to check every kim-two. Even with robotic help, he could remain hidden for years. With so few people, he could always be a few steps ahead of us."

Someone stood up in the middle of the audience. "Brandon, you expect us to believe this man? Through no proof of his own, he wants us to look out for a bogeyman. I could go out and smash stuff up and run back to town, saying someone else did it. Who did it? I have no idea, but it wasn't me. This gentleman is just trying to save his own hide. He will say anything."

As the man spoke, others echoed his words.

"I believe there is evidence. Dan, you told me you saw someone break into the buildings. Is this true?"

Dan, watching the exchange, was slow to react. He stood and cleared his throat. "Well, yes. When we were searching, we found a video feed of someone breaking into the buildings."

"Can you show us?"

"Um, sure."

He took a few moments to bring up the images.

We could not define the individual, no matter the angle or the length of the camera shot, as any single person. They did not wear a hood to mask themselves; they wore a white hat with a slight brim, as one would wear on an outing on a summer day. Glasses covered their eyes, and we could not see any distinctive facial hair as they always had something blocking their face, as if by pure happenstance.

"The data on these shows that everything was recorded years ago."

"Yes, that is correct. Whoever did this was bold enough to do this early on after the event, within a week or two. We really didn't note what these buildings were or their importance on the ship. No one reported any damages. Again, they probably assumed that it was somebody looking for food or something. I doubt if someone passing this way would take any notice."

"We know now," Brandon whispered as he folded his arms across his chest.

"Yes, but it's too late. Their purpose, their function, is no longer relevant to the ship. With the terminals being locked from more than the most basic of functions, they have no purpose."

The person in the video now sat on the ground with his legs crossed. A set of tools beside him. He worked on the door frame with a hammer and a chisel. Head tilted to the side, hat covering his face, there was just no way to know who it was.

After several blows to the top and to the bottom, he brought out a bigger bar and wedged it in. It did not take long. The person knew what they were doing. After about fifteen minutes, he had the door open.

He turned, grabbed his bag of tricks, and went inside.

He emerged just a moment later, and, so help me, he lifted his hat as if defiantly saluting those watching on the camera.

Dan ran the video faster, and it was after sunset when the man appeared again. Bag of tricks in hand, he disappeared into the night.

One thing was certain more than anything else. The man in the video did not have Anderson's build whatsoever.

\* \* \*

Amanda stood from where she sat. "I remember a guy with a hat like that," she said. "Correct me if I'm wrong, but I'm sure someone else may remember this. There was a gentleman with us when we first got here who wore a very similar hat. He was the one who was carrying the basket of grapples, and the handle broke. He stepped on one and fell. I helped him stand and had to give him his hat back. There were a bunch of people there, and I didn't know your names at the time."

"Amanda," Brandon stood at the edge of the stage. "Is there a way you could point this person out?"

"No, I mean, we were all just new passengers then. I wasn't paying attention. Does anyone else remember this?"

Robert stood so we could hear him over the crowd.

"Was he upset that it got on his shoes?"

"Yes, that was the one. We called him 'Barefoot Guy' because he came to breakfast and dinner with no shoes. Brandon, even you mentioned something to him. It was the same hat I remember."

There was a pause.

"Barefoot guy was shorter." She held her arm up, palm open and facing down as if to judge his height. "Came up to about my shoulders. I hate to say it, but Anderson is taller. There is no way that the person in the video could be Anderson. Also, we have a fixed object, and we can measure how tall the man is by his height next to the door."

\* \* \*

In the end, we did not have to vote. It was clear about everything presented that it was a misunderstanding. If I had followed the procedure given to me by people experienced in working in zero gravity, then things would've worked out much differently.

Anderson pleaded his case thoroughly, and with a show of hands, in the end, he was not guilty of murder or causing damage to the buildings or the computers.

I fumed. Sitting there with my arms crossed, I looked down at the seat in front of me. They did not put the blame on me, yet I was part of the problem.

I hated that; once again, things did not go along the path I desired. I did nothing wrong, in my eyes, and yet I lost a friend forever because of it.

\* \* \*

Brandon called an end to it. If there were any further questions, we were free to come up and ask. The public forum to determine his guilt was over. Anderson would walk away a free man.

People were slow in dispersing.

I looked at Lena before I stood. Shuffling past a few people still seated, I walked to the stage. Taking the steps one at a time, I had to keep it slow and not show any aggression.

Someone was talking with Brandon about the vine on the far end. For some, they already forgot the matter at hand.

When I got close to Anderson, everyone stopped talking. They moved back and formed a circle around us. I felt several people place their hands on me, holding me back. There was no need.

I took a deep breath before I spoke. "I am furious at you."

"I know you are." When he was standing in front of everyone giving his plea earlier, his voice never wavered. It shook slightly now.

"We need to look for answers, and I guess I was looking for someone to blame."

To this, he said nothing.

"Truce," I said, extending my good hand. I could hear those around me sigh in relief.

"Truce." He had the common sense to wipe his hand on the fabric of his pants before he shook mine. Still, it was a little wet with perspiration. Looking me in the eye, he did not smile.

\* \* \*

Brandon pulled him aside a little later.

"Where do you live?" he asked.

"I have a place up there on the Twilight Wall."

"Do many people know you live there?"

"I have friends. Some do, most don't."

"Stock up over the next day and lie low for a while. A month or two would ease everyone down a little."

"There is reading I could catch up on," he said with a weak smile. "What she did was good."

"What she did was noble," Brandon nodded. "Doing it before everyone else, she helped calm their fears. May have just saved your life."

"I know. There is a lot of space in and out of the ship. Someone could go missing for a long time without being worried about."

Again, Brandon nodded. "Go, head out for a while. I'm not saying you must watch your back; just look over your shoulder from time to time. Troy wanted things to be different, yet he is still here."

"Thanks," Anderson shook his hand. "Thanks for the forum and for letting me speak my case."

With nothing else to say, they parted.

\* \* \*

Pat Pat was highly experienced in working with spacesuits. Having worked as a rock hugger/tugger at Homeport, logging in thousands of hours in space, he quickly agreed to help me understand the basics. It kept him away from his pigs, but a few days would not matter.

He went over as much detail as Stacy had gone into depth about the fruits and vegetables. I asked him frequently if I should have brought a notebook, and this he waved off.

"I'll teach ya what ya need," he said with just a helmet on and the visor down. "To me, having worked in one so long, a lot of it is common knowledge. I must 'speak it down' to make you understand."

I nodded. Making a mistake with germinating seeds may put a growing season off by a few weeks. Making a mistake eighteen kilometers above the surface would kill me. He had my full, undivided attention.

"One thing I have to point out to you, the tanks we use have a generic coupling. I've noticed throughout the ship that there are other tanks that have the same exact shape and coupling as the oxygen tanks we use. Only use the yellow tanks. If you use any other color, then things would be bad."

"They would be bad, or they would be really bad bad?"

He shook his head. "I've found purple ones down in some storage sheds by the Sunrise Wall. Purple means argon. I see no rational motive whatsoever that you would use argon. If, for some screwed up reason, you got a purple tank instead of a yellow one, when you got so far up the wall and breathed, the argon would replace the breathable oxygen in your suit."

I brought my hand up to my throat and mimicked someone choking.

"You would not even get that far. One breath, two breaths, three, and you're done. There's no odor, and there's no sensation whatsoever. You just go. Probably think you're short of breath… and then." He snapped his fingers.

"So, what you're saying is that the person won't even struggle."

"No, the person won't even know they are dying."

"Could you flush oxygen back in?"

"You could. They still wouldn't be breathing. It gets in the lungs and settles there quickly. The lungs cannot pull in the oxygen fast enough. You would have to give them chest compressions to make the body start back up again."

"Have you ever seen it?" I asked, my curiosity piqued. The way he talked, you could kinda tell that he was nervous about the whole thing.

"No," he shook his head. "They had training videos from stationary cameras that showed accidents. This happened in a room where five people were fixing a machine. The argon quickly leaked, and they did not have time to react."

"Oh," was all I managed to say.

"So what colors do you use?" he asked again, making sure I was listening.

"I use the yellow ones," I said, looking him in the eye to make sure he knew I knew what I was talking about. "I use no other color but yellow."

"Purple?"

"Out of the question."

He looked at me for a moment and then nodded.

"Sorry to make you feel creepy there. I've given to you in a few days what they have taught us in classes that lasted weeks. Being up there," he looked upward, "Is not an easy thing. When you get up there, it is something you should not take lightly. As we can see, accidents can happen, and it's not forgiving."

I nodded again, and he picked up the gloves.

"Now you see, as with the boots, these provide feedback to the main sensors…"

Homeport, Day 5

The auditorium grew dark as the person who last recorded a message on the camera shut it off. When it lit up, a different person turned it on again, and a man sat there with the most colorful clothing. He was not looking at the camera; rather, he was looking at the cameraman. He nodded, and his eyes drifted to the right. Off-camera there was the sound of a closing door.

\* \* \*

"Hello everyone," his voice was calm. "This is Uncle Butchie coming at you live from X-ray Delta aught Fiver," he pronounced each syllable of the ship's name slowly. Hands in the air, he shook them rapidly. "Ta-da! What a fine ship it is. I'm sure that when others see that the ship is no longer where it should be, they will be very upset. The families of all the others that this excursion has broken apart. Tsk, tsk, tsk," he dabbed the corner of his eye with a lace handkerchief. "Since this message is for family members, I would like to leave a few notes for my loving family, or extended family, as it were. Mom, you know who you are; I've slipped away yet again. I know you wanted to send me to meet dear old dad, but it didn't happen. I've been here for some time, and it looks like I'll be here for longer still." His smile was a little unnerving. "It's not the best place. But we are marooned, and with it, certain comforts which are given and others were taken away. Do you know how hard it is to find a decent barber in this part of the galaxy? I mean, look at this hair. Back in the day, I would've never had it looked like this. Unbelievable. Un-freaking-believable We are on a forced diet of anything plant with the occasional slaughtered swine thrown in for amusement, it seems. I cannot be too unhappy with this place because I still live and breathe. I'm outside your influence, mother. Here, you cannot, and will not, touch me," he then rubbed his nose with his middle finger.

"To my brothers Tim and Casey, it seems I brought with me something you really need. Sorry that you won't be able to get it." He tapped the breast pocket of his silk shirt. "I was fully prepared to mail it back to you as soon as we reached Sol. It was my insurance policy, of all things. Things didn't go as planned, did they? Had things worked out, I would visit father right about then, and everything would be hunky-dory for you.

"By the way, Lawrence came with me, and he would be my right-hand man, sort of speaking, but he flew the coop. I thought they clipped his wings? Shame on you for not telling me this. Anyway, he still lives. We see him from time to time. Either he has become a vegetarian, much like all of us, or he is feasting off other young birds as his species does to get by. You know," he coughed into his fist. "That reminds me of somebody who'll remain unnamed."

"There is so much that I would like to expound upon if we were closer. We have never been a close family, though. I have my own place in town, and although it lacks the hired help to keep it up to par, it is still relaxing. It is a place only I have access to. Honestly, Mother, you really should have changed the access codes. How many times will you use that same date?

"Regardless, it is mine now, and if you get to use it again, or your children, or your grandchildren, please know that certain areas are tainted. I have found a bunch of your secrets. Things you once had are not there anymore. You see, gold, although quite heavy, once someone takes it up a mag-ele, it becomes weightless like anything else. If they then open an airlock and give just a touch, a slight push is given then that little brick slowly drifts away. Do you remember the 'slight push,' Mama? Anyway, there is no need for gold here. Refined and as pure as much as it is, the metal holds no value here.

"Berries, on the other hand, or tea leaves, well you get the right ones. They are worth their weight in gold. Am I rambling? There is so much I wanted to convey; it seems my thoughts are all over the place," he lowered his head and brought his hand to his chin. For a moment, he looked thoughtful, collecting his thoughts.

"Just letting you know it's been a fantastic journey, and I plan to be here for some time. I'll drop you a note from time to time to make sure you know there are no hard feelings. Far be it from me to hold a grudge against anybody. Bygones are bygones. Love you all. Kiss-kiss, num-nums. Addio."

Uncle Butch stood and went out of camera sight. A few seconds later, after a string of foul language, the camera shut off.

XD05, Year 12 - "Casey Jones, you better watch your speed." *Grateful Dead*

There was a call that morning for work in an orchard up alongside the arc. Vine, as usual, needed clearing from the walls, and some apples were overly ripe. They took baskets and shovels so they could bring the rotten fruit back to feed the pigs. Also, if they squeezed the apples, added sugar, and allowed the drink to ferment, it would be some fine cider in the coming year.

It was a tedious job, to say the least, but the outcome was well worth it. Seven answered the call to work, and just after daybreak, the shuttle left Hotel Lima and headed parallel along the rim.

\* \* \*

"Jones, you get up here often?" Anna asked. "I figured you more for working with the vegetables."

"Got to do what you gotta do, you know?"

"Heard that. Good to see a new face in this crowd." She waved her hand at the others sitting there. The shuttle turned on one of the side ramps, and they lined up to go up around the rim. The morning sun was shining directly across through the windows. Anna rose from her seat and sat next to Jones.

"I tell you what," Carl said. "That vine will be the death of us all. Damn shit is covering almost everything up there. It's creeping into the city, and there's no usable soil for it to hold on to at all. It's all cement. How the hell can a vine find space to grow when there is nothing for it to hang onto?"

Running over the track, not on it, the shuttle was smooth. After negotiating the slide ramp, it began to pick up speed.

"Back at Homeport, they would give it some chemical or something to destroy it. Maybe we can talk to Richard to see if there is anything here that would destroy it. They warehoused everything else; they should've stockpiled something to kill the vine."

"It's strangulating everything." It pissed Carl off. For Anna, his rants were an almost daily thing.

"We'll walk the line. Be able to keep it at bay from the orchard."

Anna gave Carl a weak smile. She turned back to Jones.

"Well, this sucks."

\* \* \*

It wasn't until the next morning that somebody came up to Brandon as he was helping in the kitchen before breakfast.

"Carl was not here last night," Cynthia said.

"Um, is he always here?" He put his fork down.

"He's never gone like this before." As she spoke, her hands were constantly fidgeting. "I think something may have happened to him."

"I'm sure everything is fine. Is there anyone else you know who's missing?"

"I talked with Helen. She said Anna's bed was empty last night."

"When were they last seen?"

"Yesterday morning, I believe. They were heading off to do a task. They were going to gather grapples at the orchard. Carl has been hell-bent on eradicating the vine up on the wall there. Like it's a personal mission. He kills it whenever he can."

"I'll ask at breakfast this morning and see if everybody has come back. If not, we'll send a group to go see."

* * *

The shuttle slowed to a stop at the intersection.

They could see the wreckage that lay beyond. There was no smoke, just debris scattered all over the place.

Jason exited the foremost door of the shuttle before it had even stopped and paused for just a second before he ran. He could hear the others behind him. There were cries of anguish.

The damaged shuttle lay over the tracks. Pieces of it were strewn about.

"No, no, no!" he heard himself yell. He climbed over the wreckage, a hand getting cut on the metal, but he paid it no mind.

Everyone had died. Four bodies lay in the shuttle's front, two were on the ribbon beyond, and one lay below.

* * *

"Oh yeah," MC stood and dusted his hands. He straightened his glasses before he turned to Brandon. "I can see the problem right there. These vehicles are strong. They have no moving parts. They carry themselves on the indigo road and pull themselves down the line by magnetics. They only go where the magnets tell them to go. Right here, you see, the ribbon has broken. It's strong, but it will wear out over time. Had everything been working properly, had we been back at Sol, this problem would've been detected long before it became an issue. I make this ribbon. I do. The problem's right there." The temperature on the ship was usually a constant. Clouds and wind had cooled it in places. Today there were none of either, and both MC and Brandon were sweating in the heat.

"Is there any way we can detect damaged ribbon?"

"Don't know. Be nice if we could have some type o' diagnostic program. They check and see from intersection to intersection, but these places in between just have no sensors."

"Would you be able to put sensors on them? We could have the computer take us on only certain routes then. Stay on the protected path."

"Don't think I have that kind of tools. I mean, if we were building the thing and had all the equipment, that'd be easy enough. Now though, shit, the ship is already built. They won't have that kinda stuff here."

"Is there any way a person could intentionally damage the ribbon?"

"Oh, hell no," MC looked at him and grinned. "Carbon microfibers. The technique used to secure the cable and hold them on the concrete stitches them into the concrete. There's nothing here on the ship that could damage this. Except for time and the sun above," He looked upwards. "If you look back here away's," MC walked several steps back down the ribbon. "You see here? This is where it tore because of age. Bots would've found this had we had any. If they were going at the normal speed of a shuttle, it would mean the whole shuttle stopped in only about two meters. Even with their safety belts on, it would've been very painful. Like most crashes, the belts hold the person in, but the internal organs get pulled hard."

\* \* \*

It was a very sad day for me. I knew the people involved in the crash. Norah was one of those killed. I had spoken with her two or three days ago. And now she's gone.

They did not want me to help in the cleanup. I went out later after they removed the bodies and helped them move away some debris. They wanted to push the shuttle from the track; however, with it where it was, no other shuttle was getting past and so it would be a deterrent in the future. Not that someone could control the route in which they took. The central computer would now realize that there was a block on the ribbon, and it would let nothing else down that line.

None of the equipment we used for harvesting and cleaning, the rakes and the baskets, were usable. Like my friends, nothing came through unscathed. We brought the tools back to the hotel and placed them in the fire pit. As they burned, we all cried. I'm not sure who we cried for. Maybe it was for them; maybe it was for ourselves.

The morning after their burials, I went back to my room, and on my wall, I wrote their names and the date. They are special, and here, where life is so limited, their presence will be missed.

Homeport, Day 5


It took more than a day to identify everybody who lived and worked at Homeport. A ten-man group of soldiers went to the main doors of the giant ring that separated the north from the east. These were closed and sealed for the first time in living memory. Starting there, the soldiers went room to room, evacuated everyone, and forced them further down the ring. Identification tags in hand, it became very crowded for a few hours as they pushed everyone onward.

Very few, if any, became argumentative as they were still in shock over the death of everyone on XD05. Everyone knew someone involved.

When the soldiers reached the southwest corridor, halfway around the ring, a secondary team started where the first team had to make sure there were no stragglers. There were none. When the second team met up with the first team, they stopped the forward search, and the process was reversed. For the rest of the day, they checked the identification of everyone and brought them back around.

In the end, they could not find Michael White. He was not at Homeport, and that limited the number of places he could be if he were still in the system.

With the whole place in lock-down, with no shuttles ferrying people back and forth, Wendy and Bob had to spend the time away from their home in a makeshift shelter of the gymnasium. Even though they lived just half a ring away, they could not return for the time being. Two times, soldiers came through and checked the identification of everyone.

Still, the result was the same, and they never found Michael White.

* * *


People lay on crew mattresses on the gymnasium floor. They complained the pillows smelled old, not from being used and old, just musty from being in storage. Sitting in the bleachers, Wendy held Bob's hands as they watched the letters home play on the large screen.

When the person finished talking, the screen went dark. When it came back on, Director Porter was there. He looked tired, to say the least. Hair disheveled, the top button of his shirt undone, sleeves rolled up; it was so uncharacteristic to see the old man so.

"We will shut down for the night," even his voice was weary. "We know that with the system on lock-down, most non-essential personnel are at Homeport. Again, we are sorry for any inconvenience. This is something new for all of us. We will resume tomorrow and start off exactly where we left off. Before we start it back up, I will give a briefing on anything we have found overnight. Thank you so much for your patience."

He nodded, and the screen went dark for a final time.

* * *

They eventually gave Wendy and Bob permission to return to their home. Wendy looked at the door to the room which Sally occupied just days ago. She went to the metal frame and stood for several moments, looking at the empty bed in the bare walls. Bob came over and placed his hand on her shoulder.

"I knew it would be awhile before we saw her again. I didn't think the last would be the end."

"She was unique, you know? Not top of the class or straight A's, but she was good. She had her wits about her. Lotta spunk."

"Friendly," Bob said, placing his hand on her back. "She always strove to see the best in situations. Even though she was here and away from your brother and his wife, clear out here on the rim, she never let it get her down.

"Yeah," Wendy mused. "She was our little twinkle."

* * *

With nothing else to do, Wendy and Bob returned to the gymnasium the next morning to watch with the others.

They knew some people, and it was interesting to see how they aged.

It was after a message home from Doc that Richard Porter came on the screen. Although it was midmorning, it looked as though he had not slept at all.

"It has been a long and trying time for all personnel. I truly thank you for your patience. Now, we cannot locate Michael White. He is a person who we are interested in, and it seems that he has slipped away. We have buckled down on passenger transportation procedures. If he is here, we will find him, although I do not believe we will get that opportunity. I am calling off the physical search for him. I permit everyone who lives at Homeport to go back to your quarters. If you live away from here and on one of the larger ships, then you may leave at any time if the transportation is here for you. We have teams already on the surface of '05, and undoubtedly we will need more as time goes on. If you wish to dedicate time there, please see your immediate supervisor. Make sure that your current job is not mission critical. Thank you. We will resume the messages."

XD05, Year 12 - "Mustang Sally, now baby, guess you better slow that Mustang down." *Wilson Pickett.*

I would take a break every so often. When the days were warm and sunny and no new plants needed to be harvested or sewed, I would request a shuttle. At the N-terminal, just before the track arced up the Twilight Wall, I would stop and don a suit.

The only existing computer terminal for the weather and such was at the Hub, thanks to Michael White. I would go there and look the system over to make sure everything was running smoothly. I would not disrupt what was already in play. Lessons from the past taught me that even little changes sometimes would have catastrophic consequences. It was better to leave well enough alone.

I pulled a suit from the locker that was fresh and fully charged, yellow tanks. Within a half-hour, I was back in the shuttle and heading upward. Closing my eyes, I rested and let the seat take my weight. It was smooth and comfortable, and I could have dozed.

I had just felt a little lighter when the shuttle jolted to a stop. The restraining harnesses tugged hard against my chest.

I screamed.

Arms out, I thought I was dead. I could not help think back to the crash, which took the seven.

The curse was silent under my breath. I was not moving. I was not tumbling up the side or falling back. My shuttle must've malfunctioned differently than theirs. MC had said a piece had come loose on their shuttle, and this dug into the ribbon, causing it to jump the track.

I had the same momentum, just different results. Probably a computer malfunction or a length of ribbon was not powered.

The gravity did not have the 1G pull it normally did on the surface. Stranded at about a third of the way up the distance of the wall, I could climb and jump a little easier.

Not sure of the inner workings or the mechanics of it all, I did not touch the indigo track. From the cab of the shuttle, it was a simple jump to one of the supporting struts. There was a slight wind, and the metal of the strut was a little slick with a coating of ice. The magnetics in the suit held me there firmly.

I looked upward. Roughly thirteen more kilometers to go, steadily shedding off the gravity the higher I went or putting it back on the closer I came to the surface. Decisions, decisions. Thoughts of Brehm came to mind. Looking downward once more, I knew my chances would be better if I went up. It's what I have dressed for, anyway.

* * *

It took time, but once at the Hub, I found a maintenance airlock that let me inside. At the control panel, I called up a magnetic-elevator and took it back down to the surface.

I did not take the suit off. Setting my helmet and gloves down at the base of the elevator, I went on a hunt of sorts. Within an hour, I found what I was looking for. I found three drums that used to hold rainwater for a garden. I tipped them over to get the water out. One by one, I dragged them the three blocks to the elevator.

The closest water source I could find was a hose in a maintenance locker. Still too far away to get to the elevator by hand, I took another hour to find a pallet and a pallet jack. I was a little exhausted when I got back into the elevator; however, the barrels were full of water, and this made me thrilled.

I watched them intently, lids off, as the elevator went back up. With my hands on the side of one barrel, I could feel the sides stiffen the higher we got up. Ice at first formed a small layer and then got deeper and deeper. By the time I was out of the atmosphere, the barrels had completely frozen. Irregularities in the water made the ice snap and crack. This was cool.

Getting the barrels into a second shuttle was a chore. Although the barrels were weightless, they had mass greater than my mass. I had to use muscle and sheer strength to get them going and then to get them to stop. The first one entered the shuttle a little too fast and cracked the paneling, and chipped a seat. I tried to brush it off, but I could not hide something like that. Hopefully, no one would notice the little bit of damage.

The second and third one I was a little more careful with. When they were in and secured with a strap, I sat back and breathed a sigh of relief.

The Hub was not pressurized now, as it was at one time, and so I could open both airlock doors for the shuttle at the same time. It sat on the track and a turnaround. If a shuttle came in from one direction, it could be rotated and sent in a different direction. There were four directions in all. Although they had no bearing on direction whatsoever, the makers of the ship dubbed the four tracks North, South, East, and West. The stuck shuttle was in the West. The one I called up had come from the East, and so it could go straight through.

I opened the airlocks for the West track. Disengaging the automatic locks on the shuttle and shutting it down completely, it sat there hovering on the track 13 kilometers above the other shuttle. Once I got it moving, it would slide down the track and nudge the other shuttle back on to the track that was working. With the shuttle back at the hotel, I could notify someone, and they could come up and fix it if warranted.

Standing on the edge of the track, I pushed on the shuttle with everything I had. Marking a place on the floor at the front of the vehicle, I had hoped to make it budge just a little bit. After several moments of trying, it had not moved.

I hovered there breathless, wondering how to get it moving. They shaped the handle of the airlock like the letter 'L.' In a moment of inspiration, I ran my spider cable from the shuttle over the handle of the airlock. Bracing my feet, setting my hands and shoulders, I squatted down and grabbed the spider line. Pushing upward, away from the wall, I gave it all I had. It was slow, ever so slow, but the shuttle moved. I unlooped the spider line and, with a quick jump, got to the shuttle and unhooked it. It carried me for just a moment before I jumped off again.

And it was gone. Slowly creeping forward, it made its descent to the surface a little faster than a snail. 'See,' I said to myself, 'Problem solved.'

I went to the terminal and did the work I came to do. The weather was fine; the water was running normally, and the air was circulating just peachy. There was an alga bloom on the north side of the lake near the Morning Wall. Nothing to be concerned about; such things had a way of correcting themselves—a ripple effect up the food chain. In a few weeks, when the algae were too high, then there would be a growth in the number of the little bugger things that ate the algae. And it would work its way up to the fish. /There would be a spike in the fish population, which would eventually lead to many of them dying because there would not be enough little buggers to feed on. The hardy ones would survive, and the rest would pass on, creating a foundation for the next.

Some others asked me if it was possible for me to make it rain a little earlier in the evenings. Normally, I did very little tinkering. Memories of Brehm, although a year or so in the past, were still fresh in my mind. Giving in, I rescheduled it two hours back every other day. Since they knew what I was doing, there would be no repercussions. When I got back down to the surface later that evening, I would let them know. It would take a few days for the whole cycle to kick in any way.

Looking all over, noticing no red flags, I shut the interface down.

Before going to the mag-ele, I pulled on a tether and went to the main window. It was here that I first arrived on the ship. My aunt was there with a soldier. They had pressurized the place. I could move back and forth without a helmet or suit. Directly above my head, twenty or thirty meters, was the tube that carried the sunlight. Looking down, I could see the world below. There were very few clouds out today, and I could see a good bit of the land. The few years have done the ship well. Whereas before, it was mostly brown with rich, carbon-filled soil, now there was a lot more greenery. The birds were carrying the seeds quite far. Most notably, where the kim-two where they had planted the trees. This gave the birds a natural place to roost, and they favored it there. Carrying seeds back and forth, they would drop them from time to time, and these places were an oasis.

I was sure that the sequoias were getting taller.

The green belts continued to the left and right. Where I was, at the Hub center, I could see almost the whole way around. The tube blocked out the land above me.

We would make it if our own boredom did not kill us. We had enough food and water to last our lifetimes. Once the pigs had numbered only twenty or so, now their numbers were up in the hundreds. The people could have pork for supper two or three times a week now. Supplementing with the fish they caught and the fruits and vegetables, it was not a bad diet.

And the beer. How could I forget about Jaughn and his beer?

I paused a few more minutes, taking it all in, and decided to leave.

Thirty minutes had passed since I nudged the shuttle. A tug and pull on a tether nearby set me in motion. I curled my feet underneath me and spun into the door of the mag-ele. Another small shove and I was at the panel to close the door.

I would meet them both at the bottom of the arc. Traveling at a pace like that of a slow walk, I could go down below and wait for the two shuttles to return.

I smiled inside for a job well done. No one would know what happened or question my motivations or my actions. This made me happy.

At the bottom, the fresh air was a welcome change to the recycled air in my suit. My helmet off, my gloves tucked inside, I would have to walk a distance to get to the bottom of the arc to meet the shuttles when they reached the bottom of the artificial gravity well. The suit that once kept me warm now cooled me down, and it was comfortable, if only a little bulky.

An hour later, almost at sunset, I heard a horrendous crash above me. I froze. Seconds later, debris started to hit the rooftops of the surrounding buildings. Still, in the shadow of the indigo road, none of it came close to hitting me. Windows shattered, building façades crumpled, the street suddenly became covered in chunks of ice.

It was all over in a matter of seconds, but still, I waited. There were no screams; there were no cries of help or cries of alarm.

I walked over to the nearest piece and picked it up. I recognized it immediately as part of a barrel I had used.

"Shit," I said, setting it back down. The shuttle must've picked up too much momentum. Rather than a simple push from one to the other, it disintegrated both on impact.

Not only had I destroyed two shuttles at one shot, but it would also be a long walk back to Hotel Libra.

At the N-station, at the bottom of the arc, I replaced the suit, making sure the battery was recharging.

Twilight was just starting when I put my hands in my pockets, lowered my head, and walked.

\* \* \*

It was almost midnight when I arrived back at Lena's. The front door slid silently open. I opted for the stairs rather than the elevator. Pausing before the bedroom door, I weighed my options. I went down the hall to the kitchen and grabbed fruit from the fridge.

I kicked my boots off into the corner, and I shed my clothes on the way into the bathroom. The warmth of the shower felt good and helped ease the muscles from the walk.

\* \* \*

"Were you with somebody?" Lena asked the next morning as I knew she would.

"No, no need to be jealous. There's only you. I was just out walking. I got sidetracked and lost track of time, is all."

"Is everything okay? I know you have a lot to think about. I worry from time to time."

"Everything is fine," I patted Lena's knee, giving her my reassurance.

Lena looked me over and could probably sense my melancholy mood.

"If you ever need to talk about anything, please let me know. I'm always here to help you."

"Yeah, I know. Been here for so long I am missing home. I wonder what Mom and Dad are doing. They were a young couple about your age when we left. I think they probably have had more children since I've been gone. I probably have a brother or sister out there somewhere and don't even know it. It gets hard sometimes, that's all."

Lena nodded. "I have two brothers and two sisters myself. Being here doesn't make it any easier. I have a whole collection of messages and videos I've saved. I look back on them every so often. It pains me to know I am no longer part of their lives, and it may be a long time before they find out what has happened and can rescue us. I will always keep them close." She put her arms on my shoulders and kissed me on the forehead.

"Hey," I said. "We're not dead yet. If I was ever to get stranded somewhere, I'm glad I got stranded here," I felt Lena smile.

"No place I'd rather be. Good friends, good food," Lena grimaced and stuck her tongue out, "We are a family no matter what they say."

"Yeah, I got you, girl."

I gave her a kiss.

"I will go work in the fields today," I said to Lena as I pulled back.

"Ah, should lighten your mood," Lena raised her eyebrows.

"It will keep my mind busy and my body too."

"I'm going to the warehouses to help with inventory."

"Oh, the joy of joys."

"Yeah, I know, right?" Lena stood and turned. Her hand still lingering on my shoulder. I gave her a playful shove. "Have fun in the fields today, kiddo."

"Have fun in the dusty warehouse." I stood and hugged her for a moment. "Now get!"

* * *

No one mentioned a word. Not that day or the next. Throughout the week and with the workers in the field, I waited to hear a rumor of something catastrophic that had happened. But nothing came up. I know I should have felt relieved at getting away with doing it. However, it was a blatant act of just simple stupidity that caused the wreckage of the two shuttles and other buildings. I could've killed somebody. I could've been maimed for life, or at the least, I could've killed myself. Once again, I was humbled by my place in the universe. Like Brehm, I could have died just as easily.

* * *

It was a week later when I left the field early and called up a shuttle. At the N-terminal, I pulled on the same suit as before. The shuttle took me up the same route to the Hub. The computer had its backtrack. I entered the Hub on the southern ribbon.

I had damaged the ribbon that went directly from Hotel Libra up the side of the Twilight Wall in some way, and we had no way to repair it.

I became depressed after that. I had destroyed some part of this great ship, not purposely, but I had a heavy hand in it nonetheless.

Homeport, Day 5

The screen went to black, and the gymnasium darkened. Many people have gathered here. They could watch it on their monitors throughout the station, but here they felt a sense of closeness—a sense of community.

When the screen came back to light, there was a man standing there. Glasses, bald head, he was not sitting, but standing in front of the camera as if he were peering into the lens.

"It's MC," someone exclaimed. "MC, MC, MC," they chanted. They mixed it with other people yelling out, "Young man, young man!" Apparently, many people knew him.

MC looked at the person behind the camera, nodded, and then took his seat.

"Yooooooo," he said with a wave and a big, toothy smile. "Hey Y'all, MC here. Been doing pretty good, pretty good. I'd say I'm pretty good. They treat me really square, and I am thankful for this bunch of people. Like to say hi to Ma and Pops, my brothers Tony, Franco, and Hector. And sis Rachel.

"Man, I gotta tell ya." he smacked his lips in disgust. "I was heading back to go on retirement, have a few beers, wait for the sun to set on a warm beach on Earth, and just chill. Here, now, they got me working again. I told them I just fixed the track; I don't plant vegetables. But that's what they got me doing, ya know? Planted so many damn potatoes that my fingers hurt. But it's all good; they treat me pretty good. Imagine that, MC the farmer. Need to stick a piece of grass or something in my mouth and walk around with a straw hat on my bald head.

"We found some of y'all's beers. They lasted for a time, but we were able to make our own. Don't tell the boss man, but a young man has a still hidden out there. Couple of us do. Shhhh, no telling where mine is hidden. So, now I'm able to have a nice cold one and play spades on the downtime. You know, I play a mean game of spades. Anywho, I let you all sit it out for now. Light a candle for MC once in a while 'cuz he misses y'all. Peace my people."

The person off-camera cleared his throat. "You still have five minutes left, young man."

"Ah, naw, I'm good, I'm good. It's all good. Save it on my account for 'nother day," MC stood, waved once more, and walked away

## XD05, Year 12

Brandon had searched the area and found MC in a conference room of Hotel Libra. It is quite possible that the card game had been going on since mid-morning. Spades was the common game. They each had a six-pack of Jaughn's beer, and he thought back to times past when people would smoke cigars, drink heavily, and play poker. There are three such spade games going on.

"MC," he said from the door. "May I speak to you?"

MC turned, looked over his shoulder, nodded, and went back to his card game.

As Brandon neared, MC brought his cards back so no one could see them.

"We have a problem with the track ribbon going to the Hub. It seems there was an accident of some kind some time ago that no one reported, and that section of ribbon is malfunctioning."

"I can go look at it. I can't make no promises like that." He played as he spoke, dropping down the deuce of spades and took the book. "Is anyone missing? If it was another accident, then probably someone else died. If the shuttle jumped the ribbon up that high, you're done for."

"Yes, I know. There is a large debris field at the base of the ribbon. We will look shortly. If you could check on it, it would mean a lot. We would have to circumvent that line and go out of our way to get to the Hub."

"Who was up there, anyway?" asked Davies.

"It gets a good amount of company. It's a place where we go to check out the ship's systems."

"There are still three other routes to take to get there," said Davies.

"I'll give it a look-see," MC said over his shoulder. "Not sure if I can do any good or not. I helped with the weaving of the ribbon. Shoot, they make that thing slowly, microscopically. Ain't nothing we have here to fix anything up there. If there is a rip or a tear, just gotta deal with it. Remember the crash? I can't fix nothing like that."

"I understand the ship is getting old. It might be a tear, maybe a loose connection to a sensor. I'd just like you to look at it."

"I can do that."

"Is it up above the atmo?" asked Jacobs.

"It's up high enough."

"Ah, then I guess I must find the suit. Young man ain't worn no suit in a long time."

"Thank you. And people, I hate to sound like a mother hen. Let's pick up a little, please. I don't mind the drinking or eating here in the conference rooms. Just when you leave, make sure it's cleaned up."

They finished their hand.

"Give me two sandbags," MC told Davies. "We gotcha Top. Going to clean up when we get done."

"Who's winning?"

"Stephan and Jacobs, but only just. We'll get them back."

Davies looked at them and growled, muttering a playful "Bastards" under his breath.

## XD05, Year 13

The wind tugged at me as I lay flat on the cool metal surface. My hands tight around the rungs of the ladder beneath me.

It was chaotic here.

The howl deafened my ears.

Spider-lined to the side, I did not want to imagine the consequences of me breaking free. If my grip left me, if the magnets in the gloves and the boots failed, I would tumble head-first into the mouth of this beast. I had heard before that the wind speed from this intake vent to the output excelled their current measuring devices. Once pulled in, the wind would carry me the sixty kilometers to the transition in a heartbeat. My body would strike the porous membrane before carrying the bits the rest of the way to the opposite end.

My stomach clenched up when I thought about the reality of it all. This wind flowed 20/5. A complete twenty hours a day over a five-day week, never stopping, never silencing.

I was lying on my stomach at just one port at the end of the station, Morning Wall. Here, the air was sucked in by the warmth of the reactor, only to push it to the other end. Tang had called it convection. With the massive warmth of the burner and the cool air at the other end if formed a natural stirring. Air was constantly being pushed away from the burner. It forced this to the far end, where it rushed out and expanded back into the atmosphere. At the surface, there was always a gentle refreshing wind. Here where the port sucked the air in, there was a rush so violent it chilled me.

I wore a spacesuit, but no helmet or tanks; instead, I wore a skullcap. Placed under the chin and over the head, it held my hair in place. If I unbound it and let it free in this wind, it would take the longest time to work out the tangles.

Two more rungs and I would be there. I tentatively let go with my left hand and eased upward a few centimeters. When I was secure, I released my right hand and adjusted.

I looked over the edge. The opening was several meters wide. Light disappeared down into the darkness. There was really nothing to see. It was just an experience of feeling all this wind, all this excitement at the center of the vortex. It was incredible. Here I lay on the edge, on the very cusp of the lungs of this great beast. Here it drew in one everlasting breath. The roar deafened my ears. As beautiful as it was, it screamed of things that created nightmares.

My left hand gripped the rung of the ladder as tight as I could. I would not let go. The spider lines were strong enough to hold me; however, I did not want to take the chance. It was here that I reached into a cargo pocket with my right hand and pulled out a marker. Placing the capped end between my teeth, I tugged. As nimbly and as slowly as I could, I wrote my name and the date beneath some graffiti already there. Yes, I knew I was doing something wrong. Lena, and Brandon, and the others would be very upset. But I figured what the hell, this is my ship now. We were down to about two-hundred people, and this would probably be the last time I came here.

After three tries, I recapped the marker with the lid still clenched in my teeth.

It was only after I got back to the hotel that I noticed I had two red dots on my lips.

\* \* \*

It took a while, but I make it back to the mag-ele. Not that it was a dangerous walk. Once down the ladder, my route took me through a lot of twists and turns inside the wall. The corridors of workstations and office spaces seem endless. I had to use spray paint on the floor to keep from getting lost. Not much, just a little spritz here and there kept me on track.

These are the things I did on my day off.

I grabbed my helmet and hopped on the mag-ele. I lay stretched out on the floor when the door opened. It was more comfortable like this, and I found myself more relaxed. My body slowly came down from the euphoria of where it had been. What a rush!

It took about an hour, but I traveled by shuttle from the Morning Wall to the Twilight Wall. Another ride in the mag-ele brought me to the Hub at the Twilight Wall. This time, suiting up was not an option. If I did not wear the helmet, the computer stopped before I reached the danger zone.

\* \* \*

Everything looked fine on the computer display. Feeling I had to do something to make my journey worthwhile, I tweaked the water going from the lake into the 'burning hell' as Jxan called it. I slowed it down some. In the grand scheme of things, what would a thousand liters a day less mean? I was getting good at this.

A vibration on my wrist told me that my suit was down to 50% battery life. Not bad, just at the edge of my comfort zone. The last thing I needed was any kind of trouble up here. The suit I had worn the day we looked for Brehm still floated nearby. There was no use searching that suit, as the batteries would have drained a long time ago. The same went for the air tanks, although I didn't need the air. My tanks filled on my trip in the shuttle.

Kicking off from a wall, I snooped around. Bathrooms, offices, workstations. It took time, but I found a storage area. These were deep cubby holes designed to keep items in the Hub's weightlessness. Ceramic magnetic tabs sealed the plasti-lite doors. If you wanted in, you braced your feet and tugged on the handle.

In the second one, I saw something that gave me a start.

There, facing outward, was a suit that was too small for anyone here. A Miss Piggy patch was on the shoulder; I recognized it immediately. I pulled it out and smiled.

It was mine. The suit I wore coming here remained stowed away all this time. It brought back memories of long ago. Aunt Wendy had helped me put it on. I remember the excitement I felt when she held the torso and, from the back, I slipped in feet first. People come in different sizes. With the pressure suit, you had to be exact. At the time, this was the only one that fit me. The Miss Piggy patch on the shoulder cinched the deal. It's why I had chosen this one.

The little hand fit in my palm. I squeezed the fingers and smiled.

I brought the helmet up and looked into the darkness therein.

"Well, if it isn't the wee Sally Weiss. You've come a long way, kiddo," I smiled, imagining I could see the young face inside, the young eyes full of awe and amazement. If I could speak to her, I wonder if she would listen to what I had to say?

When I tucked it away and closed the door, the helmet drooped forward. Instead of looking like a child looking upward at the stars in the heavens, it looked more like a child sulking. I let it be. With the Hub in a vacuum and behind the plasti-lite, it would remain forever preserved.

Rather than finding a backup battery, I went to the shuttle, keyed in my destination, and returned to the surface.

XD05, Year 13

By my count, we were down three shuttles. The two I had destroyed and the one that wrecked. It was late at night when Lena was elsewhere, and I feigned an excuse to go for a walk. I had gone four kim-two under the street lamps when I climbed the stairs of a platform and keyed a shuttle.

"Destination?" said the pleasant male voice of the shuttle.

"Is there a warehouse that holds other shuttle's?" It was a hunch I had. The ship this size built to house tens of thousands of people would hold more shuttles than the ones we used.

"Yes, there is a warehouse."

"I need to go there," I said.

"Do you have authorization?"

"Sally, 2-0-8-5-8-4-9. And could you travel one-quarter speed, please? I wish to enjoy the ride."

"As you wish."

The shuttle lifted and quietly traveled through the night. I sat in the first seat and made sure I had on the safety belt. I eased the seat back to enjoy the ride. It was late, my thoughts drifted, and soon I found myself asleep.

* * *

The shuttle chimed sometime later, and it roused me from a dream.

"Return to where you picked me up, please."

There were two short beeps in confirmation.

When I got to the stairs to go down, the shuttle had disappeared into the darkness.

The warehouse was easy to find. It covered almost a whole kim-two. I went to the main door and keyed the access panel. It gave me permission after I gave my authorization.

With the main doors open, the overhead bay lights started to come on, probably the first time in a decade that someone has stepped foot in this building. They were all tucked away. The rows were twenty wide and five high. Not just shuttle's, but other machines too.

I was about to start up three shuttles' when I noticed some of a different model. The ones we have been using to haul produce from the fields were ones that we used for the general transportation of people. They had taken the back seats out to make it easier, but the doors still sometimes gave us problems because they were too small.

A model that sat before me was specifically designed for carrying larger items. Almost twice as long with a supported bed and with a seat for only one person, it was exactly what we needed. They had not started it up because when '05 was on its way from Homeport to Earth, they had no need for such a high-capacity vehicle. All we needed at the time was transportation for people.

I smiled.

Walking over one, I keyed the computer.

"Hello, may I help you?"

"I am Sally, authorization 2-0-8-5-8-4-9. How many shuttles of this model do we have onboard the ship?"

"There are currently twenty-one."

"Could you please activate five and take them unmanned to Hotel Lima, one-quarter speed, please?"

"As you wish."

One by one, I watched them activate. Before the last one fired up, I climbed on board and threw my backpack to the floor. The seat was very comfortable.

* * *

I slept again and arrived back at the hotel in the early hours of the morning. When they found the new ones, I told no one and did not claim responsibility. Most suspected, but no one knew for certain.

Homeport, Day 6

"Hello, everyone. I am Cpl. Lena Daniels. Been here now for almost twelve years, and if I had continued to serve my military time, I would be Master Sergeant or even a Warrant Officer by now. I and a few others wear our suits on special occasions. I dusted this one off and wore it today as I send my letter home.

"I miss you, Mom and Dad, Grandma and Grandpa on both sides. Lydia, Dawn, and Benny… I hope that you have taken care of Mom and Dad. I know that my time away in the military was to follow my career to make my own path. In my times when I took leave, I always dedicated it to coming home to see you. Even in the short time I was on duty, I sacrificed so much. I would not change my life as I am happy that I served.

"Benny, I'm sure your dog is probably gone by now, but he was a little obnoxious at times," she laughed as she sat back. "He would sit there and just stare like, I don't know, I wasn't sure if he wanted to play ball or tear my head off. I could not read him.

"Dawn, I know that we had a falling out, but I have missed you so much. I thought about the argument we had, and in the time that I have been here, I have sought some kind of resolution. That is not possible with just me being here alone. Some resolution also should come from your end. I know that you are very headstrong and adamant about things. I would hope that you do not hold grudges and that you have found the ability to bury the hatchet, as it were. I do miss you and think of you. I wish things were the way they were before we started the fight. You must understand that life is so short. If we spend our day's begrudging others, then when the day is done, that's all we must show.

"Lydia, the youngest. Well, with the ship lost, you are now the youngest in the family. Not a difficult thing you say, however, the caboose of the train has a lot of responsibility. Try to keep the peace between everybody and make sure they stay on track. That's not a reference to trains, by the way." She smiled with a wink. "I have seen the responsibilities they are heaping on the youngest one here, and she has grown so much stronger than the bouncy young girl I knew before. I would hope the same is true for you. I hope that you become strong and resilient in your own right. I love you all. Please, you must know this. Note also that I'm doing well, and I have found contentment in my life.

"I run when I can, and with a diet of mainly fruits and vegetables, I can't help but keep in shape. It's very difficult to gain weight when you don't have the carbs readily at hand. Although there are some people who maintain their weight with efficiency. There have been many challenges here as we are stranded out in the middle of nowhere. The fields need constant attention, and it's not a passive thing. We need to do this to survive. If we become slack, there is a chance we will fail. Here, it is not a 'go' or 'no go' basis. If we fail, we die. Simply put. I think there are too many people here watching over everyone to make sure that this does not happen.

She chuckled, "I must close now, I would say, keep in touch, but that is impossible. I will do another video in time. I miss you all. I love you. Goodbye."

XD05, Year 14

Our days were pretty much routine. Doc would post a list of things he needed in the cafeteria, and we would go over the list as we ate breakfast. We arrive in the fields as early as possible and either plant or harvest, depending on the needs of the kitchen.

I enjoyed planting. It gave me time to work with the information that Stacy had given me. Seeds and preparation soon fascinated me. I would spend long hours making sure we did everything meticulously. If there was one error, then it would throw off a growing season or may corrupt the harvest.

Responsibilities were slowly being heaped on my shoulders, and I did not mind it at all. It felt good that they looked up at me.

\* \* \*

Word came down that Brandon wanted a town hall meeting. It was important, and he wanted us to wrap up our work before noon. Something like that is very rare, and, once spoken, it distracted everyone for the day. We got the plums we needed, loaded up, and headed back.

Although they were not doing a headcount, we could tell that almost everybody was there. I forgot how much time had passed since the Anderson trial. Going back into the large hall reminded me of that day we lost Brehm. It's been many years now. Funny how time slips away.

I found Lena and gave her a quick squeeze. She held me at arm's length and looked me up and down.

"No time to get cleaned up?"

I shook my head and smiled. "Picking plums and digging holes for the horseradish and rhubarb."

She stuck out her tongue. "Did anybody give you a clue as to what this was about?" She asked, searching my face for any hint of deception.

"No, why do you think it would involve me?" I asked her a question in return.

"It always seems that you are in the mix of it when things of importance happen. Just curious, that's all. Trying to get some heads-up intel."

I shrugged my shoulders and took a seat. She nudged my shoulder, and when I looked at her, she nodded toward the bottom. Uncle Butch was there, as colorful as ever. I do not know where or how he found colorful clothing when everyone else had standard work clothes. I don't think I have ever seen him in the same outfit twice. Dark hair slicked back. He was sporting a beard now trimmed in some outlandish way.

I waved to Tang and Cyn, Jxan, Avery, and Mia Mei.

* * *

On stage, there were several chairs. Brandon was there, of course. He was talking with two people, and when he moved, it shocked me to see Stacy there. She had changed over the years. Where once she was tall, she now bent over just a little. They say lack of calcium in our diets was really affecting our bones. Someday we would all be that way. She still had her long straight hair, although it was not as dark and was grayer now.

Before everyone was fully seated, Brandon turned and spoke up.

"I'm sorry I had to call everybody in like this, but something of importance has come up, and I do not want it to go through the rumor mill in the dining hall. I'd like for us to decide on this matter as soon as possible.

"They never meant for us to occupy XD05. It was to go back to the Solar System, and we were to leave with a whole new set of families and farmers to move in. The pigs now outnumber us, and the vine, the cursed vine, is growing rampant. Seven of our members died in the accident, and we have lost three since. I know two of them had a daily crusade to destroy as much of the vine as they could. It is not an easy task, and we have come up with many ways to eradicate it. However, it is a battlefront we have no control over. We have kept it out of the city mostly, and yet there are still some places where it has taken a foothold, and we are hard-pressed to gain that ground back.

"Our resident herbalist would like to share some thoughts. So, without further ado, Stacy."

She shuffled from her chair to the center of the stage while Brandon took a seat.

"Thank you," her voice was measurably lower than when she taught me. "I have been racking my brain trying to figure out how to destroy the invasive vine with what we have on the ship. I have searched the storehouses, the warehouses, and the outbuildings, looking for something, anything. So far, there is nothing I have that I can use that would kill the vine and keep the environment safe. There are chemicals, but it would render the land all but useless, and once they got into the water supply, it would taint it irrevocably.

"The idea came to me some time ago, and I want to explain to you the thought process of how I came to this conclusion. The vine is very susceptible to temperature change. There are certain types of gases we could use. Condense them into liquid form so they are very cold and then, instead of spraying the vine with chemicals, spray them with the super-cooled gases. Just one small spritz where the roots go into the ground would be all that we need. The vine has many tendrils. We would have to get them all. This, however, would take a very long time. It may take more time and manpower than our current process does right now, which is simply cutting the vine and letting the vines die where they lay or feeding them to the pigs.

"My next thought was that we construct cold bombs, as it were. They would not be explosive; they would just release a mass of super-cooled air over a large area, which would freeze the vine. If we did this at night during the rain, then it would cool a very large area with a small amount of material.

"As I have said before, the vine is very resilient and just one bit left alive, and it would start all over. It has to be that every single last bit of this is completely destroyed. Hacking or spritzing or letting loose with cold bombs will not do it. It must be everything or not at all. We cannot let the vine live in any capacity.

"It is my belief that we must cool the whole atmosphere. One month of frozen land would do quite nicely." There were a lot of whispers until she raised her hand. "Logistically, it is not that difficult. We would have to amp up the harvest a little to prepare. We would have not only one month without harvesting food but also two to three months afterward. That would be a growing phase before we can harvest again. Such is normal in the temperate zones of the northern and southern hemispheres of the earth. It is a natural changing of the seasons.

"Of all the choices we have, I believe this one is the easiest one. We do not have to trudge from one kim-two to another. How many times have we gone back only to find that the vine has reclaimed land?

"We can stockpile and dry out more than enough food. The sun is not our only source of heat. There are countless batteries that hold energy—more than what we need. If the swine have shelter, adequate bedding, and food, they will survive.

"The plants we use for food are resilient. Some we will have to shelter in the greenhouses. The trees can handle everything quite nicely. We will have to have a controlled shutdown, so everything will become slowly acclimated, but in two months from now, with little effort from everybody, the vine can be forever eradicated."

She took a step back from the podium, and before anybody could say anything, Brandon stepped forward.

"I will have to ask everyone for a huge leap of faith. We can go on and continue to do it as we are doing and fail. As we are getting older, our bodies are slowing down, and we are not able to destroy as much of the vine as we once did. The percentage, even a tiny percentage, that the vine gains per day will give it the upper hand. We need to do this. We need to nuke it, so it does not come back. As Stacy said, the vine is very susceptible to cold weather."

The hall was quiet except for Uncle Butch, who coughed loudly.

"I will now turn it over to Anderson. Quiet, please," he said when people started to sound their disapproval. He waited a moment for them to calm down. "Like it or not," he paused when people did not become quiet. He said it again, louder. "Like it or not, we need him. Please. Everyone. Be quiet and just listen. They have come and explained what they needed to do. I have looked at all the options, and this is the best way. This is how we will do it. Everything will start in two weeks. This meeting today was to get you to understand our reasoning behind it, not to get your approval."

Anderson came from the shadows and stood at the podium. His voice did not shake; he was calm and seemed at ease. I did not like the man. I still think he handled things badly that day and found that with him not being punished, it struck me the wrong way.

"They design the ships to accommodate humans nicely. Making it colder on the ship is little more than a simple matter of turning the heat down. If we turn the heat down, there are certain thresholds that once we go past, we cannot come back from easily. You see, on a global scheme, if it is too hot, the water in the lakes and streams and in the clouds will get pushed upwards. If the water on Earth were to heat up and cause massive evaporation, water would escape from the atmosphere. We believe this is what happened to Mars after it had formed.

"Our best bet would be to cool down. The water would slow down and freeze, forming ice, and when we turn the heat back up, it would melt and stay in the ecosystem.

"We could do this from the computer system at the Hub. I would have to go there daily and tweak it a tiny percentage each day. Calculating everything, I have come up with just a 65% drop in temperature to achieve what we want to achieve."

\* \* \*

Brandon took the podium once again. "People, this month when the world freezes over would be a month of rest. Our roles have changed since we first stepped on board. Where once we were passengers, we were now farmers and caretakers of this great ship. This will be a vacation. A time of gathering beforehand, but during the freeze, there is little for us to do. Jaughn can work on crafting more beer; MC can sit around and play cards."

"MC cheats," someone said in the audience, and people laughed.

"Yooooooo," came the all too familiar call of MC.

"Let's do this, people. Let's get this vine out of the way, so we don't have to spend our hours trying to get rid of it. Now, any questions?"

"I have one," Jeff stood after raising his hand. "The pigs eat and depend on the vine. It is a staple for them to live off. With the vine gone, won't they starve?"

"Great point. At last count, we have a lot of pigs. If we destroy the vine, then there is not enough food to sustain their population as it is. If you ask, many believe the pig population is way too much."

"Here, here," someone said, and others echoed her.

"We will have to slaughter many to trim them back down to a normal, manageable population. We can store them in freezers until we eat them. Everybody needs to put in some long days. But I promise you it will be much better afterward. We no longer have to have people go out specifically to cut the vine. What we don't harvest, we will lose, and it will become fodder for the pigs.

"Stacy will let us know what plants and trees will be hardy enough to leave and what we will need to shelter.

"What about the beer and the wine I have?" Jaughn asked. "Won't the cold weather ice it up? The glass bottles will crack."

"If you have them in a temperature-controlled location, then there will be no need. Also, sometimes the cold weather brings out the flavor of certain fruits. Year number fourteen could be a superb year for wine."

Stacy stood up. "Actually, aren't there some fruits you place in cold storage before you ferment them? I know the red plums ferment nicely in the cold. The ice breaks the cells down just a little and allows the sugar to work its magic that much better."

"I've never tried that."

"You are not the only one here who makes a mean sangria. I have some, just a little, that you may sample if you wish."

"Stacy, where have you been? I could have used you a long time ago."

She smiled and took her seat.

"Are there questions?"

I found myself raising my hand.

"Yes, Sally."

"Will Anderson need an escort to the Hub? Also, will there be people there to watch over him to make sure he does what he does and does not jeopardize the ship?"

"Sally," Anderson stood up and addressed me. "I do not know how many times I must say that I am deeply saddened by what happens to Brehm that day. It was not my fault. I would welcome anybody who wishes to come along to join me there at the Hub. Also, I must point out that at no time since then have the controls been locked out. If I did so, I could have gone to the Hub and wreaked havoc on the system. I wish nobody to die. We are all in this together, and I want to see it out to the end."

No matter what, when it came down to it, I could not like this man whatsoever. There was nothing about him I found appealing on any level. I held him right up there with Troy. Lena said since the incident with Brehm, I may have looked for things in him and expounded on that. Mannerisms I dismissed with others, I focused on with him.

He spoke more up on stage, but I did not hear a thing. His heavy lips, droopy eyes, and the way he slicked his hair back as if he were trying to be presentable or in with the ladies. I found all of this repulsive.

I leaned closer to Lena and whispered. "Would you come with me?"

"I would," she answered with her hand on mine, and her squeeze lingered.

I found comfort in this and inwardly smiled.

"You don't have to go every time. Just the first few to give me reassurance."

Again, she squeezed my hand.

* * *

The safety of the lemon trees, the oranges, and the pineapples bothered them. All of these tropical plants would perish in the winter. The trees like the sequoias, the apple and pear trees, or the other trees bearing nuts would become dormant in the wintertime, so we didn't have to worry about them. To save the others, we would have to build a heated greenhouse over the top.

Someone suggested the Albert tubes. The plasti-light containers could cover the trees to protect them. Stacy said it would work for some smaller ones, but the larger ones were way too big. They would have to do studies to find out how well the plasti-lite kept heat. If it let the heat dissipate quickly, then there was no use using it at all.

* * *

Pat Pat spent over two days bringing as many of the taller Albert tubes as he could. The kim-two next to the orchard was getting crowded. He positioned them alongside a row of orange trees. And then, with the help of a few others, he heaved some on top.

"Now you see, even though they are round, they are sturdy enough to hold their own weight. Shit, I've seen these stacked vertically twenty high."

"That will be too high for us," Stacy noted, shielding her eyes from the sun.

Pat Pat looked at her with a sly grin. "You can never be too high."

She rolled her eyes.

"We do it this way, and it'll form a cocoon around the plants. The heat stays in, and we get to eat. Jaughn still has stuff for his liquor."

"How many do you have?" Brandon paced back and forth with his arms folded across his chest.

"Oh, we have a whole freaking warehouse full of them. Not sure if they were sending them back to be used on Earth or what. We damn sure have quite a few of them."

"You know, structurally, they are sound, and they would carry the weight of any snow that gets on top. We could tarp over the top and heat the bottom."

"That would work. We can make it very dry for a time. Have Anderson slow down the atmosphere so that there is less precipitation."

Capt. Everett returned from walking across the field. "Looking good, looking good." He shielded his eyes and looked up at Pat Pat, who stood on the plasti-lite. "I paced off the field. Each row of trees has enough room between them for tubes. We place chalk of some type on top of each one to keep it from rolling, cover with the tarp where it needs to be, and we're good."

Stacy looked over at Brandon and slapped him on the arm.

"We can do this," she said. "Finally, something is going our way."

\* \* \*

The terminal that Anderson worked at had always been in 0G. On the floor right before it were two hoops to place your feet. This allowed the operator to stay in position during the time they operated the screen. If a person constantly tapped on the screen, they drifted. It was a nuisance, to say the least.

I held on to a tether close to the ceiling and dangled there like a spider. Three others had come with us. I had never seen Lena in a suit before. Capt. Everett looked over his shoulder, and Stacy, whom I had always assumed was perpetually earthbound, stayed at his side.

\* \* \*

It was midwinter when a shuttle arrived at Hotel Lima. A person exited who was wearing a utility spacesuit. He wore no helmet, and we could not recognize him. It was odd to have a stranger in our midst.

"Hello?" He said loudly outside the hotel. "Is anyone there?"

He shielded his eyes, and I could see by his reaction, he noticed other people in the windows.

Presently, I watched Tony, wrapped in a blanket, walk out to greet him. After they exchanged a few words, the man turned and left.

Many of us ran downstairs.

"That was Demetrius. The guy who sat in the chair in the lobby for a week. He was the man who was angry at being here. He has severe allergies and only had medicine for a few days. If he comes down here with all the pollen, then it will give him an allergic reaction to kill him. He was curious why the world was turning colder."

"He lives up there?"

"How could he have a garden?"

"Hey, I don't know. Maybe he comes down in the spacesuit and raids the place now and then."

"Where is he staying?"

"He said he does not want us to know. There are literally hundreds of thousands of homes at this end and at the other end that are above the frost line. He could be in any of them. He came down because he thought we were all dead. When the world turned to ice, he became concerned."

* * *

I imagine that as we finally exit the hotel, we all looked like some prairie animal coming from its den. The suits have been charging for over a month now, and we have the heaters up. Trying to put the windows up on a shuttle is very difficult with the bulky gloves, and almost everybody dons their helmet. I'm one of the few brave ones who do not. My body is warm. The suits keep it so. The cold air is biting, but it feels good. I know my cheeks and nose are red, but the cold air is refreshing nonetheless.

There are six people in every shuttle. We work in two-hour shifts and swap out with others when we go back.

Our sole mission is to look for the vine. It's a slow process. We have the shuttle down to one-quarter speed, and they tell us that if there is any doubt, we are to stop and go exam it. When we finished, we plot our progress on a map. Many of our routes overlap. Brandon and Stacy wish to be sure that there is no more vine.

We pass by the rows of the Albert tubes. We see nothing wrong.

XD05, Year 15 - "This little piggy had roast beef."

He had to admit that the whole time it was a pretty good gig. They did not expect him to work the fields, or the kitchens, or the cleanup, or the laundry. All they asked of him was that he take the barrels of organic waste from the kitchens, put them on a shuttle and run them down a couple of kim-two's and drop them over the edge. The pigs cleaned up everything dropped down to them. He searched the fields and picked up baskets of waste. The sheer number of plants was getting out of hand and difficult to control. At first, it was just simple scraps, and sometimes there was almost not enough to go around. Now, 15 years after the event, everything had multiplied.

He could feed the pigs bushel after bushel of grapples alone, and still, so much more would go to rot.

They cut corn stalks after they harvested the corn regularly. Tomato vines were pulled when they no longer bore tomatoes. Potatoes, avocados, peppers; the list went on and on.

A caretaker for the pigs to begin with, his role shifted to that of a garbageman. It was okay, though. No one else wanted it, and they kept him busy. Alone, mostly, but busy.

This day he stood at one of the ribbon intersections. Having the industrial shuttle sit still, bees found the slop in the barrels and were gathering.

There was a bunch of pigs in the far corner. They had not seen him yet. The sound of the slop hitting the surface below would alert them. They would be here soon enough.

He brought out the dolly, secured the ramp, and got his gloves from the front seat. It was a shame he had to use the gloves of the spacesuit. These are the only ones he found that were waterproof. Gloves made of leather held too much of the liquid, and he could not count the number he had ruined. The gloves from the spacesuit were airtight and watertight. Perfect for what he needed.

He lined up the barrels at the edge.

As he was dumping in the fourth one, he overextended a bit. This caused the weight of the barrel to shift, and instead of dumping down to the ground, it rolled back toward him a little. For just a split second, he remembered the catastrophic event of Sebastian with the barrel pinning him against the wall. He would not let that happen. With the momentum he had, he came backward and shifted his weight and pushed at the same time. He sacrificed the barrel. Rather than dropping as a mushy liquid goo onto the pigs below, the barrel would hit them hard.

It was the band around the edge that caught his glove, and rather than slipping off, it pulled him with it over the edge. The drop was only 3 meters. The moist slop of the fruits and vegetables already loosened up the dirt. When he hit the ground, he hit rather badly.

His upper body hit the barrel, almost knocking him out. Several of the pigs squealed in terror and ran away. When he looked back at his arm, there was a second bend between the wrist and the elbow. Rather than the glove becoming unstuck from the barrel, it had broken his arm.

"Well," he said between clenched teeth as a snout breathed heavily in his ear, "This really sucks."

* * *

Driven first one way and then another, I narrowed the herd of swine down from six to four and then finally two. With a series of gates, I could single out one pig. It was not my first choice, but he would do nonetheless. Once the hammer fell, and this one died, then I would reopen the gates, and the pigs would find each other again and wander away to eat once more.

For the one beneath me, this unfortunate grunting fellow today would be his last. I could dress him here and drag the carcass back. In the kitchens in the hotel, I would invoke the help of Doc, and we could skin him and prepare an evening meal.

The thought of pork again turned my stomach a little. Maybe time was better spent out in the orchards gathering fruit. The only reason I was out here today was that Teddy and one or two others complained that they needed more than just salads. If they thought it was so easy, then why weren't they out here?

It was an early morning for me, the sun out just an hour. I would take a nap this afternoon after everybody was taken care of. If I had children, and the thought lingered in the back of my mind as it was prone to do, if I had chosen a different path and given in to those who wished it, then my children would be here now doing the dirty work. My offspring would be the ones who would take care of me.

Hearing the pig below me grunt brought me back. I shook my head to clear my thoughts. It did not make a difference now, regardless. What they did was done. I was well beyond the age to have children comfortably if there was such a thing.

I had marked a spot on the ground and lay poised on a catwalk with a heavy hammer dangling over the edge. Too heavy for me to hold directly, a rope and pulley held it fast. I had placed apples and carrots directly in the circle. Kept reined in the ring that made up the second kilometer from the Twilight Wall, the pigs survived only on the wild grass that was there. The apples and carrots were a delicacy never before had.

The pig was distressed at being away from the others. His communication with them through grunts and squeals would go on for a little longer. Even though his family had freedom, they stayed close to the first gate.

With the trap set, all I had to do was wait until his head was in the circle before I let loose of the string to drop the hammer. It never knew I lay above looking through a peep-hole.

I took one breath, held it, and then another. The rope slipped from my fingers, and the hammer fell. Not the shot I wanted, but it would have to do. It struck the piglet on the side of the head, and the squealing began anew. It did circles looking for a way out, but could find none. Blood squirted from its head, and in a few moments, it collapsed.

Its cloven feet pawed the earth before it settled down and died.

This is something I never got used to. Once the kill was over and the adrenaline left, I would look at the helpless animal with pity.

*Getting a little soft in your old age?* I asked myself. I waited a moment longer and then stood using a spear for support.

I triggered all the other gates, and they dropped. The trapped swine ran outward and was free for another day.

* * *

As I brought the dressed pig back to the hotel kitchen on a wagon, Doc stopped me.

"Have you seen Pat Pat?" He gave me a worried look.

"No, not lately," I looked around, realizing that I had not seen him in some time.

"I don't want to alarm anybody, but I think something got him. There've been times he missed a day or two. It's now been a whole week. The kitchen slop he was feeding the pigs is beginning to pile up. Just not right."

I understood what Doc was getting at. There was a hint, somewhat subtly, for me to go find Pat Pat.

I looked back at the wagon and handed him the handle.

"I'll take a shuttle on down to his place and see if he is there."

"He's been gone a while. I tend not to get worried when people don't show up for a meal. This is becoming less of a place to find food and more of a place to congregate, you know?"

"Yeah, you do well bringing them all together." I slapped him on the shoulder and turned.

* * *

What gave his location away were the barrels sitting alongside the track. There were only three, yet they were so out of place where they were. I gave the command for the shuttle to stop. I did not bother to call out. I wanted to see it first.

After looking over the edge, it was easy to figure out what had happened. The clothing was barely recognizable as it lay covered in blood and mud. There was no sign of him. He was the one who had told us to be careful around pigs. A small family group of four or five could devour a human in a very short time.

The pigs had gone from the area. I could see the ground where they trampled.

I needed no evidence or proof of his death. I would let Brandon know what had happened and tell Doc afterward.

I climbed aboard the shuttle and headed back to the hotel.

Homeport, Day 6

For his presentation, Adams did not resort to a videoconference. Something of this importance, he went directly to Director Porter's office. He carried no papers or books with him; he needed none. Everything he was about to present to them was in his head.

He waited outside until the secretary let him in. The director was there, as were Mabel and the heads of the military.

"*Good,*" Adams thought to himself. This was everybody whom he needed to see. Richard looked more at ease than he had in a long time. Mabel tapped a stylus on a tablet as she crunched numbers.

Adams took a seat. "Whoever did this was a very crafty individual."

"Not only did they have to know the 'ins' and 'outs' of the computer system, but the degree of knowledge to put in the right variables is also nearly impossible to duplicate by pure happenstance."

"We have been looking for Michael White. I do not think it's him. Michael had the education, but I knew Michael. He did what he had to do and was happy just existing. He never ever went against the flow. He was straight and narrow as they come."

Mabel shifted in her seat. "So, you think it is someone else? Who else would have the ability?"

"I do not know. I know that for Michael White to do something such as this, it would be a tremendous leap. Is it beyond him? No. I'm a firm believer that everybody has a spark. For someone to do something like this, you would need a sense of adventure to believe they could do it even before they started it."

"Mr. White lacked this?" asked Major Ronca.

"Ambition is the word I'm looking for. Michael White had no ambition whatsoever. He was not ambitious enough to try something like this."

"So, what exactly are we dealing with?" Richard asked.

Adams got the biggest smile on his face. "It has been a revolution in what we do. So much more has suddenly become open to us. It is like finding a diamond in the coal bin." He laughed while the others looked at each other. Mabel favored him with a smile and looked at Richard to see if he knew the joke.

"Let me explain. The Lightfoot Equation we used to shuttle our ships around simply does not say 'let us go from point A to point B as quickly as possible.' The variable in question is a sentence of four hundred characters, and if there is one letter, or one number, off by just one place in the alphanumeric ladder, then the whole thing kicks it back out. After three or four such failures, it will shut down completely until it notifies those in the hierarchy and they override the previous failures.

"Somehow, our friend accomplished the impossible. They have rewritten the Lightfoot Equation in this shoebox to allow for appendages. Now, with this unique series, we still have the four-hundred-character sentence; however, some of those characters now refer to a secondary branch from the main root. So instead of a standard equation, we now have one that contains more information and is an unbroken string of over a thousand alphanumeric characters."

Richard leaned forward. "I am really not understanding what you are saying."

"Okay," Adams took a deep breath and closed his eyes, gathering his thoughts. "Say we start off with a simple string, yay long," he held up his hands. "Okay, the information we must feed the shoebox, get it, shoestring shoebox, anyway, the information we must give the shoebox can only be four hundred characters. If there is any mistake in the characters, then we must start over. Somebody has created the standard line of four hundred characters plus some offshoots. We have never thought this possible before. Before this, it was quite impossible. These offshoots are like branches of a tree. There can be more information obtained on these branches and fed back into the original trunk. Instead of four hundred characters to depict a location in the galaxy, we now have a thousand.

"Quite remarkably, the Samuel Drives can drop anybody almost anywhere."

"So, you are saying…?"

He looked between them for a moment.

"Another analogy someone came up with is a sailboat. With what we knew before, we had to ride against the wind or straight on. What we can do now is 'tack.' To go to a different place, we go at a slight angle and visit a completely new place on the stairway, a stairway we are no longer bound to. Based on what I have seen, it may be quite possible we can move freely in the universe with minimal effort."

"So, then it can tell us then how to get to the location of XD05?"

Adams looked confused. Clearly, his mind was going elsewhere, and he had to shift gears. "Um, once the ship jumped to where it has been all these years, the person covered their tracks. They had a lot of time and could access this. They erased the original string, and the command line sat empty."

"Could have they returned if they wanted to?" Capt. Klasnick asked.

"You mean '05, oh yes, someone with that amount of knowledge would surely know the equation to get them home. For them, it would be rudimentary. As if someone asked you or me to recite the alphabet. They sat there all those years in self-induced exile. They could've returned at any moment."

Richard steepled his hands. "When the '05 returned, was there any record of how it got here? Clearly, it has been unmanned for a very long time. The return command would have had to be programmed in. If we find it, we could reverse it and find the '05."

"We could not find anything. That it returned here is still beyond us." Adams held up his hands. "I know that you are all worried about your ship, as you should be, but there is something else here. Again, I must tell you the importance of someone cracking the Lightfoot Equation."

"I am sure it's very exciting," Capt. Klasnick injected. "If the '05 is somewhere out there and all we must do is plug in these thousand alphanumeric characters in the equation, then we will find them. It will be just a matter of a process of elimination."

"No," Adams shook his head. With his hands on the arm of his chair, he was literally sitting at the edge of his seat. "That's not really how it works. We cannot do it sequentially. It will take a while for us to figure this out. In all my years of reading code, we could never do anything like this. From day one, the rules have been set in stone. Now suddenly, we realize that we have been thinking narrowly. We have been so happy to stay on the staircase and all that it offers that we never knew what it would be like on an individual floor."

"If we continue to use the staircase analogy, how many steps away are we talking about?"

"As far as steps go, presently we have, on the Lucy staircase, one step for every light-year and calendar year. We cannot go back too far. It binds us to the galaxy by the massive black hole sitting at its center. If we go back too far, the galaxy has not yet formed, and it loses us. There is a point in time where several of our probes sit. Stuck in B.F.E. somewhere, they do not have the signposts to return home. If they could not traverse the light-year/calendar year, then they will have a very long time before they catch up to us. The same goes for things going upstream. We can travel as far ahead as to when the Andromeda galaxy slams into us. Once our black hole and their black hole start to mesh, then things get really tricky. So that leaves us with a nice tight stairway of operation."

"How many steps do we have in the staircase?" Richard asked.

"We are looking at 17.76 billion usable steps, if you choose to continue this analogy, from top to bottom. Our time sits close to the start of the upper quarter. There is so much more behind us than there is before us."

"All we must do then is slowly listen on each of these 17 billion steps to find X-ray Delta 05."

Adams shrugged his shoulders. "It may sound easy in layman's terms. We set the probes up, press start, and just let them go. We already completed all that information gathering with the first sweep two decades ago. '05 is there in that mass amount of data. We have to know what we're looking for."

"I gather it is not that simple?"

"No, there is so much more involved. With this new variation to the Lightfoot Equation that tells the computer where it wants the ship to come out, it is a whole different ballgame. From what I can see, it uses the same information the ship's computer would use for the ship to travel Lucy; however, there is more data. Director Porter, for every Lucy step we take, these new equations give thousands of different locations literally. And this is just the first Lucy step we take, either upstream or downstream. If we were to take two Lucy steps, we would have the first few thousand different locations and the second set of a few thousand different locations. Every step we take, the number of destinations increases exponentially."

"So, we will never find the '05 while it is away," said Richard, tapping the tabletop with his fingers. "It disappeared for a thousand plus years. Truly, during the next thousand years of our time, we should be able to find it. We mapped the Lucy staircase within five years."

"Director, if we have at our disposal one thousand probes, we could send them out to almost every location in one step in this equation. When they came back to us, then we could sift through the information. We could then have them jump one Lucy, upstream or down, and then from there, they could send them out using the new variables. The information gathered would be, pardon the pun, so astronomical as to be overwhelming. We have 17.76 billion steps with a few thousand random destinations on each one. We may have lost XD05; however, with this technology, we now have so much more to explore. Whoever did this gave us a galaxy."

None of the others shared his enthusiasm.

"I hate to burden you with this. It is not my place to cause turmoil with the upper echelon." As he spoke, Adams fluttered his hands upward. "We are here in this pseudo-solar system, taking a lot of effort to build ships that will sit in a Near Earth Orbit. People depend on what we do. As of last week, we had only one single sun that followed our sun's orbit on the staircase. When we finish '06, we can send it there, rather than Sol. The number of ships around our home Sun is really gaining in number.

"Lady and gentlemen, I foresee that a whole new era of space travel will open for us. Do you remember the expansion before? Do you remember how they suddenly channeled all resources into this vast new place that opened up to us decades ago? I believe we will have an extensive number of suns available with hospitable planets. We will move cautiously; however, there is so much out there now suddenly within our grasp that within a very short amount of time, the ships built here will be completely obsolete. They will search for people to terraform a world rather than harvest vegetables on the ship. We will no longer be needed."

The room was quiet.

"I foresee that it will only be a matter of time before we find another sun. And based on these equations, this sun does not have to be in tandem with our Sun. No matter where we are in the galaxy, which direction we are going, what time we are in, we will find our way back home."

He stood from the table then. No one looked at him as he went to the door and left.

XD05, Year 18

Doc came running into the dining hall. His chef's hat was sitting way back on his head. He had a knife in one hand and a ladle in the other. I thought at first he would hurt somebody.

"STOP!" he yelled at the top of his lungs. For a second, there was no other sound in the dining hall. "Everyone stop eating. Does anybody have any bana-berries left on their plate?"

We all looked around, but it was clear that there were none left.

"Any in the dishes? Just one bana-berry? Anyone?"

When no one replied, he had a look of pure sadness on his face.

"I made a mistake." Placing the utensils in one hand, he took his hat off and crumpled it up with the other. "I screwed up royally. The bana-berries that came in from the field were the very last bana-berries we had. I thought someone gave them to me to prepare. We were supposed to take the seeds off for the new year. Ladies and gentlemen, I must tell you, today we ate the last bana-berries. There are no more onboard." His head drooped as he turned and shuffled back to the kitchen. It was a long time before conversations resumed.

\* \* \*

We searched the fields. To ensure a fresh crop, the recent plants were pulled two days ago to make way for a new crop. These had already wilted, and it was clear that there was no hope they would survive. They shut the area down, hoping perhaps there were one or two seeds hidden in the soil that would eventually germinate into plants.

The field that Lena and I had started so long ago was doing well. Instead of bana-berries, we had to resort to actual strawberries. There was a fuss at first, but not by many.

\* \* \*

With the same fanfare that Doc used, Renn and Jeff ran into the dining hall. Out of shape and sweating profusely, they both crumpled into seats. Elbows on his knees, Jeff looked like he would collapse. Something happened, something bad. The two had to catch their breath before they could speak.

"The vine... the vine... is back!" Renn gasped loudly to everyone who gathered around.

"We were up... past the transition... sunrise side... Western quarter.

Ah, man, it's there."

Renn shook his head and wiped his brow. "I recognize that green anywhere."

"How much is there?" Viyona asked. "Just a kim-two?"

"It's back with a vengeance. It's been two years now since we had winter. We looked for it then and have not looked for it since."

Renn breathed deep and sat back in his chair. "I just lost two buckets of berries."

\* \* \*

Many of us went to look. As we drifted past the area in question, it was clear that the cold had not eradicated the vine.

"Shit," said Jaughn. "I'm done." Others echoed his response. "I mean, days upon days I tugged and pulled, I cut and snipped, and still it's here? We beat it back this far. By the time it gets back to us, I'll be long gone.

"Sally." I turned as he mentioned my name. "You'd better get a taste for it."

As I looked back out the open window, I gave him the finger without flinching.

XD05, Year 20

Get ready for a rant. I was not having a good week. No matter what I did, things were going against me.

For some reason, we were short-handed in the fields. When has that ever happened? Hudson and Tang helped when they could, but even they seemed elusive at times. We needed potatoes for breakfast and evening meals and somehow were short on rations in the kitchen. It had been a while since we had dug them up, and some potatoes had grown more plants in their eyes while stored in Doc's back room. I finished digging up two tubs myself. There were five of us out there, and for some reason, the others seemed to be in a non-productive mood.

I was filthy when we returned. I ended up taking two showers.

The second day, I got called to the orchards, and once there, we could not find some essential equipment. We had to go back to the shed two times. Once for ladders and then once again for pickers. The pickers were very rudimentary. Long poles with a wire net at the end. You put it around fruit on the branch, tug, and the fruit falls into a wire net. Simple. How could they have forgotten those? We have the technology that allows us to hover on a paper-thin ribbon from one end of the ship to the other, but we cannot get a device that will harvest the fruit for us. This day I filled three baskets of grapples and one of oranges.

As we were winding down, they wanted me to go pick grapes ready for harvest. I looked at them in disbelief. Charlie normally did this. He was our great connoisseur of grapes, but he was not feeling well and his shoulders hurt. That's the problem with them getting older; they could do less and less, and more of the burden was on me.

I dusted my pants off and told him I would help. For me, there was a catch. I wasn't about to put away the equipment here and help Charlie at the same time. It was one or the other. I let them stow the stuff away.

It was a very relaxing twenty-minute ride to the kim-two with the grapes. I almost fell asleep. There is a nice abundance on the vine this year, and it would have been shameful to let any of them go to waste. Charlie chatted the whole time, and that was fulfilling. He is quite the personable man. He would talk about his family and how he missed his wife and children. Sometimes he spoke of other girls he knew before someone married him. From what he told me, as old as he is, he was quite a lady's man back in the day. I kept quiet, mostly letting him go on and on. I gave him a knowing wink once or twice, and this put a twinkle in his eye.

It was well past suppertime when we finished. He gave me a hand in getting the grapes to the shuttle, but he would not come with me this evening. He had a little shanty there in which he stayed and rarely came into town.

I woke up in the shuttle. The ride has always been smooth and quiet. I was not sure how long it had rested with me at the hotel. That was quite the experience to wake up and not know where you were. I made something for myself in the kitchen and then shuffled up to the room I shared with Lena. I took a shower and then slipped into comfortable clothing.

Addy stopped by for a few minutes; however, she did not stay long, and after she left, I climbed in the bed. Sleep came easily that night.

I thought the third day of the week would be the easiest. At breakfast, I found out there was a spill they wanted my help with.

Bev had been moving something, some type of hazardous material that spilled, and she wanted my help with it. I asked if anybody else could help, and everyone was busy doing other things. They stuck me with it.

The stuff in question was a two-hundred-liter drum of some liquid. It was red with the labels on the side that said 'oxidizer.' It is not terribly hazardous, but we could not leave it lying there. I went out to the site, and it took most of the morning just getting the cleaning materials there. We had to go find several other drums to put it in. It was a very sticky and slurry liquid that had a faint odor of apples with a hint of lemon.

During the process of cleaning up, I splattered myself. On these work pants, my favorite, I had several drop spots. I knew this was hazmat, but it better be the 'washable' kind and not the 'burning holes in clothing' kind. I was a little frustrated, to say the least.

At one point, I was getting exhausted and going to take a break. There was an empty drum sitting with several others on a pallet. This one happened to fall as I was standing there and, even though I jumped back, it fell on my toes.

It pissed me off.

With my good foot, I kicked the drum in frustration. This only ended up stubbing my toe. We did not have boots on; we had on sneakers. I hobbled around for quite a few minutes. Curses flew.

Bev's face reddened, and although there was a look of concern in her eyes, she looked upset as well. She told me to go sit on the rock, and she would finish up. When I told her I was thinking about taking the shuttle back to the hotel, she stalled me. She said to wait a few minutes, and we would go together. The few minutes dragged on. I would like to say she was deliberately keeping me here. When the cleanup was almost finished, she would sit and chat. My responses were quick and short. I was tired, hungry, and in pain. I didn't want to sit out here underneath the sun and chitchat.

I saw a movement out of the corner of my eye. I sighed audibly. A shuttle was coming down the ribbon. It slowed as it got close and then settled down.

It disappointed me to see it was Addy. She had been in the military as well. Sometimes I thought Lena was very strict and regimental. Addy was even more so. She did not look too happy to see us, even though we were done with the project, mostly.

"Addy," I smiled at her. "Um, we were just finishing up."

"Doesn't look like you're helping at all," she scolded me. "Was Bev doing all the work?"

"Empty drum fell on my foot. I was just resting my digits." I raised my foot and flexed. "See, nothing broken, just bruised."

"Very good. I need you to get on board and strap in."

"We're just going back to the hotel, right?"

She turned to me, and her face was passive. She snapped her fingers with a short whistle. "Bev, you need to come."

"Oh? I… I…"

"It can wait. It looks like you got everything cleaned up for now. We need you both back." Giving no further explanation, she turned. I looked at Bev and shrugged my shoulders.

When we sat, Addy activated the controls, and the shuttle lifted.

* * *

As we neared the hotel, the shuttle did not slow down.

"Addy, where are we going?" I asked, firmly watching the familiar building zip by. No one was outside.

"I say again, strap in," her voice was flat and monotone. I often referred to this as her military voice, which still gave no explanation. "We are going up the wall."

Bev and I were quick with the buckles.

"If we're going too far, I didn't bring a jacket," I snipped. Addy looked over her shoulder at me for just a moment. I sensed she didn't like my little quips, and so I remained quiet.

* * *

Sensors on the shuttle would stop the vehicle from going up too far if the passengers had no protective clothing. Addy worried me sometimes. We were just a kilometer up when the shuttle slowed. I let out another sigh, thankful she did not take us up further. I did not know the lengths she would go to.

The vehicle flattened out. We went from gravity pulling us back in the seats to it pulling at our feet. Riding the shuttles up the wall was always a thrill of sorts. It had gone in about thirty meters and settled. Addy unbuckled, retracted the belts, stood and waited for us outside the vehicle.

We followed.

It was cold up here. The temperature was about 10° less than at Lena's house. Still, I had no explanation as to why I was here, and I was getting very curious; however, I held my tongue. I watched her, looking for clues. If someone had been seriously injured, she would've moved faster. Somebody may have died. My mind reeled, and I finally gave up trying to read her.

She went to one house and put her hand on the entrance pad.

The door chimed before it opened. Addy did not enter.

"Sally, there is stuff here. I need you to help me stow on the shuttle. Bev, we could use your strength."

"All this to help you move boxes. Feeling a little used here," I did not hide my frustration at her rudeness. Still, Addy did not move.

"Listen, you have a problem?" She stepped closer. "Take it back down to the surface. Right now, we have a job to do. Let's get it done and go home. Everyone else is busy. You need to learn to pull your share." She looked at me evenly, and I returned her gaze.

I rolled my eyes. I hated that people thought I did not carry my weight. We could tussle right here, but it would not be the thing to do. Addy had never backed down on her military training and was quite fit. I'm sure she would have me pinned on my back before I could blink. I didn't even think Bev would come to my aid. I looked between both of them.

Out of anger, I almost swore.

"Addy, I don't need this, all right?" my voice was loud and carried. "Show me the boxes, and we will load them up. I hope you can respect that my feet hurt, and I need my weekend to start."

She motioned with her hand.

I was expecting the lights to come on automatically. I was not expecting what happened next.

"SURPRIZE!!"

From the darkness, as the lights came on, there were suddenly people. To say I had a quizzical look on my face was an understatement. I remember mouthing words that were inappropriate.

Music blared, and there were more shouts of excitement. Tang was there, Lena, Brandon, Derwin, Evan, Tony, Jxan, Viyona. Everybody was cheering. MC let out one of his telltale 'Yooooooo's.' The place was more crowded than the dining hall. I realized that everybody on board must be here. Even Charlie, in his dusty overalls, waved to me from the back of the crowd. Renn offered a large tumbler and handed me a drink. I sipped the fruity mix and could definitely taste the alcohol.

I was in shock, a complete shock. I felt all the tension I had wrapped around me slip away like the drink burning my throat.

"What's going on?" I asked over the din. Addy walked past me and punched me playfully on the shoulder. I think it was the first time I had ever seen her smile. She and Bev joined the others. I realized Bev was in on it.

It was then I read a large sign hanging from the corners of the room. 'Welcome Home.'

Lena, grinning from ear to ear, stayed back.

Brandon stood from his chair and limped forward. Always good with words, they let him speak. The music died, and the din settled.

"I had a casual conversation with Jacob and Helen a few months back. The pig's population is flourishing. The vine is being held back at bay, but only barely so. It would take a lot more people than we have to eradicate it completely. We are getting older." There were several boos from everyone. Brandon held up a finger, and they quieted. "Time is passing, and time is nobody's friend. As things run their course, there will be a day when we many are down to just a few. The vine will strangle the crops we have, and when we are our most frail, we will have to fight our hardest. What Jacob and Helen brought to my attention was the simple fact of why are we were fighting the vine down there? If we retreat up here to live and work, then it rewards our efforts. We have already lost the battle down there.

"What we have done here is drawn a line in the sand. Where we are, it is too cold for the vine to grow, and so, this space will always and forever remain free. Over the last few weeks, we have restructured several homes here and created a greenhouse that is vine free. The sun will warm it, and the water will flow, soil. We've brought up and sterilized many tons from the surface. Everyone here has been busy bringing up plants and germinating trees. It's been one of our most productive times ever."

I didn't know what to say; I stood there in my dirty work clothes, nervously rubbing my hands, trying to clean them, and I was speechless.

"But"

"We did this for you. We also did it because we know someday you will need it for the last. Doing this now, when we are able-bodied, we know we can keep the vine from here. These buildings specifically we have made for you." Brandon raised his own glass. "May you be here longer than the rest of us, Wee One."

"How many times do I have to hear that?" I did a fake sigh.

"Hey, we're just looking out for you."

"We only wish that Stacy was here to help out," Cyn said, nudging my shoulder. "We think we got everything done correctly. With her hand, we would've been sure."

Subconsciously, I flexed my own fingers, balled them into a fist, and remembered something that she had once said. "From my mind to yours, from my hand to you," I said without thinking about it.

"Is she talking in lyrics again?" Brandon laughed, patting me on the back, before walking away.

* * *

The work they had done was expensive. Bringing the special glass panels up from the surface to homes on the wall was no easy task. The front of over ten homes was completely taken away and replaced.

Water, purified and ever-flowing, went through a series of open ductwork. Every five meters, they placed a small collection pool. With a bucket or ladle, we took water out when needed. They had an irrigation system that misted water over the plants. It was a good concept; however, they shied away from irrigation works with moving parts. If I became dependent on this and it broke down, then the whole network would fail.

More Science Stuff

Our Sun is uniquely ours. In the Galactic Spiral Staircase, our value is neither negative nor positive. It sits at zero. There are other places we wish to go to. Homeport, where the giant ships are being built, is -140,357 Lucy steps away from us, and so its signature is negative 140357. There are at least twelve points of interest throughout the space and time of the galaxy's existence that intersect the spiral staircase quite nicely. Of all the trillions of stars, the comets, and the clouds of dust and gas that are out there, these twelve are the only ones riding in tandem with us.

At the time of the return of XD05, its sister ship, XD06, was about two years until completion. Almost everything was operational on the ship. They were waiting for the atmosphere to settle and the weather system to kick in.

With these new equations that came from the shoebox on '05, things were put on hold. Attention shifted.

They needed a place to start out. The area around the sun was too busy. They wanted to start out at the beginning, as low down the staircase as they could work their way upward. If they started at the Sun, they would retrieve information from upstream and downstream at the same time.

They believed XD05 to be unstable. The eco-system had collapsed, and if they wanted to get it up and running again, it would take years of meticulous planning and rebuilding the biodiversity.

The atmosphere would suffice with the number of humans working there, but there would be a day when they would pass the point of no return, and the breathable oxygen to start to decline exponentially. They deemed it necessary that '05 would stay put and begin the long, slow haul to mending.

They sent '06 down to the first step at the bottom of the staircase. Those who worked there called it the basement. Before, it was just a simple outpost, listening for any signal from anywhere. With the ship's arrival, there is a big celebration. The inhabitants jumped from a listening team of twenty to a team of over a thousand.

* * *

The probes they now made were much more sensitive than they had been two decades ago. They gathered more data, creating a wider net. Design engineers sat for countless hours, creating something that would traverse the blackness of space. In the end, they came up with the globe about four meters across. The Samuel Drive, the shoebox, the other sensors, data recorders, data storage units, and the power supply were all crammed in this tight spot.

When the first probe arrived at the bottom of the staircase, they quickly looked it over. With great anticipation, they plugged in the very first variable. Sending it 4 km away, they started the sequence. The probe winked out of existence. During the twenty hours it gathered data, two more probes arrived in the system.

Over the next one hundred days, ten new probes arrived daily. Others returned, the bulk of the data harvested, and that information sent back to Sol.

The retrieval of data was an around-the-clock, mostly automated effort. When sifting through the data, they primarily did it with human senses.

* * *

At the end of six months, they thoroughly searched the first stair in the spiral staircase. At this point, the galaxy was still somewhat in its infancy. With every possible point on the Lightfoot equation for that step examined, they pulled everything and advanced up one light-year/one calendar year.

They started the whole process over again.

Back home in Sol, the information the probes retrieved became invaluable. Although they found no places that were favorable to the human population, there were troves of information on places we found enticing. They logged destinations and kept records. Survey teams lined up in droves for the chance to visit places, yet unseen. The probes recorded a wealth of information from these favorable places now as the humans turned to go see it firsthand. Historians brought up the past. This was close to the gold rush days of America's past.

After the initial round, over seventy-three surveyor teams struck off. Exciting at first, it soon became very arduous, and yet people did not falter. It was a special breed, and they enjoyed what they did. This is the first step in our second expansion of the universe. We had, literally, about 1 billion years LyCy that we craved to explore. It would focus mankind on this endeavor for a very long time.

XD05 remained at Homeport, both of which now lay forgotten and derelict. Our once prized possession, the vehicle that gave us the keys to the kingdom, now lay all but forgotten.

X-ray Delta 07 had a catastrophic failure with the atmosphere. They scrapped it after salvaging what they could. '09 remained without a burner, and although there were traces of atmosphere and water, everything froze.

There was a push to get everything brought back to Sol; however, '05 seemed cursed. No one would touch it, fearing that it may lose its way and become a wanderer in the stars once more. Left alone, it would eventually be part of the system they created it from. Sometime within the next few million years, the gas and dust of that system would condense. In time, a new planetary system would form.

XD05, Year 22

I had to shower to get the dirt off me and change out of the dirty field clothes. On the way back, about a quarter of the way around the circle, I stopped the shuttle when I noticed some nice flowers on a tree. Lena always liked yellow buds. They told me years before that some trees and flowers relied on seasonal changes. This variety was out of sync and had just bloomed for some reason.

A big branch snapped off, and I would try for another, but I was in a hurry. For the rest of the ride, I pulled the yellow buds off the branch and left enough stem so I could tie them together and put them in a vase. They were pretty in the sunlight.

It was late evening when I arrived at the infirmary.

There were others there talking quietly amongst themselves. When I got off the shuttle, everyone noticed me and grew quiet. I bowed my head, not daring to look in their eyes. I didn't need to lose it in front of them. I noticed Stephen first off and went to him.

"Is she...?" I asked, coming beside him.

"She still lives," he said as he reached up and placed a hand on my shoulder. "If we were back home on Earth, she would be fine." He choked up but fought it back. His eyes were red with emotion. As he spoke, I looked at the mosaic on the floor and focused on that. "She will go soon. I'm no doctor, but that's what they say."

"Does she know?" I kept my voice strong.

"How can she not know? Although she is not in the best of moods, I believe she has come to terms with it. She told us goodbye earlier and has been asking for you."

My grip tightened on the bouquet.

"Had I known it was so dire, I would've come earlier."

"No one is blaming you." he squeezed my shoulder a little tighter. "This is life," he whispered, as if his voice threatened to fail him. "This happens. In the end, we must all face it."

Someone else, I was not sure who, came and touched me on the shoulder. It was Wanda. Her eyes were red too, her hands steady. She took a step forward and laid her head on my back.

"Go, little one," Wanda patted my shoulder. It was a name I had not heard in years. "She waits for you one last time."

And I ran.

The well-lit hallways were empty. My shoes sounded loud as they slapped and squealed on the waxed tiles. I went through the double doors to the room that Jxan had once occupied.

Lena was there. Propped upright in the bed, she had two IV's of saline solution, a wristband, and was hooked up to a heart monitor. She wore the white gown and had the soft cotton blankets pulled up to her stomach.

"There you are, kiddo," she smiled, and at that moment, the years I have known her were all but forgotten.

For a second, for one breath, I remembered looking up into the eyes of Lena as she wore her soldier's uniform. Crisp and clean, it fit her perfectly. In all the things she had done over the years, she was a soldier first. Her hair, tightly bound in a dark braid, lay over her shoulder. There were no signs of gray. She was one of the first people, the first friendly face, who welcomed me when I arrived here years ago. One of the fondest memories for years was the warmth of Lena's hand.

Tears filled my eyes and washed away the image from that time. I dabbed my eyes with my sleeve and held back a cry.

I rushed to her and, mindful of the wires, hugged my love. I kissed her forehead several times and felt her respond with a smile.

We held each other for several moments until Lena trembled. She was too weak to carry the embrace, and her arms fell to her side.

When I pulled back, we were both in tears.

"I'm sorry. So, so sorry." I wiped her tears away with my sleeves. "They were having trouble with the irrigation pump up in kim-two 0349. I thought I could help and have been up there for a few days. Dee is the one who brought me the news. Why didn't you tell me?" I tapped her playfully on the shoulder.

"Oh, I didn't think there was much to worry about at first." Her voice was hoarse and spoken at just over a whisper. I had to lean in to understand her. "It's been aching for some time, you know? I thought that after all these years, it had something to do with eating ham all the time or a diet of fruit. Never thought it would be this fast."

"Did they say you will get better?"

"No, they wished me the best, and Jerry wished me a safe journey," at this, she smiled. "I missed halfway by three people. Of the 300 here, I am 147." Everyone on board was keeping count.

"Still, it seems crowded." I sniffed my tears and looked out the window for just a second.

"Better than 299. I forget, who was that?"

"That was Dylan. He went away, you remember? Stormed out one night when they had the argument, and they found him dangling from that balcony."

Lena held up her hands. "He hung himself in a place that had half a G. I mean, come on; it's a slow way to go."

"He probably didn't want to go through with it or left the option open to stop it if he changed his mind. I heard theories that by the time he was near the point of no return, there was too much $CO_2$ built up in the brain, and he wasn't his right self."

"Maybe I'm 148," she smiled a half-smile. "Maybe Johnny Tantrum is still out there. He's wearing that fancy suit still and eating off the fruit trees."

"I think we would have found him by now. That somehow, he would have surfaced or come back for some type of connection with people here. Being in a self-imposed exile that long when there are people here who will talk to you takes a lot of fortitude."

"He seemed to be a very tenacious fellow, if I remember correctly."

I looked into her eyes, and we held each other's gaze for a while.

"I don't want you to go," a whisper was all that I could manage. My voice was held in check. If I spoke louder, I would falter. I had to stay strong for her.

Lena closed her eyes, and it was a full breath before she opened them again.

"For a moment, those on X-ray Delta 05 will pause and wait for me to go. Make sure I am buried here. Be it in the far field or near the water; make sure I stay here. This is my home, and this is where I'll stay."

"Of course you'll stay here. Where else would you go?"

"I have heard rumors. Some have talked about leaving the ship when they believe the time has come. Don a suit, cut the tether; let the interstellar winds take them. In millions of years, they'll become some curiosity for an alien civilization," she paused. She had to take three breaths before she had the strength to speak again. "I believe when I die, I will be with the spirits of my family. My body is ill, but I do not wish it to drift forever. Not in that vacuum. Do you understand me, Sally?"

I nodded.

Lena touched my cheek, wiping away a tear with the back of her hand before she touched her own cheek.

"I cannot tell you when I first looked at you and realized I was in love," she said. I smiled and nodded. "It was even before that trouble began when you were still too young to experience it yourself, but I had feelings for you."

"I know, Lena, I know."

"It wasn't the night you came to my bed; it was a time well before that."

"Shhhh," and I kissed her on the lips. "Why do you speak to me about our love? I will not forget it and your memories, the memories of you, will always be with me."

A single tear rolled down Lena's cheek.

"Keep my things safe. If, in the years to come, anyone speaks harshly of me, do not stand for it."

"Ha! Why would anyone speak harshly of you?"

"To some here, some still living, that I had to protect you from. I was not so nice. Do you remember someone limping a few years back?"

I thought back, but no one came to mind.

Lena sighed. "I don't remember his name exactly. We were never on a name-to-name basis, but he was one of the ones who wanted you to have children. Taller guy, sandy blonde hair, wore the coveralls all the time." Lena caught my eye. "I almost eunuched that bastard."

I could not suppress a smile on my face. "I am not familiar with this term."

"Had he not gotten away," she barely could mime using scissors. She chuckled dryly and nodded. "No more trouble." Lena laughed, so she coughed. She found it hard to stop, but when her body let her, when the spasms in her lungs and chest stopped, she lay back in the bed once more.

"Feel it fading, girl. The strength just goes. I could walk a day ago, and now I doubt I could stand on my own."

"Then don't speak." Not letting go of her hand, I reached back with my foot and, after the third try, hooked the leg of the chair, which I brought closer.

"I will not speak. Everything... I needed to say... I have told you. I love you, I love you, and the love remains still. It will always be here. Sit with me awhile... we will remember."

"I will remember. I will do it for you; you just listen."

"Ah, yes ma'am. I guess I'm in for a tale," she spoke her last words.

"Shhhh, no more." I pressed a finger to Lena's lips. "I must find a place to begin." My mind raced, thinking about where to start. I chuckled twice and was about to start when I paused. Holding Lena's hand and looking her in the eye, I began. "I don't think I ever told you, I've told no one actually, about my trip up to the air intake six on the Morning Wall."

\* \* \*

I gave Lena her last bath. After filling the sink with warm water and soap, I used a sponge to bathe her. When this was done, I washed her hair, dried it, and then braided it, as I remember she used to wear.

She had stayed the same size all the years I have known her, and it was in my mind to dress her in her military uniform. I thought long and hard about this and opted for a white dress they found with Uncle Butch's stuff. I do not know who it belonged to before, but she looked gorgeous in it.

I did this all before rigor mortis set in.

The Albert tubes were not always these huge, clear cylinders. They sometimes came in different sizes. Leonard knew of several that were big enough for her. Also, I had never seen a real coffin before. Stefan said this would do rather nicely. I sent Tony and Leonard to hunt one down.

They laid bedding down the length with a pillow at the end. Trying to get her to lie properly here in the gravity well would be a little difficult. We would do it up at the Hub, where she would be weightless.

I quickly grabbed a few things from her room and met the others in the hospital room.

With help, I got her to a shuttle. From there, many of us took it down to the Morning Wall. I wanted her to rest there. I wanted to wake each day knowing where the sun was, so was my love.

Everyone said their goodbyes at the bottom of the wall. Slipping into a suit, I would be the only one going up. It would be a long journey for me. I wanted to preserve her exactly the way she was. If I raced up the side and exposed her to the cold and the vacuum too soon, it may damage cells of the body. My ascent would take a few hours. The mag-ele noting the lack of body heat would allow me to go with her unshielded. If someone tried to go up without a suit, then safety procedures would kick in and stop the mag-ele before it reached a dangerous threshold.

Helmet on the floor, I briefly hugged everyone present. We wept openly. Stefan brought more flowers, and Cynthia put some in her hair. It was all touching.

* * *

I stood in the corner suited up as she lay there. Slowly traveling upward, I had passed the danger zone some time ago. I thought for just a moment I noticed her chest rise and fall. My breath caught in my throat. Perhaps she still lived. I thought maybe we had done this too soon. Her body was reacting to the cold and the lack of air, and she was trying to get a breath.

"Lena?"

Her body was rising upward. For an instant, I thought she was doing it on her own accord. I was a second from pushing the emergency stop button.

We were losing gravity. The Albert tube was doing the same as I was sure I was. It was just momentum that was causing her, us, to drift.

* * *

"This is, by no means, me trying to tuck you somewhere and to forget about you." Well out of range from any communication device, I spoke with her. "I will not. I will not forget about you. I am putting you here, so I remember you. You are the East. You are the only one who belongs here. This is my heart; this is my sunrise each morning. This is where the moon sets every night. I love you, Lena. More than the sun, and the moon, I love you, and I will always love you."

With cargo straps and the tethers, I secured the Albert tube to the wall. It was a little awkward, but I straightened the bedding out.

I brought her from the mag-ele and placed her inside. I could not force the body to lie on the bedding. In 0G, things moved around where they would. I placed her down gently, and with a final goodbye, I put the end cap in place and, grabbing a tether and planting my feet, I tightened it.

She looked at peace.

I would never touch her again. I would never get to hold her. I would never get to kiss her lips. Just two days ago, I could have held her, heard her laughter, and seen the smile in her eyes.

"I'm coming back. I miss you, Lena."

The momentum I used to touch the plasti-lite was the same momentum that pushed my hand away. Here, with no gravity, my movements had an opposite effect.

I stayed for a long time. I did not want to go. Ever.

When I was younger, I had always wanted to grow up. I never wanted this. I wanted everybody to stay with me. I wanted the world to be as I knew it without change.

With no guidance or support from her, I had to face my future alone.

I positioned myself a few centimeters above the Albert tube. Peaceful at being close to her, I did not realize I slept until my suit beeped. The air mix was down to fifty percent; the battery had dropped to twenty.

"I will be strong for you. I will do what is right, and I will not falter. I love you, I truly do."

I sighed then, touched my gloved hand to my helmet and then to her tube, and pushed off. It was dark here, quiet, and still. She would not age.

I grabbed a tether and went feet first into the mag-ele. I watched her in the darkness as the door closed.

* * *

A dark cloud descended.

Over the course of the next few days, I sat in her apartment and just stared blankly at the wall. The memory of her was all-consuming. I looked at her clothing, still sitting in the hamper and needing to be laundered. I watched the door intently, listening for the beep and the few clicks as the security would open the door for her.

I cannot say when I last ate. My stomach grumbled, and I remembered making a plate of food. I pushed the fruits around for the longest time and ended up dumping it out. My hands shook ever so slightly. For not the last time, I cursed.

XD05, Year 23

Brandon called me in one day after supper.

"How are things with you?" he asked.

I looked at him and realized how I must've looked. Ever-present dirt from the fields, my arms still sticky from picking grapples. The shirt I wore had a stain from months ago that I could not get out. I wish he would've let me shower before asking for an audience.

"I am doing well, all things considered. We have been so busy lately. I haven't had time to sit and think. I consume my days with studying and other work. But I find it enjoyable." I was still having a hard time. Of all the people, I did not want him to see my pain.

"This is good," he sat with his elbows on the arms of his chairs and his hands steepled in front of him. Grayer now, more wrinkled than he was years ago. We all were older, I guess, but he aged more so. The weight he carried broke his body down faster. "I have a secret I have harbored since we got here. Something that may seem simple or trite. If it were not for you, if we did not have a young girl on board, I would've stepped back, not assumed authority, and let everyone find their own path. As a social group this small, we do not need leaders. Everyone would've gotten along well without me to guide them. This has all been done for you. Not the making of the ship, of course, but all those years ago when I first saw you, I had to make sure you somehow survived. For better or for worse, I had to make sure we took care of you."

I looked at him and did not know what to say.

He spoke again. "I had asked Lena to watch over you, and she did an exemplary job. I could not have asked for better."

"Nor I," I bowed my head and tried to hold back the tears.

"She was way too young when she passed. I wish we could've foreseen this sooner and stopped it."

I only nodded.

"I do not know when my time will come," as he said this, I looked up at him. "I hope that everything I have started will continue on until the end. I have given everybody a framework to structure their lives. It is something they are comfortable with, and I believe they will continue to follow even after I am gone."

"Do you think you'll go soon? Are you feeling pain anywhere?"

"No, I still feel very healthy. Thank you so much for asking," he chuckled a little. "It is just that in time, they will need a new leader. Someone they can look up to. My job has not been an easy job. That fiasco with Troy and the shuttle crashing are just two of the major things I had to deal with. Troy took a lot of finesse and tact. The shuttle crash that took seven lives made people ask for answers, and of course, they looked to me."

"Who do you think we should put in charge if you should happen to pass?" I asked. In my mind, I went over a list of names. "There's Derwin or Avery who have the qualifications. Avery is older, though. I can think of a few others who are equally qualified."

"No, Sally," he said, leaning forward. "It cannot be one of us elder ones. It has to be somebody who will be here for some time."

"Me?"

"Yes, exactly,"

"How? They only come if they need something lifted, or moved, or grown, or picked."

"It will be slow. There is no real sense of someone being in charge, only of someone being in control. Over the next few days, I want you to divvy out the chores. Nothing major, just a few tasks here and there," he patted my hand. "They will look up to you."

I looked at him for a moment and nodded my head.

Homeport, Day 7

After Leonard said goodbye to his children, the screen in the gymnasium darkened. When it came on again, Sally walked from behind the camera to the front. Gone were the soiled clothes from the fields from before. She did her hair in a ponytail, and she wore a bit of makeup. She looked lovely.

She set an uncorked bottle down on the desk. The contents were half gone. By the look of the deep color, it could only be wine or some alcohol.

"We're down to fifty," she said, rubbing her forehead. Clearly distressed, she did not look at the camera. She had definitely drunk some. "We lost Tang last month. I mean, come on, he was a hoot. Funniest guy I ever knew," she exhaled, reliving a memory. "I lost my Lena years ago, and I cannot shake the memory of her from my mind." Fist touching her forehead, she paused. When she spoke again, she almost cried. "She was all that I had here, and with her gone, I now seem lost. I visit her at the Morning Wall when I have the chance. I must get there soon." She looked towards the window for a moment and sniffed back the tears. "Each day, we are wasting away. We easily kept the plants and the pigs at bay when we were three hundred. Now, I let the place go to shambles. It's hard; it's so hard. It's like some sick game we're stuck in. I'm just watching them go. I have no choice. Beverly is slipping. Her mind is going, and she knows it. She's forgetting words all the time. She came to the front of the hotel yesterday and looked up and down the sidewalk. She was asking people where the sidewalk went to."

"I'm not sure if anybody comes in here to send messages off anymore. Everything is set up, and it's automated. If people do, they don't really talk about it."

"I have sectioned off a certain kim-two. You think the pigs would be happy living where they are, yet they are constantly trying to get into other areas. It's an uphill battle. I imagine when it's just me, I will retreat to my place up the wall. Um, they built a place for me up the Twilight Wall that is a giant greenhouse. I have all the plants there that I need. When the last one goes, then I will no longer be down here at the surface."

"I wish I had somebody to talk to. I am far apart in age from the others, and they all seem distant from me. They see me as some kind of 'death angel' or something. I bring them food, I search for medicine, I do their laundry and some cleaning, and yet when we notice somebody is missing, they all look suspiciously at me. I want a husband; I want to be normal. Can you blame me for hiding in my song?"

Sally put headphones on and clicked something on her belt.

Fingertips up to her ear to listen a little louder, she hummed and swayed. When she sang, her voice seemed hoarse.

"… summer hair … running in the grass … we slipped away … to the county fair"

She was so off-key and drunk, it was difficult to understand her. Someone in the crowd recognized the song and sang with her. It did not take long for others to join in. Wendy concentrated until the words came to mind.

It was the lamenting song; she realized. A song that was popular almost 40 years ago.

"La da da la la," Wendy sang until she knew the words.

"And I ran with her through the courtyard, my hand with her by the river. We walked to candlelit halls, and kissed under the moon."

Wendy cried then. Her own voice was off-key but joined the others. Almost everyone sang. Bob gripped her hand.

Sally was there, growing, living, aging, just beyond reach. A life lived long, but a life condensed. They lost so much time. She was dead now, Wendy knew, and yet she was so alive and so young. She had endured so much in so short of a time.

Tears blurred Wendy's vision.

When the song was over, Sally stood there for a moment. She brought her hands down from her ears and smiled a weak smile. She laughed a little and sniffed back the tears again. She walked away from the desk, only to come back a few seconds later to grab the bottle.

"Come on, Jaughn, we've got work to do."

Within ten seconds, the camera shut off.

## XD05, Year 23

I don't know why the sessions with the camera bothered me. Starting at first, under the ruse, we were sending messages back home to our loved ones. I think it was just a simple tactic to calm fears and to keep everybody from panicking. I think Uncle Butch initially came up with the idea, and this is probably why I was so weary of it. For some reason, he, of all people, wanted us to connect with people from our past.

I took a big swig of Jaughn's homebrew and wiped the excess from my lips with the back of my hand. As I walked out into the evening sunlight, I turned and gave a silent nod to the heavens.

"I miss you, Lena," I said and turned. Knowing full well that she could not see me, I pointed back to the building that housed the camera. "Our love is there, sweetheart," I also tapped my chest. "etched in here forever. Forever in a crystal."

I raised the bottle, saluted to her, and took another long pull.

\* \* \*

It was quiet when I returned to the hotel. This late in the day, they would be fussing over supper. Robert would want his cabbage, and others would settle on pea soup. Again. I could not, for the life of me, figure out why they had a fascination with green peas. I'm not partial by any means, but I do not think I will be able to eat them with the consistency that they do. Maybe in many years' time, but with such an abundance of other fruits and vegetables around, there had to be a better way to find a bit of flavor.

I would not eat with them tonight. At times I think they enjoyed it when it was just them. They were the elders, and although I have known them for almost thirty years, I found at times I was still somewhat of an outcast.

Walking past the chair that Mr. Stubbs used to sit in, I brushed the fabric of its back lightly with my fingertips.

I went to my old room and laying on my small bed. I fell asleep without undressing.

Homeport, Day 7

The date at the bottom of the screen jumped ahead. Doing quick math, Wendy realized that Sally was almost fifty now.

The camera came on, and Sally walked to the chair and sat down.

"Oh Gawd," said Wendy when she saw Sally's condition. For some reason, Sally had darkened eyes, almost as if someone had punched her, and both were turning black and blue. Even a little more startling were the tomatoes and other vegetables she smooshed in her hair. Her normal beautiful hair was now completely discolored with reds and greens. There was something tucked in her shirt, something between her cleavage, and Wendy didn't know what it was until someone spoke up.

"That's one lucky cucumber," they said, and although it was crass, there was laughter.

Sally looked into the camera for a moment. Her eyes were not steady, and you could tell that she had probably been drinking a bit. She turned and placed her elbow on the table.

"April Fool's," she said with all seriousness. She sat there for several moments. Eventually, she bowed her head, and it looked as though she was extremely tired and about to sleep. She breathed deeply, smacked her lips, and looked back at the camera.

Grabbing the tabletop with both hands, she pulled herself up, walked around to the camera, and the screen went dark once more.

\* \* \*

There were a few giggles about the auditorium.

"You go, girl," said someone to the left.

"Whoop, whoop," said someone else.

"I do not know what she was thinking or where she got those ideas from," Bob whispered to Wendy. "Probably some kind of inside joke."

## XD05, Year 24

I did not have to work as hard with fewer people. I could spend the day and bring in a basket of corn, cabbage, carrots, onions, and other fruits and vegetables that would last us almost a week.

After I cooked the meals, I could help them with basic housekeeping. A little picking up, getting laundry done, and emptying the trash went a long way. I found that I had long hours where no one needed me.

I walked in the city where it was safe. I carried with me my iron rebar staff, a knife that dangled off a belt in a scabbard on my side, and a satchel from one shoulder to the other hip. This I carried in case I found something I could use. Not as cumbersome as a backpack, it held quite a bit.

Not sure if it was happpenstance or just blind luck, I stood in front of the gate of where Uncle Butch retreated. It had been so long since I had seen him. I wondered from time to time if he had passed. I never really liked him on any level. The man seemed a little creepy. I would still feel the same way about him, even if he were the last man on the ship.

The fence was too close to the ground for me to climb beneath, as I had done when I was a child. I went back to the gate and stood there for a while.

I pushed the bell for the ringer and waited a few moments. There is no reply. He could just not be home, or there is a real possibility he died somewhere along the way, and I would find his body. I felt that each would satisfy me as I had no desire to speak with him face-to-face again.

I went to the screen, and curious as to whether he had changed or deleted my access code, I brushed away some dead leaves and typed it in.

Without hesitation, the gate rumbled open.

I was genuinely shocked. Uncle Butch, the devious man he was, would have surely changed the combination. Perhaps, in his sick mind, he decided not to and wanted me to visit from time to time.

I walked cautiously. He was liable to have anything set up to trap the unwary.

* * *

The trees and grass were unkempt. The pigs have stayed out; otherwise, they would have eaten this down to bare dirt. It was so much different from what I remember years ago. Clustered and decorative shrubs and bushes had never been trimmed. Growing out of control, they made the place look eerie.

There was only one building. Sprawling and decorative, it looked so out of place in the city with perfectly square avenues and buildings with plasti-lite windows. As I neared the front entrance, the small red light on top of the door blinked to green, and it slid open soundlessly. I could not keep my presence hidden. Searching for any kind of guests, he would surely know of my arrival by now.

Needlessly, I called out several times before I crossed the threshold. I would hate to see him come charging out with a spear or other weapon.

Except for my echo in the large open area, the place stayed quiet.

I ended up spending several hours there.

He liked shoes. I thought at first; he owned many many pairs as there were several sets of shoes in every room I went to. I came across several pairs that were too small for him, and then another pair that was way too big. These were not shoes directly off the shelf; these were shoes that people had worn already. More than a few of the soles were worn down. Either these were shoes he took from the trash after people threw them out, or he made a habit of taking things that didn't belong to him. I found the shoes I wore when I first got here. Uncle Bob got them for me from the Hand-me-down store before I left. At Homeport, there are a lot of kids, and when someone grows out of clothing, they send it there so someone else can use it. It's normal for kids to have worn clothing. This pair I found was my pair.

One thing I soon realized was that Uncle Butch had been gone for some time. There was evidence that somebody had lived in the house. Bright, colorful clothing littered the main laundry room. Some of it was crusted brown with dried blood. Hopefully, he had killed a pig or two. With these few people and this much space, he could almost do anything and get away with it. I recalled nobody who was missing. I accounted for everybody I knew.

Not for the first time, I tapped my hip to make sure the knife was still there.

In the end, when I was leaving, I concluded that Uncle Butch was no longer there. I could live out my days and be thankful if I never saw him again. Even though the day was warm and the building completely empty, I still felt as though he were watching me from behind one of the plasti-lite windows as I walked away.

Before I left, I went to the small shack and activated the screen. The last entrance to the place was just over four years ago. It shocked me to see that it was not Uncle Butch who had entered the place. It was a guy named 'Michael White.' That name did not sound familiar at all.

I walked out to the sidewalk and, making sure the gate was closed securely behind me; I went home.

Homeport, Day 8

The screen was dark for a time. Everybody in the gymnasium was quiet.

The timer read twenty minutes to go until the end.

Sally came back on, and she had to shuffle as she walked. There was a scar from her cheek to her neck. The skin there was a deeper purple.

When she sat down in the chair and looked at the camera, her hand went to the side of her face as if to cover the wound. She was much older, with gray hair and sunken cheeks. She hobbled more than she walked. Her other arm, she held close to her chest as if it pained her. She pulled earbuds from her ears, and for just a second, music was heard.

"The ship is dying," her voice was raspy. "I had been to the big lake at the Morning Wall, and it is drying up. There are a lot fewer fish than there were before. They don't have the room they used to have. Everything there is just smaller. The dock, where we used to jump in from, was way above the waterline. The lilies are gone. The rowboats and everything are on high ground, and I do not have the strength to get them back into the water. There is no place for me to go," she chuckled. "Everything is fine. It's just so quiet now. Joan was the very last one. When she left me, the place was at peace, and I seriously thought about joining her, and the rest, so many times since. Brehm, I didn't know him much. We worked together in the fields, but his death haunts me. I miss Lena every day," she looked toward the window in the sunlight. "I miss Tang and Viyona. I can give you a list of three hundred people who I wish were still here.

"I do not know where you'll find me. I have the timer in my room to cool it down after twenty hours of inactivity. If I die there, then I will freeze until the power runs out. I'll be dead and gone and do not care. I do not want the pigs to eat me, and so I avoid the city. This has been a special trip. Were the camera equipment any lighter, I would've brought it home with me.

"It takes forever to put a suit on, and I cannot believe how heavy they are. I want to go see Lena again," she looked towards the window at the sunshine. "I miss that girl, beyond reasoning. She has been my rock." Sally lifted her good arm and made a loose fist. "I may do one more transmission on this recorder, but even coming in here is difficult. Keeping the electricity going has been a problem. I'm sure that there is something I am not doing correctly. I was never very knowledgeable about this. The power keeps going down. I would not have expected it to last as long as it did.

"This will reach nobody who has worked on XD05. That generation has gone. I want you to know this ship held up well. It is dying, not because of something you have done. It is dying because someone has not given it proper care. The water is receding, yet if there were people here, they would replace it. '05 is a very fine ship. By my count, I have lived with her for almost sixty years. The last twenty of which she has worked like clockwork on her own. Just she and I. She will continue to run like clockwork well after my days are over.

"I must fight the swine. Resilient little ornery bastards." at this, she touched the side of her face again with her good hand. "They, and the birds, and the vine, have the run of the place now. They do not know it; they do not see the ending. I can rise above them all and have this foresight."

"You know, now," she sighed heavily. "Looking back, I have no regrets about not having children. They would've adapted easily to this environment, but I can see the ship and its downward spiraling ecosystem would take them with it. I wonder how their lives would be as they looked about and did not know beneath their feet is a universe yet unexplored.

"Goodbye, everyone. This is Sally Weiss, 2-0-8-5-8-4-9, saying goodbye."

When she stood, her arm was curled close to her chest, and she hobbled to the camera once more.

The screen went dark.

* * *

For twenty seconds, there was no sound in the gymnasium. Everyone sat quietly, stunned. The floodlights came on, and the room became suddenly bathed in the glow of light.

The dark screen flickered several times, and unexpectedly, another form came into view.

Whispers grew as people tried to shush other people.

"Dim the lights, dim the lights."

When the lights dimmed, the figure was still there. Shorter in build, steady hands moved the chair aside. The individual, with their back to the camera, looked left and then right. Raising their hand, they coughed in their fist. Walking off camera, there was the sound of some other movement.

The lights dimmed further.

An agonizing short time later, a shadow went before the camera. After some breathing, the camera shut off.

* * *

When the lights came back on, everyone stood there. It stunned many, and they stood in silence. Others yelled and demanded that the last few moments of the video be replayed.

The video flickered once more, and they watched the individual repeat the actions.

"The time-stamp is different," whispered Bob, leaning close to Wendy. "Somehow, somebody got on board the ship forty years after Sally made her last video."

After it played for the second time, Bob stood and went to the gymnasium floor.

"Play it back again, this time jump two minutes further back, please."

He stood there in anticipation until the request went up.

When it came back on, it was Sally finishing up her narrative.

"See, look there," he pointed needlessly to the big screen. "The date here is May 2198. The camera will flicker a few times." He waited as it did so, and when the stranger came on, he pointed to the time-stamp again.

"Now it shows that it is October 2238. Someone had visited the ship well after everyone passed. For some reason, they did not wish to disturb anything or to leave anything for us to find."

"Were they searching for something?" someone asked.

"I don't think we'll ever know." Bob shrugged his shoulders and walked to his seat. "I was just making an observation."

"How do we know if they have taken something?"

"Again, we won't. We don't know what was there for them to take."

"They could come for the pigs," a woman said loudly over everyone else. There was a pause, and then some laughter.

Homeport, XD05, Year 3

Who knew three years could change so much?

It devastated Wendy when '05 returned, and she found out Sally had passed. The time afterward left them both depressed. Wendy felt responsible. Even after Wendy's sister came to Homeport, and they all grieved together, she still felt she was the one to blame. Had she known, she would never have taken the young girl on the shuttle that day. There were constant supply transports back and forth. She could've gone on any of those.

The giant vacuums came through and did the best they could. There was almost no residual dust on the surface anymore. Three times the fans blew in the air what they could, and the vacuums collected everything.

Now, as Wendy and Bob passed over the city in a hover, it looked almost pristine. Broken windows randomly dotted the smooth textures of buildings, and every so often, they could see a building that leaned, but other than this, it looked vacant. To them, it looked like it did days before departure.

They did not travel to the hotel this time. Instead, they took a different route and settled gently in the city. The hover brought them to just outside a large building that looked like an air arena.

The canopy lifted, and they stepped out.

"It's quiet here," he said within moments.

"You always say that," she said, looking at him with a slight smile. "Every time."

"Well, it is. No one else is here, no birds, no insects, just a huge open space, a man-made gravity well to hold the air."

"I want to look around, you know, one last time."

This building, the air arena, had seen better days. The roof had collapsed in, leaving girders pointing upward like the rib cage of some fallen giant. The glass façade had cracked and shattered. Sunlight streamed in, adding to the pattern of disarray.

She wandered about. No set path, no set destination. She wasn't even sure if Bob followed her or stayed by the vehicle. Entering a building away from the arena, her footfalls echoed off the high ceiling of the foyer. The great vacuums removed the dust, but other debris remained. Taking the stairs upward, she found herself on the landing that looked over where she had just been.

After another set of stairs, she doubled back and found a catwalk open in the air. She waved to Bob, who sat on a bumper of the hover with his feet tucked up.

The catwalk was secure enough. Although having been here for an untold time, its structure remained true. She looked down into the ribs of the air arena but did not go further.

There was only one such place on the whole ship. No doubt, Sally must have been through here at some point in her life. It's a shame they locked the building up in transit. Sally would've liked it here. If the air arena was unlocked, she imagined Sally would've loved it.

Wendy would miss this place.

Not just the city, but the whole ship. With the findings of the Lightfoot equation, mankind's curiosity had shifted elsewhere. Priorities changed. Manpower and funding shifted. They did not need the big ships like the '05, '06, and '07 any longer. There were smaller ones now. They were cramped scout ships that would head to these new destinations to see with human eyes what was there. The data received from the drones was indispensable, yet it was our curiosity to go there ourselves. No less than fourteen exoplanets have been found that are so remarkably Earth-like. The draw of people to these places has left Homeport nearly abandoned.

With her hands on the railing, she looked upward at the curve of the ship and the blue of the sky. This was no longer their place. In just three weeks, she and Bob would arrive at their new home. As the crow flies, the planet was 40,000 years in the past and 12,000 light-years away. To them, it would be a new home with new opportunities. They would be among the first wave of people to settle. Devoid of any animal life above insects, things were about to become very interesting.

"We will miss you, Sally," she whispered. The search was thorough and exhaustive. They never found her remains. Through DNA and dental records, they could identify everybody else on the ship. They buried many in graves in kim-two 2626. They found the rest in various homes up the walls, up in the Hub's, or at the hotel.

They never found Sally or Butch. From the records she kept and the video message which her niece sent, they believe that Sally lived a long life here on the ship. Rumors and speculation abounded in the years since. They could not account for several of the spacesuits now missing. In the end, she could have donned a suit, went out an airlock at the Hub, and drifted from '05.

That everyone else was here except for them is a mystery that they will never solve. There was a deep part of Wendy that longed for this closure, but it was still denied, so it left much open.

They found the remains of over 100,000 swine. Computer simulations depicted that many more had lived on the ship. In the years after Sally passed, they were the dominant species. Something went awry, and catastrophically the whole system failed. It was easy to imagine that they resorted to cannibalism as they were prone to do when food got scarce.

Her wristband vibrated. It was time to go. Squeezing the rail one time with her hand, she turned and quickly made it to the stairs.

Bob already sat in the hover by the time she got back. The door closed, they strapped in, and the vehicle lifted quietly.

\* \* \*

Richard Porter was not the last one to leave, although he stayed until they nearly vacated the whole place. It had no purpose. In less than a generation, it had been outdated and classified as unwanted. It was with sad regret when he climbed aboard the transport that would take them back home. The answers they sought were still unanswered, and yet with this form of distraction, everyone else's attention lay elsewhere. This branch of discovery lay forever snipped. With whole worlds opening ripe for the picking, they did not need this anymore.

There was no fanfare whatsoever as his transport winked out.

XD05, Year 26

It was rare that I visited the Morning Wall. When I do, it is to go see Lena. I let the shuttle drop me off at the mag-ele and take the trip upward. It gets me there quickly, and I spend as little time as possible on the surface here.

I had always felt my home was on the Twilight-side, and there I felt safe. I always associated the Morning-side with the breakaway group. Even though everything had changed, and they had resolved the differences being here, it felt like I was infringing upon their territory. I could not help but look over my shoulder from time to time and knew it would be so until I returned home.

I took the shuttle as close to the swimming hole as I could, and from there, I walked the old familiar paths.

Heaven help me; I could smell the water. Trees had grown taller, as did the grasses. Left unchecked, they took over the place. When I walked, they pulled at my legs. I knew the path was there and followed it with memory.

I had thought growing up that the lake's only function was to grow fish and for us to swim in. Lena was always talking about the biodiversity of the ship and saying how the life in the ship itself depended on the well-being of the lakes. She said it helped the air of the ship remain moist through evaporation and the creation of clouds. I didn't believe her; I mean, come on, the ship is huge compared to the lakes. Some others I had talked with said the lake was part of a collection pool, and the water would sit here until it became recycled.

All our waste made it here. Algae and bottom feeders would feed off it, and if they missed it, the water would carry it to the 'burning hell' as Jxan called it. When the water met this ever-present heat, it evaporated. Air convection pulled it rapidly upward, where it would re-condense into clouds. If any solid waste made it through the filters and encountered 'burning hell,' it turned to a cloud of fine carbon dust.

The band of light blue of the lake was a slow curve away from me to the left and the right. From where I stood, it was one whole kilometer to the wall of the ship, the Morning Wall.

They had always told me where there was Sunshine, Heat, Oxygen, and Water, there would be life. 'S.H.O.W.' they had called it. 'Show' what you can, and I will give you life. I think it was the slogan of some larger organization or something.

Here there were algae that fed upon nutrients in the water. Deep and thick, it covered the water as the small waves lapped the shore. It was green for several meters out. I could see an abundance of life there. The fish populating the waters had no natural enemies, and so they thrived. The surface broke every so often as they splashed out into the forbidden realm which we populated. In their aquatic environment, they were at the top of the food chain.

I did not have the time, or the desire, to cast the line for fish now. I may ask and see if others would want to come down and cast a net. We had enough food to be diverse. The population of the pigs was such that I could supplement my diet with them. I did not need the fish.

On XD05, there were no tides. They had said Earth had a moon, and this moon was essential to life on the planet. It would pull at the waters of the ocean so much that it would cause the water to rise and fall from one hour to the next. Here, there were no tides and only the wind, the great convection of the heat of the sun, and the coldness of space created the endless cycle that kept the water from going stagnant. Wind pushing on the surface caused the water to ripple and small waves to crest. These were gentle.

When I was here last, I placed a stone at the exact spot where the water stopped. Now, either the rock had moved backward because of the wind and rain, or something else was wrong. The water line had receded about half a meter.

I looked upward at the Morning Wall. The sun traveled behind me as I stood in the track's shadow as it arced upward. At its center, the Hub was a mirror to the one on the Twilight Wall.

Lena lay in rest.

I stayed a while. I preoccupied my mind with many things. This was but one more. If, for some reason, the water was disappearing; it was a cause for alarm. There would be more than enough to see me through my lifetime. Afterward, well, at that time, there would be nobody here to worry about. It was not leaving the ship. It was staying here, be it a vapor, liquid, or ice. The water was going nowhere.

I grabbed a second rock. This one was much heavier than the first, and I doubt the wind could move it at all. I placed its edge right at the waterline and made a mental note to come back and check on it later.

## XD05, Year 37

I was in the fields tending to the garden, which, everyone has come to learn, meant that I was getting away from all of them. The petty bickering and infighting grew tedious. They all wanted me to referee over the simplest of things. It's not that I didn't care for them; it's just that they could be petty. Very petty. Being out here in the sunlight gave me freedom, which I have come to enjoy.

With the music turned low, I could be in my own thoughts.

From here, I could see the ship getting greener. The pigs could not grow fast enough to eat the abundance. This was the grass that spread. More natural than the vine, it was a pleasure to walk through. I could see in time where it may take over the sorghum if we were not careful.

Everything in my garden on the surface was doing quite well, and I needed a basket each of peas, corn, and sweet potatoes. There was enough lettuce and carrots for the salad. Carl must either wait another day for his apples or just go get them himself.

I stood and was stretching my back when I noticed a movement out of the corner of my eye. One of the shuttles had come down the line, and someone stood there shaking a brightly colored handkerchief trying to get my attention. Thinking there may be an emergency, I dropped what I had and ran.

"Is everything okay?" I yelled before I got there.

The person, seeing I was coming, stopped waving the handkerchief and leaned on the door frame. "Yes," he cupped his hands before his mouth and yelled loudly.

I slowed a little. It was Leonard.

He waited until I got there before he spoke.

"Sally, I think it's time," he wheezed a little, made a fist, and coughed into it.

I stood there with my hands on my hips, straw hat keeping the sun from my eyes, and just looked at him. There was no one else there. It was just him and me for several kilometers. I was about to speak, but then pursed my lips.

Looking him in the eyes, I could see how tired he was. Living here on the ship was not arduous. It was a simple life we had grown used to. It was the weight of the future, the weight of the unknown, that bore down on you day by day. I could feel its light touch now. Not as heavy a burden that the others carried, not yet, but soon enough it would be.

I nodded.

"If this is the path you choose to take, then I cannot stop you."

"It is. I am not copping out; I'm really not. The back is aching, and I cannot sleep at night. It's been many months since I've had a decent night's sleep. Medical ain't got nothing to fix it. I'll never get better. Only getting worse, only downhill from here."

I held my hand up. "I do understand. Believe me, I do. How soon?"

"Tonight, maybe?" There was hope and sadness in his eyes.

"We will have a good meal tonight. After everyone heads off to bed, then we can go."

"I'd like that." his smile, something he had not done in a while, was genuine. And this made me happy.

"The old ship is really something to see under the light of the moon. Looking down through the atmo makes the lights shimmer. The visibility is incredible."

Leonard smiled.

I looked at him and then back toward the garden. "Is there anything you want to say? Any messages you wish to leave behind on the recorder? Find a pen and paper and write a message to place in your suit. When you go up to the Hub, the vacuum will preserve it forever."

"I will write something. There are things I need to say to friends and family who have died and wait for me on the other side." he held a small notebook in the palm of his hand. "I don't know if anyone will ever read it, but I will know I'll never be forgotten."

I nodded again and looked down. "Best you get back in town. Out here too long, they'll miss you. Quietly say your goodbyes. Bring the shuttle down to the 3009 connection. It's a worker's drop off point, and they have a lot of utility suits there. These are more limber, so we can put them on easier. I'll be there after supper, and we can go up and watch Twilight together."

He smiled then and dabbed the corners of his eyes with the multicolored cloth he carried. "Thank you, Sally," he mumbled. "It means a lot to me."

He shuffled up to the controls. A few seconds later, the door closed, the shuttle lifted on the track, and silently headed back towards town.

I stood there until it had disappeared. I slapped my gloves on my leg, creating a cloud of dust.

"Damn," I cursed as I returned to my chores.

* * *

"You're a little late." I couldn't keep the humorous tone from my voice, trying to keep everything upbeat.

"They wanted to play cards. I played a few rounds. MC, I believe, was cheating again." Leonard exited the shuttle with awkwardness to his gait. He held his left shoulder high while his right side drooped. He wobbled back and forth as he walked. He carried a small package.

"Would a cane have helped you?" I asked.

"I need corrective surgery done. No one here can do that."

"A back brace. We can wrap everything up and hold it tight."

He held up his hands for me to stop. "I've tried that. Found a back brace that fits, and I wore it underneath my clothing for the longest time, even though it chafed me. I played the hand they dealt me. I had a great life here. Today, well, today was a fantastic day."

I had his suit laid out in pieces on the platform.

"Undress and sit. Everything must come off. We will start with the pants first and work our way from there."

"Everything?" he asked. I looked up and could see the embarrassment in his eyes.

"You may leave on your underclothing. I have found that shirts and pants make everything too tight." The lesson given to me echoed back over the years.

* * *

He touched me once as I was helping him slip the heavy pants on. Working his foot in, I heard him draw his breath in and knew it hurt. His hand came up, and he touched my head. His heavy hand smoothed down my hair.

"Thank you," he said. When I looked at him, he placed his hand under my chin and tilted my head back, and placed a warm, dry kiss on my forehead. "Thank you," he said again, his breath upon my skin.

The top was very difficult. When at last it slipped down over his frame, he cried out in pain. It took a moment or so for his eyes to focus. His face lost all color, and he shook. He sat down on the chair, elbows on his knees, breathing heavily. I placed my hand on his shoulder and sat with him for several long moments.

"Thank you... thank you... I... could not have done it... without you. I will not break." he rubbed his fingers through his hair.

"Hey, the rest is easy. Sit back; I'll slip these boots on for you, then we'll get the gloves."

He winced again as he sat back. "Could I take the mag-ele up without the suit?"

"You could, to a point. There are cameras, and safety measures take effect. It'll recognize you as a passenger without a suit and stop before it gets to the danger point. If you get too cold, if you begin to experience hypothermia, it would come back down."

"How do you know this?" He asked.

"I've been there. Tried it."

"Really?"

I shrugged my shoulders. "Not to end it, just to see."

He raised his foot, and I slipped the boot on. Four snaps, and it was secure. The other boot was just as easy.

"You want your gloves on now?"

He looked at his hands. "No, not yet. I've left my messages in my pocket and have no way to hold on to them."

In his discarded pants, I found the notebook. I set it on the collar of his suit near his chin.

"When you're working in space, they frown on such things, ya know? They are a distraction and get in your way. Now, I don't think that'll matter." I checked everything to make sure the seals were tight.

The suit he wore had one yellow canister for the 02 that he would need. The other was a purple tank that held argon. The thing about it is the suit could not tell the difference and would pull from both tanks, regardless.

I began to undress to put my suit on. He smiled, looking at my form. Looking around to see if we were indeed alone, he looked back at me.

"You are an angel. You know, years ago, when we were all much younger, I had secretly hoped that you had wanted children. You're exquisite, and I have often fantasized about what it would be like to make love to you."

I smiled as I slipped the pants on. Looking at him, I saw his eyes never strayed from my panties or the curve of my hips.

"What's a girl to say to that?" I picked up the top. "You have always been a very handsome man, Leonard. Were things different, were I a little older, or you much younger, and we would've met under different circumstances, who knows what might have happened?"

I kissed his forehead then and gave him a hug that lasted.

"I will grieve for you," I whispered. "I miss everybody who goes. It is not an easy thing I do for you. There's always a price we both pay."

He kissed my ear and touched my hair again with his left hand. His right hand lay to his side.

I stood then and donned the top piece of the suit. The boots were easy enough, and I flexed my ankles, making sure I had a good fit.

His gloves went on, and as he sat there while I put the helmet on his head. When it sealed, I tapped it twice on top. The package he brought, his message, laid to the front near his chin.

"There are one or two others you will take on this journey soon." He said, and I searched his eyes. "Simone Dove has talked about it more than anybody, and I believe Fathallah desires it as well."

"That will leave us down to thirty, including me."

* * *

"Keep these low," I said, pointing to the controls on his arm. "They regulate your oxygen mixture. I have modified your suit. The left tank is the oxygen mixture you need to breathe. The right tank has a high mixture of argon. When you are ready, you can switch between the tanks."

"Will it take long?"

"No, usually less than a minute."

"Usually?"

"You are not the first," I said dryly. "Through the years, several others have asked for my help in this manner. I was kind of appalled at first, but now I'm more accepting. We all miss the friendship and companionship. Some people handle it better than others." I could tell him what Stacy had told me all those years ago. I could tell him she knew I would be the one to see them all to their graves. But I refrained.

I slapped him lightly on the shoulder and motioned him toward the mag-ele door.

* * *

I did not watch him. As we took the long mag-ele ride upward, I stood to the front and to the left, watching the world slowly sink beneath us.

"What did you do back in the day?" I asked, trying to keep his mind elsewhere.

"I worked in construction," his voice was weak and hollow as it came over the radio. "I was taking a break on my fourth tour. I would head out and herd in rocks the size of houses. It would take a week or so to get to them. We strapped a return bot on them and sent them back, you know?"

I could feel the air pressure change on my suit. It would be about another ten minutes before we were out of the atmo. Sometime between now and then, I would start to feel the effects of weightlessness.

"You miss deep space?"

"That I do. I've grown used to living with my feet on the ground these past few decades, but my heart has always been aching to get back to what I did best. I did a few walks on the outside of the ship. It's not the same when you're tethered. When you're out there buzzing around like a madman, trying not to get hit by a mike-mike, it's a fantastic feeling."

"Mike-mike?"

"Micrometeorites. The thing could be zipping from one place to another, born of a collision light-years away, and you are in the right spot at the right time. The damn thing will pinhole you and keep ongoing. It's the damnedest thing."

I heard him sob for a moment. The lonely sound was coming to my ears from the headset. He muttered the words 'goodbye' several times.

"Leonard. Point of no return," I said, looking into his eyes.

"It's fine." He blew me a kiss with a wink. "I know that I chose this day and this hour. This really sucks." He turned away from me and looked back over the grand expanse once again.

\* \* \*

When we reached the Hub, he was motionless. His left hand still held the tether.

I pulled him away and turned his arm so I could see the controls; I turned off the heating of the suit. I still had dreams every so often of the time I had left the suit warm. The bacteria will thrive on creating a world in which they could live. To them, it was a human-sized XD05 where they could live and grow. The woman who had asked me to help her had bloated from the gases the bacteria created. Even though the suit was strong enough to contain it, she swelled immensely. It was not a pleasant sight.

Leonard would not do this. He was dead now. Beyond the pain and the suffering, beyond bringing back to life, his body would stiffen soon. With the heat of the suit gone, his inner core would dissipate and plummet near zero in less than an hour or so. His body would remain like this, perfectly preserved, until they found the ship.

I activated my helmet light, and with him in tow, proceeded to the airlock at the center of the Hub. There were several there now. I did not activate the overhead lights, and I didn't look into their helmets. I brought them here so they may rest. I did not wish to see them again.

I could disconnect the purple tank with only just a little of the gas escaping. Still, over ninety percent charged. If any others went this route, it would see us through.

Star 19

The star they dubbed, and will ever refer to it as, '19'. It was the 19th star cataloged by the survey team that Daniel Wilde spearheaded during the first sweep.

The third planet which formed the gas and dust around Star 19 was relatively new. Created just over 3 billion years ago, the planet's atmosphere was heavy with liquid water and oxygen. People explored them with no protective clothing. They walked on its barren surface, swam in its empty waters, and knew they had found some place special.

Yet, there was a simple life thriving in its warm oceans composed of single-cell microbes. The blue-green slime coated the rocks along the shoreline of the temperate zones. We arrived, and terra-forming began almost immediately. We could replace the native single cells that were forming with more advanced cellular life favorable to us. It didn't take much, a few low atmosphere airdrops of the bio-cubes harvested on XD05 to release enough of our homegrown matter to wipe out what had taken the planet 19 million years to create. This christened the planet and made it more like our home.

On Earth, we had eons and eons of biomass building up to form our rich soil. Here, there was none of that; 19 was still too young. We brought with us machines to pulverize the stone and to mix it with what we already had. The machines worked day and night, kicking up huge plumes of dust as they worked. Combined with the warmth of the sun, the rain, and human ingenuity, it was not long before large swaths of land were green.

* * *

Wendy stood from her work, and even though she wore a sun hat, she shaded her eyes.

The Sun, Star 19, was near its midday height. Days here were twice as long as Earth normal. Although it was 'noon,' her day had just begun. Forty-eight hours of sunlight and forty-eight hours of darkness took getting used to. Tomorrow morning, when the sun fell below the horizon, two days of nightfall would begin.

A wind blew in from the lake, bringing with it the hint of algae and fish.

It was a pleasant day.

Bob had yet to leave for work. He never complained about fixing the robotics and tinkering with the latest trends. It was a job he loved, and with Wendy, it was the same. Growing something from nothing always gave her a sense of satisfaction.

She watched a bird light on a post before it flew off once again. Like the wind, the few birds they had helped propagate the plants. Seeds dropped in their excrement sprouted grass in the most uncommon of places.

*"Sally,"* her mind whispered. Wendy smiled. It had been years since she thought of her long-lost niece. The child, had she lived a normal life, would be a grown woman by now and have a family of her own somewhere on some planet or station. They would see each other from time to time when their paths crossed on family get-togethers or holidays.

But she was gone. She was just as gone as the ship that once held her.

At home, Wendy had an archive of the messages they received from '05. Quickly doing the math in her head, she realized it had been years since they took the time to watch them. She decided she may just have to break them out tonight. Certainly, there was some anniversary or a cause for a celebration coming up. Aligning the dates in real-time with the dates on the recorded messages was always cause for a party or a nice, quiet drink.

Bob would like that.

Tossing the brown leaves in the basket, she went back to work.

XD05, Year 41

When I heard the screams, I knew something was wrong.

First was a woman's voice and then a man's voice. With all the commotion, I thought they were arguing. Then I heard my name called several times, and I tossed the snap peas down in the bowl. I was in the kitchen's doorway when they came running into the dining hall.

"It's Robert," Joan exclaimed as she saw me standing there. Mike was by her side. She had this wild look about her. "Oh my God, come quick, something's happened! Something's happened!" She pointed in the direction she just came from.

I ran but didn't know where to go.

"Sally, he's in his room up on three."

I had run past the stairs. Turning, I climbed them as fast as I could.

They were slower, and by the time I got to his room, they still had not made it up the elevator. As I neared the room, I could smell the pungent odor of urine and fecal matter.

Robert lay on the floor of his room, wrapped in soiled sheets. His back arched, he clawed the floor with his hands, his tongue was out, and his mouth worked as if he was trying to say something. I could only see the whites of his eyes.

Obviously, something happened to him I could not begin to fix. He was suffering; be it something wrong with the head or something happened to his heart, I could not determine. I know I didn't have the expertise or the medical facilities to diagnose what happened to him. Ever since he injured his knee, he has been less active, and this puts weight on him. Only now did I realize, with him lying almost nude, how much heavier he had become. I had no means of picking him up. Even with the help of everybody, we could not do it.

He made a grunting noise. Low and visceral, it lingered.

Joan, Mike, and several others had made it to the door.

"What do we do?"

"Can we help him?"

I raised my hands but could think of nothing to do. Glancing quickly about the room, I was at a loss.

He grunted again.

I went to him and knelt down. As he convulsed, he bit his tongue. It mixed blood in with the saliva. With the palm of my hand, I pushed his tongue back in, took a deep breath of my own, and then firmly placed my hand over his mouth. I pinched his nose and pressed down hard.

If I let air in, it would only prolong his suffering. He would die this day, even if he had proper medical treatment, even if we were back home. The odds were against him. This was the only humane way to deal with him.

He convulsed again, and his tongue was a warm slug coating my palm. His hands clawed the floor and not his face. Had he been of the right mind, had he some inkling of what was going on, he would've tried to remove my hands and breathe once more. Understanding the fact that he did not do this, I knew that his mind was gone.

There was no hope.

When she realized what I was doing, Joan screamed more. From the corner of my eye, I watched as Mike held her back.

It was not over quickly. The moments stretched. I could feel sweat under my shirt trickling down my back. And still, he would not die.

I let out my breath and drew in another deep one.

"She's killing him! She's killing him! Oh, God, what are you doing? Bitch!" her words echoed down the hallway. "Mike, stop her. STOP HER!"

His twitching slowed.

Still, I did not let go. I had to do this. He deserved no less.

He started to shut down from the outside in. His hands flexed, fingers stretched taut, and he shook. I watched as they slowly settled to the floor. His fingers curling into the palms and then lay still. His arms rested on the floor, and the tension eased out of his shoulders. I still do not let go.

He was close; he was so close.

His feet and leg eased down, straightened, and then relaxed. His chest heaved once, and then twice as if it were drawing a breath of air from somewhere. I felt his tongue recede back into his mouth. The slug had retreated.

Still, I did not let go. I had to be sure. Were he to come back from this, it would be just as bad.

When I could feel that all movement stopped, when I knew the life was over, I first released his nose and then took my hand from his mouth.

The sound came then. The death rattle. His body expelled his last breath of air in a noise that one does not forget.

I was breathing heavily. I wiped my brow clean of sweat. My hand hurt, and my arms trembled.

Mike had not let go of Joan. He stood behind her, one arm wrapped around her shoulders, another around her waist. She was sobbing uncontrollably. The others, Marty, Lee, and McCready, were standing in the hallway saying nothing.

I took a handful of clean linen and wiped my hand off as much as I could. There was so much mess. His room was often tidy, but now there was debris everywhere.

I had to shoulder my way past Joan and Mike.

"Ya just going to leave him there?" She asked.

"He's too heavy for me to lift. Even with the help of everyone, I doubt we could get his mass on a gurney. And then what do we do? I can't dig a grave for him. I'm sorry, but I can't. I'm not the young woman you guys knew. Think of where you were ten years ago." I looked to McCready. "Fifteen years ago. I find it hard enough now to work the fields and feed everybody. We have not used the equipment needed since Bruce passed away. I doubt it will still operate."

"We can try," she pleaded.

"We are but nineteen left now. If you think you can get him up and outta here, then, by all means, please have at it."

I walked away, but she yelled at me.

"What are we going to do when we're down to ten or five? Are you just about to let us lie around wherever we fall? This is why we need children. This is why you should not have been so selfish and thought of yourself. They would have given us the dignity we deserve. Not like this! Hey!" she yelled at me. I didn't want to hear anymore. I didn't want to deal with it again. Still, Joan yelled at me as I walked away.

"You can't just let him lay here to rot."

I stopped then at the top of the stairs. Looking back at them, I took a hesitant step closer.

"Cover him with a sheet, a clean sheet, and if you wish, you may clean him up the best you can. Make him somewhat presentable, and I will go pick flowers. Tomorrow morning, we will seal off his room and vacuum the air out. It will remain so until the end of my days. Find the others and let them know."

"This," It would not silence Joan, "this is what you will do to us as well? When our time comes, you cannot suffocate us like an aging pet?"

I paused for a moment and tried to look thoughtful. "You're right. I'll carry a knife with me."

Even from where I was standing, I saw her face blanch.

It was quiet as I walked down the three flights of stairs and out the front door.

\* \* \*

She tried, bless her heart, she tried. Joan had assembled about ten others and tried to move Robert. It was just too much for them. In the end, they draped him with one of his favorite shirts and a blanket. I brought back tulips, which were always growing near a stream by the transition point.

He was a close friend of Paul's, and so we left it up to him to speak a few words. We all stood in the hallway and listened. When we said our goodbyes, he shut the door and palmed the keypad.

"I wish this room closed. Remove all oxygen and seal tight."

There was a small popping noise as the door sealed, and we knew it was over.

* * *

It was obvious that evening that no one wanted to be around me. After I made meals and put them on the table, people ate without talking. Rather than anybody helping with cleanup, they all shuffled away. They were purposely avoiding me.

That night I did not stay at the hotel; rather, I went up to Lena's place. When I woke, I showered and dressed and went straight to the fields. There was a solitude here. By myself, I didn't have to deal with them. I didn't like their passive aggression. There were things I had to do, and if they agreed with me or not, I did them nonetheless.

I gathered more food and placed it on the shuttle's back. I could have hopped on and unloaded it at the hotel, but I was not ready yet. When the shuttle left, I stayed behind. Let them find it sitting in front of the hotel and let them get their own food. They've done it before; they can do it again.

I thought about calling up another and heading back to Lena's house. I finally opted to walk for a while to clear my mind.

## XD05, Year 50

There is so much waste now. I don't need the bushels of grapples we had to harvest in the past. Now, just one bushel of grapples will last us for a week. I walked down the rows in the orchard, and I'm stepping over more grapples than I could eat in one lifetime. I'm on my fourth bushel of the ones I am picking up off the ground. My hand grabs one too tightly, and not for the first time, grapple juice covers my palm. Jaughn would've had a heyday with all the abundant fruit. He could have surely made any quantity of cider with the plums in the next orchard, the lemons, the oranges, peach, elderberries, and apricot. There is so much that I could not keep up with all of it.

Ants are bad this year, and the honeybees have become a nuisance.

Lemons have always been good for flavoring. I could let them all rot and harvest from just one tree, and that would be enough to sustain me for the rest of my days.

The pigs got their nourishment from the ever-growing grass and their roots. The rotten fruit I gave them helped fatten them up for the inevitable harvest.

* * *

I gathered four bushels each of rotten fruits and vegetables. By the time I sat in the shuttle's seat that evening, the back was full. Somehow, they could tell when the shuttle was coming even though it was whisper quiet. I always took the shuttle to the same location to dump what I had recently picked. I swear, there were more there than there was before.

Two days of work filling up the bed of the shuttle, one-half hour of dumping basket after basket over the edge to the pigs below. Bees had gathered on the rotting food. Getting stung twice did not help my mood. If any bees stung the swine, all the better.

I did not care where the food fell. I emptied each basket with no discrimination. When I dumped one directly on a pig, I heard squealing as if something caught it. This made me smile.

When I finished, I looked at the Twilight-End. Home was up there before the clouds curved. This close to the transition, I could barely make out the ends. So far away, the buildings that gave the end a 'tree ring' look to it were too light to make out.

A memory came to me, and I spun. 'Lena.' I was close to her. I raised my hand and bowed my head. 'I miss you.' I sent her a happy thought. 'I'll come to see you soon.' I was away from her for too long. I am sure she understood, but I did not want her to feel that I neglected her. I think she would be very proud of me and happy for the things I have done.

My mind went through a list of things I needed back at the hotel. I wanted to make spaghetti for myself. I had spaghetti squash for the noodles. With tomatoes, onions, some cilantro, and peppers, I would make a kicking good sauce.

I remember Doc complaining of no mushrooms at all on board. I do not remember these, their flavor or their texture. It was something I did not eat when I was younger. Ben always grimaced when Doc spoke about mushrooms. I guess it was a cultured taste.

With my hands on my hips, I watched the feeding frenzy down below. It would really suck if I fell down there like Pat Pat. They'd have me eaten in no time.

I went through the list of things the others needed and came up empty. The three people left needed the basics, and that was it. If I made it back and one had not keeled over, I considered it a good day.

* * *

As time passed, we grew less and less. By fate or dumb luck, Joan and I were the last two.

"You will kill me, won't you?" she asked me one day, and I knew she had an inherent distrust for me that lingered from before.

I looked at Joan in disbelief. She pursed her lips tightly and looked out the window, her frail hand pulling back the curtain.

"Joan, there have been days I wanted to get away from people and needed my solitude. However, those days have long since passed. We sit and drink tea and idle our days away. I will miss you when you are no longer here as I miss Lena, and Brandon, and Brehm."

She looked at me from the corner of her eye and pursed her lips anew.

"I do not intend to kill people. I was there for the death of many, but I only ended their suffering upon their request. Robert was different. It troubles me to know I did not have his blessing to take his life. No, Joan, I will not kill you. For my sanity, I need you here as long as possible."

Even though I said it in a joking manner, when she looked at me, she did not smile.

"I have picked a basket full of grapples for the meal this evening."

"I can't eat grapples," she said, looking from the window. "They bind me up."

"If you let me finish," although stern with her, I did not raise my voice. "I have some spaghetti squash, tomato sauce, onions, and peppers."

"Fresh water?"

"Either that or grapple juice." I left the room before she could say a word.

* * *

For almost two years, it was just her and I. The others died in bed in the rooms in the hotel, and like everyone else, I dropped the temperature down to freezing and sucked out the air. We visited once or twice, giving sad goodbyes. In the end, however, the doors were closed and remained sealed.

Daily, I would tend to her needs, and at night I would make sure she went to bed properly. She was not overly hard to take care of. Feisty, at times, trying to keep her independence when we both knew it was not possible.

After she fell one night trying to go to the bathroom, I slept in an adjoining room. She said my music and room light would keep her up. I found a monitor, and I put it in my room. It was pressure activated, so it beeped and lit up on my side as if her feet touched the floor. She slept better this way, and I kept the door closed.

Toward the end, I had to change the sheets every day. She had a problem with incontinence during the night, and we could find nothing to change this. She was very embarrassed at first, and yet it was something that was so natural. If she had no control over it, then there was no need for embarrassment.

There came a time where she spent more and more time in bed. As with almost everybody else, we knew the time was drawing nigh.

I would sit beside her and let her listen to music she remembered from her youth. They were good songs. Music has always been part of my life, and I can only imagine what it was like hearing the songs for the very first time.

She would talk to me, and I would have to listen closely, as her words were less and less understandable. We had worked out a basic series of sign language for her needs. A hand tilting back to her mouth meant water, a circular motion before the mouth meant food.

I did not leave her long. I had made preparations to be with her for the long haul. I brought down all of my canned fruits and vegetables. This allotted me more time to be with her and less time in the fields gathering.

I visited the greenhouses up along the wall just to make sure that everything was still running smoothly. Also, there was no beating fresh strawberries, kiwi, or watermelon. I must confess, Doc's pumpkin pie was so much better than mine. I wish I had kept the recipe.

There was a lot of stress as I prepared for her death.

I would stand in front of the windows of the hotel and just look out at the expanse. Birds and pigs had free rein now. I daresay that I saw Lawrence out there once or twice. I think that with him being familiar with us being at the hotel, he would frequent our rooftops and come back every so often to check on us.

\* \* \*

On her day to die, Joan did not get out of bed at all.

I sat in the chair beside her, my feet propped up on the sill, headphones on with music softly playing. I know my mind should have focused on her, and yet I found it on so many other things. This has been one of the longest times I have been away from my greenhouses, and I worried about their upkeep. I had very little meat left and did not look forward to the butchering, but I knew it was something I had to do. The strawberries were ready to ripen, and I would have to cultivate a few seeds.

Again, my mind was going through a whole list of things rather than dwelling on the woman lying before me who, on this day, would take her last breath.

Her eyes did not open once. Her breathing was shallow and so slow that several times I thought it was over.

"Joan," I whispered.

I had taken headphones off and turned the music silent.

"Joan, you can go. Do you know this? I'm sure you have a family waiting there for you. You don't have to stay here with me. I have got plenty enough to do, and I can take care of myself. If you see Tang there, tell him I cannot find his papers anywhere."

The memory made me smile.

"Oh, and MC. If he is there, tell him 'Yoooooo'. I haven't heard that in so long. I miss his deep voice. I'm sure he's doing pretty good; they'll tell you he's doing pretty good. If you see Addy, make sure she's doing push-ups."

I cried then.

All those people, all those memories, and we thought we had forever.

I looked out the window at the sunshine and knew each one who passed would appreciate a day like today. We would work the fields or cook meals, or play a game of spades. Make love, or just be, and they would enjoy the day. The day would be ours.

"If you see Uncle Butch, well, if you see Uncle Butch, I believe you're in a bad place."

Her breathing slowed again. "Joan, you can go. I release you; I want you to be free. A safe journey to you and your family will welcome you home. If you see Lena, tell her I love her and that I'll see her soon. You can go."

As I reached out to touch her hand, she did just that.

* * *

I did not stay long. I paid my respects to Joan, and although my heart sank, I could not weep any more. I covered her with the sheet and dropped the temperature down in the room as low as it would go. I closed the door and would not be back this way again for a very long time. Everyone I had ever known, every family member I had, everyone I had interacted with in these last fifty-plus years, had died.

I pulled the air from the room and sealed it in a vacuum.

A thought came to me, and not for the first time. I refused to listen to my mind and shoved it to the side, burying it deep. Now they were in the grave I could go to, without fear of shame or of being ridiculed. If I took my life this afternoon, there was no one here to say it was a bad thing. I would die, and XD05 would have the silence it so long deserved.

* * *

I went to the kitchens and found a very nice old bottle of Jaughn's brew. It was clear and still sealed. After strapping myself into the shuttle, I undid the lid and drank a healthy sip. I did not travel fast. The precautions from years ago were still on my mind. By the time I started up the arc, heading home, the drink had made my head fuzzy.

I did not have a high tolerance for alcohol, and yet by the time I reached my home, I had finished half of it.

For a few moments, I stood before one opening between buildings. They had protective rails and guards so that people would not fall. I leaned against these as the drink took hold.

"I can do this," I muttered to myself. "I can do this."

I knew I had drunk too much too soon, and it was quickly catching up to me. Before I was completely incoherent, I wanted to throw the bottle out over the expanse. With this defiant act, I could watch the bottle tumble away.

Looking at it in my hand, with Jaughn's own handwriting on the label, I hefted it twice, testing the weight before my muscles tensed. I gave it all I could. Knowing I had about a meter square space to toss it through, it was almost too big to miss.

In mid-toss, his name came to me again, and I faltered.
*Brehm.*

I attempted to stop.

The bottle would fall away like Brehm. Unstoppable, meeting his fate, by my hand, I destroyed it.

Caught up in the motion, I could not stop. The bottle flew too high and shattered on the railing above.

I looked at it for a moment; liquid dripped from the ceiling, glass now lay scattered all over. I shook my head and gave a weak laugh. Such was my life.

"For everybody," I said. I gave a deep bow, knowing there was nothing more I could do to honor them. I stumbled a little as I shuffled home.

* * *

With all the preparation everyone had done when they were here, life was not that difficult. Water came through the irrigation pipes, feeding the plants that grew with such abundance in my place on the wall and below, that I did not have to go far to gather what I needed.

I could binge on whatever I wanted to without worry it would no longer be there. I had seeds in cold storage as a backup for everything I had growing.

In the days and weeks after Joan's death, there was little that I needed to work on. I cannot lie and say the depression was not there. It was. I would spend hours just staring from my room out at the vast expanse of the ship and the emptiness there. Had everyone died at the same time, and if I were the only survivor, I would've gone insane. As it was, each death brought me one more step closer to the inevitable, and yet, and at the same time, it helped my mind cope with the realization that I would be alone.

One morning, I noticed a flurry of white outside my window. It was Lawrence, that naughty bird, as Uncle Butch referred to him so often. He still lived. After all this time, he found a way.

As I stood there drinking a concoction of berries and fruits from the blender, it slowly dawned on me. All this time, all these years we have been here, he has been the only one of his species to inhabit this place. There were other birds here. When they built the ship, they used these other birds to help propagate the seeds. This helped with the randomness of trees and bushes. Compared to Lawrence, these birds were much smaller. There is no way he could breed with them. And if what Uncle Butch said was true, Lawrence was intelligent. So, all the other birds would seem to be 'dumb' in his eyes.

This bird had lived here all this time alone and isolated. In many ways, he was the embodiment of me.

I turned then and went to take a shower. It would be my first in countless days. Until that time, I did not care if I stank, or my breath was foul, or my hair was a mess. With Lawrence in mind, I cleaned up.

When I finished, I tended to my fruits and vegetables once more.

I went to the surface and slaughtered a pig of medium-size. It took a lot of work, but I dragged it to a platform before I dressed it. Warm entrails lay right there. The birds would eat it and eventually clean it up. If Lawrence ate meat, then it was an offering to him.

Just by his presence, he helped bring me around.

If an escaped white bird could survive on his own, then I could survive as well.

Blood, staining the floor of the shuttle, pooled and settled as I went back home.

After skinning the pig at my place, I showered again.

In the hallway between my house and the shuttle track, I cleaned up the broken glass, saving the label as best I could. It was here that I left small strips of pork skin. It was a second offering for Lawrence. Tang would've said I was leaving milk out for stray cats.

I stood, brushed my hands off, and went back inside.

\* \* \*

The music saved me in every way possible. I had spent too many days moping and being lethargic. For almost two months straight, I went to the air arena daily after breakfast. I put the music on randomly, strapped the shoes on, and danced with as much passion and energy as I could.

I was alive, dammit.

I did not want to hide away or cower. It wasn't my way before, and it would not be my way now.

At my fingertips, at my disposal, was this grand ship. '05 and I were one. As long as she lived, so would I.

When I slipped the shoes off at the end of the day, I was sore and breathless. I could feel my definition come back that I had so long ago in my youth. Yeah, I can do this. I got this beat.

\* \* \*

It was the music that got me through. Somehow, time and time again, it brings everything around. I remember Evan once saying that emotions were like dollars, hills, and dales, highs and lows. The further down you went, the higher you would climb, and then, sure as shit {his words}, you'd fall right back down into that valley again. I had most of my music upbeat.

Of the millions of songs I had access to, I had chosen several thousand that the computer deemed to have an upbeat tempo. It would work the brain into thinking everything would be fine. Occasionally, a song would slip through the cracks, and I would forward past it right away rather than listen.

One song came up, and I was hard-pressed to let go.

In the middle of his career, Phleks came out with the song called 'Cinnaminson's Lament.' On a different day, under different circumstances, the song would just be something a little mediocre. I could listen to it and move on without a problem. It would be a middle valley in my day and something I would climb out of easily.

Today, the song just struck me, and I paused as I was gathering avocados.

After the first few beats, my good mood faded. It was not the song. There are parts of the song that are uplifting, and I had listened to the rhythm and lyrics and harmony many times before, and it never did this. I looked at the avocado in my hand, and literally, I could not go on. From my hand, I looked at the space of my greenhouse. Not empty of life. There was plant life, there is insect life, but I was the only human life. This was missing. I went to the window and looked out. There were birds outside and a multitude of insects there. This whole ship was empty of human life except for me.

The words continued in my ear-piece. The sound, the rich deep voice, the rhythmic jump of the piano from one ivory key to the next. It was almost as if he were beside me singing, making me feel the anguish that the sorcerer felt when he lost his love. Like a flame sputtering at the end of the candlewick in the night's dark, he did not want his love to leave and yet was powerless to stop it. The sorcerer, knowing he could save nothing of her, summoned his magic and captured her last breath.

*"The presence of her lips, always etched in the crystal, her last kiss I will miss her till "* And then he pauses; the beat stretches. *"The end of time."*

XD05, Year 55 - "This little piggy stayed home."


It was my fault. I would like to blame the young boar, but I cannot let myself.

Out of habit, I carried several things with me: a backpack, some food, a little piece of rope, and a knife on my belt. I have only used the knife to cut food, wire, rope, or cloth. And also, when I walked, I used a length of rebar as a walking stick. It was heavy enough. I should have used something lighter, an actual wooden stick perhaps, but I had been carrying this for so long that the weight did not bother me and felt comfortable in my hand. It was good for helping to help open doors, hold one open, or to crack a window.

I was on the surface looking for things when I turned the corner, and there was a little runt right before me. When I say he was right before me, I mean, I literally tripped over him. I did a quick dance, trying to avoid him, but my foot kicked him in the back. He squealed so loud and long I thought I broke his leg. I think I scared him more than he scared me.

His cry alerted others.

I cursed when a bigger boar, his father possibly, turned my way. He and some others were about a block away. I knew they protected their young; I didn't know I pissed them off as much as I did.

With a squeal, the bigger boar charged.

There was no doorway I could run into. I was not limber enough to jump to a window. The only thing I could do was to hold the rebar vertically to the ground in front of me. I held with both hands, elbows locked, and I hoped that he would run into it before he hit me.

I screamed but was sure the squeals from the little one drowned it out.

I pranced. Seeing he would not stop and that confrontation was imminent, I planted my feet squarely on the sidewalk.

But I was no match. He had me beat, and he knew he had me beat. Heavier and stronger than I was, I had just a second to wait.

\* \* \*

I could see clouds and blue sky. There was a light wind, and I saw a small bird flit from the corner of a rooftop. My face was numb. I could not smile. I do not know why this bothered me, but it did. Near me, buzzing around my eyes, was a bee. I tried to shoo it away. For some reason, my right arm wouldn't move, so I used my left.

Something covered my palm, and it took a minute to realize dried blood coated it. Memories came back in a rush, and I looked around to see if I could see the boar. Neither he nor his family were there.

My left arm was free. I wiggled my toes, and there was no pain there. I slowly brought my feet up, and everything felt fine. I felt a slightly uncomfortable pain in my back. The pears in my backpack hurt my ribs.

As I turned over to free my right arm, pain shot through my shoulder. I screamed and let out a curse. It nearly caused me to black out again.

Babying the arm, I could not roll to the left, and so I rolled with my right arm still beneath me. My forearm and fingers were numb—my left hand reaching out, trying to find anything to hang on to. I found nothing. I slid my good arm underneath the strap of the backpack, slipping it off.

If I held my right shoulder still, there was no pain.

My hand was limp beneath me.

Blood soaked my shirt. Somewhere, I bled.

Using my feet and my good arm, I got on my knees. I winced as pain shot through my shoulder again.

"You bastard, you freaking bastard," I clenched my teeth so tight I thought they would shatter.

Knees beneath me, forehead to the ground, my breathing came in ragged gasps. Blood had pooled. It was on the pavement. It covered my backpack. It dripped from my head, but I did not worry about this wound. Head wounds bleed a lot.

With my good arm beneath me, I pushed upward.

My legs were so shaky. I almost went back down. I held my bad arm, curled close to my side protectively.

I just wanted to go home. That's all I wanted. I wanted to wake up and see my beautiful Lena walk in with morning tea and breakfast.

I growled. Primal, in my throat, spittle coming from my mouth, pain fired up my arm with every step.

I left the rebar there and clenched the strap of the backpack with my good hand. Barely able to lift the canvas, I let it drag on the ground.

\* \* \*

It was as I was walking past this one building when a movement caught my eye, and I saw my reflection. It was the gymnasium we had passed all those years ago. At the same spot at which I now stood, that guy that had the big muscles, Sebastian, had entertained us for a few moments as he flexed.

It was also here that he had died.

I stepped closer. This gave me a better view of my reflection and the damage. What numbed my face was a deep slice from my cheek down to the side of my neck. It missed my ear by the width of two fingers.

The rebar.

When the boar slammed into me, holding the rebar in front of me, the tip caught me in the face.

I looked at the reflection of Sally Weiss and shook my head.

"You've done it now, girl," my mouth could barely open. Barely able to talk, my swollen skin became taut. I felt more blood drip onto my shirt.

I walked over to the door and pulled. Thankfully, it opened easily enough. I didn't want to have to fight that, too.

With the door closed, I paused. They made the building of windows. Decades-old, any could've shattered, allowing pigs in. There was no breeze; there was no noise. There was just still air and empty spaces to greet me.

They had showers here. Plumbing and pipes so long unused, rust may flow as freely as water.

Taking the first step upward, pain needled my shoulder. Not ready for it, I cried out.

What was his name?

The second step gave more pain. I pushed it away.

The one soldier with the beard. We were carrying Lena back to her place after a party.

The third step is no easier. I wanted to sit down. I wanted to put my head back on the cool tile of the stairs and just rest.

The soldier had mentioned an army sergeant who gave Lena strength. He gave her something to focus on. His name is there. I could see how he pronounced it. In my head, I could not bring it to light.

On the first landing, more blood dripped.

"Focus, Sally, come on. His name, you gotta remember his name."

Metzo, that was it! Sergeant Metzo was looking for ya, Sally! Lena had explained to me the rigors of military training, and there were often times I imagined myself training alongside her. I tried to dig deep. I tried to give it all I could, but it was not there.

I wanted to lie down. The distance I had come and the distance I was going was too far. I wanted to reverse the way I had stood out on the street. To fall on my knees, and roll over on my back, and just sink back into the blackness and let it pull over me like a blanket. I wanted to sleep and not wake up.

I wept.

I openly wept.

I shuffled up the stairs. I lost the backpack then. Slipping from my fingers, I would find it later. It was in my hand when the main door closed. It was safe.

With my free hand, I pulled myself upward.

Come on, Sally. Metzo wants you to run a few laps. Dig deep; you gotta dig deep. You can do this; this is nothing. Your feet are not hurt. It's your shoulder. If your feet are not hurt, then why are you having trouble on the stairs? Dig deeper, focus. You've done this before.

"Criminy," I swore. I didn't have it.

I glanced over at the first room on the second floor. A room for working out. There was not much here. To the back sat a large window and a counter, where they handed out towels. I turned to leave when I noticed the red cross on a white cabinet there.

I tried not to smile.

* * *

There were three red tubes in the cabinet. Red for cuts, but not deep cuts. Red for burns, but not massive burns. Red for deep, sore muscles. If a person used the wrong one by accident, they would've been screwed royally.

The hospital held everything I needed. That was there; I was here. I had to find something temporary to get me somewhat patched up.

Looking at myself in a bathroom mirror made me cringe. The bleeding had slowed, and thankful when the skin moved, I did not see bone. I took the tube for the minor cuts. It contained medicine with a slight adhesive that would seal the wound and keep my skin clean.

I know the damage, but it didn't make it any more pleasant. And again, for the thousandth time, if I were back home, things would be much different. I wouldn't have to deal with boars or pigs of any nature. Medical personnel would treat my wounds and know what to do.

I shook my head and tried not to think about the 'what if's.'

My hand trembled. Odorless salve completely covered two of my fingertips with the clear gel. Already I could sense that they were numbing. I never thought about using the medical gloves. It was too late. Starting at the top, I laid it on thick. Done right, I only had to use one application. Several times I irritated the skin, and with clenched teeth, I did a dance on my tippy toes while holding back a scream.

The water ran for several minutes before the basin cleared of blood. I turned the spigot off with my thumb and pinky. The other three fingers had no sensation. The salve did not discriminate what it numbed.

Putting two tubes away, I pocketed one and looked for gauze.

* * *

Something was wrong with my shoulder. It was more than I could ever fix on my own. It turned black and blue and was very sensitive to the touch. I had a limited range of motion with my arm and hand. I held my arm across my stomach to protect it from moving. To help it mend, I could sling it with some cloth. If I had broken a bone, I would be pissed.

Needing to wash my clothing free of blood, I stood in the shower and let the hot water take away what it could. Carelessly, I had forgotten about the gauze I put on and knew I would have to change it. I scrubbed my hair, and the water at my feet turned crimson.

Knowing the hot water was not cleaning my clothes the way I wanted, I stripped down. Tossing the pants in the corner, I then held my good sleeve with my injured hand and slowly slid my good arm out. Carefully as I pulled the fabric over my head and gingerly over my bad shoulder, I held my shirt a moment before I tossed in the corner as well.

I lost so much blood.

"Stupid Sally," the words came to my mind. "Must be more careful next time. You have to. Death to ya if you're not careful."

It has been a rough day. Could've been my last day; these hands could've been dead and cold this evening. I shivered in the heat. With a wave of the hand, I turned the water off. Towels were numerous. I slid a robe over my shoulders and got my good arm in.

The place had no blankets to speak of. I grabbed three or four terry cloth robes and rolled up on a padded gym mat. They covered me. Two folded towels became a pillow.

* * *

Hunger pains stirred me in my sleep. More than the need to use the bathroom, I needed to get something to eat.

Rolling off the mat, I was careful not to hurt the shoulder.

When I fell backward, I mushed the pears in my backpack. The skin broken, the fruit decayed hours ago. I ate what I could, but of the four pears I carried, only a little remained to eat. I scraped most of it out and flung it away.

On the landing sat a cabinet. I realized it was odd they would place something this size right here. When I opened it, it surprised me to see several large containers of protein material.

The word 'Beefcake' emblazoned the front with two lightning bolts streaking through the red letters. I took the lid and the foil seal off. The aroma coming out was unlike anything I had ever sensed before. It smelled wonderful. The food, which may have been a powder one time, had condensed down into a solid brick. Tantalizing, it lay so far down, I could not even lick it with my tongue. Nothing lay nearby that I could use to chip away at it. If worse came to worst, I could hammer it with one of the smaller weights.

I placed the lid on securely and dropped it from the counter. After the fourth time, I heard the contents move around and knew I had loosened it.

After the lid was off, I reached in and pulled out a small shard. Forgoing water to dilute it, I placed it in my mouth and sucked on it like a piece of candy.

It was potent. Not sure if it was good for me, I did not care.

After a few, my stomach stopped rumbling.

I carried several bottles of water and returned to my 'nest' on the mat on the floor. The food gave me cramps from time to time, but it was nothing I could not handle.

\* \* \*

I stayed at the gym for three days. Knowing the pigs were not nocturnal creatures, I finally left at night. I carried one container of the beefcake in my backpack and another in the crook of my arm.

It felt awkward not having the rebar in my hand as I walked. Moving cautiously in the moonlight, I found it where it had fallen.

Something lay beneath it, and I thought to dismiss it simply as rubbish when it moved in the wind. Free of the weight of the rebar, the white feather stirred.

"Lawrence?" I whispered. He was here?

It never occurred to me that the bird watched me. I knew he had a long lifespan. As long as any human. He remained elusive, and I do not recall the last time I had seen him.

During my recovery at the gym, I'd thought I scared the boar, and it ran off after the attack. The confrontation was over as quickly as it began. If Lawrence were here, and the bore knocked me unconscious, he may have led it away.

I placed the feather in my injured hand, grabbed the rebar, and headed to the shuttle.

\* \* \*

When everything seemed like it had healed, I took the bandage off. To my surprise, some bandages stuck to the scab and sealed partially in the wound. I cut off as much as I could, and then, with a makeup-mirror and tweezers, I pulled the long strands of gauze one by one from beneath my skin.

It hurt.

Jaw clenched, I held back a scream every time I did it. I found it better to pull quickly and get it over with rather than prolonging the pain. With the tweezers firmly grasping the strands, I pulled my head to the side. If there was pain, I was doing it right. If there was none, I had to do it all over again.

Not only did it irritate the new skin, but it inflamed the new nerves. I had to rub some lotion from the red tube on it to soothe it down.

* * *

I looked out my window at the world below. As of right now, I had enough provisions for my future. I had slaughtered enough pigs, harvested enough food, and the water remained fresh and clear. There was no need for me to go back down to the surface. I honestly forgot what I was doing down there in the first place.

I wish I had a bigger weapon to carry with me, besides a knife and the piece of rebar. Both seemed highly inefficient with this attack. The elderly spoke of guns from time to time, and I remember these somewhat. It was something that a piece of metal would fly out from a round tube. Perhaps in my youth, I could've manufactured something like this. With my hands the way they were, it would be all but impossible now.

If one was to be made, then the others would've made it already.

I sighed and watched as clouds ambled lazily along before being sucked into the air intake tubes. I would just have to be more cautious. If I had any reason to get down to the surface again, I would just have to be wary all the time and never let my guard down. It was my daydreaming that almost got me killed. I had to be more vigilant in my endeavors.

* * *

I stayed at my place, mending my garden. With over ten buildings used, there was always something to do. The pain in my shoulder had abated somewhat, or I had just gotten used to it and tuned it out.

Again, it happened when I wasn't paying attention. I was never a clumsy person before; I don't know what happened now. I was in building 2, making sure everything was going smoothly. The grapples here were almost ripe for picking, and I did not want them rotting because I neglected them.

I was on my way to building 3 to check on something. As I walked, I read notes from my notebook. Not watching where I was going, I struck my bruised shoulder on the doorjamb. I heard the worst popping sound. My tablet fell. I screamed as I hit the ground. My shoulder was instantly numb. Instinctively, I grabbed my shoulder.

The pain there was… the pain was… was gone.

I moved my arm in the sling. I could now raise it up higher than I could before. Pressing against the sling, I straightened my arm. I felt a residual pain, but there was nothing like there was before. Bumping into the doorjamb had somehow fixed it.

I kept it in the sling for the rest of the day. That night, I slept more comfortably than I had previously.

In the morning, when I woke, I took the sling off and left it lying in the bathroom. I smiled at myself in the mirror. The scar had turned a deep purple color. I did not care; I would not see anybody, anyway. My shoulder, now back in position, felt better. Not one hundred percent, but better than it had been all week.

* * *

When I came down to the surface again, about a month had passed. I took the shuttle down. More cautious than before, I kept it slow as I passed the hotel. It was really showing its age. Some trees, now nearly as tall as I, had taken root in the cracks of the courtyard.

"Brandon," I yelled out from the empty shuttle as I looked around for my mentor, "We gotta get someone in there and cut those down. How can I kick my soccer ball around with all those trees playing goalie?"

I meant it as something humorous, but it made me sad. My shouting did nothing but startle some birds.

## XD05, Year 62

I woke early this morning and made a conscious decision not to work in the greenhouse. Things would tend to themselves, and my one day of inactivity would not destroy the whole ship. It was a vacation of sorts. This was my first stop in revisiting old places.

The dreams I had that night would not let me be. I normally don't remember my dreams, but this one from last night lingered. I had dreamt of people: different voices, different faces, many styles of clothing. They were people I had never met before in my life, but somehow, in the dream, I was familiar with all of them. It was a sunny day with blue skies above. I talked and mingled and laughed. When I woke, I lay there confused for many moments, trying to recapture what my mind had just created.

More than once, I questioned my decision not to have children. I fantasized from time to time what it would be like to have the little heathens running around getting into mischief. There were plenty of people on the ship who could look over them. It would have been a community effort. The children would all have a little of me in them, and I could see certain traits of their fathers.

By my count, my last conversation with Joan was twenty-two years ago. She still lay here in her room, as does Robert, Troy, and Cyn.

With a silent hiss, the shuttle pulled in front of the hotel. Even after it settled, I did not stand. With my hands on the railing before me, I took a moment to compose myself.

I sighed.

I looked out of the front of the shuttle, and the ribbon was still in a straight line before me. With the sun shining in its second hour now, I imagine it is bright where Lena rests. I'd have to go see her one last time.

It is a day of remembering what we once had. It will take a conscious effort, but I will not suppress memories as I once had. I need to relive the laughter and love once again.

The wind picked up, causing my hair to blow, and I brushed it back from my face absently with my good hand.

Satisfied with no pigs nearby, I slid the door of the shuttle open.

Vine had claimed the surface of the left wall. It covered several windows at the base and was working its way upward. I could stunt the growth by changing the settings of the reactor and only allowing a little sunlight to reach the surface. I had enough food stored for my time ahead. I could do this when I knew my final days were near, though I dreaded suiting up and taking the elevator to the Hub. I would rather go see Lena than waste my time at the Twilight Hub.

Shielding my eyes to the morning sun, I found my cane comfortable in my hand. Using it for support, I crossed the once familiar courtyard. The entrance doors to Hotel Lima refused to open. I waved my arms and even tapped the glass with the end of my cane. No one had occupied the place in a very long time. Thinking I would have to return home, I looked around and found the sensor had a layer of dust on it. As soon as I wiped it with my thumb, silent motors opened the door for me.

The foyer had an odd smell. Days and years of neglect had given the place a bad air. A lingering odor of septic rot. It was dark here, as only half the lights came on. It was a place where music no longer played. I made sure the doors closed before I crossed the mosaic.

Mr. Stubbs's chair had shed. The once firm cloth on the arms drooped and sagged. It listed to the side and seemed as if it were slowly sinking. It was hard to believe that in all these years, no one has ever moved it from its place.

The elevator doors were quick to open. I could have taken the stairs, but I had to be careful. Falling now and breaking a bone would be deadly. I did not want to die a lingering death like Philip.

I had only taken the elevator a handful of times to Lena's floor, and it seemed as odd now as it had in the past. I had always viewed it from the stairwell.

The door to her room was closed but unlocked.

Someone had been through. They disheveled her things, but not overly so. They did not bother with the paper notebooks or the pencils; these still sat at the writing desk. The contents of the footlocker were on the floor. They had looked through her clothing and did not bother to put anything back. I could see the extra uniform that Lena had meticulously kept. Here also were her dog tags and the simple rings she wore when not on duty. I gathered these and the journals.

I did not want them to stay here. With trees, grass, and the vine taken over, this hotel would soon succumb, and in fifteen to twenty years, it would fall as it gave in to the elements. I needed to take Lena's prized possessions to a place safe from harm.

I pause for a time at the door of my old room. Room number 321 was unlocked. With the end of my cane, I pushed the door open and just stood there for a few moments, looking in. Miss Priscilla lay on my bed. Frail and fragile, I let her be. I know that if I picked her up, she would fall apart in my hands, and I would rather have the memory of her as she was than the notion of how she is.

Above my desk was the wall with the names of everybody I had written out years ago. It was my ledger of everyone who had passed. The dates now seemed inconsequential; it was only the names that I wanted to remember.

I read them slowly.

On a whim, I took the pencil and etched tomorrow's date by my name. It tired me. Let me rephrase that. I was beyond tired. Like Leonard, the guy who could not sleep because of something being wrong with his back, I now felt that way. I did not want this anymore. So, I had decided I was going to go see Lena one last time, and there we would stay. Whenever they found the ship in years to come, they would find me with her.

I looked at the other names. *"Oh Brehm, how would you have died had you not died on the day?"* It was a thought I often thought as those who still lived here grew less and less. I would have conversations with Brehm from time to time. Not that I was overly close to him. Until the day he died, we had only spent time together in passing. It was that one day, those few seconds where I literally held his life in my hands, that made him forever a part of my life. He died that day. We could just never find him. He was no Robinson Caruso, bandaged up with a broken leg, eating off the land and waiting for his body to heal before he returned to us. Something had happened. I had put him in a situation that caused his loss of life, and he was very near to my thoughts.

I gathered a few other things from other rooms that were otherwise occupied. They were belongings of people who have faded through the years. These went into a container and then onto the shuttle.

* * *

I made several trips that day. Everything of any importance went into containers. One by one, I took them to the lobby elevator, from the elevator to the front door, and then from there, I made short quick trips to the shuttle. This gave me a reason to go see Lena. I would take a couple of keepsakes so that the elements on the surface would not touch them.

After the Hotel doors closed, I walked to the front of the shuttle and looked up to the canopy of trees.

It was, quite possibly, my last time in the building.

* * *

So much has changed over the years. I do not know when I remembered the canopy over the top of the indigo ribbon. And yet there it was as if it existed there my whole life. It is one thing that the vine did not touch. Perhaps the roots were too thick to find a place to hold on to in the nano-carbon ribbon. The vine did not discriminate where it wanted to go.

XD05, Year 65 - "Sail on silver girl, sail on by. Your time has come to shine; all your dreams are on their way," *Simon and Garfunkle*

My suit was nearly impossible to get on, and it took a lot of time, patience, and effort. I knew now how the others felt when I would sit patiently and watch as they donned their suit just before we took the trip up the wall. There was one gentleman, Leonard, I think it was, who had a very difficult time, yet I waited for him and helped him out where I could. Now, I had nobody but myself.

In the end, my arm hurt too much to place it into the suit that was my size. I had grown so used to having it curled up against my chest that the muscles just would not react to keeping it straight out. I found a suit designed for someone much larger in the torso, and this is what I used. My arm still curled against my chest, the arm of the suit lay empty.

I checked the air tanks. There are several sets in a row. Two held no charge whatsoever, and a third and a fourth one had faulty seals, which failed as soon as I tested them. Standing there and hearing the hiss of air was quite disconcerting.

If this happened while I was up above the atmo I would not get to see her again. And this was my main purpose. I wanted to see her one more time. I felt my death creeping up on me. Slow and steady, death would not leave until it got what it came for. I set my resolve to see her, and then after that, well then, I suppose, death could have me.

The last set of tanks I tried worked to my satisfaction. The yellow paint had chipped, and the open area of the tanks had rusted from being exposed to the weather. They would last as long as I needed.

The weight, which at one time felt so comfortable, became overbearing. I had to lean forward on the bench, gather my feet beneath me, and push upward with all I had. Once I stood, I was okay. My steps were slow and steady. I knew I shuffled like the old person I was, but I could not chance falling over. If I did so, I could break a bone and have to lie there until the pigs found me. And besides, I *was* an old person.

This was the only way I could get the tanks into the shuttle. They were way too heavy for me to carry or drag. If I had placed them on the floor, I could not situate them so I could put them on my back. I had to start off this way.

For Lena, the chance was worth it.

My gloves were in the helmet sitting in the shuttle.

It lifted on the track and began the slow journey to the Morning Wall.

\* \* \*

Every kim-two I passed had pigs. The damn bastards were everywhere and had taken over completely. If everyone were still here, we could have one a day and still not make a dent in this population.

Near-Earth Orbit


When the orders came down the pipe, they said something of interest was in the area designated as OVON01.

When the survey ship arrived, the computers automatically scanned the area for anything. The five-member crew sat in the forward observation while they left the computers do their cycles.

"We have nothing here, sir," Jamila said, looking at her screen. "A planet named 'Jamila' would be nice, or a drifting moon called 'Jacob,' but we have zilch."

"For once they slipped up, I show nothing on all frequencies," Jacob sounded frustrated. They had all been hoping for another big one—something with excitement.

"There has to be something here; otherwise, they would not have sent us out here."

"No, we're between stars," Tatiana looked at them around her monitor. "A cold planet if there is one. We have four neighbors. The closest is 12ly, two that are roughly 17ly away and one on the border of the 25-year mark. Probably a rogue moon or something just wandering through the neighborhood."

"It's dark, as dark as it will ever be. We're in the middle of nowhere."

"Is there any way to enhance?" Layne asked.

"I will amp it up. With no star in the vicinity, then there's no hope for life. I mean, come on, open a portal, look outside. It's dark."

"We have nothing we can hold claim to."

"Bust," said Jacob in his deep Southern drawl.

They all heard the beep.

"Got something," Emma said needlessly. "It's not moving."

"This is space; everything is moving," Layne said.

"To us, it's relatively stationary, sir. Not your rogue moon, Tat, or asteroid. It's sitting quiet and pretty."

"Could we get to it?"

"5,000 clicks, give or take. It would burn up a third of the fuel. It is within the secure distance." To jump, LyCy required no rocket fuel. Each vehicle required the means to maneuver in space and carried rocket fuel as a precautionary measure. If they jumped in and suddenly found themselves in the path of an oncoming planet, they needed something to maneuver with in-system.

"If it's just something in space, let's go home and get another assignment. No need to look. If we get excited over every bit of rock, we found tumbling in space, we get nowhere."

Layne held up a finger. Everyone was quiet.

"It's not tumbling," he breathed. "It's rotating on an axis."

"A slow rotation."

"What's the size?"

"Dims are unique. Hundred and twenty-three kilometers in length."

"In length?" Layne drifted over. "This thing has a shape?"

"Apparently, it does. Thirty-six kilometers in diameter. Spinning perfectly on its axis."

\* \* \*

They strapped in and did a hard burn a quarter of the way out. After some nudging to correct the course, they coasted. Everyone suited up. As they neared the craft, with a few short bursts, they rotated the scout vehicle, so it faced the opposite direction. The rockets fired again. When they came to a relative stop, they were 20 km from the surface of the ship.

"Should we send word back?" Jacob asked.

"No, possibly, quite possibly, regulations will cover this under salvage rights. We found a derelict object in space. We have the authorization to investigate before we report back."

"It's the '05," Layne muttered, not for the first time. There was a giddiness in his voice; his hands shook as he cinched the buckles.

He made motions in the air with his hand. As if he were trying to figure out the timeline for how the '05 got here, how could it be present at this place and present still elsewhere?

Of course, if he had a telescope strong enough, he could find Earth, and on it, according to the light that was traveling through space, he, or his parents, or someone in his lineage, existed there. Taking a slice from the galaxy at this point in time, the time he existed in the present, he could exist in two places at once. He, his crew, and the '05 existed at the same time; it was just thousands of light-years separating them. By the rule of Parallel 15, they could occupy the same physical space of the universe but at different times.

"We, in theory, took a shortcut. The '05 took the long road."

"Now they know where it is, they will trace it back and find out when it got here," Jamila said. "They could create a paradox and rescue everybody."

"No," Emma shook her head. "On the old stairway, the XD05 is its closest right now. If we go one light year-one calendar year up or down the steps, that puts the ship so far away from us, it will take lifetimes to get to it again."

"Rat's ass," said Jacob, shaking his head. "I go back one LyCy, I fly out under sleep, double hard burn, wake up, and I'm there."

Tatiana's slapped him on the shoulder. "Ain't going to send someone like you on a fool mission like that. It's a light-year. Take a ship ten-thousand years to cross it."

"You'd get rid of me for time."

"A long time. Could I get extra pay for him, you think?"

"Everyone," Layne kept the sense of humor in check. "Check your buddy. Make sure everything is functional. Most of you have not used suits beyond training. No roughhousing, no horseplay. We go do this by the book, or they'll be retrieving you in a few days after you drifted off."

"Copy that, big dawg."

Layne looked at him oddly and shook his head. "Do you honestly know how long ago that was? Can't you guys let anything rest? Focus people."

Jacob whispered, "Big dawg, big dawg, big dawwwwwg," under his breath a few times. Layne gave him a curt look, and Jacob gave him a thumb up.

\* \* \*

With sounds they felt only through the vibrations of the feet, they knew the tethers held them to the great ship.

Jacob reaffirmed it. "Grappling complete. Locked in. Mag-hooks have connected to their counterparts. A firm handshake."

"Steadfast?"

"We are. The system is a little antiquated, but we are in for the ride now."

The tightness of the airlock did not go unnoticed. Able to fit only one person at a time, the rest would have to wait inside or out as the team cycled through.

"Sgt. Layne," Emma motioned to him. She smiled at him behind her visor. At the use of his military rank, he rolled his eyes. "You are our Captain. You've been here before, and you have the honors."

\* \* \*

My arm hurt from being confined in the suit. I moved it when I could; however, there was just no getting around that I would bind it until I reached the surface, and I shrugged everything off. Here at the Hub, it was the mass, not the weight, which was my burden.

I stopped for a moment. Needing to rest, to come to a full stop, I did not grab onto a tether. I grabbed onto something more solid. When I pushed off again, this gave me more momentum. The tethers were slower.

As I was letting go, I thought I felt a vibration. I quickly grabbed the next metallic thing and came to a stop. For there to be a vibration this far up the ship's wall, something catastrophic may have happened to the world below. My mind reeled at the implications, and if something terrible happened, then it would be my end.

I slowed my breathing as if my ears could pick up the sound over the suit's ventilator. I was about to let go when I felt the most curious rhythmic tapping from the metal I was holding onto up into the palm of my hand.

It tore me. If this was the end for me, then I should go spend it with Lena, although I wanted to see what was going on. The closest portal that would let me look out upon the ship was about thirty meters away.

I could only explain the next sensation that came as a grinding sensation. Metal scraping against metal caused a distinct vibration that lasted about fifteen seconds.

"Oh, Lena," I could not forsake her now. As I turned and went toward her, the lights at the end of the corridor danced wildly. I had so little time to make it.

* * *

It was just like déjà vu. In the darkness of space, all portals look the same. This one could've been the same portal that they used all those years ago. Helmet lamp on automatically. He was glad to see that there were no bodies this time.

The airlock cycled, and he pulled himself inward. When he was clear, he tapped the button, and the door closed. It was in his mind to say after all this time, the power still worked, yet he was thinking of it in a different tense. In his mind, he thought approximately ten-thousand years had passed when here it was probably only about fifty-five to sixty. Most things wouldn't degrade so much in so little time.

He brought his helmet lamp around and also one on his wrist. Looking around, the openness of the Hub appeared to be dark and empty. He spent a lot of time on the '05 when it was operational. He had several chief rotations on either Hub. And also, before they decommissioned it, he helped with the salvaging crew. Needless to say, he was familiar with the Hub. Curious as to the rooms he once knew, he pushed off. Everything looked as it always had been. He had last seen service on it, clicking off the numbers in his head; it had to have been about thirty years ago. So much had changed during his life between then and now.

Grabbing a tether, he pulled himself back and headed toward a corridor. A teammate had made it through the airlock, and he saw the flickering of their lamp. He noticed a partially opened door down the hallway. If something jammed, it would be very difficult to find the leverage to pry it open further. Layne grabbed the edge and pulled. They could make it through, but only just so.

His helmet lamp shone on the area in front of him. The one on his arm was a stronger lamp and more directional. He could point it around to illuminate areas that the helmet lamp missed. Looking down the corridor, he noticed there was a full suit hovering there.

"Guys, I think we have one body."

He pulled back from the door and turned. Two more of the crew had made it through the airlock.

When he turned back, he had the strangest feeling that the suit had moved closer.

"Emma,"

"*A-yeah?*"

"Come check this out. It looks like it's getting closer." No sooner had he said that than the person in the suit reached out for a tether.

"She's here! She's alive!"

He reached out his hand through the door, not wanting to let go as he would lose a firm anchor. Even though her one arm was closer, she turned at the last moment and reached with her other one. He fumbled a little, and when she hit, she pushed him backward with her momentum.

"Are you okay?" He asked.

She did not respond, but when he looked at her, he could see she was talking.

He pulled her in so that their helmets touched.

"*... I'm going home, Lena. I'm going home...*"

"Are you Sally Weiss?" He asked.

He could not hear her as she pulled away. Looking at her through the helmet, he could see that she was laughing. Water droplets drifted around the inside of her helmet.

She cried.

\* \* \*

They all worked to get me through the door. That one moment made me question my decision to wear the oversized suit.

They were transmitting on a different frequency than what my suit was picking up and so I could not hear them. All communication had to be done by helmet to helmet. One person would hold me close and relay messages as the others tried to pull me through. They had me move back a little as they used what leverage they had against the stubborn door.

It was very different to feel someone move and to have someone else's hand on my arm or on my own hand. All these years. All these years.

They grabbed me once, and it felt like they shook me. My head bobbed, and I was thankful that they could not hear me. Without wanting to, I made the most peculiar noises. I felt like a doll being shaken. A memory came back of the first time I arrived on the ship.

It took ingenuity, but they finally could make the door wide enough. If it meant my rescue, I would've removed my suit right there.

When I finally made it through, there was a tremendous cheer as everyone huddled together in one floating mass. I could only hear them when the helmets touched. If they had only known how deeply thankful I was that they were here.

Two people were back through the airlock. They were there to help guide me back to the ship. I went in, and as it cycled through, I felt a twinge of anxiety. Here, quite suddenly and unexpectedly, I was leaving the ship that was my home for over seventy years. My mind raced. Did I leave the water on in my greenhouse? Something cooking? It would be soon time to harvest the avocados, yet now it seemed so trite and insignificant.

They took me by the elbow and ushered me to the ship they had. When the person grabbed the empty arm of the suit, I think they were a little shocked.

Back from their airlock, standing with two others who had quickly removed their suits, they helped me with mine.

The one gentleman, the one who had first found me, was the one who spoke first.

"You are Sally Weiss?" he said as they removed my helmet.

"Damn right I am," I said, and I could not help but smile. Still in my suit, my hands shook.

"We'll get you home," a woman said. They undid the buckles that held the suit on. "Is there anything you need from the surface?"

Again, my thoughts were all over the place. I thought of Lawrence, the great white bird which Uncle Butch brought. If he still lived, they could find him.

"Lena is still here. Her body is just inside."

"Ma'am, if there's no one else living, then we will leave her. They will retrieve her later."

I could only nod. The suit peeled away, and I shivered. They brought me a blanket and took me to a seat, which they strapped me in.

"Headcount, 3... 4... 5 and now 6. Got everybody. We are ok for our LTL checkout."

They disengaged from the hull. I felt the vibrations as the cables let loose and retracted.

The ship used small puffs until we were back some distance. These became longer and longer to get some distance. At four kilometers, they engaged the rockets.

I must have had a startled look on my face.

"When e get back far enough we will engage the Samuel Drives. It will take time, three hours, but we will be home."

"Welcome aboard, Sally," said the man, and everyone echoed.

"Thank you," I whispered. "Thank you."

* * *

The clothing I wore was rather embarrassing. Something which I had worn for days or weeks, perhaps. I honestly did not know.

They found a spare set of clothing. The ship, a trite as it was, had a small shower in the bathroom. Some surveying trips could last for days. The showers came standard; they informed me.

I had to make sure I was dry. With the ship in Zero-G, they took a lot of precautions not to have droplets of water drifting about. When I finished, they wrapped me back up in a blanket and buckled me in.

"We looked all over for you, Sally," said the leader of the group.

"I can imagine that even a ship this size is difficult to find in the galaxy."

"No, we had the ship. Somehow or another, it returned to us."

"It did?"

"Yes," someone chimed in. "The day after it left, it returned. Our time only one day passed, ship time, it had been many years."

"They said thousands," the leader said. He gave them a look, raised eyebrows, and they seemed to understand that he wanted to tell the story.

"Estimates say about ten-thousand years had passed."

"I'm sure you wouldn't find me." I looked at them and chuckled. "I would have been long dead by then."

"Your DNA recorded in the database was absent on the surface. They never found your bones. They found the people in the airlock at the hubs, but not you.

"The vine had taken over, covering everything. I was in the military at the time and happened to be there. This has been the second time I've cracked those same doors open."

By the way I looked at him, he could tell that I did not believe him.

"Someone wrote the names of everybody on the wall in your bedroom. There was a soccer ball there and a doll you had, Ms. Pamela?"

"Miss Priscilla." The name brought back memories briefly. "Her name was Miss Priscilla."

"She lay on your bed. There were over twelve others entombed in their own rooms."

I looked at him; I tried to think of a way he could deceive me, and I came up empty every time.

"I am hungry," I said, looking about. "Do you have any food?"

Someone unbuckled and pushed off to a room to the back.

"What would you like?" they called out.

"Anything," I said, my mouth watering already with the anticipation of real food. "Anything, but pork." They could not figure out why I chuckled dryly.

XD05 - "When lonely days turn to lonely nights, you take a trip to the city lights, and take the long way home." Supertramp.

It is said that after my rescue, they gave the ship a thorough inspection. For some reason, there was a catastrophic failure in the depths of the computer system all those years ago. Even after all their exhaustive searching, they still could not find out exactly what had gone wrong or how the information got all screwed up. X-ray Delta 05 was drifting from one step on the LyCy stairway to another. Even though they had discovered so much in the years since the ship returned to Homeport, they did not wish to taint their findings further. Having access to the original data, they incorporated this knowledge into the shoebox brain of the ship.

When all was said and done, they only occupied the ship for another three months before they sealed it up again. They made extra precautions to not create any other paradoxes.

When I got to see the body of Lena, the one that traveled with the ship, they estimated that she was about ten-thousand years old. She was just a few years older than the ship itself.

They believe the initial journey of the ship placed it between the stairway below and the stairway above. The stairway it had to be on was exactly on the opposite side of the galaxy. The ten-thousand-year journey it took brought it to the LyCy step above. Once it was there, the program kicked in and sent it back to Homeport. When Layne and the reconnaissance crew came out and found me, they took a shortcut.

The ship, left to drift by itself in space, took the long way home.

\* \* \*

I want to say everything worked out.

It didn't, not really, not if you think about it hard.

They took me back to Earth. The place that time had denied me for so long. My parents had passed years ago, and they left children behind who are now adults and had children of their own. They had a concern for me, although I think they would never fully accept me as a sister. I stayed a stranger to them.

I had the strangest feeling on Earth. When I looked up at the night sky, it terrified me. I felt the need to get back to my enclosed sky. Looking up and seeing only the endless vastness of the universe, I felt as if I would fly away. I reached back for my spider line, although there was none.

I thought of Brehm and had to look away. From that day on, for the short time I was on the planet, I always wore a hat and never looked upward. The sense of vertigo made me dizzy.

There were advances in technology and medicine while I was gone. They worked with me daily, and in two months, I looked younger. They rejuvenated the tissues in my arm, and it felt like new again. I, myself, had started a rejuvenation process. I felt more spry and energetic. Muscle mass was slow to come back, and yet it did. My skin carried fewer wrinkles, although the scar stayed. For me, it was a badge of honor. I did not mind it in the least.

XD05 was derelict. Nobody wanted it. Everyone was busy exploring the new worlds that have been found. They created '05 to help a struggling civilization get more growing space. When I returned, there was a momentous push to get it up and running to its former self, and although many people volunteered to contribute, it never really went anywhere. I had to get special permission to get everything going. Within two months, they replaced the burner with a new one. The ship went dark for three days and suddenly came alive anew.

* * *

They brought the ship to Sol, where it now resides. At first, I commanded a fleet of about forty maintenance robots who worked around the clock, getting the place back up to par. In time, I will swap half of those out with specialized gardening robots. I like to call them my lil' Stacy's. I plan to make food enough for a few, not thousands or millions, just a select few. There are curious travelers who wish to stop in and see the place. They all stay anywhere from a few days to a month before it satisfies their curiosity, and they journey onward.

I find that the human race is now made up of nomads. With over three hundred planets to visit and with transportation from one to the other costing so little, people wish to just travel.

With the advances in technology, also came advances in medicine. They have replicated the DNA in the people who opted to be frozen. As of now, I have no less than forty children running around. Lena, my dear sweet Lena, has just turned ten. She got her arena wings early on, and, as with me when I was young, she would spend whole days there riding the micro breezes. She is growing up just like her parent. She will not have the experiences that my Lena had, although she is quick with a joke, and even at this young age, her sarcasm is kicking in. If I close my eyes and listen closely, I can hear my Lena in her young voice. It's incredible to watch.

The others are here too. I can see Brandon in the likeness of his child, and, believe it or not, there is a young man who looks exactly like a young man. We sat down in the evenings over the course of one week, and we watched the video that they prepared for us many decades ago. Young MC watched the older MC and has mimicked his mannerisms almost perfectly. Every morning when he sees me, I get the long drawn out "Yooooooooo." It sounds just like MC.

Jaughn has been mixing drinks, and Doc has taken an expressed interest in cooking. It has all made me wonder if it was something that they have always been prone to do.

* * *

There was never any trace found of Uncle Butch, or Lawrence, for that matter. Both remained elusive to all their scanners. To this day, I do not know what became of them. They have identified the remains of all the people whom I have traveled with except for Uncle Butch and his naughty bird. Stories abound, and his relatives are not happy at all.

Between the Morning Hub and the Twilight Hub, there is a tube traveling the full length of the ship. This is where the globe travels that deliver light to the surface. Here on a sensor jutting out a few meters from the surface, they found the remains of Brehm. In the vacuum, the only thing to harm him was light coming from the burner. For centuries, it baked his suit daily. There is no way they could tell the actual cause of death. I would like to hope that it was quick and that he did not suffer.

I miss him. I miss the many others they could not replicate. In my wildest dreams, I think it would be exciting to have three hundred children running around, and, reversing the roles, I would be the eldest among them.

* * *

We have stayed aboard the ship. Given to us by the powers that be, it is a home for me and those with me. I think eventually that my children will move on, but for now, they are content living here. I provide everything for them. We have a more diverse ecosystem than I had before. We have become farmers and herders.

Cattle roam the kim-two's with high Timothy grass. We have a large clutch of chickens, ducks, and rabbits. Gibbons and chimps travel in their own family groups high in the abandoned buildings on both walls. We have a family of dogs and a couple of cats to round it off. We have set special precautions up to make sure the pigs we have do not escape the kim-two they are in. Pat Pat would never forgive me.

Like the others of my species, they have not denied me the ability to travel. If I wanted to, I could assign somebody to watch over the children for a time and travel the stars. However, I do not believe my home is on other worlds where the sky above me is endless.

* * *

Lena, my Lena, remained forever frozen. Brought back from where she lay in storage at Homeport, they placed her where I had always gone to see her. In the mornings, I would watch the sunrise and knew she was there. Not a week has gone by that I do not go visit. It is a luxury I did not have before.

* * *

I stand for a time at the edge of the air arena floor. Young Lena enjoys her speed and is lapping everybody as she almost flies around. Her laughter fills the emptiness when the music fails.

Phleks is playing. With a heavy beat and a rhythmic tempo, it is his famous song called 'Entwined.' I wait for a moment with my eyes closed and my head tilted backward, letting the pounding pulse and the lyrics fill me. My head bobs slightly in tempo, and I c feel my toes tapping.

Lena races past. I see the flash of color of her clothing and hear her distinct laughter. Wee One is fast. Arms outward, I duck walk to the arena floor. Taking those few steps, I feel the familiar pressure as micro-blasts of air push me up and keep me upright. Without hesitation, arms in, leaning forward, I chase after her.

Made in United States
North Haven, CT
12 September 2025

72823746R00202